LEAVING PHOENIX

www.JefePress.com
Ordering Information
Quantity sales: Special discounts are available on quantity purchases by
corporations, associations, and others. For details, you can contact the
publisher and author at:
jefepress@yahoo.com
jafe.danbury@yahoo.com

Orders by U.S. trade bookstores and wholesalers:
Please contact Jefe Press or visit www.JafeDanbury.com

ISBN 978-1-7333440-2-9 (print)
ISBN 978-1-7333440-3-6 (e-book)

First Printing, 2021
Printed in the United States of America
This is a work of fiction. Names, characters, locations, and incidents
either are the products of the author's imagination or are used fictitiously.
Any resemblance to actual persons, living or dead, businesses, companies,
events, or locales is entirely coincidental.
Cover concept by Jafe Danbury
Cover design and formatting by Damonza.com

The author is very grateful to all of the above-listed music publishers for
the granting of licenses for use in this book, and to the artistry of the
writers and performers on these wonderful songs. The book is better for
their inclusion. Thank you, each! — Jafe Danbury

ALSO BY JAFE DANBURY

THE OTHER CHEEK: Boy meets girl. Girl beats boy. Just your typical love story...

"It captured me from page one. The characters are so well defined. Jafe writes with true feeling for his characters. Although a very entertaining read for anyone, I can also see how this book could serve as a beam of hope and a beginning of healing for anyone found in the same situation...."

~ P. MINNICH

"Danbury is reaching an audience not often addressed in realistic fiction... I absolutely flew through Danbury's work, absorbing one of Rich's emotions after the other and fearing Tami right alongside him. I recommend this book to anyone who has survived abuse, thinks they may be a victim, or knows and loves someone who is dealing with a controlling significant other. Danbury is making important strides with The Other Cheek.

~ LITERARY TITAN

"The Other Cheek by Jafe Danbury throws light on the existing but ignored aspect of domestic violence... This book challenges us to see the vice of domestic violence from a broader perspective. I loved how realistic this book turned out to be. Its authenticity comes from the fact that nowhere did I find it going overboard. In fact, the story remained true to its intent and shook me. It also strengthened my faith in the belief that not all that appears is true. There could be something more malicious and horrifying beneath the surface."

~ "TOP 10 FICTION READ OF 2020"
K. GAUTAM, BOOKISH FAME

"A truly compelling read! I've been thinking about this book for days. Thank you, Jafe, for telling this moving story. It had to be told. A must read for anyone who is or has a loved one in an abusive relationship. This should be a movie."

~ K. PORTER

"I loved this book! It is honest, not over the top, and real. Female on male domestic violence does happen. Most men do not report it. Whether out of shame, fear of being arrested, losing his children or his job, fear of his spouse's retaliation, or whatever other factor is involved most men choose to live with it until someone gets hurt or dies.... Danbury strikes the nail on the head with this one... I would give a copy of this to the guy in your life about to start dating. Maybe to the guy you suspect is in a similar situation. This is for women, too. For every woman who has a man she loves in her life... This is Danbury's debut novel, and I dare say we will be reading much more from him in future, at least I hope so!"

~ THE BOOK DRAGON

"This book was riveting. It opens your eyes to the other side of domestic violence. Once I started reading, I couldn't wait to get to the next chapter. The author uses intros, fade outs, and inserts of music in the most brilliant ways. I recommend this book; it is excellently written and keeps you thinking about what really goes on in the world."

~ K. STYLES

"A fascinating twist on the issue of domestic abuse, with the victim the husband and the perpetrator his wife. The story is compelling and totally believable and reminds the reader that most people never know what is going on behind closed doors except for the people behind the door. The pop-culture references from the 1980s and 1990s are a bonus: you can hear the music in the background. When an author can transport you to another time or another place, you know you've got a good read in your hands. I recommend Mr. Danbury's book and look forward to his next offering."

~ W. GABLE

THE OTHER CHEEK:
Boy meets girl. Girl beats boy. Just your typical love story…

FINALIST MEDAL: "BEST FIRST NOVEL"
2020 NEXT GENERATION INDIE BOOK AWARDS

LEAVING
PHOENIX

JAFE DANBURY

PART ONE
DESERT ROSE

CHAPTER 1

THE REPTILIAN MAN topped off the tank of his pristine, ebony, four-year old AMX Javelin, fastened the fuel cap, and slithered inside for a carton of cigarettes and some Tab. He wasn't on a diet—far from it, at 170 pounds—but he preferred the taste of saccharine to sugar, and it had the requisite caffeine for the long drive ahead. He didn't bother asking his passenger if she wanted anything.

After several minutes, he emerged with his stash, wearing his ever-present wraparound shades, and took pause as the morning sun slapped his pockmarked face, hard. It wasn't even 8:00 and the day promised to be atypically hateful for this time of year. Dressed all in black, including his alligator boots, he matched his ride, yet both fell short of the pitch of his soul.

Not unlike a diamondback, he exuded an aura of danger, and he slinked his way to the passenger window where he handed the paper bag of road snacks through the window to the petite, ginger-haired teenager. She wiped her eyes and risked a glance inside: a carton of Kent Menthols, two bags of pork rinds, Pemmican jerky, three Slim Jims, and a sixer of diet soda. Not even a donut. Her empty stomach growled in protest.

As he settled in and started the engine, he regarded the frightened girl, who looked younger than her seventeen years with her freckles, and her bob, plus she'd just finished a cry. He was only five years her senior, yet he felt more like her father than her...*partner*. He pulled four hundred-dollar bills from his pocket, money he'd collected from a cocaine sale twenty minutes prior.

"Before I forget, take this. The clinic's $360, which leaves you forty; it'll cover the bus, and you can get yourself a burger, or whatever, after," he said casually, dropping the drug money on her lap.

She picked up the bills and looked blankly out the window as they drove away. They proceeded in silence for several blocks. The streets were relatively quiet, as it was still early, and a Saturday. From their humble apartment, the clinic would've been closer, and he could have easily dropped her off there instead, but his "errands" were in the opposite direction and had been deemed more important. The bus stop was up ahead, after all.

Her eyes were completely unfocused—as if dilated—against the violently bright sky. The only thing she noticed were the gray floaty specks trapped in their gelatinous membranes.

How long have those been there?

After a couple of miles, they rolled past the drive-in theater. The huge red letters on the giant marquee got her attention, cruelly displaying this week's double-feature:

IT'S ALIVE
&
GONE IN 60 SECONDS

Her tiny, childlike hands found their way to the rapidly growing bump that had replaced her until-recently flat tummy, and she began subconsciously caressing it. Even though she'd dressed in her off-pink sweatpants and an oversized, gray ASU tee-shirt—one of his—the growth had become impossible to conceal, especially considering she was approaching her third trimester. For many weeks she'd worried about how he'd react, dreading the day he returned from being away. It turned out he hated surprises, and she'd found out the hard way, via the belt.

The Javelin slowed, stopping at the curb adjacent to the empty bus stop. It idled loudly, the throaty notes thanks to the high-performance exhaust system. He looked at his watch: 8:10.

"Good on time. Should be here any minute," he said. He might as well have been seeing his daughter off to school. He turned to the girl with a stern look now, emphasizing the importance of the instructions that would come next. "Appointment's at 9:30, you'll do some paperwork, then get on with it. Don't mention my name, don't list me on any damn papers. Just get rid of it. Get rid of it, then take the bus and go on home and rest up. You understand?"

She looked back numbly, partly in disbelief at his profound lack of sensitivity, and what he was forcing her to do. But there was also horror in knowing this was the man who had impregnated her in the backseat of the very car she was riding in—on Easter Sunday no less—and at the drive-in they'd just passed. During *Dirty Mary, Crazy Larry*. She was carrying his spawn, and he was making her out to be the problem here.

"Are we clear?"

She nodded weakly. "Yeah…"

"Okay. Now, I'm heading out straight from here—right now. I'll make LA tonight, Frisco tomorrow. Should be back in about a week—week and a half, maybe, depending on how things go. If it's going good, and looking longer, I'll let ya know." He pulled out a couple more crumpled bills. "Get yourself some groceries. And don't forget to feed the fish. I'll see ya soon, 'kay?"

As he reached over to touch her face, she pulled back involuntarily. The bruise on her left cheek had been courtesy of him two nights before and was still a bit sore. So was the welt on her back from his belt. He shifted his attention to the rearview and the approaching transit bus.

"Alright. Here's your ride. Call ya soon, Rose. Love ya, kid."

"Love you too," she muttered unconvincingly as she exited the vehicle. With a chirp of his tires and a roar from the tailpipes, he sped away with renewed purpose.

The sound of the bus's airbrakes refocused her attention and she slowly turned toward the source. With its large door now opening to collect her, she likened it to the mouth of a blue whale, and herself as a powerless, insignificant krill, about to be swallowed whole.

CHAPTER 2

FORTY-FIVE MINUTES HAD seemed like an eternity, yet Rose secretly wished the bus would never arrive at her destination. What would happen if she never got off? Where would she end up? Maybe the earth really was flat, and they'd just fall off the edge. She'd be totally fine with that.

Anywhere would be preferable to where she was going.

They'd made twenty-two stops before hers, and each tempted her with the momentary opportunity to change her mind—to escape this vessel and the insanity she found herself in. But she knew what would happen if she tried.

He'd probably kill her.

As her chariot approached the curb outside the Planned Parenthood clinic, the first thing she noticed was a small cluster of people on the sidewalk, holding signs. Two clusters, actually, as if opposing teams, and they weren't exchanging pleasantries. The first group consisted of two young men and three women—all college aged, in their twenties, she guessed. They were conservatively dressed, and the guys wore thin neckties. Their signs were all pro-life in nature, which didn't fare well with the other group, who appeared a little older, more battle-ready maybe, more casually dressed, and decidedly more vocal as they waved their pro-choice banners, all the while shouting the boilerplate Planned Parenthood slogans to counter the protesters.

The bus made its noisy arrival and the door swung open. Rose closed her eyes for a long second, took a deep breath, and made her way down the aisle. She took a brief pause at the doorway, as the next step down to the curb felt akin to walking off the plank, into shark-infested waters.

"You sure this is your stop, darlin'?" the motherly driver asked. Rose looked at the woman blankly, searching her kind face, and nodded.

"Yes, ma'am," she replied softly as she stepped down and was quickly enveloped by the small mob. The driver shook her head sadly as the door closed, and the bus pulled away, belching a cloud of diesel exhaust in its wake.

"You don't want to do this, sweetie," the lead pro-lifer gal said urgently, putting a comforting arm around her shoulder. "Think about it. Think about your innocent child!" Her sign displayed a sonogram of a fetus and the handwritten words: *ABORTION STOPS A BEATING HEART!*

This was immediately met with a challenge from the pro-choice side, as a Birkenstocks-wearing hippie type brushed her hair back and wedged herself between them, proclaiming Rose's very right to make the best choice for herself and her future. She too carried a sign, which read: *OUR BODIES! OUR CHOICE! OUR RIGHT TO DECIDE!* Stuffing a Planned Parenthood pamphlet into Rose's hand, she began clearing a path for her. "You have your whole life ahead of you, honey. You don't want to be saddled with a child. It's your life, it's your body, and we're here to help! Come with me...."

Another pamphlet, this one religious in nature, found its way into Rose's other hand as she weaved her way through the gauntlet toward the front door. Another very helpful pro-choice advocate rang a buzzer on the door, which was met with an electronic click, indicating the girl behind the counter deemed it safe to unlock it.

Rose squeezed inside, leaving her new "friends" on the sidewalk to present their passionate arguments to the next arrival, and judging from the crowd in the waiting room, that would probably be soon. She heard the door's lock click behind her. The locks had been added recently and were solely for the safety of the staff. Rose looked around and noticed the only empty seat.

An unseen female staffer, somewhere in a back room, let out a belly laugh, which seemed completely out of place for a medical clinic—especially one that offered abortions.

The clerk at the front counter covered the mouthpiece of her desk phone and shushed her associate, all while trying to suppress a giggle. Rose wondered if she was in the right place, because she seemed to have crashed some kind of office party.

"Can I help you?" the clerk asked, pulling it together.

Rose looked around to see if she was addressing someone else, but she wasn't. She approached the counter nervously.

"Yes. I—my name's Rose—I have, uh, I have a 9:30 appointment," she managed, her eyes darting around.

"Okay, Rose," she replied, setting down the phone and handing the frightened young girl a clipboard of forms and a pen. "You'll need to fill these out. Don't leave anything blank. If you're not sure, ask. Signatures go here…here…and here," she added, pointing them out. Another belly laugh came from the other room, at which the clerk briefly lost her composure, then just as quickly recovered. "It'll be three hundred sixty today, Rose. You good with that?"

Rose pulled out the crumpled bills and slid them across the counter. As the clerk collected the funds, she couldn't help but notice the bruise on the young girl's cheek, but it wasn't her place to judge, nor to report. She'd seen the same, and worse, way too often. Besides, this was shaping up to be another busy Saturday, and she had a schedule to keep. She handed back two twenties, along with a receipt, and directed Rose to the waiting area. "Just bring 'em back to me when you're finished, and we'll get things started."

"Okay," she whispered, pocketing the change and her two pamphlets, and made her way through the crowded room. The empty seat was wedged between two attractive, athletic-looking young women, who appeared to be in their mid-twenties, and considerably more seasoned than she. They could either be on the same volleyball team, or hookers; she wasn't sure. Neither seemed to have a care in the world as they joked back and forth, and this clearly wasn't their first rodeo.

"This seat taken?" Rose asked shyly.

The blonde, sporting an impressive set of store-bought breasts, turned to her and smiled, sizing up Rose in a matter of seconds.

"No, honey, please sit," she said, clearing her small bag from the chair. "How're you doin' today?"

Rose smiled nervously as she took her seat. "Thank you."

"No problem. I'm Tiffany, this here's Francine," she said, gesturing to the slender Asian girl to Rose's left.

"Frankie…you can call me Frankie," she said, as she took a draw from her large Slurpee. "What's your name, sweetie?"

"Um…Rose. Hi."

"First time here, Rose?" Tiffany asked.

"First time, here—or anywhere," she replied, her embarrassment showing.

"Well, don't you worry about a thing, Rose. It's a piece o' cake, okay?" Frankie offered. "Heck, this'll be my third time!" she chuckled, punctuating the moment with a peek at the stud in her freshly pierced, Slurpee-blue tongue.

"Gotcha beat! Fourth time for me," Tiffany said breezily, proudly emphasizing her achievement by holding up four well-manicured fingers. "Guess that makes us both frequent fliers!" she added, playfully slapping Frankie on the shoulder. This provided a brief moment of levity, but only between the two, as Rose awkwardly shifted her attention to the task at hand.

"Sorry, honey. I know you've got forms to fill out. We'll let you get on with it. Don't forget to sign in the three places there. It's just standard stuff, don't even got to read it, really. They're here to help you out, and you'll be back home before you know it."

"Piece o' cake," Frankie reminded her.

"Thanks," Rose said, as she began putting pen to paper. She'd never, ever felt more alone. The din of the room, and the casual chitchat and chuckles, were constant, but faded almost completely into the background as Rose focused all of her attention on the paperwork. It felt like a final exam she hadn't studied for, but she dutifully initialed next to each of the stated *Risks and Hazards*, as well as the numerous *Patient Consent Statements*, even though she didn't really know what they meant, but figured they must know what they're doing. *Piece o' cake…*

Her stomach growled again.

She handed the clipboard and pen back to the gum-smacking counter girl, and headed back to her seat, wondering if a lightning bolt was going to strike her dead before she got there.

As she sat down, only then did she notice that Frankie was no longer there, nor Tiffany for that matter. *The doctors must really be busy back there.* She lowered her face into her hands, took some deep breaths, and began a silent prayer of forgiveness. *Dear God, I*

"Rose," the voice interrupted, devoid of any emotion. Startled at hearing her name, she looked up to see a thirtyish nurse, in a white smock, standing before her. Her name tag said ELLA, but she didn't bother to introduce herself. It wouldn't have killed her to at least attempt a smile when she added, "We'll take you back now."

CHAPTER 3

THE NURSE PUNCHED a four-digit code into a door next to the front counter, heard the lock click open, and ushered Rose back into the inner sanctums of the clinic. The walls were devoid of color; there wasn't a painting or a plant to be found, and no effort whatsoever had been put into trying to cheer up the place. That is, other than the decorative skeleton hanging from the ceiling in the reception area. It was almost Halloween, after all. As they turned the corner, she pointed to the first door.

"Bathroom's here. Gown's hanging on the hook, back of the door. Get changed, meet me in Room 2," she said coldly, pointing to another door across the way.

Rose nodded solemnly and closed the bathroom door behind her. The nurse hadn't waited for a response, and briskly continued down the hall and entered the back room, where she began washing her hands.

There were two other clinicians in the back room: one was rinsing instruments at an adjacent sink, while the other counted baby pieces—*products of conception*, rearranging them in a stainless-steel tray in an effort to reconstruct a tiny human. This was done to confirm they hadn't left anything inside the mother during the procedure. *Retained tissue*, as they referred to it, could be problematic, and was a brief mention in the unread waivers the patients signed.

She'd just finished emptying the suction machine's cannula––a plastic vacuum tube, which had been deployed in an adjacent room—with all of the emotion one would have while sucking up litter out of an SUV's cupholder.

"I'm short a leg here…you seen an extra leg?" she said too casually, as if reporting a missing drumstick from a customer's bucket of KFC.

"You check the Crib?" her cohort replied, gesturing to the biohazard fridge where the "products of conception" were kept.

"I'll look again," she sighed, as she began rummaging through the trays and baggies contained therein. Atop the fridge, some jaded comic genius had thought it a good idea to leave a copy of Hemingway's *A Farewell to Arms* for a little levity. Another had slapped a six-inch, yellow, diamond-shaped sign on the fridge door: *Baby On Board!* Neither were even in the same zip code as Funny, yet this was the way these clinic workers—long ago desensitized to their deathly chores—dealt with the insanity of the job. Surely, at some point early on, each had crossed that line and surrendered to the dark side, letting their hearts callous to a point where they could get on with it. And even, somehow, find some twisted humor in it along the way.

"Found it!" she said with a chuckle as she slammed the fridge door, all too happy to have completed her jigsaw puzzle, and checked the box on her paperwork.

Planned Parenthood… The name Infanticide Incorporated must not have tested well with focus groups.

Room 2 was a bare-bones study in white walls and stainless-steel fixtures. The only color to be found—and you'd have to be looking for it—was in the two droplets of blood at the base of the table where she now sat, shivering in her paper-thin clinical gown. *Seriously, they*

could hang meat in here. A single knuckle rap on the door alerted her to the arrival of staff. The door swung open, and the nurse entered first, then handed the clipboard to another person—a tall, thin, and altogether-unfriendly looking man—who gave it a scan as he closed the door behind them. No *good morning,* eye contact, or anything of the sort. It was as if a pissed-off version of Kramer from *Seinfeld* had arrived, and Rose was an annoying speedbump on his busy pre-lunch schedule. With no introductions being made, Rose conjured up her own names for them.

"Lay down please, Rose," *Cruel Ella* said, as *Dr. Loquacious* finished washing his hands. As Rose complied, the reticent doctor began feeling the mound that was her stomach, shifting his fingers around to different areas as if taking measurements, his hands the micrometers that had performed this task a thousand times. He might as well have been selecting a bowling ball.

He wasn't known for his bedside manner, obviously, but for his efficiency. He scribbled a note on the chart, metering out his brief eye contact for the nurse and softly uttered a cumulative total of two syllables upon finishing his perfunctory assessment, "Sa-line."

Rose's eyes bounced back and forth between their faces, as if watching a tennis match, in hopes of a clue to the cryptic declaration. The nurse turned her back and busied herself at the counter for a few moments, while the doctor's brow furrowed at the sight of the blood droplets that had eluded the staff's mop. He'd have a word with the clinic director, as this was a serious breach. The nurse turned, revealing a syringe. Rose had her answer, and she squirmed involuntarily at the sight.

"Okay, Rose. You can lie back…all the way," Ella said, offering the first hint of anything resembling a smile.

Rose did as she was asked, returning her gaze to the needle poised over her. She hated needles. "This will help get your tummy numbed up a little before we continue." *Continue?* The needle found its mark, and Rose winced as she felt it sinking in, relieved that it wasn't altogether too painful. "There we go," the nurse said, placing a cotton ball and a small bandage on the site, before placing the syringe in the locked disposal box on the wall. While the nurse busied herself at the counter, Rose glanced over at the doctor, whose gaze still eluded her. She couldn't help noticing that he seemed to be more interested in his shoes and the clock than his patient, as he waited the requisite few minutes for the regional anesthesia to take effect.

When the nurse turned around, she was again brandishing a needle, only this one seemed monstrous in comparison. As she handed it to the doctor, he approached Rose, all the time looking at the target, not the person. To Rose, this new syringe had all the menace of a samurai sword.

"Relax," the doctor said in a hushed tone, as he readied the injection, appearing to be mapping his angle of attack. "Will it hurt bad?" Rose managed, feeling as if she might cry. The nurse stepped in closer, offering the frightened girl her hand.

"It's okay, Rose. Here, squeeze my hand and take some slow, deep breaths. It'll be over before you know it." Rose closed her eyes, clamped onto the clinician's hand with a vice-like grip, and took a series of protracted breaths. The next thing she felt was the sensation of the long needle sinking deep into her abdomen. Thankfully, and to her pleasant surprise, the sensation was more of pressure than acute pain, as the previous injection had done its job—for the most part. Still, it was uncomfortable, and she tried not to think about what was taking place inside her.

Rose continued focusing on her breathing as she resumed her silent prayer, wishing she was anywhere else in the world other than where she was. She'd lost all track of time, and it seemed like it was taking forever.

By design, the lengthy needle had not only penetrated her abdomen but had been plunged deep into her child's amniotic sac, where it withdrew nearly a cup of amniotic fluid before another redeployed, delivering its liquid cargo of concentrated salt solution.

As the saline poured in, mixing with the amniotic fluid, the child began inhaling the toxic cocktail, and would continue to struggle and convulse as it swallowed the poisonous salt. Additionally, the highly concentrated solution would begin its heinous process of painfully burning away sections of the child's skin, sizzling it for the excruciating hour or so it would take to terminate its life.

Once satisfied with his delivery, having calculated the requisite time and trajectory, the doctor carefully retracted the needle, wiped the site and nodded to the nurse.

"Rose, the doctor's finished. Everything went well. You can let go of my hand now, and open your eyes, okay?" Rose released her death grip, allowing the blood to return the nurse's hand. As Ella placed a bandage, she regarded the young girl laying there before her. "You okay, Rose?"

She blinked her eyes open and thought she saw a modicum of compassion coming from the medical professional hovered over her. "It's over?"

"The procedure's over, yes. Can you sit up, please? We need to get you started on some water, then you need to walk around a little while before we can send you home, okay?"

Yes, technically the procedure was over. What she hadn't fully elaborated was the fact that it'd likely be sometime tomorrow when her body delivered a tiny, chafed corpse.

Rose nodded and slowly swung her feet over the side of the procedure table. She was handed a cup and finished its contents quickly.

"That's right...good. Now, why don't you follow me down the hall."

Rose looked around the room but didn't see the doctor. Elvis had left the building, without so much as a word.

Thank you...thank you very much.

CHAPTER 4

ROSE PUSHED THE peas around their tiny corner compartment of the Swanson TV dinner tray, not really feeling it this year. She wasn't into the veggies anyway, and she wished they'd offer an option with more cranberry sauce and way more stuffing. And where was the pumpkin pie? Regardless, she'd been particularly hungry, and this was her second tray tonight.

Setting down her fork, she poured herself another tumbler of Boone's Farm Strawberry Hill and turned the channel to CBS. *A Charlie Brown Thanksgiving* was almost over, but it was a repeat of the one that aired a year before. *Maybe it'll be become an annual thing.* She took a swig of the artificial fruit-forward beverage and lit another cigarette, one of his.

Rose had never been a drinker, nor a smoker, but here she was, all alone, doing both. On Thanksgiving. She wasn't old enough to buy liquor but had stumbled upon a couple of bottles stashed on the cereal shelf, behind the Lucky Charms.

It'd been five weeks since her...*partner* had dropped her off at the friggin' bus stop, all alone, to *get rid* of what he perceived to be a *problem. Get rid of it...* Add to that the fact that he was still gone—after he'd said he'd be gone a week to ten days, tops.

Happy Thanksgiving, Rose…

It'd been a month since she'd experienced the ultimate horror of delivering a baby who she knew was going to be dead on arrival. The "salt out" procedure the day before had sealed its fate, and the twenty-four plus hours of chugging water, walking around, and waiting for the impending labor was excruciating.

The labor itself hadn't been too terribly long but it was painful, and seeing the end product—a tiny, perfectly-formed, yet chemically-burned, dead baby, *a girl*—had taken its toll on her physically, emotionally and spiritually.

For the weeks since, she'd been consumed by guilt, and she attempted to find solace at the bottom of a cheap bottle of wine. Actually, several of them.

She took a swig and turned her attention to the cartoon. Linus took it upon himself to lead the prayer as the *Peanuts* gang assembled at the backyard table and found an opportune segue to provide some 1621 history of the first Thanksgiving. Peppermint Patty was launching into a hissy fit when Rose suddenly started feeling a bit… off.

Shouldn't have eaten that second one…

But, no, it didn't feel like that. This wasn't one of your run-of-the-mill *Revenge of the TV Dinner* feelings. She snuffed out the cigarette and sat back in her chair, hoping this would soon pass.

That's when she felt it, and her eyes went wide. She might have been a little buzzed, but of this she was absolutely sure: She'd just felt *a kick*.

Jeezus…

CHAPTER 5

"**R**OSE," HE SAID, doing his best to regulate his voice and his breathing now. *The machine again.*

He took a deep drag of his Kent Menthol before dropping it into the half-full can of Tab, where it sputtered out. "Pick up…" This was his third call today, and one thing he *hated* was being ignored. He'd be having a little "talk" with her about that when he got home. Maybe another taste of his belt would get her tuned up. The clock radio displayed 8:55, reminding him to get a move on.

"Look, Rose, it's 9:00, Tuesday night. Don't know where you are, or what you're doing, but we're finished here for now. Tonight's show's cancelled, so the tour's done, and I'm heading out now. LA tomorrow sometime, home Friday—but gotta detour to see a guy in fucking *Douglas* first. I know it's been a coupla months, but I'll be home for Christmas, Rose. We'll have Christmas together, baby. I'll call again from the road, and you'd *best* be there."

He carefully returned the phone to its cradle before releasing his volcanic fury, violently sweeping the phone, an adjacent lamp, a full ashtray and several empty soda cans to the floor. "Fuck! Fuck!

Fuck!" he bellowed, a cumulative frustration at having been disre-
spected this way, and the pressures of managing an up-and-coming
band he'd discovered—and recently signed. They'd been slated to be
the opener for Moby Grape and Lucky Strike, but the Winterland
gig was cancelled, and this was a shitty note on which to end an
otherwise pretty great tour of supporting slots. The Winterland
appearance would've been great exposure. "Screw it," he said, as he
zipped his duffle bag and grabbed the car keys. Surely every room on
his corridor, and on the floor above, felt the concussion of the heavy
door almost ripping from its hinges as he slammed it behind him.

TEN MINUTES LATER...

Rose scurried about the apartment in a full-blown panic, hastily
throwing clothes, personal items, diapers and baby formula into
a couple of bags. Her now three-week old baby girl was wailing
from the bedroom as Rose rifled through the kitchen cupboards,
grabbing some granola bars and whatever else she could find. She
continued to be amazed at just how hearty a cry could come from
something that was roughly the size an eggplant and weighed under
three pounds. Recently released after three weeks in the NICU, she'd
been born a premie, and on Rose's eighteenth birthday. Rose took
this, and the fact that her precious daughter had apparently been
born with surprisingly few complications, as a sign from God. Add
to that, the fact that, through some *miracle*—because that's what it
truly had to be—she'd escaped the especially heinous fate that her
twin sister hadn't.

Her train of thought was interrupted at the sight of something
she'd never before noticed: a dark ceramic jar in the very back of the
pantry. She hoped it had something sweet in it.

As she pulled the container toward her, she carefully removed
its large cork lid and looked inside. Her jaw dropped and she caught
her breath. *Something sweet, all right...Jeezus!* The sizeable wad of
bills—mostly hundreds and some twenties—was rolled up neatly,

like a round hay bale. She had no idea how much money she held in her hand, and she didn't have time to count it, but it was heavy, and she surprised herself when the entire wad found itself into her diaper bag without hesitation. "Thank you, Jesus!" she rejoiced, replacing the jar behind the box of instant potato flakes and returning to her crying baby.

"Shhh, it's okay, Phoenix... Shhh, my sweet angel. Mommy's here," she said softly, rocking the tiny survivor in her arms. "We're going somewhere safe, where he won't find us..."

CHAPTER 6

"DEVIL'S HIGHWAY" 666
JUST NORTH OF DOUGLAS, AZ
FRIDAY AFTERNOON

IT DIDN'T MATTER, he figured. The guy was in a ditch, face down, and a good fifty yards from the highway. Covered with some tumbleweeds and a few large rocks. Buzzards would find him before anyone else would. Except maybe the coyotes. They'd definitely enjoy that asshole. Either way, the guy'd had it coming, and a bullet to the back of the head was too good for him.

"Nobody rips me off," he muttered, jabbing a Kent Menthol between his teeth and firing up his Zippo. "Nobody!" *Click.*

He'd have to find a new connection now, and he was pissed about that too. The proximity to the border at Nogales had made the supply chain pretty reliable. His connection, not so much, and there was a price to pay for shorting him on coke. He wasn't even really a drug dealer—not professionally, anyway. It was a means to an end, and strictly a way to generate capital to fund his real ambition: music producer. The cash had come up a bit short, thanks to the guy in the ditch, but he had another stash, which should be enough to fund the band's recording session, plus the pressing of albums and tapes. Cassettes were the future.

He was heading north again, on this treacherous, godforsaken stretch of winding—and rumored to be cursed—piece of desert highway. He'd have to reconnect with Interstate 10 and barrel back west, toward Phoenix. Way the fuck out of his way, this place, and not a word from Rose since Frisco.

He was coming in hot.

A hundred yards ahead, he noticed a dark critter inching its way across the blacktop, hoping to make it to the other side. The Javelin accelerated, closing the distance with the small armadillo.

"Sorry, dude…wrong place, wrong time," he whispered, taking a deep drag on his grit.

Stomping down hard on the pedal, the car roared toward the tiny creature, whose little legs and limited armor were no match for the 315-horsepower beast that obliterated it at 100 miles per hour.

"Boom!" he yelled out, punctuating his joy with a very creepy laugh. "Better not've fucked up my car, you little shit."

Turning west onto the 10 now, he wasn't looking forward to another three hours of hell in the saddle, but there it was. "Miss me, Rose?" he said to himself, tossing his cigarette out the window. "I've got a little surprise for ya."

GLENDALE AZ
HOME SWEET HOME
DINNER TIME

Dog-ass tired, and thirsty as hell, he pulled into the carport and killed the engine. Reaching into the back seat, he retrieved the cold sixer of Tab he'd stopped for at the Circle K. The duffel he'd grab later. First things first. He wanted to say hello to his girl. Maybe she'd have dinner ready. *That'd be a first.* He tucked the .38 revolver into his waistband.

Theirs was a second-floor apartment, on the end of the L-shaped complex, and overlooking the small, kidney-shaped pool. A couple of boys were making a ruckus as they enjoyed their very splashy cannonball contest. Reaching the top of the stairs, he brushed the remaining Douglas murder soil from his black shirt and jeans, wiped the telltale boot dust onto the back of his pant legs, and slipped his key into the lock.

"Hey!" he said, loud enough to get the boys' attention. The splashing stopped as they looked up to the man. For extra menace, he slowly removed his wraparound shades, revealing the black leather patch over his left eye, and gave them both the snake-eye as he slowly shook his head in displeasure. They seemed to get the message loud and clear, as they grabbed their towels and hastily retreated.

"Rose, I'm home," he called, pushing the door open, revealing the darkened living room. Not a single light was on, except for the aquarium light across the room. He flipped on the wall switch and was immediately hit by the overpowering stench.

"What the fuck?! Rose!" he called out, setting down the soda on the coffee table. *Gawd, it smells like someone died in here!* "Rose! Where the hell are you?! What's that fuckin'—"

Crossing the room, the smell became stronger, and the sight of the floating, long-dead puffer fish, bobbing in the murky tank, made him stop in his tracks. It was all he could do not to upchuck his pork rinds. "Jeezus!"

Turning the corner to the bedroom, he noticed a couple of her half-opened dresser drawers were missing inventory. Crossing to the kitchen, more quickly now, he scanned the room, which indicated they'd either been robbed, or somebody had left in a damn hurry.

As he flung open the pantry door, he immediately pushed aside the box of tater flakes and went for the wide mouth ceramic bowl in the back. The one he'd crafted on the potter's wheel in his eighth-grade art class. He futzed with the cork stopper and tossed it aside. After several moments of staring into the abyss of the empty vessel, he let it slip through his fingers and crash into tiny pieces on the kitchen floor. It was gone. All of it. *Little bitch…*

"*RRRROSE!!!!!!!!*"

CHAPTER 7

CAVE CREEK ESTATES-ADJACENT
HOME SWEET HOME 2.0
SATURDAY

ROSE HADN'T HAD the luxury of time when it came to getting her ducks in a row. She knew that the Pirate—that's what she was going to think of him as now, because of that lame eye patch—was back in town, would be livid as hell, and looking to hunt her down for making off with his cash. *It was all drug money anyway. Not like he'd ever done anything respectable to earn it.* That was her justification—that, and the fact that he'd beat her up on more than a few occasions and forced her to abort her child. One of them, anyway. Under no circumstances could he learn about Phoenix. There wasn't the slightest doubt that he'd kill them both without batting his one good eye.

Escaping with a scant couple of bags and the clothes on hers and Phoenix's backs, she'd settled for accommodations that were, shall we say, less than ideal. But when one's in fight or flight mode, it's any port in the storm, and she'd offered six months' rent up front on this nondescript mobile home, situated on a deep cul-de-sac lot with a dirt driveway, in a neighborhood of similar castles. At about eight hundred square feet, its two bedrooms and one bath were plenty for her and her tiny new roomie.

As the crow flies, she'd only managed to put about eleven miles distance between the old apartment and this new place, but Phoenix was a pretty big area, and she'd left no tracks that she knew of. The new digs happened to be situated only a half mile from where she'd spent the past three and a half years of school, at North Canyon. Getting preggers hadn't been part of the academic program, and it definitely threw a monkey wrench in her plans for college—and perhaps naïvely, even to pursue a career as a singer. That's how she'd met the Pirate—and thinking back on it, she only now saw the irony in the fact that his first name was Roger (as in Jolly…not!). She'd fallen for his "I'm a music producer, I can get you recorded" bullshit that one chance encounter at the coffee shop, when she sang a duet gig with a school friend.

Her mustard yellow, beater Ford Pinto was only a couple of years old, but not in the greatest of shape, and its paint was already succumbing to the unforgiving Arizona sun. Had she bothered to give it a test drive before she paid cash for it two days prior, she would've been alerted to its rough ride, but she hoped to have it tuned up soon. Like everything else, it would have to suffice for now. Thankfully, she'd made it a point to secretly get her driver's license over the summer, not that the Pirate had ever let her drive his beast. But at least she was street legal, and the four-speed stick wasn't too tough to grasp.

Shaking herself from her reverie, she got out of the car and clutched the tiny papoose to her chest. With her free hand she grabbed the two grocery bags and pushed the door closed with her foot.

No need to lock it.

"C'mon, little angel…let's get you inside."

ACROSS TOWN
ROUGHLY ELEVEN MILES AWAY
SAME MOMENT

The Pirate, er, Roger was inspecting his left, front wheel well as he directed the high-velocity car wash wand on the remnants of armadillo that had soiled his precious ride. He tossed his cigarette at the drain and swore under his breath, angry with himself for having not washed away the roadkill the day before. But after three punishing days on the road, that'd been the last thing on his mind.

Rose, being the first—and only—thing, had slipped away, and with all of his seed money. And killed his fish. That little whore was gonna pay, and when he was finished with the armadillo, hunting season would officially begin.

He was locked and loaded.

PART TWO
PRICKS AND STONES

CHAPTER 8

ROGER (THE PIRATE) hadn't started off as such a bad guy, really. Spanked as a child? Sure. And often. But that doesn't excuse anything, ever, and he'd probably had it coming—at least some of the time. He had, however, been dealt some pretty bad cards.

His strict German father had exhibited early disappointment in his only child, who he'd considered lazy and a failure in the making. He viewed his smallish son a weakling, mostly due to his size, his disinterest in baseball, and his incessant obsession with the devil's music—rock 'n' roll—to the exclusion of anything else. He was sure he'd never amount to anything. Sometimes, he wondered if he was even really his.

Juergen Offermann had immigrated to Tucson after the war and, after establishing sufficient residency, was offered a teaching position in the engineering department at the University of Arizona at Tucson. It wasn't his dream job, but it utilized his talents—at least on a fringe level—and he'd managed to meet his future wife, a junior in one of his classes, that spring semester of 1954.

They married six months later, had a child the following year, and his hausfrau wife settled into her role. After two years at the university, Juergen had become disenchanted with the administration, and threw caution to the wind in his desire to be an entrepreneur.

He couldn't afford to fail in this venture, especially now that he had a family, but he resigned his position, made a business plan, studied the competition, and opened his first shop in Phoenix, where he immediately moved the family.

He could be considered modestly successful and was an intensely proud man who focused most of his energy on the two dry cleaning businesses he'd started from the ground up—the one in Phoenix, and another in Glendale. He'd mustered considerable imagination in naming them both Offermann's.

A man of few words, he'd often let his belt do the talking when he got home, especially after he'd had a few glasses of his favorite German brandy, Asbach. Mrs. Offermann was occasionally on the receiving end of that belt as well, as she was too mousy to effectively protest the treatment she and her son received, and neither had any idea of the pressure he was under.

The industrial-sized chip on their son Roger's shoulder, and the lion's share of his soul scarring, had most rapidly accelerated during his painful years in the public schools. It started early, in the second grade, as his left eye started going south—literally, as in *lazy*. Because of this, he was teased mercilessly by boys and girls alike, and he was the only kid at school whose condition necessitated wearing an eye patch. He dreaded every single day, and the innocent smile he'd exhibited in kindergarten eventually disappeared altogether, as evidenced by the hardening of his features in each successive school portrait.

Things really started coming to a boil as he got into his middle and high school years, often resulting in some rather brutal after-school fights. Though relatively small of stature compared to most of his peers, he would answer any taunt offered by the jocks, and any initial fear was quickly supplanted by the ferocity that came from a well stoked and white-hot hate, which made him remarkably effective with his fists and more often than not, victorious. He started commanding more respect eventually, entirely due to his badgerlike tenacity. As a result, the taunts began to decrease dramatically in his junior year.

That summer, as Roger was finally seeming to be developing a modicum of self-esteem—as ill-gotten as it was—he began suffering an especially cruel hormonal shift that manifested itself in a worst-case invasion of acne, which proved impervious to cleansers, dietary change, and even extensive tetracycline regimens. The result was a deep and savage restructuring of the dermis on his face and neck, and the latent pockmarks had left their ruthless reminders.

Only one schoolmate—a newbie who didn't know better—had been stupid enough to taunt him with "Crater Face," and did so at his peril, as Roger's piston-like fists had pummeled the boy's face into something worse looking than Roger's. His new reptilian appearance, combined with the black eye patch, cemented his persona and his sense of menace. With the adoption of an exclusively black wardrobe and wraparound sunglasses, he slicked back his hair to complete the picture.

He had no friends, and now no enemies, and that's the way snakes—and pirates—liked it.

GLENDALE, AZ
CHRISTMAS EVE
FIVE YEARS LATER
HIGH NOON

Sitting in the empty strip mall parking lot, he looked up through the windshield, shaking his head as he stared at the ridiculous, now-defunct sign: OFFERMANN'S

"Jeezus—" he muttered, flinging the flaming cancer stick out the window. He turned the key, revved the engine loudly several times, and left a long trail of burnt rubber in his path.

This little trip down memory lane hadn't been a random one.

He'd rolled back into town two weeks prior upon hearing of his mother's passing. His childhood had been pretty jacked, arguably, but he had always managed to reserve the one tiny speck of a soft spot in his heart for his mom, who'd done her best to raise him—and protect him—to the best of her ability, from his asshole of a father.

Though she never understood what really happened, losing her husband in a car wreck had been exceedingly tough on her. Also, truth be told, pretty liberating. But still tough. It was true that Juergen's car had been discovered at the bottom of a gully outside Scottsdale. A bottle of Asbach had been found in the car along with him. What nobody could know, however—with the exception of Roger—was that he had been nearly beaten to death before having his Volvo nudged over the side of said gully, and by a nineteen-year-old who'd finally had enough of his bullshit.

Auf wiedersehen, Herr Offermann!

Last to enter, and first to exit, Roger had sat in the rearmost pew during his mother's service. His parents hadn't been religious people, and this was the first and only occasion he'd ever darkened the doorway of a chapel. He planned to keep it that way.

This return to the desert had come after several exhausting, yet fruitful, years of creating his brand and claiming his stake in the San Francisco music scene. He was becoming a known commodity now, and in some circles, he had a nasty reputation for *always* getting what he wanted, from bands and venues alike. His own bottom line was what mattered most, and the label he'd created, Picaroon Records, was especially fitting, considering his affinity and talent for plundering everything from the naïve treasure-seekers who'd signed his predatory contracts. The eye patch wasn't an entirely bad trademark either. Business was good—for him—and he planned to build on that when he returned. But while he was here, he had a little something he had to take care of first.

After those initial months of scouring metropolitan Phoenix to no avail, he'd decided to abandon his search for Rose—not entirely, because he'd never allow her to go unpunished. No, when the time allowed, he'd resume the search.

And the time was now.

Rose definitely wasn't in Glendale, he decided. Having canvassed every friggin' inch of this place since his return, he needed to plot a new grid.

Where would she have gone, and how would she have gotten there? She hadn't had any wheels…not even a driver's license—or did she? He wracked his brain as he began driving east. She had no family in the area, not anymore anyway.

His initial searches had involved scouring areas closest to their apartment: Glendale, Peoria, central Phoenix, but he'd not yet hit paydirt. He'd long ago eliminated Scottsdale and Tempe. Chandler was too far south. Gilbert? Nah.

Then he thought back to where he'd first met her, at that little dive…not far from the high school…other side of Interstate 17… not far at all! *As good a place to look as any! Hmmm…*

With new coordinates selected, he stomped hard on the gas. Andy Williams came on the radio, launching into "It's the Most Wonderful Time of the Year." Roger wasn't having it. He pushed the cassette into the deck and was all too pleased by the fortuitous Lynyrd Skynyrd selection that cued, as if just for him, because he was "On the Hunt."

CHAPTER 9

THE MOBILE HOME
CHRISTMAS EVE
ABOUT SIX HOURS LATER

IT WAS TRUE what they said, whoever'd said it. It might've been Dorothy, from *The Wizard of Oz*, but Rose didn't know for sure. It went something like—and apologies to Howard Payne—"even if it's humble, there's nowhere like your home," or words to that effect. Even if it was a mobile home with a dirt driveway and set in the middle of a cluster of similarly sketchy mobile homes with dirt driveways, it was theirs. And Rose was thankful for it.

Had it really been five years since they made their escape? She'd originally envisioned this to be a short-term rental while she figured things out. The owner had been very cool, not asking too many questions and allowing her to pay a lump sum of cash for the first half year. It was spartan, but it met their needs and, so far, they hadn't been found.

The cash from the jar was long depleted, and Rose had taken a job at the local bowling alley to keep food on the table, and Kimbies on her girl. Babysitters were expensive, and the manager let her bring her little one to work, provided she kept an adequate eye on her. It was only three days a week and a ten-minute drive, and after a while she became resigned to the task of spraying disinfectant in all those stinky bowling shoes. There were worse occupational hazards, she figured. Times were lean, but they had a roof over their head, enough to eat, and she felt safe.

Even with the passage of time, though, there were still occasional nights when she'd wake up in a cold sweat at the sound of one of the neighbors' cars rolling down their gravel driveway.

Rose finished hanging the two Christmas stockings, spacing them about a foot apart on the handle of the oven door, as there wasn't a fireplace mantle handy, and she didn't own a hammer anyway. The two kitchen hand towels that had previously occupied that space were returned to a drawer. For a fleeting moment, she imagined hanging three stockings instead of two and wondered if the girls would've been identical. Phoenix had inherited much of her own attributes, including her stunning head of hair. Had her twin as well? She'd never know, and it pained her deeply.

The tree, at only three feet tall, didn't occupy much space in the corner of the main room, and she'd done her best to make things as festive as possible for her five-year-old angel. Rose looked forward to her expression when she opened her main gift.

"Phoenix, let's come inside now, sweetie, it's gonna be getting dark soon."

"Just a few minutes more please, Mama?" the tiny voice replied.

Rose opened the screen door and smiled as her little beauty made figure eights in the dirt on her new red tricycle. She fondly remembered her own first trike and the feeling of independence that came with newfound mobility. There was just something about having wheels, be it two, three or four. Which reminded her, she'd need to get the right front tire replaced on the Pinto next week.

"C'mon, sugar, let's put your trike away and have some dinner. And then…" she trailed off with the cliffhanger.

"What?" Phoenix asked, stopping in her tracks. "Then what, Mama?"

"And then…we get to open some presents!" she replied, giving her little elf a warm hug.

"Yay!" she squealed, running inside.

Rose shook her head and smiled. These were the moments she cherished. Though she'd had doubts early on about her ability to be a good mom, she was enjoying the motherhood experience. She shuddered to think she'd almost been denied that opportunity altogether. "Wash your hands, Phoenix. Soap and water!" she called after her, grabbing the seat and a handlebar as she carried the trike around to the back of the house, to the small storage shed.

The Javelin slowly crept through the last of the remaining neighborhoods to explore. Roger had exhausted every avenue these past several hours, and he hoped to cross this one off his list before it got too much darker. *How could anyone choose to live in these dumps?* The mobile homes were configured on adjacent cul-de-sacs, fanned out as if spokes on a wagon wheel. The Pirate was saddle-sore, hungry, and pissed, and that wasn't a good combination.

He extinguished his headlights and let the car idle as quietly as possible as he inched past the units, scouring each property for any outward signs of familiarity. Not seeing any, he pulled over to the curb and rubbed his eye—the one that had been doing the heavy lifting, then got out and walked around to the other side, where he could be unseen as he took a long-overdue leak. He let out a long sigh of relief and looked over his shoulder, where some movement across the street caught his attention.

Rose was making her way back toward the front, laboring with a coiled garden hose. She began unfurling the kinks and positioned the cheap plastic sprinkler in the middle of the tiny patch of grass that was hanging on for dear life.

Roger couldn't believe his eyes—er, his eye. *Could it be?* Even though he was parked a couple of units back, and partially hidden by a mesquite tree, he ducked down behind the car and watched closely as Rose went over to the spigot and adjusted the flow. Her hair was long and wavy—not that short bob she used to have—but it was an unmistakable mane, and shades of red he'd only seen once before. And on the same person. The corners of his reed-thin lips slowly curled upward, forming his twisted version of a smile.

Thank you, Santa.

Rose had never taken even a remote interest in learning how to cook, and she remained culinarily challenged. She was fine with that, as she could boil water with the best of them, and that was a handy skill when preparing their twice-a-week mac 'n' cheese from a box. One thing she knew was that she'd never again subject herself to another TV dinner. Too many bad memories.

She'd picked up her version of the Christmas meal from the drive-thru an hour before and began preparing a plate for Phoenix. It was one of those compartmentalized plastic plates for kids, with the dividers, and as she placed the two scoops of sweet corn, and one of coleslaw, in their respective zones, she couldn't help but think that this looked eerily similar to a retooled version of the TV dinner she loathed. But the KFC components were a serious upgrade and a treat they both enjoyed—except Phoenix wouldn't eat the Colonel's mashed potatoes, as she deemed them too salty. Still, she'd popped for the family bucket and extra sides. She'd just gotten paid, and it was Christmas—plus it'd last all week. She went about removing the skin, and the eleven herbs and spices, from Phoenix's chicken breast before cutting it into bite-sized pieces.

Rose had already given Phoenix a bath and gotten her changed into her Scooby jammies, so she was ahead of the game. She was happy knowing that her little one was quietly enjoying the almost-new Mattel Honey Hill Bunch doll she'd found at the Salvation Army store, the one with the auburn hair like Phoenix's, and striped pants. Phoenix's favorite place to enjoy her treasures was sitting in her tiny beanbag chair, which was set deep in the back of the bedroom closet. That's where she was now and would remain until called for dinner. They had their little routine.

Rose paused to take another swig of her peach wine cooler and turned on the radio sitting on the counter. The velvety smooth voice of Bing Crosby came on, singing his Christmas classic, "Do You Hear What I Hear?" Apparently, she didn't because with a tiny *click*, the screen door had just closed stealthily behind her. It was the shadow she noticed first.

"Miss me, Rose?" the voice said, a terrible, unmistakable, hissed whisper.

The fine hairs on Rose's arms stood at attention and her breath escaped her. With her back still to him, Rose palmed the steak knife she'd been using. She slowly turned around, her eyes wide as saucers, as the sight confirmed her worst nightmare.

"It's been a while... look at you, all grown up like," he said menacingly, taking his sweet time as he regarded the startled prey standing before him.

"Did you really think I'd ever stop looking for you, Rose?" he continued, not waiting for an answer. He cradled her delicate, dimpled chin between his thumb and index finger while she stood there, frozen with panic and disbelief. Avoiding a look at the patched man, her eyes darted around the room. All she could think about was that her baby girl was in the next room, and her maternal instincts told her that she'd do everything in her power to keep this wretched man from finding out about her child.

Bing was singing about a child shivering somewhere...

Rose gripped the knife tightly, her hands still by her side. She knew she'd only have one chance at saving her little girl from this maniac—the same demon who'd beaten her into submission and made her "get rid of" her daughter's twin.

"How did you find me?" she asked weakly, interested in time more than an answer.

"Does it matter?" he replied. "You look good, Rose. I like what you've done with your hair," he said, grabbing a hank of it in his fist. Her eyes began to water. It hurt like hell. "I believe you took something of mine, Rose…and I *really* don't like it when somebody takes something that belongs to me. You should know that." His tongue darted out long enough to moisten his lips and Rose could've sworn it was forked. She listened for any sound of movement coming from the next room. So far, there'd been none. She needed to keep it that way.

"I'm sorry I took the money," she managed, relieved to feel his grip loosen slightly on her hair. "You were gone a long time…I needed some…it was a mistake."

He took a moment to consider this attempt at an apology. It wasn't going to save her, but he considered it just the same. "You're right, Rose, it was a mistake. And sometimes we have to pay for our mistakes. You…*inconvenienced* me, Rose, and I'm a very busy man these days."

"How can I make it up to you?" she said, grasping at straws. "Can we go outside and talk about it?" The knife's handle felt secure enough in her hands.

"Ahh, that's rich, Rose," he said with a menacing grin. "Hmm… let's see…." His free hand found her breast. She shuddered, then made her move, thrusting the knife blade and making purchase with the side of his neck.

"You *whore!*" he hollered, as he released her hair and put his hand to his wound. It was a glancing blow, not a gusher, as she hadn't managed to achieve a kill shot, but it hurt like a sonofabitch. His other hand found her throat as his thumb dug into the side of her larynx and the remaining fingers began slowly cutting into her air supply. The knife dropped to the floor.

Rose managed one final bellowed word, praying a neighbor might hear her killer's name before her wind was depleted: *"Offermann!!!"*

Rose's fate was being sealed, right her in her kitchen, on

Christmas Eve, by this soulless monster, and all she could think about were two things: *God, please save my daughter!* And *Daddy, where were you?*

He held her like that, increasing the tension on her slender throat, for a full couple of minutes. As her feet left the ground, she flailed, desperately clawing at his arm, but his strength, and the pressure being exerted, were just too great. She had failed her daughter, she now knew, and her eyes rolled back, in full surrender, lifeless and devoid of any embers as the last bit of breath left her body.

Bing's song segued to the orchestral intro of "The Christmas Song" by Nat King Cole. Roger shook his head, then let Rose's lifeless form drop to the floor. Without further thought, he grabbed a drumstick from the bucket and thrust it between his teeth, tearing off a chunk of the Colonel's finest before returning to the porch to retrieve the metal gas can he'd left there.

As he distributed big splashes of the petrol about the kitchen floor, he managed to get a bit on his right arm, with the lion's share of the remainder soaking the counters, the cabinetry, and Rose. Nat was singing about roasting chestnuts, and the irony wasn't lost on this murderer.

A pair of innocent eyes peeked out from around the corner. Unbeknownst to him, as he was busy covering up a crime scene, this snaky pirate monster was etching an indelible image in a young five-year-old's memory. Taking a step out onto the porch, he retrieved his Zippo from his right pocket and turned the wheel. His shirt caught first, causing him to screech in pain as the flames engulfed his arm, traveling its length from his hand to the shoulder. He shook his arm wildly, dropping the can and the lighter into the kitchen, which immediately burst into an inferno.

The last thing young Phoenix saw was the man running away on fire and the flames consuming the kitchen, her mother, and Christmas altogether. Consumed by shock, she let out a silent scream as she ran out the back door, clutching her doll tightly. She'd heard her mother call out his name, and she'd never forget that evil face. She'd never forget the *"Awful man!!!"*

PART THREE

PHOENIX RISING

CHAPTER 10

THE EARLY BIRD got the worm, and even though it was forecast to be a sweltering 116 degrees on this Saturday, Phoebe was out the door at 7:30, ready to hit the ground running. Well, walking. Like most days here, it called for flipflops, and she wished she could wear them, but after several childhood surgeries to correct a club foot, she needed the extra arch support that only a good pair of walking shoes provided. She liked to take her sweet time checking out the garage sales in this neighborhood, and she might even log a couple of miles today.

A seasoned garage-sale pro, she liked to visit the nicer neighborhoods, as they tended to have better stuff and not just the random piles of old clothes and such in the driveway. Up ahead, on the right, she noticed a target-rich environment, a cluster of several homes with signs up, and items being carried out from their garages. She was first in line, as usual. *Score!*

She slowed to get a better look at the offerings, then parked, in the middle of the cluster so she could load any treasures into the car more efficiently. There were still a few minutes before the homeowners would officially open up shop, so she took a moment to gather her considerable red mane into a ponytail and affix her ASU ballcap.

Phoebe was pretty partial to the ballcaps, and she had several, but the ASU one was her favorite—that, and the one with the Arizona flag emblem. Though she'd have no way of knowing it, she'd inherited her amazing mane of flaming red hair from her mother. It was a fiery spectacle to behold when she chose to liberate it, and it included a few shades of red and orange that Crayola hadn't included in the box. At first glimpse you might expect it to spontaneously erupt, like a campfire. Or solar flares. But she found it to be a smothering burden in this Arizona heat, thus she tended to rock the ponytail-in-the-ballcap look more often than not. As she barely clocked in at five-feet tall—and only if she wore the right tennies—her youthful appearance could be mistaken for a child at times. Her fair skin hadn't seen too much of the desert sun, and her freckles and dimpled chin completed the adorableness.

"How's my little Prick this morning?" she asked, turning to her passenger. The little Chihuahua mix took no offense, as this was his name, and he had no clue it was a play on cactus. Plus, it suited the little prick. "Yes, you get to come with me," she added, clipping the leash to his tiny martingale collar. She avoided unnecessary chances when it came to critters and carefully placed him onto the sidewalk. After letting him mark three different mesquite trees, they were on their way up the first driveway.

"Good morning," Phoebe said, directing a smile to the proprietor, who waved back. She was still in her pjs and holding a large coffee cup. Phoebe didn't wear any makeup on garage sale days. Those were the accepted terms for both sides in this marketplace. She made a beeline for the long table at the top of the drive that was littered with boxes of record albums. "How much are your LPs?"

"Different prices, they have colored dots on the top corner. Most are two dollars, some are more. More you buy, the better discount I can give you."

"Perfect, thanks!" Phoebe replied, as she started flipping through them. A real eclectic bunch and everything from Mendelssohn to

Metallica. *Yes!* Prick let out a yip, as he was already bored, and knew that his mama was going to be here for a while. This wasn't the little guy's first rodeo, after all.

"Shh, quit complaining, we just got here," she said softly as she tossed the critter a tiny piece of duck jerky. "Mama's in the candy store, and you need to be patient."

She started hitting serious paydirt immediately, and tried to keep a poker face as she began setting some albums off to the side:

Head East ~ *Flat as a Pancake!*

Climax Blues Band ~ *FM/Live!*

Danny Kirwin ~ *Second Chapter!*

Lani McIntire and His Aloha Islanders ~ *Aloha Hawaii!* (Okay, she'd never heard of him, but this was a leather-bound series album on four, thick—and very fragile—10-inch records.)

And it has a $2 sticker on it, which equates to fifty cents a record!

"Would you take six dollars for these?" she asked, presenting her selections for consideration.

"Sure, honey," the woman said. These albums had all been her ex-husband's and had followed her around for several moves. She just wanted to unload them. "I'll throw in one more for free, just pick one."

"Thank you so much," Phoebe said, selecting Dan Fogelberg's *Phoenix* album as her bonus item, before handing her six one-dollar bills.

Garage Sale Rule Number One: Always carry lots of singles, it makes it easier to bargain.

"Thank *you*," the woman replied. As Phoebe started to turn away, the woman asked:

"You want all of 'em?"

"Excuse me?"

"I'll make you a good deal if you take all of 'em," the woman said, gesturing to the eight boxes full of albums, all properly stored vertically.

Phoebe had noted immediately upon arriving that they all seemed to be "near mint," in both jacket and vinyl condition, with the exception of that old Hawaiian one. "How much?"

"How much you got?"

Phoebe opened up the front zipper compartment of her fanny pack and extracted a wad of ones. "Sixteen dollars?" she asked, feigning embarrassment.

"Sold! I'll help you load 'em." *Woo-hoo!!*

After Phoebe folded down her 4Runner's rear seat and finished arranging the bounty, she thanked the kind woman again and squinted as she glanced around at the offerings in other nearby driveways. Other bargain hunters were starting to arrive, and she thanked her lucky stars for her good fortune in scoring an entire record collection for twenty-two bucks.

She had several dollars remaining in the secret compartment of her fanny pack, a little bit of cargo space still, and it looked like the guy next door had some cool things. *What's that? Is that a friggin' lava lamp?!!*

She looked down at her little sidekick. "Come on, you…we're just getting started."

"Yip!" replied the little Prick.

Three hours later, and satisfied she'd sufficiently canvassed the neighborhoods, Phoebe was more than pleased with the great stuff she'd scored. From her experience, most of the good things were snapped up pretty early, and most sellers' stuff was pretty picked over in the first hour or two. She needed to get home.

As she arrived at the house, she backed into the long driveway for unloading and continued to the very back, where her guest cottage was situated. A studio granny unit, and formerly inhabited by an actual granny—her adoptive father's mother, who'd passed away five years before—it was perfect for her needs, as it afforded her a little privacy. It had a tiny porch area for her succulents and an adequate dog run on the side for her occasional fosters.

Phoebe tapped the horn, signaling that she had returned, and "Pop Pop" acknowledged her with a wave from the kitchen window. He was quite fit for fifty-five, ruggedly handsome, and blessed with a full head of sandy blonde hair. At six feet three inches, he was an imposing figure, and towered over his daughter. Always quick with a smile, he came out the side door, wearing his faded USN tee-shirt, drying his hands on a dishtowel, and leaned down to give her a hug. "Find anything worthwhile?"

"Oh, man…you have no idea, Pop Pop! I hit the motherlode today!" she said, beaming, as she hoisted the rear hatch to reveal her loot. "See for yourself…"

"Whoa!" he cheered, overlooking everything else as he became laser-focused on the albums. It looked like a record shop on wheels, and he shared her love for quality vinyl. "That must've set you back some change! Guess you'll be wanting some more hours to pay for all that, which I can arrange."

"Twenty-two bucks, American, for all of 'em! All killer, and no filler! Some are still sealed, even!"

Pop Pop turned to face her, waiting for the punchline, because, surely, she had to be kidding. "True story," she confirmed, making the "Scout's honor" gesture.

"That's my girl!" he replied. "Any Grand Funk?"

"Tons."

"Yowza… Let me help you get these outta the sun," he said, as they unloaded the eight album boxes, and the two other boxes of…random stuff. Her cottage was small, and these ten boxes now occupied much of the main room.

"Okay if I use the turntable for a few hours later?"

"No problem, Feebs," he said, as he set down the last of the random boxes. "Tell me that's…a…lava lamp!!"

"Yessir, and it works—I tested it!"

Pop Pop got his nickname from his daughter when she was first adopted, as that was her way of pronouncing "papa." He'd never corrected her, and the term of endearment had obviously stuck, so he was totally cool with it. His real name was Dave...LaFlamme. No relation to the musical genius of "White Bird" fame; he'd checked.

He lifted the lamp from the box, exercising extreme care as he held it upright, admiring the condition of the vintage device. It was a rare one in that it had the peachy-white wax floating in a clear liquid. Its gold-colored metal base was devoid of any dents or scratches, and it had the little drilled holes where the light escaped when it was plugged in. The original cord was in perfect condition as well. This was definitely '60s vintage.

"I hate to ask..."

"Five bucks!"

"Mercy!" he said with a laugh. "Where were you when I was negotiating for my truck?"

He'd had a similar lamp when he was in college, but with red wax. One of his stoner buddies had ruined it by shaking it, and the waxy blobs disintegrated into smaller BB-sized pieces, which never properly came together to reform into their original "lava" masses. Sometimes he was more of a kid than she was—especially when it came to music, vintage stuff and memorabilia.

"It's a beauty," he said, mostly to himself. He might have to join her on the next garage sale adventure. "Grilling chicken later. I could grill you some mixed veggies. Make a salad. Gonna be around?"

He'd said the magic words, and nobody grilled better chicken than he, but she had gone "cold tofurkey," becoming a full vegetarian, literally overnight, a couple of years ago. If she missed anything from the meat world, it was Pop Pop's chicken. That, and tacos. Man, she missed those too. *And salmon filet...stop!*

Her new mantra had become "never eat anything that had two eyes and a loving mother." She wasn't sure what had prompted that decision, but smart money would say it was from her passion for rescuing critters. Or maybe even something buried in her subconscious.

"Wouldn't miss it, Pop Pop! What time?"

"How's 4:30?"

"Perfect! I'll probably have headphones on, so if I lose track of time, come find me."

"You bet. Have fun!" he said, winking at her as he closed the cottage door behind him. He knew she would, because that record collection looked like any audiophile's dream. The stereo gear, kept in the den of the main house, was Pop Pop's pride and joy—well, one of them anyway.

He made his way to the kitchen, returning the dishtowel to its perch on the stove handle before continuing down the hall to the shrine. He had to clear the decks for Phoebe and reshelve the pile of CDs he'd neglected to put away the day before. He didn't want to set a bad example. He couldn't help but smile whenever he entered that room.

Aside from the perfectly calibrated Technics turntable, the system consisted of matching Kenwood components, including a stereo receiver, a magazine-loading six-CD player, and a single-deck cassette recorder. He'd added a rather basic Radio Shack mixer, and the speakers were some still-wonderful-sounding Pioneer HPM-100 four-ways, delivering two hundred watts, which offered excellent dynamics across the spectrum, and were loud enough for the neighbors to enjoy. *Ahem.*

The den was where he kept the guitars as well, and it truly was a music-themed room. A man/adoptive daughter-cave. His Arctic white Squire Strat hung on the wall from its rosewood neck's headstock, as did his cherry sunburst Epiphone Les Paul. Next to the Epi, there hung a fifteen-year-old, Japanese-made Yamaha short-scale bass, with a deep honey tone finish. Pop Pop had taken it in trade for some engine repair services, and the smaller size accommodated Phoebe's tiny hands. Though he'd never been able to afford the nicer guitars—he dreamed of a Rickenbacker or a Gretsch—his humble collection suited him for his purposes.

Once a month, they'd be liberated from their wall mounts and transported, along with his Mesa Boogie amp, to his buddy's house in Mesa, for their garage band jams. Phoebe came along, on occasion, and in addition to laying down some solid bottom end, she contributed some fine vocals. She could be a little Suzi Quatro, when she let herself go.

Another of Pop Pop's passions was the auto repair shop he'd taken over ownership of in 1972 and renamed Pop's in 1985. The shop employed three full-time mechanics and an admin. Plus Phoebe, who'd shown early aptitude for mechanical systems and had become quite proficient with most of the shop's tools. She was qualified to do most tune-ups, could work on shocks, brakes, and electrical systems, and could even hold her own with mounting tires.

Which brings us to the center of his universe: Phoebe herself. He and his ex-wife, Suzan, had adopted Phoebe when she was barely five years old. The little they knew of her story had broken their hearts, and upon hearing how she'd been rescued from what appeared to be an arson fire—one that had reportedly killed her mother—they felt compelled to take the little girl into their fold and offer her at least a chance at having a decent upbringing. Due to the nature of the "accident," and eyewitness accounts that mentioned seeing a man fleeing the scene, they thought it best to change her name from what had appeared on the forms, from Phoenix to Phoebe, hoping she'd adjust easily enough, since she was so young. And she had.

Shortly after adopting her, they were advised that Phoenix/ Phoebe would need a series of operations to surgically correct what had developed as a club foot, likely a defect from birth. She'd been a trooper through all of it, as she'd had to endure a series of casts and braces, and use crutches for a period of time, but she had come through remarkably well. But it had taken time, and Phoebe had endured more than her share of teasing from the kids at school.

The next few years of procedures and accommodations had proven too much for Suzan to handle, and she divorced Dave when Phoebe was ten years old. They'd never been successful in having a child of their own. Try as she might, Suzan had never really felt that special bond with Phoebe, not the way most mothers do with their daughters anyway, and it might have been due to the fact that they weren't biologically connected, or that she felt her child was somehow…defective.

Though Phoebe and her Pop Pop shared no inherent DNA, their bond was tighter than anyone could imagine. He'd been a very active father in the PTA, had done his level best to encourage her in the Brownies and Girl Scouts, and he shared the things he loved with his precious girl. His love of music, his talents, his passion and skillsets in the shop, and an appreciation for good barbecue.

Shortly after the divorce, when she was about twelve, Phoebe started asking Pop Pop some rather pointed questions, questions that he could no longer dance around, and it was then that he thought it only fair to tell her the truth, that she had been adopted. Though he didn't provide much in the way of any backstory about her birth parents—mostly because he really knew nothing about them—he felt strongly about being honest with her and felt that, at twelve, she was mature enough to know it.

He'd been right. Phoebe seemed, even as a preteen, to be mature beyond her years. Deep down there seemed to dwell an old soul. And perhaps some ghosts he wasn't privy to. Phoebe had taken the news pretty well and spent the next several days processing it all. As time went on, she developed a desire to learn more about her birth mother and hoped to make contact with her when the time was right.

The trauma from twenty years before had tripped her synapses, and she'd subconsciously blocked the horrific experience and any memory of shared time. Though her research hadn't yet born fruit, she remained hopeful. She tried to imagine her mother, and wondered about her father, but she couldn't conjure him up either.

But, for now, Phoebe felt loved and contented. Pop Pop remained her best—and only—friend.

And it was a two-way street.

For that reason alone, Pop Pop knew he'd have to share the letter that had come that morning.

Maybe after dinner.

CHAPTER 11

BASED SOLELY ON the sheer volume of framed portraits lining her cottage entrance, it would be easy for any visitor—not that there were many—to conclude Phoebe had a deep and abiding sense of family.

The collection couldn't be more random, really, and it spanned many generations, even ethnicities. Smaller ones adorned end tables and nooks, while the larger portraits—all seemingly disconnected by both content and framing choice—occupied the entire wall leading from the front door to the back. Each had been a garage sale find, including the two four-by-sixes next to the phone, frames still containing the cheesy preprinted photos from when they'd been purchased at some Kmart somewhere. She'd hung two new ones just now, a couple of eight-by-tens, both obtained that day from the lava lamp dude, and they were pre-populated with pics of random people, and probably the garage sale peeps' dead relatives, for all she knew. She didn't care. The face of the old Asian guy was great, as was the serious-looking woman with the chopsticks in her hair.

She'd started this little hobby a year ago, when her deep sense of yearning for knowledge about her "real" family really kicked into the next level and remained unfulfilled. She knew it didn't make sense, but somehow there existed an obsessive need to construct a family—even if it was a global one and from random characters.

Thankfully she hadn't gone full-blown Sarah Winchester obsessive yet, but she wouldn't need much of a nudge. She was grateful for Pop Pop, yet she couldn't help feeling like a part of her was missing.

Phoebe lowered the Murphy bed and laid out the three dozen albums she'd narrowed it down to. She'd taken a good hour to go through all eight boxes, and these were the beauties from which she would create her favorite form of art: the mixed tape. Actually, a couple of mixed tapes, while she was at it. She'd tried the Memorex, Denon, BASF, Sony—just about all of them—but she kept coming back to what was now her go-to blank cassette tape: the Maxell High Bias xlii ninety-minute marvel. After a few bad experiences with the one hundred-minute ones, which seemed too thin, she'd gone back to the nineties, because they seemed more robust and less prone to jams in the deck. One less song per side, sure, but she'd opt for reliability. She grabbed the Maxells, plus another—a TDK, which were good too—from a drawer and headed over to the main house. She was the self-professed "Queen of the Pause Button," and these mixes would be her crowning achievements.

About five hours later, and after several unanswered taps, Pop Pop opened the door to the den and peeked inside. Phoebe had her back to him and had indeed surrendered to the studio headphones. The sight of her joyfully bobbing her noggin, fully immersed in a passionate place of rock 'n' roll vinyl groove, brought a big smile to his face. He looked at his watch and decided to give her another thirty minutes undisturbed. He could relate; it was his favorite thing too.

After all, she'd learned from the King of the Pause Button.

Phoebe closed her eyes as she savored the last bite of the perfectly simmered veggies Pop Pop had prepared for her. He'd grilled them in a self-made pouch constructed from heavy-duty aluminum foil. His technique involved cutting the fresh veggies into bite sized pieces, as if to go on skewers, only they wouldn't be.

His trip to the farmer's market that morning had yielded some choice mushrooms, lovely zucchini, a couple of yellow squash, carrots of a medium girth, young red potatoes, three colors of mild peppers, optimally ripe Roma tomatoes, a little yellow onion, and some fresh sprigs of rosemary. These were all lightly coated in a good virgin olive oil, seasoned with a dusting of minced garlic and a dash of parsley (very little salt!), a splash of cheap red wine, and carefully sealed in their foil tomb so as to assure proper steaming on the Weber. Judging from the look on her face and the sighs of pleasure coming from the other side of the table, he'd stuck the landing.

"Soooooo good, Pop Pop. You've gotta teach me how to do this. Please!"

"Happy to share the magic with you, Feebs! Glad you're enjoying it. More bread?"

"No, no…thanks. Salad was awesome as well. I am beyond happy," she replied, setting down her fork and wiping her smile with her napkin.

"Truth be told, the chicken wasn't my very best effort," he confessed. "Think it could've used a little more Beau Monde—but still better than you'll find anywhere else!" he added, setting a naked drumstick atop the considerable pile of dead soldiers already on his plate. "Dessert?"

"Depends…."

"Be right back," he said, a big smile on his face as he excused himself from the table.

Phoebe watched him as he walked toward the refrigerator. This gentle giant of a man was such a loving parent, friend, and boss. She silently thanked her lucky stars to have landed in this home, and in his loving care.

"Close your eyes," he said from across the room.

"'Kay."

"Are they closed?"

"Yes!" she chortled. "What's with the big surprise? I know it's not my birthday…and it's not your birthday…."

"Okay…open!" Pop Pop said a moment later, carrying a white box containing the grandest of all earthly desserts ever created. It was the absolute favorite of both, and it had probably been a year since they'd last had it.

"One blueberry-lemon cheesecake with lemon curd, madame," he said, attempting his best wannabe-French accent. "Specialty of the house, here at Chateau La Flamme," he continued, placing the entire cake in the middle of the small table and gently liberating it from its packaging.

It was almost too pretty to eat, with its generous layer of lemon curd, and the top's circumference was adorned with a crop of gigantic fresh blueberries that looked more like black olives. They were both terribly full, yet there always seemed to be room for this. He carved out two huge slices.

"Oh my gawd, Pop Pop," she said, as if staring at a treasure chest of gold doubloons. "Is this that one from Hilltop Bakery?"

"Accept no substitutes!" he said, watching her take the first bite. "As good as you remember?"

"No," she mumbled to the best of her ability with a mouthful. His look of disappointment prompted her to finish her answer. "No…it's better!!" she said with a chuckle.

"Bon appétit!" he chirped, happily digging into his own precious slab.

Other than the occasional, "Oh my gawd," little was said as they worked it to completion.

It was, indeed, the pièce de resistance, and deep down they were individually reflecting on the fact that they'd not likely have anything approaching this yummy again…until the next time this very same thing came around.

"Thank you, Pop Pop," was all she could manage.

"You bet, kiddo," he said, the corners of his smile dipping slightly.

The moment seemed as good as any, he decided, pulling out the envelope from his breast pocket. "This came for you today, but I thought it was for me. Opened by mistake…apologies," he said, sliding the envelope across to her.

"No worries, Pop Pop," she said, looking at the return address. She didn't get much mail, and this one appeared to be from out of state. "Who do I know in…California?" she asked under her breath as she removed its contents. He didn't offer an answer and instead watched his daughter's face as she went about reading the handwritten page.

Phoebe took her time, giving the letter a thorough once-through before cycling back for a second pass. Its penmanship was neat, and it'd been written in a man's hand. Her brow furrowed, then she looked up.

"What is it?" Pop Pop asked, already knowing the answer, but wanting to hear it from her.

"It says…he's related to me somehow, but he doesn't elaborate, other than his first name and that he knew my mother, and that he might have some information for me," she said quietly, a sense of disbelief nearly robbing her of her ability to speak.

"Hmm," he muttered.

"Did you know about this person and not tell me, Pop Pop?" she asked, an almost hurt expression on her face. "How long have you known about this guy *Liam*?"

"No, I didn't know, Feebs. Honestly. This came today, and I opened it 'cause I thought it was mine. But, no, I wasn't aware of this till now. You know I've never been dishonest with you, sweetie, and I never will. Okay? This is news to both of us."

She knew this to be true, and she nodded. "You think this guy's telling the truth? Think he might really be a relative?"

"I did a little search of the address. Appears to have been mailed from a nursing home in California—Monterey County, actually. There's no other contact info, but I'll try getting ahold of the place tomorrow, if you'd like. Seems legit, from the surface anyway."

Phoebe shook her head slowly, digesting the message a third time before folding the letter and returning it to its envelope. "Yeah, that would be great. Thanks," she said softly. This was suddenly hitting her like a ton of bricks. "I'm tired, Pop Pop. Think I'll just get to bed early, after I walk the Prick, if you don't mind," she said, getting up from the table and giving him a quick hug. "Thanks again for everything. Love you," she said as he watched her exit the main house. The screen door slammed behind her.

"Love you too, Feebs," he said, mostly to himself, as he pocketed the letter.

CHAPTER 12

POP POP WAS scribbling some notes on a legal pad and already on his third cup of coffee when he heard the screen door slam behind him. He knew he had to replace the pneumatic door closer, but it was the furthest thing from his mind at the moment.

Phoebe shuffled in, all bunny slippers and sweats, and made a beeline for the coffee maker. She always came over to the main house for her morning coffee, and he'd made a second pot. "Morning," she said groggily.

"Mornin', baby," he replied, looking up for the first time in a couple of hours. He glanced at the wall clock and couldn't believe it was already 10:40. "You must've slept well, Feebs."

"Not at all, really," she replied, adding a splash of half & half and two sugars to her cup. "Couldn't…active mind," she added, taking a seat next to him. "What's that stuff?"

"Mm, just jotting some stuff down. I had an active mind too. Been doing a little research into our new California friend here," he managed, before surrendering to a yawn as wide as the Grand Canyon. His bedhead, and the bags under his eyes, indicated he'd probably pulled an all-nighter.

"Ah, yes…Liam. Anything?"

"Yeah, well, I managed to get through to the nursing home— kind of an assisted living/rehab place, I guess—and it took some doing, but I managed to get a name. He looked up at her, and she at him, searching his face and dangling on his little cliffhanger for several moments.

"And...?"

"Sorry. And...turns out Liam is short for William. Last name of McGinn. Sounds Irish."

"Ya think?" she replied teasingly. "Red hair, per chance?" she said, fluffing up her own.

"My intel didn't glean hair color yet," he replied, taking another pull from his mug. "I did manage, however, to find out a little bit more about this William McGinn."

Phoebe leaned in, squinting down at his chicken-scratch notes, then back to his face, her brow furrowed. "I can't really read your writing, but does that underlined word say *cop?*"

"Yeah, it does," he replied. "Ex-cop, anyway. Formerly worked homicide. Get this: City of Phoenix. Can you believe that?"

"I dunno. Who's your source for this intel?"

"Let's just say I know a guy...called in a favor last night, and he got back to me about an hour ago."

"Okay...So, Liam—sorry, William—McGinn, ex-Phoenix PD, hair color unknown, now living in California. That's what we know. Good start!" she said, looking up from her coffee to find a very serious expression had taken over his face now.

"What is it, Pop Pop? What aren't you telling me? Is there more?"

His expression told her that there was. He didn't know how to begin, but he was a man of his word, and he hoped and trusted she'd be able to handle what he was about to say.

"Liam had a daughter, Feebs. Name of Rose. Rose...McGinn."

Phoebe's eyes searched his face, plumbing the depths, absorbing this new information as if it were gulps of oxygen after a near-drowning experience. "Go on, Pop Pop."

"She died young, she was only around twenty-one or twenty-two. Died in a house fire, over near Cave Creek, back in '79." His voice began to tremble. Phoebe squeezed his hand, encouraging him to continue.

"Rose was his daughter. She was also…your mother," he said, his eyes welling up.

Phoebe's lip began to tremble, and it was hard to see through the foggy veil of tears.

"Wow…" was all she could manage, and they both sat there in silence for several minutes before she could muster up her next thought. "So, he's my grandpa then?"

"Seems so, sweetie," Pop Pop said, wiping away his own tears.

"And he didn't come for me? Where was I? Where was he? What happened? I don't understand!" she said, as she got up from the table and began slowly pacing the kitchen. "How could he not tell me?"

Pop Pop stood and pushed in his chair. He put an arm around Phoebe. "It wasn't that easy, honey. There's a bit more to the story, I'm afraid."

"Well, we might as well just lay it all out there, right?" She looked at him and her earnest expression let him know that she was ready for whatever he had left in the quiver. "Lay it on me, Pop Pop. Please. Please, don't hold anything back. I need to know… everything."

He took a long thoughtful look at his adopted daughter. With her red-rimmed eyes and her Minnie Mouse sweatshirt, she looked about twelve. Life wasn't fair, and as much as he wanted to protect her from any of the world's unpleasantries, he had to face the fact that she was twenty-five now and had already experienced more than her share of darkness. More than she was even aware of.

He respected the young woman she had become, appreciated her maturity, and he took her prodding as an invitation and the green light he'd needed to proceed any further.

"Okay, Feebs, but not on an empty stomach. Let's get cleaned up. Get some breakfast—" he said, glancing at his watch, "—lunch maybe, and go for a little drive…."

Los Dos Molinos was known for their lava-hot entrees, and Phoebe was certain her tastebuds had experienced third-degree burns. Pop Pop had taken her to the Alma School Plaza one, in Mesa. Its location, next to the auto repair shop in an industrial setting, might be off-putting to someone not in the know, but they'd been coming here for years, and they needed to sweat out the truth over this joint's specialty relleno dinner: a whole green chili wrapped in a fried egg, stuffed with cheese, and smothered in spicy green chili.

Pop Pop had added meat to his, and an order of their Dutch-oven cooked pork carnitas to bring home. Some rice and beans, fresh guac, fiery salsa, a couple baskets of chips, and a few cervezas. And a house margarita each. Phoebe wasn't a drinker, but she might just become one today—if for no other reason than to put out the fire.

But truth be told, the margaritas Pop Pop had ordered were the perfect pairing with the next item on the menu: the mother of all truth bombs, served open-faced. As the server cleared their dishes, he took a sip.

"You doin' okay, Feebs?"

"So far, yeah, I guess…man, what's in this thing? Whoo!"

"I don't know, sweetie, but I don't see any open flames, so I think we're okay."

"So…" she said, sliding her glass to the side, her look direct, but not confrontational.

"So…okay, Feebs. I mentioned about Liam being with Phoenix PD, and about his daughter—your mother, Rose." He took a deep breath and exhaled slowly through his ballooned cheeks. "Turns out Liam was one of the officers who'd responded to the fire that killed your mother. He was the one that found her, Feebs. He was the one who found his daughter, Rose, in the burned down house. Turns out it was an arson fire."

Fat tears rolled down both of Phoebe's cheeks at hearing this, and her emotions were a strange cocktail of sadness, regret, and a developing anger at hearing this last part.

"Arson? As in somebody deliberately set her house on fire?"

"That's what the police report says, honey. And being the investigating officer at his own daughter's crime scene…it pretty much destroyed him. And his career. He nearly drank himself to death over many years. That's why you never heard from him—that, and the fact he didn't even know about you all these years," he said, shaking his head.

"And you didn't know…."

"No, honey. We adopted you when you were five, not long after this happened. You were just a little girl, and probably too young to remember. We—Suzan and I—tried our best to make a happy home for you, honey. I don't know if we succeeded, but that was the goal."

A minute went by as she absorbed everything. She wiped away her tears and rested her hands atop his, giving them a reassuring squeeze. "Don't ever doubt that, Pop Pop. Of course, you did! I don't know if I've ever properly thanked you for everything you did for me. It must've been hard on you too."

"Every day I get to spend with you…that's thanks enough, Feebs," he said, his tear ducts betraying him, poking holes in the dam that was his masculinity.

"I love you, Pop Pop," she said, coming around to his side of the table, where she got enveloped in a deep hug with the bear of a man. The server came by with the check but didn't wish to interrupt the moment, so he walked away.

"I love you too, Phoenix."

It'd come out of his mouth. He felt a slight slackening in her hug. Her face surfaced again, her eyes finding his.

"What'd you call me?"

"Phoenix…that's the name your mother had given you. We

changed it to Phoebe to protect you, Feebs. Just in case there might still be a bad guy out there…I hope you understand."

She looked up, studying the ceiling for several moments, as if plotting to paint a fresco. Her eyes found his, and there was a smile.

"Phoenix…I kinda like it!"

CHAPTER 13

THE TO-GO ORDER of carnitas and a small pile of tortillas were properly bagged and sat on the seat between them. There were a few bumps on this stretch of road, and Phoenix stabilized the goods with her left hand.

"Mind if we swing by the shop for a minute?"

"It's Sunday."

"I know. Just want to check on something really quick."

"Cool with me," she replied, looking out the window, her brain buzzing like a hive of bees, with all she'd learned today.

Pop Pop smiled to himself and took a left turn at the next corner. The shop was only a couple blocks away. They pulled into the driveway and parked against the block wall, next to the Dumpster and below the modest signage that declared they were at POP'S. He climbed out and came around to her side and opened the door.

"You want me to come in too?"

"Yeah, if you don't mind. Won't be long. Wanna show you something."

"Okay," she said, placing the foodstuffs on the floorboard.

Being Sunday, it was very quiet, and devoid of any activity. Tomorrow morning would be a different matter but, as the owner, he sometimes liked to stop in when there wasn't anybody there. It helped him think, and he could get a read on what to expect the next day, once the doors were rolled up and he'd swung the plastic sign around to the OPEN side. He dug the considerable ring of keys from his pocket and once inside, punched in the security code.

"Want me to finish the brakes on the Camaro tomorrow, Pop Pop?"

"We'll see, Feebs. C'mon back, I wanna show you something," he said, guiding her around to the rearmost bay. She rarely had cause to visit this part of the shop and what she saw there was a large drape covering what appeared to be a rather sizeable vehicle of some sort. Its shape revealed no clues, and she couldn't imagine what was underneath the sheet. Even with the overhead lights the service bay was rather dark, so he rolled up the heavy steel door and let some daylight in.

"There, that's a little better."

"Did you buy a Chris-Craft, Pop Pop?" she said with a chuckle. "You wanted to show me your new boat?" She punched his shoulder kiddingly.

"Well, not exactly, but…well, have a look. Go ahead, honey. Pull the covers back."

She gave him a quizzical look and decided to humor him. "Okie dokie." She yanked away the cloth dramatically, as if revealing the white tiger in a cage. "Ta-da!" she exclaimed, going with it. It wasn't a tiger, however, and her breath escaped her entirely.

For a full minute time stood still, and the whole world seemed to have been muted.

"Beautiful, right?" Pop Pop said with an irrepressible grin. It was perhaps the most beautiful thing either one of them had ever seen.

"Oh. My. Gawd…Pop Pop, is that what I think it is?!"

"Depends. What do you think it is?" he said with a laugh.

"It only looks like my favorite fucking —oops…excuse me, Pop Pop—*friggin'*—car in the whole entire friggin' world. Is it?!" She looked up at him, reading his expression. "Is it a 1970 Plymouth friggin' Road Runner?!?!" she asked, almost tripping over her jaw now.

"You have a keen eye, and discerning tastes, Feebs! Yes, it is indeed!"

Her eyes were hubcaps as she regarded the pristine Hemi orange beast. Since she'd been obsessed with her identical toy Hot Wheel version of this exact car since she was in middle school, she already knew that this beauty had to have a 426, was probably capable of zero to sixty in about five and a half seconds, and a quarter mile in about thirteen, at a bone-rattling 106 miles per hour. She'd never seen a real one and had wondered if they really existed. This car was a unicorn, and she ran her fingers across the glossy orange hood which had the functional air grabber and the same wide, black striping as hers. It had full Road Runner badging and even had the reflective decal strip of "dust trail" extending from the bird's feet and continuing past the door before it disappeared into the side scoops. Original steel wheels and the raised white lettered Polyglas GTs. This thing was absolutely bad ass!

Pop Pop watched every move on her face, and he knew every thought that had to be going through her splendid little red head at that moment. With everything that had been laid on her today, he was overjoyed to see her—distracted—with something she loved so much.

"Oh, my goodness…okay, just tell me what it needs, Pop Pop. Brakes? Tune-up? Shocks! I get dibs on this one tomorrow!"

"Actually, it's not needing any of those things, Feebs. She's mechanically sound, runs like a top, and this one has the working telescopic air grabber—there's a switch for it under the dash. It's always been garaged, meticulously maintained, and is wanting for nothing!"

"Whoa…no way! Why's it here then?" she asked, wondering why this beauty wasn't on exhibit in a hermetically sealed case in some museum, or in Jay Leno's private collection, anyway.

"The 4Runner's getting old, Feebs. On her last legs. You'll be needing some wheels."

71

"Shut up!" she said with a laugh. "No, seriously. I mean it. What's it doing here?"

"I know a guy," he said, pulling a single key from another pocket. It was attached to a leather fob with a plastic insert displaying an image of the famed Warner Brothers cartoon character. He held it out in his palm.

"Here, see if it starts for you."

"You mean it?" she asked, plucking the key from his hand like it was the Holy Grail.

"Driver's door should be open."

Phoenix placed her hand on the chrome door handle and slowly swung it open. Not a creak. The interior looked all original, and with great ceremony, she slid her tiny behind onto the black upholstery. It felt akin to a queen sitting on her throne for the first time. She put her hands on the wheel, then slid her right onto the knob of the four-speed stick. For a moment she wondered if she might be dreaming and, if so, she surely never wanted to be woken from it. She could barely reach the pedals, so she slid the bench seat forward several inches.

"I hope you don't mind, but I took one small liberty...under the dash, there."

Her eyes traveled to where he was pointing. At about knee level and mounted within easy reach now that she'd adjusted the seat, she saw that he'd done a slight upgrade to the sound system: a beautiful, high-end Blaupunkt AM/FM/cassette stereo.

"Holy—"

"I removed it from that red Porsche—the one that was totaled. Works great! The AM radio in the dash there, its original, and still powers up, but it needed a little help. Oh, and there are three-ways in the door panels and a couple six by nines in the back. Plenty of power."

"What's the deal, Pop Pop?" she said softly. This entire day had been too much to process, and this equated to sensory overload.

"Happy Birthday early, Feebs. She's yours. A 4Runner for a Road Runner, if those are acceptable terms." Phoenix laughed, then immediately burst into tears for the third or fourth time today. At least these tears were happy ones. This was way cooler than her Hot Wheel.

As she slowly slid the key into its slot, she looked back up to Pop Pop. He just nodded his approval. The beast came to life immediately on its first turn, a throaty roar coming from its twin pipes, as it idled at nine hundred revolutions per minute. She tried the horn, which delivered its trademark *Meep! Meep!* sound.

"No coyote's gonna be able to catch you, sweetheart."

CHAPTER 14

PHOENIX HAD SLEPT like the dead, all the while her subconscious labored to piece together the billion-piece jigsaw puzzle that had been dumped on her the day before. She probably would've slept half the day away, but the dog had jumped up on the bed at 6:30, pawing at her face and signaling it was time for breakfast. And he needed to go poop.

"Mm…hey…okay, little Prick…just a second…jeez!"

She swung her feet over the side of the bed and stepped into her bunnies before hoisting the Murphy bed back up against the wall. Grateful that Pop Pop had offered her the day off, she shuffled the few feet to the bathroom area and washed her face. After she'd patted herself dry and tousled her considerable mane, she took pause at the sight of the beautiful creature looking back at her in the mirror. *Where'd she come from?*

"Good morning, Phoenix!" she said with a smile. It felt so weird saying that but, somehow, it felt good. It felt…right. A yip from the Chihuahua mix reminded her that he needed her attention.

"Yes, you little Prick, we're going out right now."

After a potty break, and a serving of kibble, Phoenix put the pooch in his crate and rolled through the shower before heading over to the main house for her coffee. She was needing a caffeine jolt in a big way. As she passed by the garage, she couldn't resist a peek through the window to see if there was really a 1970 Road Runner in there, as she'd wondered if it had been part of her dream cycle. It was indeed parked there, and the sight of it brought a huge smile. "Meep! Meep!"

Pop Pop had been kind enough to move some boxes around in the one-car garage the day before, extending the length of usable parking area by a couple of feet to make room for her new ride, which—at seventeen plus feet—needed a little extra space. This meant parking his F-150 XL off to the side of the driveway for the time being, but he was totally fine with that. It was basically a work truck, and it had ceased being pretty a couple of years back.

The screen door slammed behind her as she made her way over to the machine that would provide her with some much-needed, life-giving nectar. That and a bowl of cereal, and she'd be good to go. The glass coffee urn was still hot because Pop Pop had only left an hour before. She dumped some dairy and a couple of sugar packets into her favorite Little Mermaid mug and made her way over to the kitchen table.

A cereal bowl, spoon, a glass of orange juice, and three cereal boxes were waiting for her. "Thanks, Pop Pop," she said to herself. He was always thoughtful that way. Today's offerings included raisin bran (yecch!), some shredded wheat, and box of Lucky Charms, which she chose because…she was Irish. And it had those marshmallow things in there, if that's what they really were. After pouring on a little milk, she got to it.

A couple of magically delicious bites in, she heard a beeping sound coming from around the corner, where the office area was. She tried to ignore it, but it persisted. *Maybe Pop Pop left me a message.* Curiosity got the better of her and she carried her breakfast bowl as she investigated.

Like many, the "office" was a repurposed empty bedroom and

totally utilitarian. It didn't have to look pretty and was half full of stacked records boxes, while the other half had a cheap laminate desk with a cordless phone, a standalone Panasonic answering machine and a combination copy/fax/printer deal. The Panasonic was quietly minding its own business and there were no beeps or flashing lights to signal a new message had come in. That left the other contraption, which was new and looked a bit complicated. Its display window was illuminated, however, and its top paper tray began noisily regurgitating a few pages of documents. The only decorative item was a framed five-by-seven-inch photo on the desk, of her and Pop Pop at her high school graduation.

Phoenix took in the memory, and a couple of bites of marshmallow-laden oats, while she waited for the device's cycle to complete itself. After the last of the three printed pages landed in its tray, the machine indicated it was finished. She was about to walk away when she caught a glance at the document atop the stack. That's when the cereal bowl slipped through her fingers and—like her psyche—shattered into several pieces.

It had been a pretty long day at the salt mine and as Pop Pop pulled into the driveway, his thoughts turned to the carnitas in the fridge. He'd probably rustle up a nice fruit salad for Phoebe. *Er, Phoenix.* Man, this was going to be an adjustment for them both.

As he reached the end of the drive, he remembered to pull into his new spot. His attention was quickly redirected to the two trash receptacles and a large, open packing box, all of which seemed to be stuffed full of various photo frames. He recognized several of them. *Huh?*

His typical quick tap of the horn to announce he was home had gone unanswered, so he peeked into the garage window. The Road Runner wasn't there. *Must be enjoying a little drive.*

Once inside, he tossed his keys on the counter, deactivated the alarm system, and pulled out the carnitas, as well as the assorted fresh fruit from the crisper. Also calling to him, from its perch on the second shelf, was an ice-cold Guinness Extra Stout. *Thank you!*

It was nearing 5:30 and Phoenix would likely be home any minute, he figured, but he could enjoy a frosty beer. *Weird about the picture frames.* He'd have to ask her when she got home.

As he sat down at the kitchen table, he pulled off his Diamondbacks ballcap and took his time transferring the contents of the can to the frosty mug he'd retrieved from the freezer. There were several hard-and-fast rules in this life and one of them was: Never rush a Guinness pour.

Next to the day's mail, he found a small stack of official-looking documents he didn't recognize. Amongst them, some twenty-five-year-old hospital records and two reports from his "guy" at the Phoenix P.D.

"Holy mother of God," he muttered to himself, as the information on the pages began delivering body blows. "Oh, sweet Jesus!" Pop Pop pounded his fist on the table, unconcerned with the beer cascading from his mug. As he got through the last page, his brow furrowed, and he buried his teeth into the fleshy part of his large hand and began sobbing uncontrollably.

Phoenix had indeed gone for a little drive, but it hadn't been particularly enjoyable. Not in the slightest. As she sat there in the parking lot of her old high school, she stared vacantly out the window as she saw the blurred shapes of the girls' soccer team running about, in spurts and seemingly random circles, like scorpions in a hot skillet.

Her thoughts drifted as she heard the squeals of the athletic team in the distance. She'd hated her years here, as she had at the middle school before. Memories of always being picked last for teams in P.E. and relentlessly teased during her formative years, it was all crashing down on her hard. Her foot surgeries had made it difficult for her to participate athletically, and she'd never even been asked to dance, plus—to this day—she'd never kissed a boy.

Years of taunts along the lines of "Phreaky Phoebe" and "Pheeble Phoebe" still haunted her and they'd done a big number on her self-esteem. The tears resumed, streaming down her cheeks.

Phuck them!!!

Phoenix had already driven all over Gilbert today, and much of Mesa, trying to get her head around the latest shit sandwich she'd just been served—and hadn't ordered. It could probably be argued, and quite successfully, that there wasn't anything in this life that could even approach the shock of finding out that your entire life had been a lie, and that you were, in fact, the survivor of an unsuccessful abortion.

Yes, her young mother, Rose McGinn, had decided that the child growing inside her wasn't worth the trouble and had chosen to have her aborted! And, as if that wasn't enough, to find out as she just had—that you were actually a *surviving twin* of a successfully murdered would-be sibling…this was the worst scene from the worst horror movie, and she was living it.

The intense guilt trip had begun hours before, courtesy of the malignant data that had just been installed and was now rampantly infecting her inner hard drive. She wished she could just simultaneously hit the control, alt, command, and power keys on her brain—if only her life could somehow reboot entirely—but she was no longer even sure of her motherboard.

A sister…it might've been nice to have a say-so in that…. And, why, God? Why did I, Phoenix Phriggin' McGinn, survive, when my sister didn't? How phucked up is that, Big Guy?!

The blowing of the coach's whistle signaled the end of soccer practice, snapping Phoenix back to reality. And reality was sucking hugely right now. She stared at the little bobbing hula girl she'd added to her dashboard, a garage sale find she'd liberated from a box that morning. It watched over her, serving to remind her that she'd never ever been to Hawaii, had never seen an ocean, and hadn't even been out of the state of Arizona. *Add all those to the future wish list....*

She turned the key, and her orange hot rod roared to life. The sky was starting its surreal palette shift into the red tones, signaling it was probably time to get back home.

Pop Pop had finished creating the fruit salad, and it was a masterpiece. In addition to the boilerplate offerings of apple, orange, grapes and banana, he'd included four varieties of fresh berries, two freestone peaches, and some cantaloupe. He'd taken great care in making it picture perfect, and it was worthy of the front cover of *Sunset* magazine, though he didn't remember any of its preparation. The carnitas simmered on low. He'd already fed the Prick.

The unmistakable sound of a Hemi 426 coming up the block prompted him to turn off the burner and begin plating. As the Road Runner rolled into the garage, Pop Pop prayed for guidance in how to handle the ensuing conversation. As the garage door closed, he wiped his hands on his jeans, threw up a Hail Mary, and went outside.

Phoenix was still staring at the garage door when he came up and initiated a fatherly bear hug. After a few moments, resistance became futile, and she reciprocated the hug, the car key dropping to the ground. She went limp, and her shoulders heaved with the release. No words were spoken, as none were needed, and regardless of any attempt, they wouldn't have been close to adequate anyway. They stood that way for several minutes as the sky shifted toward purple.

"C'mon in, sweetie," he said, giving the top of her head a kiss. And she did.

Her head was elsewhere as she picked at her salad, but she slowly made progress, almost enjoying every bite. "Thank you, Pop Pop."

"Don't mention it, honey," he answered with a weak smile. He hadn't touched his own carnitas, and these were the first words either had spoken. With the silence now broken, he sunk his teeth into the pork-filled tortilla.

"I've decided I'm going to go," Phoenix blurted, sliding her empty plate off to the side.

"Oh?" he managed with a mouthful. He swallowed before venturing, "Where, honey?"

"I've *got* to go see him now."

"Wait, who are we talking about?"

"Liam. William. *Grandpa*...if that's who he really is. I'm going to go see him. In California," she replied, looking at him directly now.

Pop Pop set down the other half of his burrito and wiped his mouth. "Wait, you're sure?"

Phoenix nodded resolutely. "Yep. I need to do this," she said, before quoting from a favorite movie of theirs, *The Big Lebowski*. "New shit has come to light...."

"That it has...."

"So, I'm thinking day after tomorrow. Wednesday, if you're okay with me being away from the shop?"

"The shop will be fine, Phoenix. Have you given any thought as to how long you'd be away?"

"Not sure...no idea, actually. But I have to."

"You need some help with airfare?"

"Nope, I'm good. Good excuse for a road trip, right?"

"You want to drive? To *California*?"

"I'm a big girl, Pop Pop. I'll be fine! It's not like I'll be gone forever. I just need to figure out a few things. Hopefully Liam can help connect some dots."

He knew he wasn't going to have any success talking her out of something she'd already decided upon. "Will you at least consider taking along my gas card?"

"Only if you feel strongly about it," she said with a hint of a tired smile.

"I do."

"Okay...deal," she said, shaking his hand. "Thank you, Pop Pop."

TUESDAY

After her obligatory walk with the Prick, Phoenix spent the next two hours filling several dozen small nail holes with Spackle and touching up the granny unit's interior paint. She was done with her menagerie of framed strangers on the walls; they had served their purpose. She added two small K-Mart framed pics of wannabe siblings to the trash can. She could visualize her family tree a little better now, even though all of its limbs had been cut off, and the trunk had long died.

She really didn't have any idea how much to pack, but she began setting a few things she wanted to take by the cottage door: one large duffle of clothes, two pairs of walking shoes, her bass guitar—just in case—her Blueberry iBook Mac G3 laptop, the lava lamp, her folio of mixed tapes, curling iron, toiletries, chargers, etc. Plus, the dog crate, dog bed, dog food and stuff for her other companion, the bird. She'd already taken a second look at the interior of the Road Runner's trunk and gauged her load accordingly. Riding shotgun would be the Prick, and the bird—a young, rose-breasted cockatoo named Angus—would be in his medium sized cage.

"Hello!" said the bird.

"Hello, Angus!" Phoenix replied. "Yes, you're coming too," she said, filling a medium packing box with various critter supplies. She'd thought about the impracticality of bringing Angus along, but he was pretty snippy when it came to who got near his cage for cleanings, feedings, and the like. Plus, she didn't want to saddle Pop Pop with all that, so she'd decided to book him a seat.

She made a few trips out to the car with her belongings, everything but the animals and their stuff. Satisfied with her packing job, she closed the trunk and locked it. As she took a long look at the rear of her car, she remembered the one thing that was missing: the bumper sticker she'd picked up. She ran back inside and retrieved it, then wiped the left rear bumper clean before peeling off the strips to reveal the sticker's adhesive. Careful not to get any unsightly air bubbles, she affixed it firmly, then stepped back to admire her favorite slogan:

MEAN PEOPLE SUCK!

Yes!

Tomorrow's road trip called for another special *themed* mixed tape, and she took her time as she thoughtfully perused all eight boxes of albums before retiring to the den with her stack. This ninety-minute tape would likely be three hours in the making, but it would be a gamechanger.

Pop Pop had ordered their favorite delivery pizza, and it was a half and half deal. It always started out, as its base, a large vegetarian, with the red sauce—hold the onions. On her half, they'd hold the black olives. On his half, they'd add Italian sausage. On the whole deal, they'd add pineapple. It worked, and they dubbed it "the Swineapple." After dinner, they'd played a few rounds of their favorite boardgame, *Sequence*, and Pop Pop took two out of three.

Over a couple bowls of good Neapolitan ice cream, Pop Pop went over the road maps with her, gave her his extra gas card, and eventually his blessing. "The gas card will probably heat up pretty quick but use it as much as you need. Don't worry about paying me back. Don't expect to get great mileage with the Hemi, and always follow the basic rule when driving—especially in Arizona: don't ever let it get below half tank before refilling. Got it?"

"Yes, Pop Pop. Thank you for being so great with all this," she said.

"Just looking out for my little girl. I only want you to be safe and to be happy," he said, biting his lip slightly. He didn't want to let her know he was having a hard time with this, and he looked away before his moist eyes gave him away.

"Love you, Pop Pop. So much forever," she said, giving his hand a squeeze. "I've gotta get to bed. Long day tomorrow."

"Love you too, beauty. Sleep well. By the way, I called Mike at home, told him to open the shop for me, that I'd be in about ten, after I see you off."

"Awesome. 'Night." Phoenix got up from the table, walked around behind Pop Pop's chair and wrapped her arms around him, then disappeared beyond the slamming screen door.

After properly tucking in Prick and covering Angus's cage, Phoenix experienced a bit more difficulty with readying herself. Tossing and turning with an active mind was the worst kind of curse, and it would likely be another sleepless night of nonstop flashbacks and trying to figure out the un-figure-out-able. Could her pillow literally be made of memory foam?

With a monster drive ahead of her, she was determined to get at least a few solid hours of shuteye, so she strapped on her darkest eye mask, seated the wax earplugs deep into her canals, and did her level best to become one with the cicadas.

PART FOUR
LEAVING PHOENIX

CHAPTER 15

THE CAR WAS packed, maps were on the dashboard, and her travel folio of cassettes was within easy reach. As soon as Prick was finished marking the recycling bin, they'd be wheels-up. Best laid plans, but the previous night's sleep had been spotty at best. Knowing this, Pop Pop had filled his largest travel Thermos with strong French Roast, a generous splash of half & half and the requisite two—make that three—sugars; it was a big vessel. He handed it to Phoenix while she monitored the Prick's prick for any progress.

"This should get you started," he said. "Might want to refill it —and top-off the car, while you're at it—when you get to Yuma. Oh, and take this too," he said, handing her his Visa card.

"If you insist…thanks, Pop Pop," she replied, smiling warmly and pocketing the card before laying into the dog for being overly selective in picking his optimal place to pee.

"There! Just do it…c'mon, we've gotta go!" No sooner had she barked at him than he yipped back at her, then lifted his leg.

"It's about time…sheesh!"

"Call me when you get to the motel. Promise?"

"Promise," she said as she loaded the little guy into his crate.

She tossed in a greenie for his teeth. "Really, I'll be fine, Pop Pop. Try not to worry, okay?"

He nodded. This was way more difficult than he'd ever imagined. "Okay," he said, then pulled her into a two-minute hug. Neither wanted to let go, but Phoenix was the first to release.

"Gotta go. Love you," she said, smiling as she adjusted her ASU ballcap.

"Safe drive, sweetie. Call me if you need anything. Call me if you *don't* need anything. Just call me, please," he said as she slid into her orange chariot and started it up. The beast's engine sounded melodic, and he couldn't help noticing that she made that car look even better. He gave the hood a light tap with his hand and sent up a silent prayer for her safety.

He waved continuously until she turned the corner. *Meep! Meep!* And she was gone.

The car felt solid, muscular—like a friggin' thoroughbred even. If a bird can be a thoroughbred. Phoenix had a heavy load on her mind, but she still found it hard to suppress the smile that came from knowing she'd be checking off one of the boxes on her long-neglected wish list.

"Road trip!" she yelled out to the universe. This got an excited yip from her little companion, and even a "Hello!" from Angus.

"Hello, Angus! Ever been to California?"

"Hel-lo!!" from the back scat.

"Yeah…me neither! Here we go, little guys," she said as she approached Interstate 10.

Once the Superstition Freeway hit the junction of the 10, the first decision of her road trip would be presenting itself shortly. Pop Pop had marked the connector that would take her slightly south, past Casa Grande, before joining up with Interstate 8, which would take her due west through Yuma, placing her pretty much at the border of Mexico, before crossing into California. A straight shot and roughly three hours, he'd said. Gas up, caffeine up, stretch the legs, he'd said.

Or...this might be fun....

Phoenix had never been accused of being the most impulsive person you'd ever met, but she surprised herself when she sped right past Casa Grande and the junction of the 8. Continuing southeast on the 10, and blowing off Pop Pop's map markings, she found herself gravitating to Tucson and beyond. She'd read things about a groovy artists' town called Tubac—a haven for collectors of Talavera pottery—and by golly, that's where she was heading. *How random!*

As this was all unchartered territory for her, Phoenix decided to heed Pop Pop's advice and at least gas up in Tucson. The town held no attraction to her, other than a slight curiosity of knowing just how sketchy the Buffet Bar & Crockpot really was. She'd heard stories of Tucson's oldest dive bar, which had been around since 1934, and she momentarily toyed with the idea of at least stopping in to buy a ballcap, if they sold 'em. But just as quickly the thought passed, as she wasn't really a drinker, she didn't particularly enjoy the smell of urine, and God only knew how long those hotdogs had been sitting in that funky crock pot. Besides, she was a vegetarian...*hello!*

A quick stop for petrol turned into an opportune moment for the pooch to leave a little gift in the dirt patch out back. She made a mental note to pick up some more poop bags when she could. The day was young, but already turning out to be another scorcher, so she decided against the coffee refill and instead opted for a gonzo-sized Slurpee, a fifty-fifty mix of Cherry and Cola. And a bag of Red Vines.

Back on the road, she passed the Tucson International Airport and continued south on Interstate 19. As she chomped on a few ropes of licorice, she decided to test out the sound system Pop Pop had so graciously upgraded. She hadn't even turned it on in the four days she'd owned the car, and that amounted to sacrilege. Without taking her eyes off the road, she unzipped the cassette folio and liberated the first in the series of mixed tapes she'd prepared for the trip. As she inserted it into the Blaupunkt's slot, she cranked up the volume in anticipation of the first blast of sound. This mix, like all of the ones she created, started out strong right out of the gate, and the percussion/keyboard intro to Head East's signature hit, "There's Never Been Any Reason," filled the car with concert hall-like intensity.

"Yeah!!!!!!!!" she screamed, suddenly a front row teenage concertgoer.

"Hello!"

"Hello, Angus! Woo-hoo! And to you, little Prick—hello!"

Her copilot was rather nonplussed and couldn't compete with the crushing power chords. He went with a weak yip, accompanied with some stink-eye attitude.

She'd have to learn the bass line to this one, she decided, because guitarist Mike Somerville had come up with one of the all-time great power riffs. Basically, a G-B-C-D deal. She joined John Schlitt on the vocals, at the top of her lungs:

Did you see any action? Did you make any friends?
Would you like some affection before I leave again?
I've been walking behind you, since you've been able to see.
There's never been any reason for you to think about me.

She was already finding great power in this, and a tremendous release that could only come with singing arena rock at the top of your lungs while jamming down a less-traveled Arizona highway in a friggin' classic Hemi Road Runner with your dog and a bird.

Save my life, I'm going down for the last time.
Woman with the sweet lovin', better than a white line.
Bring a good feeling ain't had in such a long time.
Save my life I'm going down for the last time.

The prominent synth solo was every bit as trippy as anything Styx had done and sounded almost Keith Emerson-esque. Head East's harmony vocals put them in the same league as Queen, REO Speedwagon, and the best of 'em. Prick could've done without the synth solo, and he curled up further into his blankie. Angus, on the other hand, was fully into it and was bobbing his head from the back seat, like a feathered version of his AC/DC namesake.

Save my life, I'm going down for the last tiiiiiiiimmmmme!

Damn, Pop Pop done good! She couldn't wait to tell him.

Any great mixed tape—one that you'd be proud to give to a friend, and one that was truly representative of your hard-earned title of "Queen (or King) of the Pause Button"—has certain necessary characteristics that make it great. Amongst those are: theme (if you choose one); song selection (duh); your choice of lead-off song (every bit as important as choosing your team's lead-off hitter in a championship game); the all-important follow-up song choice; knowing the ebb and flow of the mix; plus—very importantly—the amount of silence between songs. Like any respectable art form, there were so many considerations and variables, and when it came to creating an epic mixed tape, any good mix-master had to consider their audience. Even if it was just…yourself.

To wit: song #2 maintained the same fever pitch, opening with in-your-face power chords as it mercilessly slammed into the rear bumper of Head East's number, with a scant one-second pause: "Hold On Loosely" by .38 Special. *Yessir.*

Song #3 also provided a made-to-order one-second cue as it segued into "Miles Away" by Fleetwood Mac. An almost tribal tom-tom lead-in by Mick Fleetwood joined by some impossible-to-ignore guitar fury by "the two Bobs," Bob Welch and Bob Weston, along with John McVie's thunderous bottom end got this one going.

By the time song #4 came around, it was time to throttle back briefly, as it gently segued into Dan Fogelberg's beautiful minute-plus instrumental intro "Tullamore Dew," which was attached at the hip with the more visceral up-tempo rocker, "Phoenix," and had become one of her new theme songs. So, she and Dan sang it with passion.

Collective Soul's "Precious Declaration" had been impatiently waiting in the on-deck circle and, with the first pitch, knocked it into the cheap seats. Phoenix stepped on the gas a little harder, harder still as the Hemi was finally given permission to demonstrate what it'd been designed to do, and before she knew it, she had hit the triple digits on the speedometer. She lit up her vocal cords as well, entering the primal screaming phase, like a banshee on fire.

By this time, Phoenix was only about half-way through Side A, and risking permanent damage to both her eardrums and vocal cords, and the pooch wasn't digging it too much. So it was a good time to take a break, turn it off…for a little while at least. Lots of road ahead. She didn't want Angus to get a case of whiplash, after all. The little Prick let out a sigh of relief as she returned to the posted speed limit.

This highway was absolutely lousy with saguaro cacti. They were everywhere, for as far as the eye could see, and as a lifelong resident of Arizona, she'd never tired of the sight. This stretch in particular was a target-rich environment, with tens of thousands of them—each seemingly as different from one another as fingerprints, and it held her fascination for several miles.

That's when she spotted the anomaly.

Hiding in plain sight among his saguaro brethren it stood, defiantly different and impossible to ignore for anyone with a trained eye. Slack-jawed, Phoenix checked her mirrors and slowed, pulling off to the shoulder and never taking her eyes from the freakish growth that served to…beckon her…signal her…perhaps even warn her of some impending evil. She wasn't sure which. She shuddered in momentary disbelief as she regarded this weathered giant of a cactus—the only one she'd ever seen with its arms downturned, like hands on its nonexistent hips. She got out and approached it cautiously.

She remembered a legend she'd heard, quite possibly an old wives' tale from school. Regardless, it'd stuck with her. Something about these outliers having supposed powers that could forecast bad luck, but she'd never believed it. Standing here now, however, and squinting up at the face of this gnarly twelve-foot tall, woodpecker ravaged, monstrous beacon of potential doom staring down at her, she had to wonder if there was any truth to the story. Though seemingly impossible, this thing was even creepier than those pissed-off apple trees that had always freaked her out in *The Wizard of Oz*. An unexplained frosty shiver ran down her spine, which in itself was unusual, especially on a 111-degree day.

She made haste back to the car, secured her lap belt and punched the gas, spitting up a cloud of gravelly soil as she barreled ahead.

For the next several miles, chills from the encounter—which felt akin to meeting up with the Devil at the Crossroads—remained, and the sense of foreboding showed no signs of going away any time soon. That was until, up ahead on the right, she saw something gleaming white on the horizon. It was so far away it was probably a mirage, she'd decided, as it was so bright, and seemingly out of place, like a giant igloo in the middle of the desert. Two anomalies, and the day was young! As she continued ahead, it took a few minutes for the blinding object to take some kind of recognizable shape. *A mission! And well timed!*

"Hang with me, guys. We may have to make a little stop," she said to the critters as she exited the main highway and took the frontage road leading to the driveway, and eventually the parking lot outside the massive Mission San Xavier del Bac.

Completed in the late 1700s, this gleaming house of worship was still an active Catholic mission and open to the public. Still,

Phoenix couldn't help feeling that this radiant structure seemed decidedly out of place here, like some wayward, spiritual mothership that had crash-landed on its way to Roswell. Like most missions, it had a storied history and had suffered through just about every calamity imaginable—from earthquakes to lightning strikes, as well as serious leaks requiring evacuation for a time. The façade had been restored in 1953, and it had been named a National Historic Landmark ten years later. A five-year rescue effort had been initiated by conservators a few years back in order to restore the interior. The fresh white paint made the exterior of this diamond shine brightly, and Phoenix felt drawn to the structure and the apparent power within it, like iron filings to a magnet. She was absolutely compelled to step inside and say a long-overdue prayer for safe passage. Her quick mental math told her she probably hadn't been inside a church since she was ten.

"Mama will be right back…five minutes, tops," she promised, as she found a half-shaded spot. She was well aware that any longer than that—in this heat—and she'd have a couple of barbequed critters, which would be *no bueno.*

She cracked open the windows and locked the car. As she approached the chapel, she was blown away by the two bell tower structures on either side of the arched main entrance and its two massive wooden doors. Stepping inside, she was immediately taken by the impressive fresco ceilings and ornate, gold-painted sculpture work and figures. There were about a dozen people inside, spread amongst the pews, praying quietly. Out of respect to them, and in the interest of time, she sat in one of the rear ones.

She immediately honed in on the crucifix above the altar, surrendered to the weight of her eyelids, and found herself kneeling for the first time in as long as she could remember. She knew she had to make it a quickie.

"Dear Jesus, Dear Lord, Dear Heavenly Father," she whispered, "I humbly come before you in prayer. I am not without sin, Lord, yet I have had great sins done against me. Some I know of, and others I may not yet be aware of. I have come upon dark times, Lord, and I find myself here, drawn to your house, today, in hopes you might bless me with understanding, healing, forgiveness and, if you see fit, safe passage. And please keep me safe from that creepy cactus I saw. I'm pretty sure it's evil. It sure felt like it, anyway, and I wanted to call it to your attention. Please deliver me, Lord, and I ask these things in Jesus' name. Amen."

Upon opening her eyes, Phoenix watched as a surreal shaft of sunlight sneaked through the glass and found its target on the crucifix—as if on cue. The moment was perfect and didn't need any help from a heavenly chorus of angels. She took this as a sign, crossed herself, and scurried back to her critters.

With a minute to spare.

As she could see no reason to stop in Green Valley, it was roughly forty-five minutes down Interstate 19 to Tubac. After her too-brief stop at the Mission this meant, for Phoenix, church was still in session. The Blaupunkt and the critters remained silent, which provided the perfect meditative atmosphere as she continued south. She was at one with the saguaros. And, hopefully, God.

The Plymouth hummed along beautifully as it traversed this stretch of road, and the comforting sound lulled her into a place that—to the best of her knowledge—she hadn't visited.

She'd just finished reciting the Lord's Prayer, so it seemed natural to segue into the Twenty Third Psalm. She was amazed to find she still remembered it after all these years, and she allowed herself an embellishment.

"The Lord is my shepherd; I shall not want. He makes me lie down in green pastures. He leads me beside still waters," she said, pausing for the last noisy slurp of her Slurpee. "He restores my soul. He leads me in paths of righteousness for his name's sake. Yo, even though I *drive* through the valley of the shadow of death, I will fear no evil, not even the saguaro dude, for you are with me; your rod and your staff, they comfort me. You prepare a table before me in the presence of my enemies; you anoint my head with oil; my cup overflows. Surely goodness and mercy shall follow me all the days of my life, and I will dwell in the house of the Lord forever. Amen." *Wow, where'd that come from?*

"Hello!!"

"You're right, Angus!" she said, glancing back at the little guy. A look at her cheap Timex told her that her little shopping jaunt in Tubac would have to be focused and targeted, as she still had a four-plus hours schlep northwest to Yuma. She didn't want Pop Pop to worry, and she'd promised to call him as soon as she settled into her motel, wherever that was going to be.

She was seeing several signs now, some of which indicated her proximity to Nogales and the border with Mexico. She couldn't help but think of one of her favorite songs by the same name, from the *Sense of Direction* album by Climax Blues Band. She just happened to have that tape with her, so she popped it in. The lyrics told of a harrowing true incident the band had experienced there, back in 1973. She knew the song by heart, so it was easy karaoke:

> *Southward across the border*
> *On a cool vacation drive*
> *To the country of disorder*
> *Where they sure don't take no jive*
>
> *We did not buy their sisters*
> *And we did not buy their smoke*
> *So when we landed in the jailhouse*
> *We thought it was a hell of a joke*
>
> *Hey, policeman, give me a smile*
> *I want to take your picture, it won't take a while*

Hey, jailer, won't you give me a grin,
Move over, let me squeeze you in

Where are you going with my money and shoes?
You know a boy can't sing the blues in his stocking feet

We landed in the icebox
It was a cool fifteen by three
Fifteen fallen brothers
Were shiverin' next to me

There was the man who sold his sisters
And the brother who sold his smoke
So when they landed in the jailhouse
We knew that it wasn't a joke!

Hey, policeman, give me a smile
I want to take your picture, it won't take a while
Hey, jailer, won't you give me a grin,
Move over, let me squeeze you in

Where are you going with my money and shoes?
You know a boy can't sing the blues in his stocking feet

By this time Pete Haycock had launched into another one of his epic guitar solos, and the Tubac exit presented itself. Phoenix ejected the tape and began following the signs that directed her into the quaint, artsy, don't-blink-or-you'll-miss-it little town. As inviting as the place sounded…*ahem*…Nogales would have to wait for another day. She had some shopping to do.

The tiny streets and narrow alleys that comprised the shopping village of Tubac made for a pretty user-friendly shopping grid, if you knew what you were looking for, and she did. The typical visitor might allocate an entire day—or even two—to properly peruse the outdoor markets and quaint shops, which offered a wealth of treasures. One could easily furnish their entire home with the beautiful local paintings, sculptures, photography, leather goods, and crafts. Phoenix had come specifically for the Talavera ceramics, and Tubac was, if nothing else, a target-rich environment.

She'd allowed herself a scant one-hour shopping window and tried not to succumb to the sensory overload she might experience there. Focused as she was, she engaged in a little friendly haggling on the prices and came away with exactly what she had come for: a lovely Talavera road runner for Pop Pop, a couple of Talavera quail, a Talavera Prick—well, Chihuahua anyway, to oversee her succulent garden. Something else had jumped out at her from a display in one of the better jewelry shops: a turquoise and silver pendant of a phoenix, which was highly ornate and hung from a fine chain. That one was meant to be, she decided, and it immediately found its rightful place, on display around her neck.

Phoenix popped the trunk and extracted several clothing items from her duffle with which to protect the ceramic items, both from each other and the bumps in the road. Once everything was tucked in for the long journey ahead, it was back the way she'd come. She'd gas up again in Green Valley, on her way to Yuma. After that…California!

It had already been a long day, emotionally and physically. As a result, she rifled through her tapes until she came across a mix she'd envisioned would help when the drive seemed arduous. Like this three-hundred-mile stretch to Yuma. It was nearing 4:30 and time to see what this baby could do. Best to get this party started with something Angus approved: "Radar Love."

"Hello!!"

By the time she pulled into Yuma, Phoenix felt like she'd been ridden hard and put away wet. Her eyes stung, like two burn holes in a blanket, and it was all she could do to navigate her way to the neon sign and plunk down Pop Pop's credit card at the first cheesy motel she could find. After bringing in her duffle, sneaking in the dog and the birdcage, and sliding the chain into the groove on the door, she was toast.

California would have to wait until tomorrow.

It was a little after 9:00 when she plopped down on the too-soft mattress and dialed the number, hoping it wasn't too late. It picked up on the first ring.

"Are you okay? Where are you?"

"Hi, Pop Pop…sorry to worry you. Yes, I'm fine. Just decided to take the scenic route is all."

"You didn't get my messages?"

"No…not until…just…now, anyway," she admitted, as she glanced at the screen on her Nokia, which confirmed three missed calls. "Sorry about that, not much reception out there."

"I'm just glad to hear you're okay, sweetie. You know me."

"I know. I love that about you, you know that."

"So, to my earlier question: where are you? Did you make it to San Diego?"

"Not exactly. Like I said, I took a slightly different route, did a little shopping, a little soul-searching, and wanted to see what the Road Runner could do out in the desert," she confessed.

"So…."

"I'm in Yuma, Pop Pop. Please don't be upset."

"Yuma? Holy cow. Okay. And you just got there?"

"Mm-hmm," she managed through a yawn. "I decided to save the San Diego stretch for tomorrow. By the way, I've gotta tell you that the Runner is friggin' awesome, Pop Pop! She's a sexy beast and, so far, she's performed without a hitch. This car absolutely loves running in the desert!"

"That's a good report, sugar. Glad to hear it," he said, smiling for the first time in several hours. "I hope you're paying attention to the posted speed limits...kinda."

"Yep...pretty much," she said with a tired laugh, "I only had her up into triple digits on one occasion—y'know, to properly test the engine—and it's in perfect tune!"

"The only way to know for sure," he replied with a laugh. "And the critters are good?"

"Yeah, Pop Pop. They've been troopers so far, for sure." Another yawn. "Excuse me...."

"No problem. Now, other than being tired, how are you? How's Phoenix doing? You holding up okay with everything that's been going on?"

"Yeah, pretty much. The desert's probably the best place to figure stuff out."

"True," he said, having searched for many a truth of his own out there.

"Oh! I almost forgot to mention that the stereo system is... what's the word I'm looking for? Sorry, I'm tired. Let's just say it's *bitchin'*—it's perfectly paired to the car. I can't thank you enough, Pop Pop!"

"Don't mention it, kiddo. By the way, before you head out again tomorrow, have a look in the glovebox. I can neither confirm nor deny, but I may've left you a little something there...."

"Aww, as if you haven't already done enough. I'll be sure to look, first thing in the morning, Pop Pop. I've got to get some sleep," she said as she got up to cover the bird.

"Hello!"

"Goodnight, Angus!" Pop Pop called out to the bird. "And to you, little Prick!"

The little guy was already lights-out.

"Goodnight, from all of us, Pop Pop! I promise to call you at a more reasonable hour tomorrow—and from California!"

"Sweet dreams, and safe travels, sweetie. 'Night."

Phoenix released her ponytail, shaking out her mane to its full volume and brushed her teeth. Hoping to improve her chances of a decent night's sleep, she placed her lava lamp on the nightstand and switched on the lava flow.

With the blackout curtains drawn and the room's lights off, she surrendered to the slow, hypnotic motion of the wax, staring at the peachy-white blobs of lava until they shapeshifted into her dreams.

There were two peachy-white blobs floating in the tight confines of their small, shared vessel, each in their own perfect pouches of amniotic fluid. With a couple of twitches, her wombmate had managed to change position slightly, resulting in her facing outward more, now prominently in front and closer to the source of the muffled sound of unfamiliar voices outside.

The second blob, the one behind the first, could only sense a disturbance in their space as the first large needle penetrated the outward wall and found its target. Her sibling's legs twitched slightly as some of the amniotic fluid was slowly withdrawn from her protective sac and was replaced, moments later, with something much more caustic.

The kicks became stronger in reaction to the saline poison that had mercilessly invaded the sac protecting the blob, which was, in reality, a baby—and a twin sister. Over the course of the next hour, the other one floated behind the first, herself untouched, but helpless to render assistance, as the first baby breathed in and swallowed the salt, its toxic cocktail poisoning it from within, while also managing to render painful burns to its skin, deteriorating the fleshy parts until the dead, burned and shriveled child would be delivered by the mother, sometime within a pickling period of about 72 hours. There was a sensation of popping sounds, sizzling, of undeniable suffering taking place, and an awareness of kicks in protest to a murder. There was the presence of something salty in the vessel, even though it was mostly experienced vicariously.

Her sister, through her involuntary movements, moments before, had somehow repositioned herself to take the brunt of the punishment, somehow jockeying for position in order to take one for the team, and sparing the sister she'd never know.

Leaving Phoenix…

There was a loud pounding coming from the outside of the door, jarring a severely disoriented Phoenix out of her deep sleep and her disturbingly vivid nightmare. Aside from the illuminated lava, the room was still dark, and her heart raced as she tried to figure out where she was, and why. Her hair was soaked with sweat, as were the sheets.

"Are you okay in there?" called the voice. It sounded like a Hispanic woman—maybe a housekeeper—but a glance at the clock radio on the table told her it couldn't be. It was only 11:20, and still nighttime.

"Um, yes. Yes, I am okay, thank you!" Phoenix answered to the door. She must have been screaming. The dream—the nightmare of all nightmares, actually—had been utterly and justifiably scream worthy.

"Somebody called the office and said it sounded like you were in trouble. You're okay, then?"

"Yes! I'm awfully sorry if…if my TV disturbed anybody. I'll keep it down. Thank you so much. Good night!"

"Okay…goodnight then," the woman said. Phoenix could hear her walking away.

"Hello!!"

"Shhh! Go back to sleep, Angus."

Yip!

"You too, Prick. Sorry, guys. Whew," she muttered as she sat on the edge of the bed and stared into the peachy-white weirdness, that rare and devastating porthole into what she envisioned had to be her earliest subconscious memory. Several moments later she switched it off. And she had no plans to ever switch that thing on again.

"Jeezus...."

Sleep didn't return. Nor would it anytime soon. Not after *that*. Following a tortuous attempt at it, Phoenix shuffled into the bathroom, stripped herself of her soggy pajamas, and initiated a long, hot, and semi-restorative shower.

For an hour.

She'd taken one of the two laughably inadequate motel bath towels and folded it into a square, which served as a soggy bathmat upon which she could sit in the corner, knees under her chin, as the water rained down on her, and her tears flowed down the drain.

The remaining towel was rough and barely sufficient to dry herself, but she wasn't prettying herself up for anybody; she was going to get an early start on the next leg, to San Diego. The clock radio's display tried to talk some sense into her with its reminder that it was only 1:35, but there was no reason to stay in this dodgy place. Sleep would elude her tonight.

Thankfully, her room was at the far end of its row and furthest away from the office, which made sneaking the bird's cage, the dog's crate, and the undeclared critters back into the Runner a little less stressful. Phoenix packed the duffle and put the lava lamp in the trunk, mindful of the Talavera treasures. The lava lamp, it had been decided during her come-to-Jesus soak, would be a gift to Pop Pop upon her return. It had fulfilled its purpose with her.

"Hello!"

"Please don't start, Angus. Way too friggin' early, buddy. Mama needs some coffee and a breakfast sammich," she replied, starting up the car. "Ooh, glovebox...almost forgot!" she said to herself as she reached over. As promised, sitting on top of the original map-sized 1970 Plymouth Belvedere Satellite Operator's Manual—all sixty-eight pages of it—was a cassette tape she didn't recognize.

"Aww...that Pop Pop," she whispered to herself. It had been years since she'd received one of his masterful mixed tapes, and she looked forward to it. But first things first: she needed petrol, coffee, and some sort of meatless breakfast concoction.

Yip!

"Yep!"

While Runner enjoyed her nineteen-gallon refreshment, Phoenix went about cleaning a few hundred bugs off the windshield and checked the engine oil. It was still perfect, and just looking under the hood reminded her how much she truly loved this glorious machine.

The pump didn't provide her with a receipt, so she ventured inside, where she filled the largest self-serve coffee container they offered. This was going to be a four-sugars morning, and it was her little secret.

"Hi," the attendant said. It was all he had in him, as he'd started his shift at ten and had been inventorying the cigarettes for over an hour.

"Yeah, hi. Uh, I need a receipt for pump seven, please. And need to pay for this coffee."

"No problem. Just a moment," he said, punching up the receipt and the sale.

While she waited, a glance at the nearby hotdog display proved horrifying. The illuminated case brought out all the glory in the presentation of the rows of rotating wieners, gliding upon the hot steel bars that assured all sides were equally blistered by their heat source. As a vegetarian, it was a truly ghastly sight in and of itself, but the bubbly lesions on these nitrates-laden, seemingly decades-old byproduct-filled sausage casings were a cruel reminder of what her twin had undoubtedly suffered.

"Anything else?" the clerk asked as he handed her the receipt and her change.

"What?" Phoenix said, jolted back to the present and almost tearful.

"Will there be anything else?"

"No…no, thank you!" she answered too urgently as she turned to leave. The clerk shrugged and returned to his cigarette tally. He had another four hours of crazies to deal with before his shift ended.

A couple miles down the road, Phoenix found the drive-through at the Yellow M—as she and Pop Pop had always called it—and from the comfort of her car, enjoyed the savory-for-two-AM goodness of her meatless Egg McMuffin, a sleeve of hash brown potatoes, and two orange juices. She saved a small bite of cheese for the Prick and tossed her trash in the receptacle. She needed to clear her head of all the guilt, the horror, and the ugly truths that comprised the traffic jam in her head. She ejected the cassette from the deck and inserted Pop Pop's. Now, she was ready for California.

"We'll see what you've got, Pop Pop!" she said as she reentered westbound Interstate 8.

The border checkpoint took all of two minutes, as there was only one other night owl in her lane. With nothing to declare, she pressed forward and conjured up the mental image of another box being checked on the wish list. She might've marked the moment she crossed the Colorado River too, but it was too dark, and she was too tired to notice. The other signs, however….

"Welcome to Cal-i-forn-i-yay, little Prick! You too, Angus! Woo-hoo!" she hollered. "Here we go!" And, just like that, they'd left the last of the saguaros behind. Literally—as in, they stop at the state line—because they grow nowhere else but on the gravelly slopes and rocky ridges of the Sonoran Desert. Talk about an exclusive deal!

And with that, she ceremoniously hit the *play* button. After a few seconds of the tape's leader, the first cue was none other than the cartoon voice of Woody Woodpecker and his iconic line, *"Guess who! Ha-ha-ha-ha-ha…ha-ha-ha-ha-ha…"* followed by that maniacal laugh, which ushered in the challenge to the listener to identify the artist as it slammed right into Pop Pop's next needle drop: "(I'm A) Road Runner" by Fleetwood Mac. This got an eye roll, but a nod of appreciation from Phoenix. Even though her category on *Jeopardy!* would've probably been "70s and 80s Music," she had a hard time identifying this one. The vocal was straight out of Savoy Brown, but it wasn't them. There was a bit of Christine McVie-esque piano in it, which led her to guess the answer in the form of a question, "Who is Fleetwood Mac?" Of course, she was correct, as Dave Walker, ex-Savoy Brown, was on vox and harp on this one, with Bob Welch taking a backseat and Christine, then Christine Perfect, on keys.

"Nicely played, Pop Pop..."

It was true that she'd learned the art of the mixed tape from the master himself, and he'd cued up Grand Funk's Hammond organ-heavy, boogie instrumental "Flight of the Phoenix" just for her. He'd brought his A game to side A, and it was—with the exception of the Danny Kirwan numbers—an eclectic study in 70s and 80s funk and rock. That is, until the final song, which she'd never heard before. Considering the mix master behind this effort, she paid particular attention to this one as she continued west towards her next gas stop: El Centro. As the opening strains of the song filled the vehicle, they began to overflow her very soul with Seal's first lyrics.

> *Fell on my feet this morning*
> *Two angels heard me cry*
> *This is your fate hereafter*
>
> *The future is my friend*
> *It hurts, but it treats me well*
> *Take hold and be its master*

As the song progressed, it was all she could do to see through the tears on this dark stretch of highway. She wasn't sure if she'd make it any further than Holtville.

"Dammit, Pop Pop," she said as she pulled over onto the shoulder and began convulsing for the next five minutes.

Gold as the sun
As you turn me on
And bath in its sun red,
I'm alive, older and strong

Let me be someone.
I'll take hold and be its master

Gold as the sun,
As you turn me on.
With echoes of laughter
As I cry out loud

Got my feet on the ground
Your hands found me.
Saw my blood on the ground
And it changed my life

So many parts that I have to play
A tangle with life set me up that way
Now I know,
These are the words that I have to say
Won't you let me
Won't you hear me cry...

Got my feet on the ground,
...feet on the ground.

Your hand's falling...
Saw my blood on the ground,
And it changed my life

Your face in the crowd,

You're my future.
Saw my blood on the ground
And it changed my life

Got my feet on the ground.
...feet on the ground

Your hands found me
Blood on the cross,
And it changed my life

Yeah, yeah yeah yeah
Fell on my feet this morning

As the song faded out and there was nothing else left but the end leader to signal the conclusion of the side, Phoenix noticed the unmistakable pulsating red and blue lights from a CHP vehicle pulling in behind her.

The strong, laser-like beam from the officer's three cell flashlight was blinding as he approached her passenger window. She could've used a squeegee to wipe away the tears.

"Everything all right, ma'am?"

"Yes, officer. I'm sorry to have had to stop here," she said, looking at him. Her face was a wreck. "I...I just had something in my eye, I'm fine, really."

"You're sure?" the young patrolman asked, shining his beam around the inside of the car.

"Hello!!"

"Not now, Angus."

"Rose-breasted cockatoo? My sister had one of those. Where are you headed, ma'am?"

"My destination's San Diego, and I plan to stop for gas shortly, in El Centro."

"Okay, as long as you're not too tired to drive. Anything to drink tonight?"

"No, sir. I don't drink. At all. I'm good. Promise. I plan to be sleeping in a good bed when I get there. Just a couple more hours, I think, right?"

"Sounds about right. Okay, please drive carefully, ma'am. Pretty dark out here. I'll wait here until you safely pull back onto the highway. Thankfully not much traffic at this hour."

"Thank you so much, officer. I'll take my time. Thanks for checking on me," she said as he extinguished the beam. After checking her mirrors, she put on her turn signal and pulled out onto the highway. The CHP car then passed her and, moments later, disappeared into the night.

"Pop Pop, are you trying to kill me? Oy!"

It was a quick pitstop in El Centro. Phoenix topped off the tank, used the very sketchy restroom, did a caffeine reboot, and bought a large box of Kleenex tissues—just in case the B side of the tape continued to rip her to shreds. Prick went wee-wee, got a new greenie, and they were back on the interstate. Another couple of hours, as the road runner flies, she figured. Might even sneak into Mission Bay before rush-hour traffic, God willing.

True to form, Side B ratcheted things up. Pop Pop had pulled no punches with this one, and he'd hoped it wasn't too strong thematically. But he also knew his daughter, knew what she could and could not handle, and his heart was in the right place. Still, as entertaining and road trip worthy as the song selections were, it was a particularly brutal mix, considering all of the shoes that had dropped recently. She strapped herself in for the second serving and hit *play*.

There was no Woody Woodpecker intro here. It jumped straight into the throwback era, with Patrick Hernandez's 1978 disco curiosity, "Born To Be Alive." It took her a good fifteen seconds to try figuring out the instrumental intro, but once the lyrics kicked in….

Oh, my friggin' goodness!!

Over the course of the next three minutes, the chorus repeated itself several times, pounding a less-than-subtle message into Phoenix's soul. Thank Christ this was the short version and not the extended dance remix, because she wasn't sure if she could withstand the longer one.

Okay, Pop Pop…I get it! Thank you!

From there, it continued building relentless layers, and school was definitely in session as Pop Pop cued up Queen's "Keep Yourself Alive," "Stayin' Alive" by the Bee Gees, Simple Minds' "Alive and Kicking," ELO's "Living Thing," and only slightly letting its foot off the gas with "Love Is Alive" by Cary Wright. Then it slammed right into Annie Lennox's "Little Bird," Skynyrd's nine-minute "Free Bird," and ended with Tarney Spencer Band's "No Time To Lose".

Forty-five minutes had gone by quickly, even though it had seemed like the longest type of freeform torture. At least Angus had found great joy in the disco period.

That's the one to beat, Pop Pop…jeez Louise.

Phoenix wiped away what had to be her last available tear. There had to be a finite supply, right? She blew her nose again and tossed the tissue onto the impressive pile that had accumulated on the passenger's floorboard.

Phoenix switched the stereo off with a swift flick of her wrist. The remaining leg would be driven in absolute silence. At least for the critters. Because inside Phoenix's head were a gazillion buzzing thoughts and feelings, all competing for attention, and it was absolutely deafening.

CHAPTER 16

NO REASONABLE JURY would consider the statement claiming that the stretch from Yuma to San Diego was a punishingly long drive, because it wasn't. Now, if you factor in sleep deprivation on the level Phoenix was experiencing, that'd be a whole different argument and one you'd win. And she was officially burnt toast when she pulled into the check-in space at the Bahia Resort Hotel at Mission Bay.

Thankfully, she'd made a reservation here the night before because, judging from the multitude of cars, they appeared to be at capacity. Per her new routine, she checked in as a single human with no critters. She'd opted for this place because it was supposed to be overlooking the water and, she figured, her requested room type might afford easy and stealthy potty breaks.

Her ground-floor room, thankfully, was as advertised, and the establishment was a low-profile, no-frills hotel with cabana type rooms, and it was only two stories. Her patio slider exited to a small sandy area and a walking path, which would suit her perfectly. At least she hoped it would. It was still dark outside, and she had never anticipated climbing into a bed more than she did right now.

Once Angus was covered and the Prick had his little schlep on the path, it was time for Phoenix's needs to be met, and they were few: a comfy bed, some quiet, and the absence of an alarm.

The *Do Not Disturb* sign was on the door and the room phone was unplugged.

As she'd previously promised Pop Pop she'd call when she arrived in San Diego, she opted for texting him confirmation of safe arrival. It was only a little after 5:00, so she figured he'd understand. Plus, she wasn't even sure if she could properly verbalize intelligible words on the phone at this point.

> *Pop Pop, made it to San Diego. Left/arrived early. 5:00 AM here! Need sleep. Call U later. Your tape: OMG!!!!!!!!! Love you, PHX.*

Two shrill alarms alerted Phoenix to the fact that it was time to get up. Angus got things started, because he was ready to have his black-out sheet removed. After all, it was almost 2:30 in the afternoon. The backup alarm, Prick, started yipping in reaction to Angus, and the combination was enough to wake up the dead. Which was how Phoenix had slept for the first time in over a week. Like the dead.

A slight gap in the thick slider drapes admitted an unsolicited laser beam of sunlight which drilled her right between the eyes. Add to all that the sound of the housekeeper's vacuum in the hallway and the sound of kids playing outside her patio slab, and she slowly began processing the data.

With great effort, she swung her feet over the side of the bed and swept the sleep gravel from her eyes. Another volley of shrieks from the troops forced her hand. "Okay!! Jeez!!" she hollered as she pulled the sheet off of Angus's cage. A quick glance reminded her she needed to clean his cage today.

She shuffled over to the slider and peeked through the heavy drapes. The afternoon sun was blinding, and it created a beautiful pattern of shimmery diamonds on the bay water, only a matter of yards from her. A half dozen youngsters, wearing their water wings, were making sandcastles and sticking their feet in the water, all while being closely monitored by two sets of parents who'd staked claim to this stretch early, planting their lawn chairs, cooler, and umbrella in the sand. Seagulls were jockeying for position as they searched out easy snack opportunities, one stealthily snatching a sandwich from a beach towel. There were several small sailboats moored on the nearby piers, as well as what looked like an old steam paddleboat. It was all so different, all so beautiful. *I'm in California!*

After a quick potty break for the little guy, Phoenix took a nice, long, hot shower. She emerged feeling much refreshed, as the combination of deep sleep and proper hygiene was a Godsend. As she wrangled her hair into its scrunchie tie, she paused to reflect on any dreams she'd had during her nine-and-a-half-hour slumber. She couldn't come up with anything—absolutely zip—and she was actually grateful for a night off from…everything.

The little patio section of the resort's restaurant was still serving, so she treated herself to a rare, sit-down meal. Even though she'd only been gone a couple of days, it felt like an eternity, and she decided she and her tastebuds deserved this quiet, sane moment. The menu featured a vegetarian burrito, which was smothered in a mild, fresh salsa. Served with some brilliant breakfast potatoes and a side of fresh seasonal fruit, she was in hog heaven and decided if she ever had to choose one, this would likely be her death row meal.

A quick stop by the front lobby netted her what she was hoping to find, a stack of newspapers. She grabbed a half dozen of them and returned to the room, where she proceeded to clean Angus's cage.

Phoenix never watched the TV news and rarely kept up on current events, really, except when she cleaned Angus's cage, which gave her an opportunity to peruse the headlines as she spread the layers of newsprint along the cage bottom.

It appeared that George W Bush and Al Gore had thrown their hats into the ring for the presidential race, but she didn't pay it much mind. She had to laugh, however, when she scanned an article about some apparent end-of-the-world hysteria they were calling Y2K, and the mounting fears that everything would crash to a halt because programmers hadn't figured out the 00 year. Just when she was coming to the good part, Angus dropped a golf ball-sized splat of what looked like tainted tartar sauce right on the paper.

"Hey! I was reading that!"

"Hello!"

"Yeah…hello to you, too," she said as she wiped down the bars and closed things up. Angus didn't like this travel cage much, and she decided—IF she needed to spend any considerable amount of time in California—she'd have to pop for a larger freestanding cage for him.

Phoenix stepped out onto her little patio slab and sat down in one of the two fake, woven wicker chairs. The sun was already starting to get a bit lower on the horizon, and her body clock felt pretty wacked. She watched as the two families gathered up their offspring, and their trappings, and headed back down the path. Probably dinner time. She'd just had breakfast and was pretty well rested now. *What a concept!*

Which led to her next question, to be followed by a big decision: *Do I just stay here another night, catch my breath, maybe check out Sea World…San Diego Zoo in the morning?* It only took her a few moments of contemplation. She had no interest in witnessing the poor orcas, nor the dolphin shows, mainly because she felt pretty strongly about how miserable those beautiful creatures must really be behind those not-quite-genuine smiles, stuck in their manmade captivity, and forced to entertain the tourist masses, day in and day out, all in hopes some underpaid teenaged handler will toss them some bits of fish from their bucket.

Same went for the zoo. Um, no.

No, she might as well keep pressing on, she figured. North this time. What the hey.

According to Pop Pop's gas station map, which was now spread out on the bed, if she left soon, she could probably reach the Pacific Grove area of Monterey County around midnight, maybe a little after, factoring in potty and petrol stops. Traffic should be at a minimum once she got past LA, in theory, and it would likely be a seven-and-a-half-hour schlep.

"Okay, troops, here's the deal," she said to her captive audience of two. "I know we didn't get to see much—any, really—of San Diego, but we will again next time, okay? We're wheels up in twenty minutes, once mama gets things loaded and we check out. Everybody good?"

"Hello!!"

"Prick?"

Yip!

"Okay then, good meeting. Let's go potty, little guy."

There'd been a couple of large thermal urns of complimentary coffee in the lobby, and she pumped herself a Thermos full for the drive. No half & half, just that Coffee Mate non-dairy jive, and Sweet & Low, no proper sugar. Oh, well…any port in the storm, and the price was right.

After navigating the maze of frontage roads leaving Mission Bay, Phoenix found the northbound ramp of Interstate 5, and they were officially on their way. Once she was on a straightaway, she ejected Pop Pop's torture cassette from the deck and inserted one of her own making. She had about half a state to cover tonight, and she didn't need any unscheduled therapy stops along the route. She'd ride in silence for now. Besides, the Hemi purred beautifully.

Being as most of her drive would be in the dark, she'd opted out of taking the scenic route. It reminded her of a humorous postcard she'd seen in the resort's lobby gift shop with the caption, *SAN DIEGO AT NIGHT*, which was paired with a photo of pitch blackness. She chuckled again.

Instead, she'd decided on the more direct—and infinitely more boring—straight shot up the 5 and, other than a quick stop for gas, it would be another five hours before her next junction, where she'd transition west on CA-46, somewhere north of Bakersfield. *Yeehaw!!*

Phoenix had anticipated catching a little traffic, being as there seemed to be an inordinate number of commuters trying to get home after a long day at the salt mine, but this seemed a little ridiculous. She rode a virtual lava flow of taillights all the way through Orange County and until she got beyond the vast web of chaos that was metropolitan LA. *What a friggin' pit.* She was glad she didn't have to experience seeing it in the daytime. *And, man, they drive like friggin' a-holes!*

She'd had to keep her wits about her for hours, and now that she was approaching the outskirts of "beautiful downtown Burbank," she decided it was time to water the horses.

"Potty break, guys," she said, as she slowed to exit at the Mobil station. "Well, not you, Angus, but you know…stretch your wings." As she pulled into the lot, she parked at the pump nearest the entrance. She put Prick on his leash and locked the car before pulling the trigger on the fuel nozzle. Prick was on a mission once he hit the ground and immediately found a trashcan to pee on. It was probably coincidental that he'd managed to spritz a *Dodgers* bumper sticker that had been affixed to it at ground level.

A few feet away, a disheveled woman was foraging through an adjacent trash receptacle, picking out bits of recyclables. Phoenix tried to discern her age and circumstance and guessed her to be in her forties. She had maybe even been attractive once upon a time, but the mileage had taken its toll, and she was mumbling back to the voices in her head. The Prick wanted no part of it.

Yip!

"It doesn't go with that!" the woman hissed, looking up from the can, admonishing herself, or perhaps one of the personalities deep inside. Then, just as quickly, it was back to the bottles and cans.

A wave of sadness threatened to overtake Phoenix, so she offered her five dollars, returned the pooch to his carrier, relocked the doors, and watched the pump's spinning numbers, hoping for three cherries that never came. She returned the nozzle to its cradle and went about cleaning California's entire moth population from her windshield before going inside with her Thermos.

"Nice Mustang!" the attendant said to her as she approached with her Red Vines, two small sleeves of powdered donuts, and a large Sunny D.

"Thanks! Not a Mustang though," she said, placing her items on the counter. "It's a Road Runner. Plymouth. You know... *Hemi?*"

"Yes, of course I hear you," the guy said, scratching the side of his turban and looking at her like she'd just condescended to him in a Martian language. He shrugged. "Nice car...."

Phoenix smiled in acknowledgement. "Oh, and I need a receipt for pump one, please."

Upon returning to the car, Phoenix handed the poor woman one of the packages of donuts, which got a nod of what looked like appreciation, and she was again entering the bloodstream of the interstate.

She took a long swig from the large vessel of Sunny D, wondering where this delicious beverage had been her entire life and pushed the cassette until it dropped into the slot and the little reels began to spin, cuing Side A. She had another two and a half hours before her big left turn on CA-46, and this would likely be a two-tape leg. *All right...let's get this party started!* And with that, some screaming guitar and pounding drums obliged, as Alice Cooper's "Under My Wheels" proceeded to rock her world.

If anyone were ever to ask what it might be like to drive on the surface of the moon, Phoenix could riff on the answer for days. Jeez o'

Pete, this was a seemingly endless, and particularly brutal stretch of absolute nothingness, and she was grateful to finally be off CA-46. At least Highway 101 was properly lighted, for the most part, and she found a more civilized path emanating out of Paso Robles. A couple more hours, she figured, and she looked forward to a long, hot bath to soak away the aches from her saddle-sore bum.

The lighted sign indicating she'd arrived at her destination, the Chrysalis Lodge and Cottages, was literally a sight for sore eyes. It was a little after 1:00 when she coasted into the tiny lot, as quietly as she could.

There was one space still available, and Phoenix took it. With considerable effort, she was able to extract herself from the car, and she took a couple of minutes to get the kinks out before she hobbled over to what appeared to be the front lobby office. It was dark, as were all of the ninety-something rooms at this hour. It was quiet enough for her to be startled by the pinecone that came crashing down nearby.

She'd have to chalk this up to a rookie mistake because, in her hasty exodus from San Diego, she'd neglected to advise the lodge of her anticipated arrival time. The office was dark, and she had no choice but to wake up the help. She hated to bother anybody, but she had an urgent appointment with a mattress, and there was no way around it.

The young woman on duty was pleasant enough and even provided a water bowl and a Milk Bone for the Prick. This being a pet-friendly establishment, Phoenix was happy to not have to be concerned with any stealthy maneuvering this time. She even paid the pet deposit.

You could've set a stopwatch for five minutes and had time to spare, because the quick pee-pee and poo-poo, covering of the bird, and brushing of teeth was executed in record time. Phone ringer off, *Do Not Disturb* sign on the door, jammies installed, and she was lights-out by 1:30.

"Night, guys."

"Hello!"

"Please don't start. Mama's tired."

In a perfect world, Phoenix's plan had been to sleep in until 11:00 at least. But it's not a perfect world, after all, and the two critters–both of whom had slept for most of the trip north–had mutually decided it was time to start the day. At 5:42.

A series of loud squawks preceded Angus's usual greeting, and when the Prick joined in, he was really living up to his name. It quickly escalated to a squawk/screech/yip fest, and it became impossible to ignore.

"SHUUUUUT UUUUUPPP!!!!" she bellowed from somewhere beneath the down pillow.

"Hello!!"

Yip!!

Phoenix found a gap in the pillow and peeked over at the clock radio, which confirmed her nightmare. "No way! Guys!! Go back to sleep!! For the love of God…it's…too…early!"

But they weren't having it. It was time, and they felt strongly about it. Phoenix knew there was no way around it, and she couldn't risk having the dog pee in a hotel room. She furrowed her brow, trying to remember where she was exactly. Oh, yeah.

"All right, all right already…I'm coming!" she said with a groan as she labored to sit up. She took a good look at the room for the first time. It was pleasant enough, nothing fancy, but it was perfect for her three-star needs. She hadn't even noticed until now that there was a fireplace. *Cool.*

As it had been darker than a well digger's wallet when she

checked in, she figured a potty walk might afford a look around the premises. And after her shower, maybe venture out a little further.

According to the tour book, she was a stone's throw from both the Point Pinos Lighthouse, and the Monarch Butterfly Sanctuary. The timing of her visit wasn't ideal for the monarch sightings, however, as they typically migrated to the sanctuary in November and were done mating in February, but she vowed to return now that she knew where to find them. Amazing creatures, these, who, like herself, emerged from their chrysalides incredibly transformed with newfound wings.

Prick found a suitable pine for his purposes and did his thing. Phoenix's eyes scanned the treetops, and she did manage to see a solitary butterfly flittering by—one who'd apparently defied convention, not unlike herself, and not gotten the memo. There was something therapeutic about these trees. The sounds they made when the wind found them, the smell of the eucalyptus, and a tangible, organic, transformative vibe. *Om.*

After a restorative shower she grabbed a granola bar and decided to expand her horizons. On foot.

About a mile's hike from the lodge, she spied what had to be either another mirage or a bona fide wish list item. Either way, it was insanely beautiful, and the exquisite, flowery paths along Ocean Boulevard led her to one of the most incredible sights she'd ever seen: Lover's Point Park.

The waves were smashing violently against the rocky coastline, and she saw shades of blue and green she never knew existed. Scores of brown pelicans flew in perfect formations, like so many pterodactyls. A nearby bench beckoned her, and she obliged. The sounds, the smell of the ocean too, were something she'd never experienced, and she closed her eyes as she turned her face to the sun to mark the moment.

Every one of her senses was being turbo-charged, she now realized, and she was thankful.

This was otherworldly in every respect; it resonated in her

bones and in her very soul. She wasn't sure how to quantify it, but she felt more truly alive in this moment than she could remember ever feeling. There were changes taking place internally, and new synapses were being formed. She could feel multiple layers of new truths forming in their strata, and an inner confidence seemed to be crystalizing at the same time. Could part of it have to do with being in this magical place? Truly, this had to be where God hung out on his day off. *Too bad I'm not on vacation.*

Phoenix knew, though, that it was more than just being in this place. Processing life-changing information, thoughts, and deep emotions on this level wasn't for wimps, and there was nothing like large chunks of alone time, driving in the middle of nowhere and without distraction, to help things congeal.

She'd been praying for truth, for safe passage, and for understanding, and she'd embarked on this pilgrimage for a reason. She'd been led to this place. *Be careful what you ask for.*

As lovely as her surroundings were, there were more truths to be uncovered, emotions to be processed, and still heavy lifting to be done, as she still had a rendezvous with destiny.

Whatever came her way, she just hoped she could handle it. *Where there's a Liam, there's a way.*

Back at the lodge, she informed Pop Pop of her whereabouts and general state of being. It was great to hear his voice, and she appreciated his vote of confidence, as he'd given his blessing.

As Phoenix had decided this would be a day to recharge herself, without an agenda, she pulled out her Mac iBook and plugged it into the room's ethernet. She hadn't been online in well over a week, and recently discovered that just surfing around on this new thing called "the Internet" could be entertaining. Like eBay, where she was logging into now.

It was truly amazing, this online marketplace, where you could find—literally—*anything* in the whole wide world. It was like the world's greatest global garage sale, and it was open 24/7/365! She gave a moment's thought to the whole "Y2K" deal everybody was freaking about, wondering if eBay, too, would disappear, but it was not her circus, not her monkey.

Though she'd already picked up the Road Runner Talavera figure in Tubac for him, she still wanted to find something else for Pop Pop. He'd been so incredible with all this, and it was the least she could do. Perhaps it wasn't a very manly thing to collect, but he did have an appreciation for interesting blown glass pieces, having visited the Murano factory in Italy on his honeymoon. And with that, her search began.

Before she knew it, she'd spent two hours sifting through thumbnail photos, item descriptions, and every kind of blown glass piece imaginable. The critters were napping, so she decided to indulge herself for a few more minutes.

Her eyes were tired, but one particular thumbnail picture caught her eye, and she clicked on it to expand the listing. What popped up, in the detail of the larger photos, caused her to burst out laughing hysterically. There was no friggin' way this listing was for real! But it was.

The item was a blown glass pitcher in dark blue tones, which was also highly glossy and reflective. On its face, it was pretty enough, but what made it...ahem...unusual was the fact that the seller hadn't factored in its reflectivity when taking these hastily uploaded photos. Also, he might've given more thought to his ward-room, because this slovenly fellow was buck naked, and when she clicked on the enlarge function, she could clearly make out his... manhood. There were eight photos, and each was more disturbing than the last, especially the close-ups. *Oh, my friggin' goodness!*

After rolling around on the bed laughing for a good five minutes, Phoenix went back to the listing. The pitcher, it turned out, came with two small matching cups, and with shipping it was only sixty dollars. Pop Pop was worth that, and as she wiped the tears from her eyes, she chuckled as she hit the BUY NOW button. She decided, for fun, to add a note to the seller: "Nice three-piece set!" before making her payment through PayPal. She couldn't wait to give Pop Pop the backstory on this gift, so she saved the photos.

A very quick check of her email account revealed that, besides her PayPal purchase confirmation, there was just one other message. As she didn't really use email much—she didn't have any friends to speak of—she knew it had to be from Pop Pop, and it was:

Good luck tomorrow, kiddo. Call me after your meeting with Liam, please. If you want to.
Love you,
PP

—

I will, Pop Pop. BTW, the RR's driving great, and this place is pretty amaze-o.
Love you, too!
~ PHX

With that, she signed off and closed the clamshell lid.

"C'mon, little Prick. Let's get 'er done," she said as she attached his leash.

Yip!

"No, I'll feed you when we get back. Be right back, Angus."

"Hello!"

"Yes, you too," she said, pausing to chuckle as she thought about just how well versed she was in the various dialects of critter talk. She hoped this wasn't, like, one of those seven warning signs that you're a weirdo or something.

After she confirmed her little ankle biter had indeed heeded the call, Phoenix looked up just in time to see a beautiful doe and her two young fawns, as they cautiously emerged from a protective cluster of trees. She stood there motionless as not to scare them off, and smiled at the sight. The late afternoon sun joined the party, wrapping the picture in a warm and splendid magic-hour light. It seemed like she'd stepped into a Kinkaid painting.

Today had truly been a display of God's greatest hits, and she made note of this. *Pacific Grove…* Pacific *Groove*, was more like it!

"Thank you," she said to her Creator, wishing she could've shared this magic with Pop Pop, with the mother she'd never really known, and the twin sister she'd been denied. There was nobody else around, so, with that, she pointed her face to the sky and shouted an unapologetic declaration to herself and to the universe:

"I, Phoenix, am—for whatever reason—*alive!!!*"

PART FIVE

PRICKLY PAIR

CHAPTER 17

THE EUCALYPTUS MANOR Care Center was nestled beneath a grove of its namesake trees, which permeated the air with their thick, unique fragrance. Eucalyptus wasn't something Phoenix had experienced before, and she wasn't entirely sure it didn't smell a bit like cat urine. But the grounds seemed pleasant enough from outward appearances.

As she entered the homey, single-story facility, she was greeted by a matronly caregiver at the front desk. "May I help you, miss?" she asked, looking above the readers propped on her nose.

"Hi. Yes, good morning. Please…I am here to see one of your patients, a William McGinn. I'm not sure if he's expecting me today," she said, remembering to remove her ever-present ballcap.

"I see," she replied, looking at a patient roster. "I see, yes… Liam. He likes to be called Liam. And you are—?"

"I'm sorry. My name is Phoenix. I'm his…granddaughter." Saying the words out loud for the first time seemed surreal.

"His *granddaughter*," the woman said as her face lit up. "I don't think we've had any family visit him here before. How nice…I'm sure he'll be quite pleased. Are you from the area?"

"No, no, I'm not. I'm from Arizona, actually."

"Arizona," the woman muttered softly to herself. "I see," she said, as if Phoenix had declared she was from the moon. "Let me just check with my staff to see if he's up for a visit today. You can have a seat in the waiting area there. If you'll just excuse me...."

"Of course, thank you very much," Phoenix said, her stomach full of butterflies as she took a seat in one of the two available chairs. She took a couple of deep breaths, hoping she was making the right decision, and that this wasn't some wild goose chase. *What if he doesn't like me? What if he's some senile old fool who's just playing on my emotions? What if—?*

"Miss?" the woman said, returning to the front counter, and breaking Phoenix' doubt cycle. "Yes, Liam is getting dressed now and will be ready to see you in a few minutes. Would you like something to drink? Some water? A soda while you wait?"

"Oh, no, thank you. That is, unless you happen to have some Sunny D?"

"I'm not sure what that is, but we don't have anything like that, I'm sorry. We'll be right with you," she said, returning to her paperwork.

"No problem."

So, he really does exist....

Phoenix hadn't bothered to rehearse for this meeting. Every waking moment—plus the sleeping ones—had been preoccupied by the recent barrage of truths and in processing the sensory overload of emotions that came with them. She hoped she was equipped to follow through with this...this...bit of spontaneity. She had a million questions, surely, and she'd just have to play it by ear. *Holy moly... Are you ready for this?*

"Phoenix."

Hearing the caregiver's voice snapped her back to the present moment.

"Yes?"

"Liam is ready to see you now. Please follow me."

The Manor wasn't particularly large, and as she followed the attendant down three hallways, it appeared to be a mix of mostly non-clinical guest rooms, with a few patient exam rooms here and there. Several elderly clients were gathered in their wheelchairs in a common room, where the television was loudly blaring a Richard Simmons exercise video. Adorning the walls were several paintings, mostly by local artists, and they seemed to mainly represent Lover's Point and Monarch butterflies. The eucalyptus smell had disappeared, only to be replaced by that of various cleaning products and medical supplies.

As they turned the last corner, the attendant stopped and gestured toward a door which was slightly ajar. "Here we are," she said. She gave the door a light tap with her knuckles. "Liam? You have a visitor."

There wasn't an audible reply, but she swung the door open and stepped inside. "You can come in," she said, turning to Phoenix. "He won't bite," she added with a little laugh.

"Who says I won't bite?" a man's voice replied from behind a drawn medical privacy curtain.

The attendant gestured for Phoenix to step further into the room and next to her.

"Liam, you have a young lady here to see you. Her name is—"

"—Phoenix," he said, finishing her sentence. He pulled the curtain back, letting it slide around the curved bar, revealing himself as he finished zipping the fly of his loud, orange and green plaid trousers.

As he regarded his young visitor, a glimmer of recognition flickered in his eyes. The brilliant red hair, her stature, her features, her demeanor. It was like he had stepped back in time and was looking at his late, estranged daughter.

Rose....

He caught his breath for a moment before proceeding. "Phoenix, my dear. My, you are lovely, indeed. It is great to see you. Thank you for coming all this way at the invitation of an old man."

"Hello—" Phoenix said, pausing, as she didn't know what to

call him. "Hello, Liam," she continued. "Sorry, I don't mean to be awkward. *Grandpa?*" she said, blushing through her freckles now.

"We'll figure that stuff out, my dear. You can call me whatever makes you comfortable."

Liam wasn't old in a chronological sense. He was only 72, but high mileage, as years of torturous self-abuse, regret, and a life lived largely at the bottom of a vodka bottle had taken their toll. He still had an impressive, full head of wavy reddish hair, now tinged significantly with gray, and his pale blue eyes were still full of mischief. His bushy eyebrows reminded Phoenix of caterpillars.

It was a smallish room and he gestured to the available chair, as he sat on the edge of his bed. "Please, make yourself comfy."

"Liam, you let me know if you need anything, okay," the attendant offered as she turned to leave. "You want the door open or closed?"

"Either way, sweetheart," he replied as he watched her leave. "I don't mean anything by it," he said, to Phoenix now.

"By what? I don't understand," she said, smiling at this new acquaintance, this new possible relative.

"Sweetheart. Darling. Honey. Sweetie. My dear...I don't mean anything by it. I'm not being flirty. It's just...truth be told, I don't even remember her name!" he said with a chuckle. "Helps me out, y'know. I don't mean anything by it, and they don't seem to mind. A couple of 'em even like it!" he said, adding a wink.

Liam extended his hands, palms up, and, after a moment's hesitation, Phoenix placed hers in his. He was cool to the touch, due to circulation issues, but, somehow, there still seemed to be a warmth that was generated, transferred. Whatever it was—and maybe it was just this long lost, generational connectivity—it was tangible. It felt good. There was electricity there.

"I'm sure nobody minds it. It's sweet, even," Phoenix said. They looked into each other's eyes for a long moment, plumbing their depths, assessing, even appreciating the invitation to connect.

This was no stranger, she quickly surmised. This man had been the father to her mother. This man has experienced any parent's worst nightmare, losing their child. *This man has been dealt blows nobody deserved.*

As have I, she allowed with a moment's introspection.

This man has answers to my questions.

"Had lunch?"

"Um, no, I haven't," Phoenix replied, surprised by the question, as it was only a little after 10:00.

"How about joining me. I know a place!" he said with a laugh. "Can't talk on an empty stomach, can we?"

Mealtime in the Manor's cafeteria was like at any other facility, with the possible exception of the ever-present fitness guru, Richard Simmons, blaring loudly from the speakers of a Sony Trinitron's oak cabinetry: "Round…and round…and front…take it back… again—"

Liam, with a little help from his walker, shuffled toward the set and turned the volume knob down several notches, which elicited a few complaints from a small group of elderly aerobics queens.

"Can't hear yourself think in here!" he admonished, before adding, "Just want to enjoy a quiet meal with my granddaughter here. Thanks for understanding."

Phoenix rather liked the sound of being called that, more than she'd expected to. She walked alongside Liam, offering her support at the elbow, as they approached the food counter.

"Don't get the fish. Gave me the runs for a week last time," he said. "Not kidding."

"I wasn't planning to, but thanks for the warning. Actually, I'm a vegetarian, so I might just opt for a salad," she replied, smiling at this crotchety character who seemed to possess no filter.

"Vegetarian, huh? Hm…well, you didn't inherit that trait from me, but I'm sure they must have something around here for you," he said, scanning the contents of the steel meal bins. "Me? I couldn't be a vegetarian. No way," he added, pointing to the chicken enchiladas under the heat lamp. "I'll have some of those, with beans, rice…and some of the mac 'n' cheese," he instructed the attendant, who went about serving up his desires. "Thanks, sweetheart," he said to her.

Phoenix winked at him, then scanned the array of meat-laden offerings. Hot dogs, chili, and some kind of mystery fish that apparently should have a warning label. Not much for her here, but she wasn't particularly hungry anyway. She mainly wanted a chance to have an uninterrupted conversation with this man she'd traveled so far to meet.

"What can I get for you, miss?" the attendant asked.

"Let's see…um, do you happen to have a salad bar?"

"No miss. No salad bar."

"Okay. No problem. Just a bowl of the fresh fruit, please. Oh, and some cottage cheese, thanks."

"Fruit and cottage cheese, you got it."

"You're a cheap date," Liam said, again with a mischievous laugh. "My treat!"

After they'd collected their trays, they navigated the beverage bar, which was, sadly, lacking a Sunny D spigot. Liam got a Dr. Pepper, Phoenix got a peach Snapple, and they found their way to a window table, as far away from the television as allowable. Phoenix pulled out his chair and guided him into it before taking her place at the small table.

Liam regarded her small bowl of fruit, which was mostly grapes, pieces of orange, chunks of red apple, and slices of yesterday's bananas. "You sure that's going to be enough for you?"

"Oh, yes, it's fine, thanks. I had a cereal bar before I came, so…"

"Me? I mean, I like a salad now and then, don't get me wrong. Fruit, it's okay too. But I couldn't do it—the vegetarian thing. I'd miss my tacos, my burgers, my fried chicken…all of it! Y'know?"

"Sure. I can understand that. I used to enjoy all those things, too, and especially tacos…those were hard to give up. But it's a choice, and I can usually find things to make it work."

"Okay, then," he said, cutting into his enchiladas. "Your mother liked fried chicken too."

This inside pitch threw Phoenix, nearly knocking her over. She set down her fork and looked down at her food for a moment, taking a couple of slow, deliberate breaths before looking back at her lunch date. The silence was palpable.

"I'm sorry, did I—?"

"It's okay," she said with a small sigh. "Liam…Grandpa, I'm going to have to ask that you break me in a little more slowly here, if you don't mind. I mean, I hope you can understand that, until a few days ago, I thought my name was Phoebe, and that I'd been surrendered to an adoption agency when I was five, by a loving mother who, for whatever reason, couldn't keep me. And with your letter coming to me, out of the blue…well, my whole world has been completely rocked now, and I'm just doing my best to process it all and hold myself together," she said, before her eyes started welling up.

"My poor child. I am so sorry. I'm an old man, and I can be a little rough around the edges, but that's not an excuse to be an asshole."

"Grandpa, you certainly aren't an—you know. At least I'm pretty sure you aren't, we just met. It's just that I had a long, exhausting, soul-searching drive out here, and it's given me a ton of time to think about how much of my life—pretty much all of it—has been a lie, and how much has been taken from me, including my mother, and I didn't even know about any of it until now." She wiped her eye and smiled weakly.

Liam pushed his tray to the side and pulled a cotton hankie from his breast pocket, handing it to her. "Here, sweetie…"

"Thank you," Phoenix said softly as she dabbed her eyes. Despite her best efforts, her emotional balloon seemed to have suffered a pinprick of a leak. "You did nothing wrong, it's just…I'm a little sensitive at the moment, and I'm feeling a tidal wave of emotions right now," she managed.

"Understandable, kiddo. I get it. Really, I do."

"I wish I could remember my mother better. I'm having a hard time even picturing her, and it tears me apart," she confided.

Liam gently squeezed her left hand, rubbing his thumb back and forth along its back. When she reciprocated the gesture, he tried another tack. "Your mother...my daughter...our dear Rose, she would be so proud to know how strong, and how beautiful—inside and out—her daughter, *you, Phoenix*, have turned out."

Phoenix' lip quivered slightly, but she managed a small smile. She was trying with all her might not to make a spectacle of herself in front of him and as a guest in this crowded place. She silently wished someone would crank up the TV so Richard Simmons could bail her out here. "Thank you, Grandpa."

She took a stab at her fruit bowl, spearing a large red grape. "And, you probably know by now, that...*jeezus*," she said, pausing to regulate her breathing before continuing. "—That I...had...that—there was a *twin*. A *sister*...I don't know her name because I don't think she ever had one...because she...*oh, gawd*...she was *aborted*. Like I was—or would've been, anyway. And somehow, for whatever twisted reason, I, *Phoenix*, survived, and...well, here I am, and I don't know if I deserve to be here. I'm *alive,* and I'm not entirely sure why. *That's* what I'm dealing with right now, and—excuse my French—but I've got to tell you, it's all hitting me. It's hitting me like a *motherfucker.* Y'know?"

If Liam had been surprised by her language, he didn't show it. He was absorbing all of her run-on feelings, and they were all mixing into the ingredients that comprised his own potent, emotional cocktail.

"I'm sorry, I—I don't usually swear like that," she said, her embarrassment showing now.

"You have nothing to apologize for, Phoenix. You think I give a shit if you swear like a motherfucking sailor?" he said, half kidding. When she chuckled, he knew he'd made his point.

136

"Language," a woman scolded from an adjacent table.

"Sorry, sweetie," Liam replied to her, before sharing a private giggle with his granddaughter. "What do you say we get out of here?"

"But you just started your lunch. Aren't you—?"

"Nah, the food sucks around here anyway. I mean, what do you say we get *out* of here? Like, this *place. The Manor.* It's not like I can't leave when I want to. I checked myself in here, a long time ago, and with your help, we can jolly well check me out. How 'bout it?" His expression suggested some underlying boyhood mischief and his smile, now that he'd flashed it, was hard to resist.

"You mean it? Like check *out*, checkout? For good?" she scrunched her brow. "Where would you go?"

He nodded. "I know a place…hell, I *have* a place!" he said with a laugh.

Phoenix cocked her head as she regarded this elfish man with the goofy grin, wondering if this proposal might be violating some strict Eucalyptus Manor Care Center protocols, but she shrugged. "If you're sure it's okay. If you're sure that's what you want to do."

"I've never been so sure about something in my life, sweetie," he said, laboring to get out of his chair.

"Okay, then," Phoenix said, coming around to help him.

"Mind terribly if we continue this little conversation later? We have much to discuss, of this I can assure you," he said, winking. "But for right now, *let's blow this pop stand!*"

CHAPTER 18

IT WASN'T QUITE as simple he'd made it sound; it wasn't like he and Phoenix could just bus their lunch trays and walk straight out the front door together, never to be seen again by the good folks at the Manor. There were a few formalities involved, as with any such care facility, but Liam had, long before, set up provisions to skedaddle. Eventually. When the time was right.

And the time was right.

He did indeed own a home in the area, and he had employed a long-term house sitter to manage things in his absence. And it had been an absence, of several necessary years.

In his former life in Arizona, the stress of a career with Phoenix PD's homicide division had driven a wedge between him and his wife, and the long and inconsistent hours he kept hadn't been conducive to being the world's most attentive father to their young daughter, Rose. This reality eventually came to roost in her teen years, when she abruptly quit school and ran away from home at the age of sixteen. Liam didn't really know her exact whereabouts after that, or much about what she was doing with her young life, but it wasn't like he was making a Herculean effort to leave no stone unturned.

After a shift, Liam would, invariably, have a couple of Old Fashioneds upon walking in the front door, and his wife would already be at least one ahead of him. If he'd been an alcoholic then, he was a functioning one, and a damned good detective. Metropolitan Phoenix didn't have an exorbitant amount of arson fires, but Liam had outstanding instincts, and was usually the lead detective on the scene, when they happened.

Like he'd been that day.

Liam's love affair with vodka had started twenty years ago, immediately upon discovering the remains of his only daughter in the charred shell of the kitchen area of her rental mobile home. Being first on the scene and confronting any parent's worst imaginable horror, it had been an all- too-easy next step to discover a love for Absolut, absolutely, and massive quantities of it. It was the only thing that could, at least temporarily, block out the pain.

And there was pain in every waking moment for Liam.

His work suffered, and he'd been let go from the department after an investigation into his behavior, and upon being caught drinking on the job. That's when what was left of him made the slow, dizzying spiral down the drain and teetering on the abyss.

His wife had divorced him, and the only other relative he knew was now dead. Murdered, even, which provided more than enough fodder to write a series of truly sad country songs, but he wasn't talented that way, so he focused his obsessive thoughts on Rose's death. On her murder. It taunted him with unsolved unknowns, it tortured him with guilt and regret, and it drove him to the bottle every chance he got. And that was often.

Regret on this level was a bitch, and he eventually threw in the towel. A longtime friend at the department tried unsuccessfully to snap him out of his destructive cycles, but Liam had no interest in anything, especially himself. What was there to live for at this point? That's when, one day, after emerging from the fog of a particularly horrific, weekend-long drunken binge, his friend talked him into checking out some rehabilitation. In California.

Liam took several months to snap himself out of his addiction, sell off his Phoenix home, and attempt to pick up the pieces. An initial fact-finding trip to California introduced him to things he hadn't ever experienced, and—for the first time in decades—it manifested itself in his attempting to embrace some healthier life choices, seek the professional treatment he needed, and decide to purchase a home in which to live in this idyllic coastal paradise on the outskirts of Pacific Grove, adjacent to 17-Mile Drive.

Shangri-la really did exist.

Liam's round of treatment was, from all appearances, successful. He enjoyed walking the vibrant purple, flowery paths along Ocean Boulevard with his two new best friends, a mother/son pair of exquisite German shepherds, Gracie and Luke, all while inhaling the unspoiled goodness that the surf offered up every day. There was no better tonic in the world.

The wood benches spread along the trail there were his church pews, and the pelicans, otters and gulls, his choir. It seemed that it was literally impossible to have a less than magical day in this perfect place, and for the first time he felt like there might be some sparks of life left in his broken soul. That was, until his fall.

Off the cliff....

The day of the incident had started out perfectly enough, with an exquisite breakfast of game changer apple-oatmeal pancakes, a side of crispy bacon, fresh-squeezed orange juice, strong coffee, all enjoyed at a sunny window table at his favorite haunt, Holly's Lighthouse Café.

After his meal, Liam had walked a few blocks down to Ocean Boulevard, where he took up residence at one of his usual benches to enjoy the parade of brown pelicans flying in formation and jockeying for position on the guano-covered rocks along the shore. It was when he stood to get a better view through his binoculars that he lost his footing, careening off the plant-covered path and onto a sizeable boulder below, which managed to do a number on several vertebrae. That ended his therapeutic walks, and the pain and frustration led to depression and a return to the bottle.

Thus, his admission to the Manor, where he took up residence during his long stint there in what he called *Therapy 2.0*. It had been a tougher go this time around, as pain, reduced mobility, and a resultant sense of hopelessness had been added to the mix, but he'd done due diligence in getting past his demons. Most of them. All except one, anyway. And now he was ready to check out, with no plans to return, God willing.

After their lunch there, Phoenix had escorted Liam back to his room, and they made plans to reconvene the following morning, after he'd sorted out his release documentation and packed his belongings. Phoenix returned to her lodge room and sent off a text before her stroll with the Prick-master.

> *Pop Pop! Just returned from lunch with Liam…OMG, what a character!! He's for real, and he's checking out of the facility tomorrow, with my help. He says he has some important stuff to share with me, so…hopefully that'll come tomorrow, once we get him relocated to his home here. I'll keep you posted. Nervous! Excited! (confused too) :-/*
> *I'm fine though. Love you, Pop Pop! – PHX*

Prick set the pace as they made their way along the well-manicured path that paralleled the dramatic shoreline. Phoenix tore off a small piece of duck jerky and gave it to her tiny companion, who now joined her on one of the benches. She let out an extra-long sigh, representative of the feelings she'd bottled up inside her for several days, punctuated by the emotions served up by today's meeting with this man who was apparently her grandpa. And her only living blood relative. This was heady stuff, and if there was ever a place seemingly designed for the purpose of solving life's big questions, it was here, looking out on this otherworldly-beautiful body of water from these lifegiving benches. She tilted her head toward the sky, drinking in the last of the day's sun and breathing in the abundant nutrients her soul craved.

I'm...alive.... Thank you!

Phoenix's Zen experience lasted for the better part of thirty minutes before being interrupted by a series of yips, and the sound of her own stomach rumbling. She took this as a cue to walk back into the village where she stumbled upon a new-to-her sammich shop, Goodies Delicatessen. Their Veggie Lovers Dream Come True, on whole wheat, seemed as though it had been created with her in mind, and she purchased it to go, hopeful she could make it back to the room before she rifled through the wrapper and inhaled it whole. A nearby store hooked her up with the Sunny D product and, dinner in hand, she was highly motivated to get back to the lodge.

After feeding the Chihuahua—goofiest name for a dog breed ever—she did a quick cleaning of Angus's cage without taking time for the newspaper's current events, attended to the bird's nutritional needs and then, finally, her own.

Oh, my goodness...best sammich ever....

Settling in, after the bliss of her meal, Phoenix logged into her eBay account, and had to giggle at the notification that Pop Pop's "three-piece set" had been shipped. No other emails, so she logged back off, closed the clamshell, and set about brushing her teeth.

Tomorrow was going to be a big question mark once she and Liam checked out of the Manor, as she really had no idea what to expect from there. She'd floated the question about whether she could bring her pooch along, and Liam'd offered no hesitation. One thing she did know, he had a lot to share with her, so she'd better get a good night's rest.

And she did.

Phoenix awoke at a few minutes after seven, slowly cracking open one eye slit at a time, surveying her surroundings as well as her inner self. It was an odd feeling and something that seemed curiously foreign to her of late, and after a few moments of reflection, she determined that the feeling could only be one thing: *refreshed!*

The critters had allowed her this chunk of healing recharge time without making so much as a peep or a squeak, and she was grateful that the pillowtop mattress had granted her wish. She made her way to the sink and splashed water on her face, taking a long moment to regard the young woman in the mirror. There seemed to be some subtle changes happening with each passing day, both inward and outward, and she took these developments as positive ones. She allowed her reflection to smile at her, and she returned the greeting.

After a nice hot shower, she made sure Angus's food and water bowls were good for the day, took the little guy out for his potty break and, after giving him some kibble, she selected one of the two remaining clean shirts and undies she had in her duffle. *Laundry day tomorrow.*

She dialed the room's curtains so that Angus wouldn't be cooked while she was gone, hefted her laundry bag and the Prick, and headed out to the car. The dirty clothes were chucked in the back seat, Prick was secured in the "shotgun" seat, and she was pleased to happen upon a nearby McDonald's, where she ordered an Egg McMuffin sans meat, plus a tiny sleeve of their breakfast taters, and a coffee with double sugars and mystery creamers.

The drive to the Manor was only about fifteen minutes, so she got busy wolfing down her chow. She wasn't sure what tape was still in the deck, so she rewound what was in there then hit play. Gloria Gaynor, along with Phoenix, together busted out what now had to be considered the definitive version of "I Will Survive," which was immediately followed by "Wake Me Up Before You Go-Go" by Wham! Her window was down as she sang at the top of her lungs, and the air was heavy with eucalyptus. She was even starting to like that smell.

Before she could even get halfway through Climax Blues Band's tour-de-force live version of their jazz/rock instrumental, "Meso-popmania," she found herself entering the driveway to the Manor. Hers and Pop Pop's maestro, Peter Haycock, was launching into another impossible guitar solo, and the entire band was firing on all cylinders as she approached the entrance, so she decided it best to turn the volume knob counterclockwise, from eleven to about two.

There was a shady spot open, and it was marked *VISITOR*, so she grabbed it. After cracking the two front windows open for her little passenger, she locked the car and walked the fifty yards up to the lobby. She sent up a silent prayer, hoping for a not-too-crazy day and for the strength to deal with whatever came her way. *Amen.*

"Good morning," the attendant said, welcoming her warmly.

"Good morning," Phoenix responded. "I'm here to—"

"Yes, I remember you from yesterday," the attendant said, anticipating her. "You're the granddaughter. You're here for Liam."

"Yes…"

"He's just finishing up his breakfast, and we'll be bringing him out in a few minutes. If you'd please take a seat, we'll let him know you're here."

"Perfect. Thank you," Phoenix replied with a smile as the attendant picked up the phone. As she found her chair, she picked up the morning's newspaper which she quickly scanned. More concerns about the impending end-of-the-world Y2K scare, more election jive…*and more cage liner for Angus.* She re-folded the paper and tucked it under her arm.

After fifteen minutes of squirming in her seat, a door finally opened and Liam emerged, in a mandated wheelchair and with a young college-aged female attendant. He smiled upon seeing Phoenix, and the attendant wheeled Liam right up to her.

"I can walk from here, sweetheart," he said. "I'm not crippled, y'know."

"I know you're not, Mr. McGinn. It's just the rules, and only until you're in the car, okay?"

"If you say so, dear," he said, sharing a private eye roll with Phoenix.

"Good morning, Liam," Phoenix said, standing now. "Er, Grandpa," she corrected. "Are you all set?"

"Yep! Got my discharge paperwork right here," he said, holding up a manila folder.

"Awesome, I'll just go pull the car around then," Phoenix replied and headed out the front door.

"So…what's your name again?" Liam asked his young assistant.

"I'm sorry?" she said, a bit thrown.

"Your name."

"Oh, um, I'm sorry…Shannon's my name, Mr. McGinn," she said, smiling but embarrassed.

"Shannon… Irish name. Very nice name. So, Shannon, do you have a boyfriend?"

Just then, Phoenix pulled up to the curb, saving the day with a *Meep! Meep!* of the horn.

"Well, Mr. McGinn, it looks like your ride is here," Shannon managed, trying not to be totally creeped out by her client. "Here we go," she said, as she got the chair in motion and out into the sunlight, and none too soon.

At the sight of the gleaming orange muscle car, Liam had all but forgotten his question and the lack of response. He was staring at an impossibly bitchin' machine, and one of Detroit's finest.

"Ho-ly mother," he said under his breath just as Phoenix came around to open the passenger door. She'd already moved the pup to the back seat, next to her laundry bag, and she assisted Shannon in extracting him from the chair.

"A 1970…and the Hemi, no less," he said. "I always wanted to ride in one of these."

"Well, today must be your lucky day, Grandpa!" she said with an especially cheerful smile, that this man recognized beauty when he saw it. "Here you go," she said, pivoting him so his rear end faced the seat before lowering him into position. Once his head cleared and he swung his feet forward, a huge grin spread across his face—like that of a boy with a new BB gun on Christmas morning.

Shannon pulled the wheelchair back and gave him a wave. "Goodbye, Mr. McGinn."

Liam waved back in reaction to the sound of his name, but without looking at her. His attention was firmly locked in on the cabin of this dreamy retro spaceship, one he'd long fantasized about.

"Okay, you're good to go. Comfy?" she asked, clicking his lap seatbelt.

"Oh, yes, dear. Very. Wow…" he replied, looking at the instrument panel, the shifter, the utter perfection that surrounded him. As Phoenix climbed into her seat, Liam reached up to the hula girl and gave her a poke, setting her bobble dance in motion. "Ha!"

"Yep! A reminder of somewhere I need to go someday," she said, looking at the old-time youngster sitting next to her. "Ready to go?"

"You bet."

She clicked her own belt and pulled away slowly, making a wide turn and heading back down the driveway. "Anyplace in particular?" she asked with a laugh.

"Oh, yes, I guess you'd need some directions," he said, returning a chuckle. "When you get to the intersection down there, hang a right."

CHAPTER 19

LIAM SPOKE VERY little during the drive, preferring to direct Phoenix with hand signals and the occasional one-word navigational response. He rolled down his window and reacquainted his soul with the sensations that he'd been removed from since being interned.

His nostrils flared at the smell of the trees. His senses celebrated the sound of the leaves rustling in the breeze, the ethereal beauty that surrounded him, and the warmth of the noonday sun when it occasionally peeked through the foliage. He also was enthralled with the melodic, throaty purr of the Hemi engine—even if it cancelled out the natural sounds when she accelerated. To him, it all melded together perfectly, like a well-rehearsed symphony.

With his credentials, they'd been granted passage through the Pacific Grove Gate, and—with the Pacific Ocean to their right side—they drove along Spanish Bay Road before joining 17-Mile Drive near Point Joe.

Phoenix couldn't believe her eyes as they followed the surreal coastline, which lead them along the Monterey Peninsula Country Club property and Spyglass Hill Golf Course. Hailing from the desert regions of Arizona and never been exposed to golf, she was, for the first time in her young life entertaining the idea of pursuing it. There were occasional families of beautiful young deer at the edge of the tree line and an abundance of suicidal squirrels tempting fate as they scampered across the road.

"So," she said, breaking the silence while trying to gage their progress. "We must be close, I take it, if this is only a seventeen-mile drive?"

"Huh?" he grunted in response as he turned to her.

"Your place. Are we close? Do you live on the ocean?"

"Me? No…I wish. I'm fortunate to have some family money, but not *that* kind of money. I'm just taking you the scenic way around. It's been a long time for me, plus you've never seen it, so I appreciate your indulging me," he said, turning his gaze back out the window. "We're going to just follow this for a while. I'll let you know."

"No problem, I was just curious. It *is* spectacular, and, oh my God…these homes are insane," she said, now taking time to appreciate some of the magnificent properties belonging to the rich and maybe-even-famous.

"That, over there, they call Bird Rock," he said, pointing to the guano-covered mass off the coast. "Tons of gulls and cormorants today," he said to himself. "Just up ahead's another one, a little smaller, called Seal Rock. On a day like today you'll see lots of sea lions, probably some leopard and harbor seals too. God, I've missed this place," he said, his voice trailing off.

"I can imagine," she concurred.

They continued along, with Liam pointing out the various turn-outs and favorite tourist landmarks, but they wouldn't be taking time to stop today. He'd been away from home too long, and today seemed to be a popular day with tour groups.

"Cypress Point," he said as they hooked left to follow the coast. At around Midway Point, not far from the "Ghost Tree," and just past Cypress Drive, Liam directed Phoenix to veer left toward Stevenson Drive. "We'll save the other half for another day."

"There's another half?"

"Indeed, there is."

A series of turns later, they found Forest Lake Road and were on the backside of Spyglass Hill Golf Course. *Good thing he knows where he's going...sheesh!*

"Almost there," Liam said mostly to himself, and Phoenix thought she detected an extra dollop of joy in his voice. A yip from the backseat signaled approval; he needed to pee. As they approached a mostly obscured driveway on the right, Liam announced, "And that there's Pirate's Cove," pointing to a hard-to-see, all-gray, modernistic home on a recessed property. "I'll tell you about that later. Keep going."

"O-kay..." she said, her brow furrowed and curiosity aroused as they drove another mile.

"Take this driveway here," he said, pointing to his left. "And careful you don't scrape the back end of this beautiful buggy on the mailbox as you do."

"Roger that," Phoenix acknowledged as she carefully navigated the turn and proceeded up the driveway to the single-story ranch property. The wood-paneled home appeared older, more basic, and lacked the opulence of the other palaces they'd passed along the way, and that was the way Liam liked it. He hadn't moved here to be in competition with the neighbors. There was only one neighbor that interested him, and that's why he'd purchased the property.

"Okay, sweetheart, here we are. Just pull up by the garage there, and we'll attend to your pooch's needs before we go inside."

"Wow, Grandpa, I'll bet you missed this place," Phoenix said, as she retrieved the little guy from the rear seat. "C'mon, Prick."

"Hey, that's no way to talk to your grandfather. I'm moving as quick as I can here."

"Sorry. The dog. It's his name. I forgot to make proper introductions. Liam, Prick. Prick, Liam," she replied with a laugh as she monitored the peeing.

"Okay, then," he said, shaking his head as Phoenix came around to his door and helped him to his feet. As he hung onto the door frame, she retrieved his walker from the trunk and unfolded it for him as he looked up to the tops of his trees. A smile crept across his face as he took in this setting. As he grabbed the handles of his walker, a familiar sound broke the silence. The front door of the house opened, and two beautiful German shepherds spilled out, barking their welcomes.

"Gracie, girl! Luke, my boy!" he cried joyfully as they bounded over to see their master who'd been away so long. Phoenix just hoped they wouldn't topple him as they approached.

"Oh, yes...look at you! Yes, Daddy's missed you! My sweeties..." he said, the love in his expression obvious. "Phoenix, meet my babies! Gracie and Luke!"

"Wow..." she said, quickly stuffing Prick back in his travel crate and rolling the window down slightly before closing the car door. She kneeled down to pet the shepherds. "Oh, my goodness! Beautiful dogs, both. Hi, baby," she said. It was all tail wags, kisses and hugs for several minutes before Liam acknowledged the housekeeper, still standing on the porch. He waved.

"Welcome home, Mr. McGinn!" the young man said. Even from thirty feet away, he appeared as big as a sequoia.

"How quickly you forget, young man. *Liam*, please, call me Liam. Mr. McGinn was my father!" he replied with a laugh.

"Okay, sorry, Liam. Good to have you back," the tree-sized man said, stepping off the porch and joining them.

"Good to see you, Curt. Everything good?"

"Yes, sir. Did a few fix-up items this week, mostly plumbing, a little electrical. Your septic's in good shape too."

"Bless you, Curt. Oh, where are my manners? Curt, I'd like you to meet Phoenix. My granddaughter!" he said, gesturing to her as she turned to smile up at the giant. Standing next to each other, their size differential could mistake them for a ventriloquist act.

"Nice to meet you, Curt."

"Pleasure's mine, er, Phoenix, was it?"

"That's right. As in Arizona. Where I'm from, actually," she said almost shyly.

Even with her ballcap, and wearing no makeup to speak of, Curt could recognize her beauty immediately. She was tiny but, like they said, sometimes good things come in small packages.

"Arizona...never been. Heard good things though. How long are you here?"

She turned toward Liam and shrugged. "Actually, that's a very good question. I've been staying over in Pacific Grove the last couple of nights. Kind of winging it, truth be told. Came here to meet up with this gentleman," she added as she hooked her arm around Liam's.

"Gotcha," Curt replied, still slightly shellshocked at the sight of her. "Well, let me help you unload," he said, snapping himself out of it. "Stuff's in the trunk?"

"Yes. Just one bag. I'll pop the lid," she said, walking to the rear of the Road Runner and inserting her key.

"Is this what I think it is?"

"Is what—? Oh, the car. Yes. I mean, probably. What do you think it is?" she said with a coy grin.

"My buddy has a shop in the valley. He's had a poster of one of these on the wall in his office forever. Plymouth Road Runner, for sure. Let me guess...a '69, right?"

"Close! '70. My dream car, and I've only had it about a week, believe it or not!" she said, shaking her head at the thought as she grabbed Liam's bag and slammed the trunk. "Hemi. She's such a bad girl," she added, almost craning her neck to share her smile.

Curt smiled back. It wasn't one of those cocky *I know I'm good-looking* kinds of smiles, because he wasn't cut from that cloth. Even though he'd been blessed with what some might consider a disarming smile and perfect teeth, he wasn't fully aware of it yet and didn't possess the requisite confidence gene to back it up. He was a big guy—not unlike Baloo from *The Jungle Book*—thus, he came across as a gentle giant. Still, based on his size, one would probably be wise not to test the limits of that character trait.

"Here, let me take that," he said, rolling up the sleeves of his red flannel shirt that made him look like a clean-shaven version of the Bounty paper towels guy. Showing his chivalrous side, he reached for Liam's bag.

"Thank you," she said, looking away shyly. *Get it together, Phoenix…what the hell!?* This was truly uncharted territory here, and she had absolutely zero experience, nor anything resembling preparation for moments such as these. Mainly because there'd never been a moment like this. She felt something akin to a blush, and it freaked her. *Don't be a friggin' idiot!*

"That's all there is. We'd better head inside and get Liam situated," she added, recovering just enough to initiate a transition.

"Right," he said, hefting the duffle and trying his best not to stare at Phoenix's perfect little butt as he followed her onto the porch and they proceeded inside. *Get a grip, Curt!*

"Grandpa? Where are you? Where do you want us to put your bag?"

"I'm in here!" he replied from the next room. Turning the corner into the family room, they found Liam in his Lazy Boy recliner, smiling widely. At his feet were his two furry companions. His *family*. If she chose to accept an invitation, Liam would happily add Phoenix to that short list.

"I have to tell you, it's wonderful to be back, in this fabulous chair, with my loved ones."

Phoenix smiled in acknowledgement, fully appreciating how happy he seemed here. The family room looked like time had stood still, locked somewhere in the 1970s, with its paneled walls, red brick fireplace, cottage cheese ceiling and rust-colored shag carpeting.

I wonder if he'd like a gently used lava lamp…?

"I'll bet," she said instead, surveying his castle with a look of encouragement.

"Um, Liam, I think I'll be going, if that's okay with you. I have a shift tonight, so I'll leave you two alone to reconnect, okay?"

"That's just fine, my boy. I'm in capable hands here," he said, saluting him.

Curt turned to Phoenix and extended his hand. She wiped the moisture from her palm before returning the handshake. The size differential was almost comic and not too unlike a baby placing its hand into the pocket of a catcher's mitt. Still, it was a nice, cushiony place to be in, this hand, and it radiated a comforting warmth. "Nice to meet you, Phoenix."

"Nice to meet you as well, Curt," she said with a smile.

"Um, I left the front door key on the kitchen counter if you need it, okay? And I think the visiting nurse is scheduled to do a check on him this afternoon, around four. I made a grocery run, so there's stuff in the fridge. So, I'll…just…be on my way. My, uh, phone number is on the fridge. A little Post-It note there. If you need to get ahold of me for anything." *My Gawd, man!*

"Thank you, Curt. I'm sure we'll be fine, but it's good to have the number," she replied, nodding excessively as she studied her tennis shoes.

"Okay, bye, Liam. I'll call you tomorrow morning, okay?" he said, turning to exit, pausing to glance at Phoenix again. He flashed a smile and it seemed to light up the room.

"That'll be fine, buddy," Liam replied, still grinning. He'd secretly enjoyed watching this awkward little meet-and-greet session, and it reminded him more than a little bit of how terrifyingly shy he'd been at his first school dance a hundred years ago. He hated to leave Curt twisting in the wind with this, but he had to figure out this stuff on his own. So did Phoenix.

The front door closed quietly, and Phoenix watched Curt climb into his two-toned, dark chestnut metallic F-150 and navigate the driveway out to the main road. She wasn't aware of it, but she let out a pretty colossal sigh that only Liam was privy to.

"That Curt, he's a good one," Liam said, winking at his granddaughter. "Why don't you take off your ballcap and stay awhile, sweetie? You hungry?"

"Me? Um, no. I'm not, really," she replied, liberating her mane and shaking it loose. "Are you?"

"Starved!" he said with a laugh. "Let's have some lunch, then after that we'll try to solve the world's problems, okay?"

An inventory of Liam's cupboards and fridge had netted some decent offerings for Liam's palate but not hers so much. She prepared a can of Campbell's Bean with Bacon for him and opened a can of Campbell's Green Pea for herself, which she ate straight from the can, cold, with a spoon. It seemed silly to dirty two saucepans after all. She paired his soup with a turkey sandwich on wheat bread and some bites of cheddar cheese to share. No Sunny D to be found, so she poured the closest thing, two glasses of orange juice.

"Delightful sandwich, sweetheart. Thank you," he said as he sank his teeth into the second half. "Did you find enough stuff for yourself? I didn't know about your veggie preference or I would've asked Curt to pick up some things for you."

"No worries, Grandpa. Really. I'm perfectly content with this," she said, setting her spoon into the now-empty soup can. "Speaking of Curt, how do you know each other?"

Liam took a long moment to chew his bite before wiping his mouth. "Well, before I had my fall—in more ways than one, as you probably know—I had a couple of trees on the property that needed to come down. I asked around, and he was referred to me. He did a great job with those trees, hauled 'em away too, and has been doing some work around here in my absence. When he has the time. He has a regular job, so I appreciate it that he can help me out."

"What, might I ask, is his regular job?" she queried in an

attempt to sound casual as she popped a chunk of sharp cheddar in her mouth.

"Not entirely sure on that, kiddo," Liam replied, washing things down with some O.J. "He used to be a part-time handyman, then, not too long ago, he took a job with some outfit in Salinas. Salinas… I call it *Silly-ness*," he said, punctuating it with a laugh. "Hard worker, though, and a nice young man."

"Seems to be," Phoenix agreed.

"And he's single!" Liam said, watching for her reaction, which was almost a spit-take.

"That's nice, Grandpa. I'm sure he's a great guy. Not looking though, thanks. I'm from out of state, and this is a working trip for me, don't forget."

"Well…" his voice trailed off before adding, "never say never, is what I always say."

"Can I clear your plate?" she asked, happy to change the subject as she got up to retrieve his items.

"Sure, that was lovely, Rose," he said, which caused her to pause momentarily.

"You mean 'Phoenix'" she reminded him.

"Yes, of course. I'm sorry," he said, catching his error. As she reached over, a huge shock of her fiery waves cascaded down across her face. He studied her closely as she raked it aside and smiled. *Even the little dimple in her chin.*

Phoenix was rinsing cutlery at the sink when he added, "I can't get over how much you look like your mother." She wasn't at all prepared for these types of remarks, especially the out-of-the-blue mentions such as this, that he meant no harm by. Still, she tried to consider the intent and the source as she towel-dried their utensils.

"I've never seen a photograph of her," she managed. "Perhaps you can show me one."

"Indeed. I can do better than that, sweetheart. Come in here and sit with me," he said, reaching for the large brown scrapbook that was propped against the base of his recliner.

Phoenix entered, drying her hands on the towel, and he gestured her to the folding chair. "Here, pull up it closer, next to me. I want to show you something."

She took a deep breath as she grabbed the chair and placed it next to his left armrest, readying herself for whatever he had to share. As she settled in, she noticed that there happened to be a large box of tissues on the little table, within reach. Just in case....

"Goodness. O-kay...."

Liam's hands were laid flat on the surface of the album's front cover. He turned to Phoenix and he mustered every bit of sensitivity he could as he spoke. "Phoenix, my dear, please tell me to stop if you find any of this too difficult. I just want you to know everything. You deserve nothing less. Deal?"

She exhaled deeply and returned a tight-lipped smile as she wiped the corner of her eye and nodded. "Deal."

"Okay then," he said, moving the book closer so they could both see as he opened the faux leather cover to the first page, which was blank, except for one hand-written word in large red letters: R O S E. "I'd like you to meet Rose. My daughter. Your mom...."

Phoenix squirmed briefly as she prepared herself. He turned the next page with great ceremony, and the first images were in black and white, with annotations in his hand that stated the year, 1956, and other specifics, beginning with a hospital birth photo of Rose. The caption read, *Rose: 8 hrs. old.* It was uncanny just how much hair this little girl had, having just entered the world. There was a longish curl running across her forehead, and you could tell her remaining hair had been combed back. Even though the photo wasn't in color, the reddish tones jumped off the paper. "This is your mother, my dear. Only hours old and born with a tremendous head of beautiful hair. Beautiful child," he said softly.

Phoenix's eyes were already starting to moisten as she stared

156

intently into this time tunnel of an album that was transporting her to another dimension, one she knew nothing about. She was transfixed, and wild horses wouldn't be able to drag her away from what she was experiencing right now, after all this time, and after all her questions and prayers, directed to God, to the universe.

She really did exist....

More early family pictures adorned the next few pages, a younger and rather handsome version of Liam, some in his uniform, most in his casual clothes. He had a full head of wavy hair, and it was evident which side of the family Rose had inherited hers from.

He and his wife looked happy here—the new, proud parents—and they seemed to adore their young daughter. Phoenix committed each photo to memory, absorbing every detail and nuance. She was reconstructing her life today—her real life, anyway—and being able to get a glimpse into her mother's world was a gift. "That's your grandmother, Phoenix," he said, pointing to one close-up photo. There wasn't much joy in his voice in declaring that, she noticed, and she hoped he'd elaborate when the time came.

"Very pretty woman, your wife. My grandmother, I mean," Phoenix replied, offering a smile.

"Yes…" he said softly, turning the page. Even in her elementary school photos, some of which were in color by this point, Rose had been an exceptional beauty. She didn't smile often for photos, but she had stunning features, all framed by that incredible head of hair. There seemed to be fewer family photos during this period and mostly school portraits.

"Work kept me pretty busy during this time," Liam admitted, seemingly ashamed. "I missed out on many of Rose's events growing up. The school recitals and things of that nature. Oh, that girl could sing like an angel," he said, wiping his eye.

Phoenix handed him a tissue, then grabbed a couple for herself. "I like to sing too. Maybe that's where I get it from."

"I have no doubt, sweetie," he said, squeezing her hand. "My career with the Phoenix PD took a bit of a toll on our marriage, I'm afraid. And, with my relationship with Rose, later on," he said, before a little whimper escaped. "Dammit." He sighed, dabbing his eyes with the tissue.

Phoenix offered no response, because she couldn't think of an adequate one, other than to put a comforting arm around his shoulder. She was tamping down her own emotions, and they were beginning to crest like a wave.

"I'm sorry, I just have regrets sometimes. If I had it all to do over again…."

"Totally understandable, Grandpa. You can't beat yourself up about it now, though. I can tell that you were a good father and provider and that you loved Rose—my mother—very much. I can only imagine the pressures at work," she said, bracing herself for any mention later of his having found her remains. She shuddered.

"This here—" he said, pointing to her sophomore photo, "—is one of my favorites. About a year later…she ran away from home," he revealed, turning to Phoenix. "She was only sixteen. I was drinking too much back then, and I'm sure that didn't help. I have myself to blame for that," he said, honking his nose.

Phoenix handed him a couple of fresh tissues and as she returned her gaze to the photo, she couldn't help but feel she was looking in the mirror. There was Rose, but there was Phoenix, blended. A shiver ran up her spine and the fine red hairs on her arms stood up. Even though Rose's hair was now cut shorter, almost in a bob, the resemblance was unmistakable. She turned to Liam and confirmed what he'd said earlier. "I can't believe it…I look just like her," she said, her voice trailing off like the remaining air had been removed from a vacuum chamber. "Oh, my God."

"It's true, you do. Forgive me if I stare at you sometimes. I don't wish to be rude, but I can't help it. When I first saw you, when you came to see me at the Manor, I thought I was hallucinating. I thought I saw my long-lost Rose walk into the room. I hope you can understand."

"Of course, I can…." she said, recovering enough to smile at her grandfather.

He nodded appreciatively, then turned to the next page, which was blank. "Do you need to take a break?" he asked.

"Me? No. Thank you. This is amazing… I mean, is that it? Or is there more?"

His flat palms returned to rest on the blank page, ceremoniously, and he waited a few moments before he responded. "There's more, yes. But some of it is less than pleasant," he said, cautioning her in a voice that was now a loud whisper. "Some of the things on these next pages are very painful, Phoenix. For me, to remember the worst moment of my life. And for you, to look at the horrible incident that took Rose from us. We can skip this part, or maybe revisit it at another time if you'd prefer. I just want you to know—"

Phoenix looked at his hands, and how they rested on the surface of the blank page, serving as a barricade against the horrors that could be found beyond that boundary. She took several moments to consider what he'd just said and debated the best course of action. She did need to get back to the bird, and she could use that as an excuse to—

"No. Let's proceed, Grandpa. I'm as ready as I'm going to be, and it was answers I came all this way to get. Only if you're up for it, though. I can't imagine how hard it's been for you."

He squeezed her hand again, a bit harder this time, which was all the confirmation she needed, and she braced herself as he licked his thumb and forefinger and flipped to the next page.

As the page was laid flat, Phoenix saw that the entire surface was covered by clippings and a large newspaper photo of a burnt dwelling. She couldn't tell what kind of structure it was, as it appeared to be either a large trailer or a mobile home, but she knew this had to be where her mother had been found and that it had been

Detective Liam McGinn that had made the grim discovery that day. The newspaper's banner was dated December 26, 1974, which would make it the day after Christmas.

Phoenix looked away for a moment, collecting herself as she readied for any supporting material that might come. "This was...."

"Yes. This was where Rose lived, sweetie. And it's where you lived, as well," he said, meeting her eyes now, letting that nugget sink in for a moment.

"I don't understand. I don't remember this place. At least I don't think I do." She squinted hard at the photo that most clearly showed the home and the yard. "Wait, I think I do remember this place—I was very small, I don't know how old—but...I used to ride my tricycle there," she said, pointing to what would've been the front yard. "Oh, my God...." she said under her breath as she put her hand to her mouth.

"Are you okay, honey?"

Her hand remained at her mouth and she nodded, still staring at this charred structure and knowing her mother had been inside. "Christmas. It was Christmas, and—" she managed before losing it. Her shoulders started to heave from the weight of twenty-plus year-old repressed memories she didn't even know were there. She could no longer see through the waterfall of tears and she pivoted to Liam, who joined her in a long hug, steeped in understanding, in sympathy, in mutual pain that ran deeper than the Marianas Trench.

"I know...I know...."

They sat in silence for a while. Liam had closed the album and Phoenix had shut her eyes, processing this enormous data dump, one that for twenty years her subconscious mind had shielded her from.

After about twenty minutes, she slowly opened her eyes, and she couldn't help but notice that it almost seemed like she now had 3D vision; she saw things with such renewed clarity.

"There was a man."

"What's that, dear?" Liam asked, snapping out of his own dark trance.

"A man. I saw him."

"You saw someone, Phoenix? Are you sure?"

"I'm sure," she said, her expression confirming the fact. "He was hurting Mama," she managed before gasping for air.

"Easy…easy, sweetie. Take your time. Do you need to lay down for a while?"

She shook her head several times. "No, no thanks," she replied, wiping her eyes. "When I peeked into the kitchen, I saw him hurting Mama."

"Who? Who did you see, Phoenix? Do you think you could describe him?" Liam asked, his senses now on full alert as well.

"He…he wasn't very tall, but he looked very mean. He was rather ugly…with bad skin…and—oh, my God…" she said, pausing at another flash of memory. "He had a patch. On his eye. An eyepatch!"

Liam was nodding slowly now as he took in these details, these liberated accounts from horrific memories suppressed in a then five-year-old's subconscious mind. The decades of guilt, self-loathing, and pickling himself in alcohol—to the point of even questioning his own sanity at times—had overshadowed his ability to see his investigation through, and all he'd seemed to have were his suspicions, a sketchy witness's hearsay account, and an incomplete mosaic to dwell on. Phoenix was providing aggregate here, helping to properly set the pieces he'd obsessed over since that day he found the charred, lifeless body of his only child. The day the world stopped turning.

A moment later, the next revelation came. "Mama called out a word," she said softly.

"What was it?" he asked anxiously. "Do you remember what she said? What did she say, Phoenix?"

"The last thing I heard…as he was hurting Mama—" Phoenix

uttered between hyperventilated breaths, "—right before the fire started…I heard Mama say something! I heard her yell it! She screamed, *Awful Man!!*"

Phoenix had barely managed to shuffle the few feet to the family room sofa before collapsing, utterly drained and in a comalike state. Liam remained planted in his recliner for the better part of an hour, collating his thoughts and emotions, before grabbing a couple of blankets from the basket at his feet and covering his granddaughter. Once she was tucked in, he kicked his walker into overdrive as he made his way down the hall to his office.

He planted himself in his desk chair and swung around to the four-drawer file cabinet. He didn't have to search for what he was looking for; it was a readily accessible and well-worn file that he'd consulted often over the years. He lifted it from the drawer and laid it atop the desk. He switched on the lamp and took a deep breath before opening it. It was a thick file, as it had been collecting reports, files, clippings and scribbled note pages for over two decades. On the tab was written one word, in red, by a fine-point Sharpie: **R O S E.**

"Okay, you son of a bitch," he muttered as he flipped a few pages of police reports before landing on what he was looking for, a manila envelope containing several faded photos he'd gathered of a "person of interest" he'd obsessed over, but had never been able to do anything about, for all these years. The man that still haunted his dreams, still stoked the fire in his belly, had long ago driven him to drink, and was the primary reason he hadn't thrown in the towel all those years ago: the Pirate.

Offermann.

Awful Man.…

Liam grabbed his yellow legal pad and began transcribing what

Phoenix had just shared. His transcription was pretty much word for word, as his detective skills—at least notetaking—hadn't completely atrophied. He spread the photographs out so he could study them, then picked up the one that offered the best close-up look at the monster he'd long suspected was his daughter's murderer.

A neighbor in the trailer park where Rose had lived had described hearing a woman's scream, followed by a man's. Moments later he'd seen flames spreading from the kitchen of Rose's mobile home, and a male figure fleeing the scene, first on foot, and with his arm in flames, before jumping into a black two-door car—"Maybe a Mustang, but I can't be sure," the witness had said. "Looked like he had some kind of mask, or a patch…something like that…on his face. Creepy-looking dude!"

Things were starting to gel quickly for Liam. Now, he'd just have to find a way to prove it all. He pulled open the top drawer of his desk and retrieved an artifact he'd found at the scene. It was still in a tiny plastic evidence baggie with a zip closure. He held it under the light and studied it with new scrutiny: a charred shell of a Zippo lighter, embellished with a raised skull-and-crossbones on it.

"What ya looking at, Grandpa?" the soft voice asked, almost startling him into tomorrow.

"Jeezus, Gawd…you scared the living daylights out of me!" he said, flipping the file closed and spinning around in his chair. "I thought you were—"

"I was," she interjected, stepping into the office and putting her hand on his shoulder. "Sorry, didn't mean to frighten you."

"Yeah, well…no harm. I was just—oh, hell—I was just thinking about what you told me, and that got me to thinking about some suspicions I've held for a long, long time. When you described what happened, and the man—well, it just…maybe confirmed what I'd known all along."

"Tell me, Grandpa…please tell me what you know, or what

you think you know. Please. You can't leave me hanging here…not now," she pleaded.

Liam slowly nodded. "I know, honey. Just a second, while I get you a chair," he said, getting up. As he did, he stealthily slipped the lighter back into the top drawer and pivoted to the closet, sliding the door aside to retrieve a folding chair. "Here. Sit next to me," he said, unfolding it.

"Thanks," she said as she planted herself and scooched it up closer. "Is that a police file?"

"Kind of, but not entirely. It's stuff I've been collecting, studying…hell, *obsessing* over, really, if you wanna know the truth. I've had my very strong hunches all these years, but that's all they've been—hunches—until now. What you've now allowed yourself to remember, and the details you've recounted, it all breathes life into this cold case file of mine. Bless you for that, child," he said, pausing to wipe his eye.

Phoenix was closest to the Kleenex box, and she handed it to him.

"Something in my eye," he lied. She said nothing but rested her head on his shoulder as he got through his moment. "About what you saw…and heard, dear. You said you remember your mother saying something. You heard her call out…what was it again?"

"*Awful Man*…that's what I heard," she confirmed, sitting straighter.

Liam flipped open the folder, revealing the series of photos he'd been reviewing. "Please take a look at these, Phoenix, and tell me if you recognize anyone. Take your time, dear."

Phoenix leaned in, scrutinizing each picture closely. There were photos of three different, unsavory characters. They all shared a few basic characteristics like age, face shape, and hairlines. Even though Liam had eliminated two of them as suspects years before, the pictures remained with the file. Phoenix absorbed every available detail, before picking up one of them. Staring back at her in close-up was the face of the devil himself. The slicked back hair, the acne-scarred skin, the threatening scowl, and the cold, soulless eye—the other being covered by a black eyepatch.

She studied it for several minutes, mentally scanning every dot and picture element, every horrendous detail, before letting the photo slip from her hand, as it gently floated down, landing atop the others.

"Do you need more time?" Liam asked, looking up at her. She shook her head.

"No," she whispered softly.

"No, it's not him?"

"No…" she said to no one in particular, as she stared blankly at the wall now. "No, I don't need more time. It *is* him. It is the Awful Man," she said softly.

Liam returned to the photo and ceremoniously turned it over, revealing an annotation written on the backside: **Offermann**

She sat back in her chair as the last bit of oxygen left her lungs and was redirected, repurposed. A spark had met its unseen fuel source, and Phoenix's pilot was lit. The blue flame, small at first, grew stronger…hotter…more incendiary…and was rapidly accelerating to a furious and uncontainable white-hot inferno. God help anything in its path.

"Yes, that's him," she said, her voice gaining resolve and volume. "That's the fucker who killed my mom!" she exclaimed, jumping to her feet. Ordinarily she would've been surprised to hear herself curse like that, but it just rolled right off her tongue.

Though she wasn't fully aware of it, she was, in this moment and with everything that had been thrown her way, morphing into a new version of herself. *Phoenix 2.0* was emerging from the flames, and this bird had been assigned a mission. Her fist slammed down hard on the desk, causing Liam to jump.

"Do you know where this asshole is? Is he still alive? How do we get this fucker?"

Liam did another double take as he listened to her now, wondering if someone had kidnapped his sweet granddaughter and replaced her with a fiery beast, or a drunken sailor.

"Okay, hold on. One question at a time. Thank you for the confirmation, sweetheart. I know how hard this must be for you, believe me. This *asshole*—your word, but I'm happy to use it in this case—is Roger Offermann. Asshole supreme. And, yes, he's still alive. For now, anyway…." He wanted this guy bad.

"What do we do? Where is he? What do you need me—" The questions all ran together before he cut her off.

"Whoa, whoa, whoa, *whoa* there, Phoenix…hold on for a minute. Yes, I know where he is. But we don't want to scare him away, do we? We have to think this through. We have to be methodical. We have to be smart," he said, tapping the file. "This weasel—and no insult to weasels—has been running around free for twenty years, thinking he got away with this—" he managed before choking up, "—this…murder. So far, everything in here is circumstantial, and we have to be smarter than him, understand?" he said, tapping the file again.

"Yes," she answered. Her voice was soft, but another log had been added to the fire in her belly, and there was no way it was going to be snuffed out. "So…how do we proceed?" she said, meeting his eyes with a look of steely resolve that let him know, in no uncertain terms, that she was all in. Liam's expression slowly changed, his features scrunching before he answered.

"Depends."

"Depends on what?"

"No…*Depends*. Please get me one from the bathroom cabinet. All this excitement…I think I just soiled myself."

While Liam finished getting freshened up in the bedroom, Phoenix paced around the tiny office space nervously, like a caged cat, as she perused the attaboys and photos adorning the walls. Several framed citations, an award of merit, an eight by ten black-and-white of Liam's swearing-in ceremony. And another eight by ten, of Rose in her freshman year, a year before she'd—by her own hand—opted to cut off her hair, which in this picture was cascading down well past her shoulders. As Phoenix studied the picture, she could see behind the tepid smile, as the eyes quietly belied a sense of angst, of sadness, maybe hopelessness. Phoenix spun when she heard him.

"Rose was thirteen there, I think. Before she got ahold of the scissors," Liam said. "Okay, I feel better. Sorry you had to experience that, sweetie."

"Don't worry about it, Grandpa. I was going to say 'shit happens,' but I thought better of it," she said, finding her smile. The doorbell chimed and a glance to the wall clock confirmed their suspicions.

"Must be the visiting nurse," he said, closing the file and returning it to its priority slot in the cabinet. "I'm not sure how long the nurse will be here, Phoenix. If you'd like—"

"No, I've got to get going, Grandpa. I left my bird at the cottage, and I need to get back."

"Bird? What kind of bird?" he asked as they headed to the door to receive the guest.

"Cockatoo. Rose-breasted. Poor guy's been cramped in his travel crate since I left home."

"Bring him with you tomorrow, okay? My ol' umbrella cockatoo finally kicked the bucket a year ago—he was older than me. Still got his big cage in the garage. Yours while you're here, okay? Won't take no for an answer."

"That would be amazing, thanks," she said, giving him a quick hug before he swung the door open.

"Mr. McGinn, I'm Patty, your visiting nurse," the slender young Filipino woman said. "Here to see how you're doing, okay?"

"C'mon in, Patty. Thanks for coming, sweetheart," he said, as she stepped inside. Liam gave Phoenix a quick wink. "Where do you want me, sweetie?" he said as he closed the door. "Oh, and I don't want you to think I'm being fresh. I don't mean anything by it, Patty, okay?"

"No problem," she said with a laugh. "Anywhere we can sit comfortably, Mr. McGinn, would be fine."

"Okay, sweetheart. Oops…did it again. This way then," he said, leading his visitor to the family room.

"Grandpa, you seem to be in very capable hands, so I'll just be on my way. I'll come by again tomorrow morning around ten, okay?"

"Perfect, honey. Don't forget to bring your bird," he said loud enough to be heard from the next room.

"'Kay!" she answered as she liberated the Prick, attached his leash and grabbed his travel crate before closing the door behind her. She hadn't left the porch when she quickly stepped back inside and grabbed the house key off the kitchen counter where Curt had left it. She glanced at the Post-it number on the fridge, shook her head, and proceeded back outside.

Liam had given her one of his copies of a pocket guide map of 17-Mile Drive, which included points of interest, landmarks, and an overview of the Del Monte Forest and Pebble Beach. She unfolded it to its full twelve by eighteen-inch size and spread it across her lap as she started the Road Runner. 17-Mile Drive was indicated by its thick red lines on her pocket map. She had considered making a left turn out of Liam's driveway to follow Stevenson Drive, north, back to Pacific Grove, as it seemed to be more direct. And there was the option of the long way, via the other, as-yet untraveled section of 17-Mile Drive. But, just as quickly, she recounted the last thing Liam had pointed out in passing before they'd arrived at his home: *And that there's Pirate's Cove….*

Phoenix took a right out the driveway and figured it'd been roughly a mile of road to the Awful Man's. With a white-knuckled grip, she strangled all the life from the imaginary snake that was her steering wheel, as she drove that short mile that felt more like an eternity. She eventually approached the area where she knew his driveway to be and slowed to a crawl in hopes of getting a better look of the property from the road. The trees were thick here, and it didn't help that dusk was approaching. She checked her rearview and pulled to a stop, at a small turnout across the street.

As she reached for the door handle to explore more closely, an approaching set of headlights, paired with a throaty engine sound, caused her to pause. The vehicle slowed as it approached the entrance to the driveway, and she couldn't quite discern the make and model. But it was sleek, and jet black, and the windows were tinted to match. Then, as it made the sharp right turn onto the drive, she made out the shape, having worked on one in Pop Pop's shop: a particularly evil-looking Corvette Stingray.

Phoenix gasped for air, her pulse jackhammering at the sight of evil personified. Her face flushed with heat and her blood approached boiling as she watched the taillights disappear down the sloping drive. She took several moments to regulate her breathing and process this new intel, then made a mental *X* mark on the map. It was all she could do to resist roaring down that driveway and bashing in the monster's skull with the lava lamp, but she thought better of it. Liam had made it very clear that they needed to be smart about this.

A yip! from her passenger confirmed the little guy was a very good judge of character.

"Shhh...I know, buddy...."

Phoenix regarded the circuitous bold red lines on the map, remembering they'd been about midway on the circuit when they turned off earlier. She could either retrace her steps along the coastal route or continue on, rejoining near Pebble Beach and making a serpentine drive on the untraveled stretch. It looked like a longer, particularly winding stretch of road.

But that's what she needed right now.

She needed time to think.

It took her nearly an hour and a half to get back to her cottage, having become lost twice on the circuitous drive back to Pacific Grove. *More like the seventeen-hundred-mile drive....*

The Prick had been a trooper all day, especially on the way home, so she rewarded him handsomely with extra portions of duck jerky at the completion of his potty run. Angus paced back and forth on his very short perch. She'd forgotten to leave a light on in the room, and he didn't dig the dark at all. Plus, the room was freezing! She quickly pulled on her jacket.

"Hello! Hel-lo!! Hello!!!"

"Sorry I was gone so long, Angus!" she said as she tossed her keys on the nightstand and began attending to his cage. She swapped out his cage lining, rinsed and refilled his water bowl, and served him a few extra high value treats with his chow. "There ya go, handsome. Tomorrow you get to come with, okay?"

After refreshing the dog's kibble and water bowls, she kicked off her shoes, pulled off her socks and removed her ballcap, which had seemingly shrunken a couple of sizes. "Holy mother of God," she sighed, as she peeled back the spread and collapsed onto the bed. She stared at the ceiling for several minutes and said a silent prayer. *...and deliver us from evil...*

Sitting back up, Phoenix grabbed the second pillow and propped it behind her as she grabbed her callus-removing foot file from the nightstand and began the long overdue process of shaving off the dead layers from the heels of her feet. The dried, dead skin was considerable and fell like a snowdrift, piling atop a magazine she'd placed to collect it. Five minutes later, she'd liberated her feet of the dry scales and creased the magazine into a funnel shape as she poured the shavings into a small baggie for disposal. She was about to get up when the phone rang loudly, startling her. She stuffed the baggie of dermis into her coat pocket and answered the call on the third ring.

"Hey, Pop Pop!"

"There you are! Everything okay, honey?"

"Yeah…just exhausted. Long day, I don't even know where to begin."

"I'll bet. How are you and Liam getting along? I take it you got him back home?"

"Yes. This morning. We're getting along fine, actually, and…." She pinched the bridge of her nose as she paused, letting out a sigh that Pop Pop picked up on.

"What? What is it, Phoenix? Did he share any new developments with you?"

"New developments? Hm, let's see…yeah, Pop Pop. Gawd… let's just say that I am now *completely* up to speed and, excuse my French, but it's a motherfucker to absorb all the pieces!"

"Mm…no doubt, honey," he responded, choosing brevity as he sensitively gave her space to elaborate—only if she wished to—but he wasn't going to pry. "You okay?"

"Yeah…mostly…no, not really. I don't know how to feel, to tell you the truth. I took a walk down memory lane with Grandpa— that's what I call him now—and I have a better sense of who my mom was. It's the other stuff that hit me like a ton of bricks. Not only when and where she died, but *how*, and…oh, gawd…here's the mother of all truth nuggets: the *who*… The *who*, Pop Pop! Turns out I was *there* when it happened! I *saw* him—I just didn't remember it 'till today…. He's real, he's a monster, he's *alive*…and I know his name. I know the sonofabitch's *name*, Pop Pop. And…wait for it…I know where he lives…."

"Dear God…you're sure about all this?" he replied softly in a whisper of disbelief.

"I SAW HIM TODAY!!" she bellowed. "Sorry, didn't mean to

yell at you, but…yeah, I'm sure. He's the friggin' devil, and just thinking about him makes me shake with rage…."

Nobody spoke for several moments, with the exception of Angus: "Hello!!"

"So, how was *your* day, Pop Pop?" Phoenix said, breaking the silence with a laugh.

He let out a nervous laugh in response, grateful for the release it provided. "Where are you now, honey? Are you back in your room?"

"Yeah. Monster day. I've never felt so tired in my entire life. I'll be lights out the minute we hang up. Going back to Grandpa's—Liam's—tomorrow morning. I'll keep you posted, okay?"

"Please do, honey! And please be careful. Let me know what I can do to help, okay? I mean it. Call me tomorrow. Promise."

"Promise. Goodnight, Pop Pop. Love you."

"Love you too, sugar. 'Night."

She plugged in her phone's charger and forced herself to get up and brush her teeth. She tossed the cover over Angus, hung her jacket on the back of the wooden chair, and switched off the light, plunging back into the deep end of her bed, where she completely surrendered to the undertow of painful memory.

CHAPTER 20

THE PIRATE--AKA THE Snake in certain circles, but never to his face—rolled over to his nightstand and, after several strikes of the lighter, managed to light up his Kent. He took a deep drag and held it like a bong hit. Next to him, his latest conquest stirred at the smell of smoke, which prompted him to exhale deliberately in her direction.

"Get up," he said casually. He was almost annoyed that the young, wannabe starlet he'd just bedded was still there. "C'mon. Time to go."

"Mm…wait…what?" the girl mumbled. She was a few days shy of seventeen and had consented to a romp with this snaky guy she'd met two hours earlier, who'd made her grand promises of stardom.

"You can let yourself out, darlin'. I'll call you," he lied.

She sat up, covering her nakedness as she pulled the sheet up to her chin. But it was too late for modesty. She'd already shared her treasure with this pirate whose track record of plunder was unmatched. With the possible exception of Gene Simmons.

"When?" she asked, looking through the smoke.

"What?" he replied curtly.

"When…when are you gonna call me? You said we'd record my demos this week."

"Yep. We will. But right now, you've got to get the fuck out of my bed. Capiche?" he said without looking at her. He snuffed out his grit, climbed out of bed, and slithered his naked self across the purple bedroom to the closet, where he slipped on his black velvet robe, cinching the waste belt.

"What the— Whatever. Okay. I'll go. Just call me. Please. Like you promised," the girl said quietly. "By the way, I'm not somebody who just sleeps around, I hope you'll know," she added, foregoing her panties as she stepped into her painted-on leather pants and slipped her blouse over her head. She shook her long blonde perm. "Oh, and my dad's a cop, all right? I'm not eighteen, and you'd better not be blowing me off. Just sayin'."

Offermann smiled eerily as he pivoted to face his challenger. She immediately felt regret for having said the last part, as he slowly crossed the room, coming to a menacing stop, inches from her. "I'm sorry. I'm not sure I heard you correctly," he hissed, his face close enough for her to wince at his ashtray breath.

"Nothing. Okay…I was making that up because I was upset. I'm eighteen, okay. My dad…he sells insurance. Not a cop," she said, trying not to lose bladder control.

"Really. Insurance. That's good. Do you have insurance?"

"What?" she replied, clearly confused.

"Insurance. You know. In case something happens to you?" he said through clenched teeth as he placed his right hand on her throat.

"C'mon. Really, you're scaring me. Just let me go. You don't even have to call—" she managed before his thumb found her larynx and he applied gentle but sustained pressure.

"I promise…you'll never hear from me again," she pleaded as she fought for breath. He stood there looking at her, his one uncovered eye bearing down with a look of disdain. And just as quickly, he removed his grip, thumb first, then his hand completely.

"Okay, I'm glad we understand each other, darlin'," he said, taking a step back to allow her passage to the door. "Let's just forget we ever had this conversation, shall we?"

"Works for me," she said as she grabbed her shoes and quickly made her way out to the hallway. He followed her toward the foyer and the front door, opening it for her. As she stepped out onto the redwood porch, he tossed out an insult for good measure. "Besides, do you really think for one minute you have even the slightest bit of talent?" he said with a laugh. "Seriously, I could record a moose farting and sell more copies than anything with your name attached to it."

She rushed out, not bothering to look back. A cascade of tears obscured her vision as she made haste down the driveway toward the main road on foot.

"Just thought I'd save us both some time, darlin'," he called out with a cruel laugh. Once she'd made it to the road, he closed the door and turned the three deadbolts before firing up another Kent. "Amateurs."

He made his way to the restaurant-worthy designer kitchen and poured himself a Scotch. With its three ovens and two six-burner commercial-grade stoves, it was a study in overkill. Especially since he rarely bothered to cook.

Carrying his drink, he pushed a button, activating an otherwise-hidden door and took the short stairway down to his favorite room of the house, opening its door handle with a whoosh as he stepped into the humidity-controlled space.

He flicked three switches on the wall, each powering different banks of canned overhead lights, and another, on a dimmer, that handled the focused halogens. The walls were painted a deep, midnight blue and didn't benefit from the lights at all. The sole purpose of the many halogen lamps was to showcase his babies. And there were many.

Although the room wasn't huge, one ignored its lack of size when they regarded the contents, displayed as if in a mini hall of fame museum. His babies, his treasure, his collection. Each with a story before he'd acquired them, each with their own sentimental and monetary values. These weren't just guitars. You could go to Guitar Center if you just wanted a guitar, but that place wouldn't have works of art like his.

There were a variety of vintage axes, each with their storied pasts. Many had been used on famous recordings by their even more-famous artists. There were some pristine Gretsches, two Sixties-era Epiphone Casinos, and a twelve-string Rickenbacker that was reportedly once owned by George Harrison, but he had no proof. One of Clapton's old multi-colored, psychedelic Strats. Another Strat—beat up, but rumored to have been one of Rory Gallagher's. Several Gibson Les Pauls, said to have belonged to the likes of Peter Townshend, Peter Green, Peter Frampton. And, speaking of Peters, he had a rare, all-aluminum, custom made Veleno guitar, rumored to have been one of Peter Haycock's, though not his gold-plated one. This one had probably been stolen at a Climax Blues Band show, but Offermann didn't care. It was shiny.

He kept them all tuned to the best of his ability—thus the humidity-controlled space. The Veleno, it seemed, defied tuning no matter what the temperature was. But, with its V-shaped headstock and polished aluminum sheen, it remained a favorite.

Offermann didn't play any of them. He never really even learned how to play guitar, as his early obsession with the instrument had been quashed by his bastard of a dry-cleaning store magnate father, when he'd first expressed interest while in middle school. But he was having the last laugh now, as he thought back to his domineering father, who'd told him, at a very early age, that he'd never amount to anything.

Yeah? Well look at me now, you bastard! Oh, wait…you can't… Because I killed you!

Yes, Offermann had made a success of himself over the past twenty years. Almost always at others' expense, but he'd always been singularly focused on one thing and one thing only: himself. He'd launched several successful bands, and after years of predatory management, and eventually bleeding them dry, he'd enriched himself substantially. And it helped him with funding this little addiction of his.

He'd long ago tired of the LA scene, having sold his home there at the top of the market and settling into this tranquil setting,

176

which, for his purposes, was roughly mid-point between the two anchor cities of LA and San Francisco, and provided a lower-key hideaway from both.

This was the only subterranean room of the house. There were no real view windows to allow an outsider to see in, but he'd had two small ventilation windows installed, near ceiling level, a couple feet above ground level from the outside, at the rear of the house—that he could activate by remote control. He decided he wanted a little night air, so he hit the button that cranked both windows open several inches, before sinking into the black leather couch with his Scotch. With the windows open, he allowed himself a cigarette. And the sound of crickets.

His robe loosened on its own, no help from the bit of spare tire he'd acquired over the past decades. Life on the road, especially as manager of several top-flight rock 'n' roll bands, had seen more than its share of extremes and debauchery, and his expanding waistline was evidence of years of the excesses of booze and room service dining on the record labels' tabs.

Other than having put on a few pounds, the only change to his appearance had been adopting the tragically hip and over-deployed look of the short ponytail. His slicked-back hair, though still dark, was thinning, which he wasn't happy about. He compensated for this by letting his hair grow longer in the back and displaying the rebellious pirate ponytail. Without it, he might look like any other sleazy, fiftyish, record producer with one eye and unfortunate skin.

It was quiet at this time of night and, now that he'd allowed himself some opportune pleasure at the expense of yet another clueless teeny, he tossed back his drink and fell asleep.

CHAPTER 21

I T HAD TAKEN all her energy just to secure the critters before pouring herself into the car seat. Phoenix yawned deeply and dislodged what felt like a Grape Nuts-sized piece of sleep gravel from the corner of her eye. *Jeezus.* She'd slept fitfully at best.

As she pulled away from the lodge and drove past Asilomar, she began reflecting on the new movies that had looped in her subconscious all night, fueled by the buttload of new and more-than-disturbing truths about herself, her mother, her would-be twin—and a killer on the loose. The subconscious, after all, had a funny—and very effective—way of peeking under all those rocks we had no idea even existed, and uncovering all of the hidden, festering nuggets, both good and bad.

She drove in silence for a spell. No tunes, or anything else to compete with the shitstorm of emotions and crazy thoughts competing for attention in her still-sleepy head. *They were, after all, just dreams, right?* She shook her head in an effort to arrive at some clarity of thought.

As she found her way to the entrance of 17-Mile Drive, she couldn't help but feel overwhelmed by the merciless barrage of images from Liam's album, the disturbing perp photos staring back at her from his file, the supporting information Liam had provided for context, not to mention her actual face-to-face encounter on the road with a certain…monster.

She thought back to her own memories of the horrific event she experienced twenty years before. Could she really trust it? *It was such a long time ago.* Add to that all of the due diligence her subconscious had done to process it, collate it, and try make sense of it all. It was all too much.

Still, as much as she tried to avoid it, Phoenix began to entertain the sickening notion that she was closer to it all than she had previously imagined. That perhaps she already knew the answer to a question she'd been too afraid to investigate. And as if these truths weren't unsettling enough, Phoenix's mind had now arrived at the worst realization of all.

Nah!! Get a grip, Phoenix!!!

Something continued to gnaw at her. A nasty, insidious possibility that had been liberated from the muck and exposed for what it was. *Don't go there!!!* As much as she fought against the notion, it was starting to make too much sense. Just the thought made her violently ill, and she pulled over to the side of the road and unbuckled her seatbelt just in time to crack the door and heave her guts onto the pavement. She felt like she was in vapor lock as her head hung there, barely suspended above the pavement and, if she'd been a drinker, she could probably compare it to a worst-case wine hangover. But she'd only spilled her Sunny D…and her soul.

She imagined a malignant code flowing through her system like so many cancer cells and felt, somehow…raped…and powerless. She shuddered. But what were her options, really? She couldn't free herself from it. It wasn't like doing an oil change and radiator flush on a Buick Roadmaster. *That* she could handle. And what was she going to do? Take cuts in line ahead of Keith Richards for a blood exchange transfusion?

Her mind painted a series of horrific pictures and scenes that no rational person could be expected to deal with effectively. Without years of therapy, anyway. They were traumatizing on several levels, and it seemed she was powerless to control the narrative. Little did she realize that they were also imperceptibly helping to strengthen her, to forge new steel, to laser-focus her attention and resolve. She couldn't give up her power.

The only thing she could do, she decided, was to play the cards that had been dealt her. Maybe even tap into the dark, evil parts of the shared DNA that had served the killer well. Use portions of it even—not for evil's sake, but solely to harness its power, just enough to level the playing field....

Maybe I'm not powerless to control the narrative.

She pulled herself back inside, closed the door, and reentered the road.

"Hello!" Angus called to her from the rear seat, offering pleasant distraction.

"Hey, buddy," she said, sneaking a peek over her shoulder. "You doin' okay back there?"

"Hell-o!!!"

"Okay, glad to hear it. Almost there, guys," she said to her crew of two. She'd checked out of her room half an hour before, at the prodding of Liam, who'd offered up not only his spare bedroom for her, but also a proper birdcage for Angus, and she felt compelled to take him up on his generosity. Besides, Pop Pop's credit card had to be hemorrhaging by now, so she needed to do some cost containment.

The Prick would sleep with her in her room and, at least so far, he and the shepherds had seemed to get along without a problem. She glanced at her reflection in the mirror. "You've got this, Phoenix," she said with something resembling conviction, as she passed some now-familiar coastal landmarks and rounded the midpoint, before proceeding toward Stevenson Drive.

The Pirate would have to wait a little.

With nothing more than a cursory glance, Phoenix passed by the evildoer's nest and continued on, watching carefully for the entrance of Liam's driveway, which he'd alerted her to the day before. As she rounded the turn, she suddenly saw it and braked hard enough to send the Prick's crate sliding forward several inches. He didn't dig it at all, and he let her know in no uncertain barks.

"Oops, sorry, buddy," she said, restoring his position up against the seatback. "Okay, we're here, guys. Be on your best behavior, please."

She made the sharp turn, mindful of the mailbox and continued up to the spot in front of the garage, as she had the day before. As she killed the ignition, the front door opened, and the shepherds bounded toward the car like it was Christmas morning. Liam waved from the doorway.

Phoenix waved back to him and stepped out, closing her car door quickly before her two passengers were mistaken for a meal. "Good morning, Grandpa!" she called to him before directing her attention to Gracie and Luke. "Hello, my friends! Hello, babies! Oh, look at you!" she said as she hugged them individually and collectively. They were exquisite animals, both, and she'd forgotten how much she enjoyed the breed.

Liam whistled from the porch. "C'mon, guys! Luke! Gracie, come!" —and they did, galloping back inside, which afforded an opportunity for Phoenix to retrieve her critters and safely set them down next to the car.

"Ah, glad you remembered the rose-breasted!" Liam said, joyful to have the added company. "Why don't you bring them both inside, and I'll show you your room—and the bird's new condo!"

"Sounds good, Grandpa," she replied, carrying Angus's cage first and setting it on the landing, after which she liberated Prick from his travel crate and gave him an opportunity to pee. "Hey, not on the tires! Over here," she said, yanking his collar sharply and redirecting him toward a small sapling. "There you go." After he'd finished his "number one" duties, she grabbed his crate and walked him up to the porch. "Where do you want us? Which room, Grandpa?"

"Down the hall, second door on the right," he called from inside.

"Okay…uh, are your pooches put away for the moment?"

"Yep, in their run, out back."

"Okay," she said, then quietly to the Prick, "This is going to be our new home for a little bit, bud. Not sure how long, but it is what it is, and we have to be good guests. ¿Comprendé?"

His not-quite-a-yip signaled compliance, and they proceeded down the hall, as directed. As she got to the second doorway, she looked inside to find an attractive guest room outfitted with a single bed bearing a colorful Spanish-style comforter, an antique looking four-drawer dresser, a matching nightstand, and a small wicker chair. On the other side of the bed, there was some floorspace big enough for a small dog bed.

"Whatcha think? Will this work for you?" Liam asked, peeking his head in behind her.

"This is great, Grandpa. Really. Perfect, thanks so much," she said, turning around to give him a hug. "And Angus. May I have a look at your cage?"

"Please. Follow me," he said, leading her to the end of the hall and his bedroom. My umbrella used to sleep in here with me, and he liked the view from my slider," he said, pointing her to the gray, powder-coated cage on wheels. It was nearly five feet tall, three feet wide, and two feet deep, and would seem cavernous for Angus. "It's all cleaned up, and there's already a liner. Water bowl, food bowl, treat tray, and couple of toys," he said, thinking back to how much he missed his own feathered friend.

"Oh, grandpa, I can't believe this…talk about perfect! Poor Angus has been going stir-crazy, and this'll be a godsend, really, for the time we're here, however long that turns out to be."

"You can stay as long as you'd like, sweetie. Please know that."

"Thank you," she replied gratefully. "We don't want to overstay our welcome, and we'll have to see what plays out, y'know?"

"Absolutely" he said with a nod. "Why don't you get settled, then we can have a little lunch before we put on our detective hats. Deal?"

"Deal," she said, returning his fist bump.

Angus might as well have been at Disneyland; he was enjoying this new space that much. He'd expressed his satisfaction with a ten-minute back-and-forth shuffle on his wooden perch, accompanied by a Tourette's-like burst of variations on *"Hello!"* and Phoenix was happy for him. Prick was enjoying a nap in his crate, bedside, while his mama went about making a couple of BLTs—well, one BLT and an LT for herself. A large can of Campbell's Cream of Tomato and the rest of the pepper jack, and they were good to go.

A proper working detective's lunch.

"I might just have to keep you around, sweetheart," Liam said, polishing off the last savory bite of bacon-y goodness. "I haven't had a proper sandwich in a long time—well, other than yesterday's, which was also a masterpiece."

"Thank you, Grandpa. Glad you liked it," she answered with a warm smile. "I noticed you're low on a few things, so I'll make a run to the store later. Wherever that is…" she added, remembering she'd not seen any stores along the way. "If you write down some directions, I—"

"Just make a list, honey. I'll have our friend, Curt, pick up whatever we need, okay?"

"Really? Don't want to bother him."

"Don't be silly. He does that for me sometimes. You don't need to be making a grocery schlep to the village right now. We have some crimefighting to do. You ready?"

"I think so," she replied, not too convincingly.

Liam cocked his head, pausing to give her another opportunity to answer. "You ready?"

"Ready! Yes!"

"That's better!" he said. "Now, why don't you bring that file in and we'll work here at the kitchen table."

"Roger that," she said, clearing their plates before she peeled off for the office. The folder was sitting in the middle of Liam's desk. Atop the file was the evidence bag containing the charred Zippo lighter. She brought both, along with his legal pad of notes, and two pens.

Returning to the kitchen table, she set the items down and noticed Liam staring off through the window, lost in thought. "I, um, think I have everything," she said, which snapped him back to the moment.

"Mm, okay. Good," he said, surveying the pile. "Here, sit closer," he offered, sliding her chair alongside his. As she took her seat, Liam picked up the lighter and turned it over and over in his hands. "You may be wondering about this," he conceded, his brow crunching as he conjured up the years of torment it'd had over him.

"You think it might be his?" she dared asking.

"Bet on it," he replied, handing it to her. "That day I—after the fire, when I found—" he began through a cracked voice. He took a small drink of his juice before continuing. "When I—I found Rose...there, in the kitchen there—in that burned out mobile home...." He bit his lip as his voice trailed off. Phoenix placed her hand on his shoulder.

"We don't have to talk about it right now, Grandpa. I know it's hard—"

"No! Now's the time," he said, resolutely and more sharply than he'd intended. His eyes met hers. "There's no better time than right now, sweetie. Sometimes we have to face the painful thing, look it square in the eye, fight through the pain or else it will consume you. And then...the bad guys win."

"I understand, Grandpa," she said, dabbing her eye.

"This," he continued, grabbing the lighter, "—this was left behind. By the man who killed your mother. The man who killed my daughter. The man you saw that night: Offermann," he said, looking at his granddaughter again. "Awful Man."

"Oh, God," was all she could mutter as she stared at the deadly, decades-old crime scene implement that had caused so much pain. "Were there usable prints? Can we tie him to it?" she asked hopefully.

"On its face, no. Nothing usable from it, so we'll have to find another workaround," he said, not sounding like he had any answers after all this time.

Phoenix had no response, as this was her first murder case. Instead, she closed her eyes and sat back in her chair, quietly plumbing her brain, her soul, and hoping for a tidbit of wisdom from the god who'd brought her thus far down this mysterious path. So far, He'd been batting a thousand, connecting her with a grandfather she didn't know she even had, uncovering pre-Phoebe truths about her own life, revealing family and would-be family members—and their terrible fates. No, this trail wasn't going to end here. That much she did know.

"I need to meet him," was what came out of her mouth, as if by a stranger.

"What are you talking about, child?" Liam said, truly mystified at this utterance.

"Meet him. Meet Offermann. There's got to be a way. And there's got to be a way to incriminate that slimy bastard!" she said, this apparently coming from Phoenix 3.0. "Help me find an in, Grandpa. I need to have a face to face. That's the only way we can nail him!"

"Listen to yourself, Phoenix. We're not asking for an apology from some kid who stole your school lunch. This guy is bad mojo, he's a killer with no remorse, he has no soul, and it's way too dangerous."

"Grandpa," she said with a sigh, "I've had some time to think about this…and, by all rights, I shouldn't even be here. I mean, think about it! I shouldn't even be—alive! I feel like I've been living on borrowed time here, and I'm getting to a place where…well, I think I've come to the realization that I'm not afraid! Of anything. This is bigger than me. Your letter! My God, I would've never known about you, or about my mom, or that I…almost…had a sister! And…me! I would still be a clueless, directionless dweeb who was living a friggin' lie and never having a purpose. Phoebe is lost to me now. I'm crawling from the wreckage, Grandpa, and I have never felt stronger in my entire life about something. I need this! I deserve this! And there's nothing that's going to stop me from bringing this evil down. It's not for me. It's for Rose. For your daughter. My mother. My sister. I've found my…destiny! Help me, please, Grandpa!"

Liam looked deep into her eyes. There was an abyss of pain behind them, he knew, and other than playing the protective grandparent card, he didn't have an opposing argument that was worth a damn.

"You know I can't just let you waltz into danger, honey. Let's think this through," he said.

"If you have a better idea, I'd love to hear it," she countered.

Despite his decades of investigation experience, Liam wasn't coming up with any new strategic nuggets, so he carefully weighed what he was to say next. "We're going to need a team."

They'd agreed on that much and adjourned the meeting for now, while they both gave it a good think. Phoenix did her best thinking while she was driving, she'd found, but she was landlocked at the moment, so she'd asked for some old towels and rags, a good bucket, and the use of the driveway. Washing the car was a good activity for figuring stuff out, she reckoned, and she'd changed into a pair of cut-off shorts, a tank top and her flipflops.

The Road Runner's grill and windshield were caked with a fair amount of bugs and even a few butterflies who'd been too slow to get out of the way. She felt bad about those. With some good suds and a lot of elbow grease, she returned the orange beast to her former glory, rinsing, drying, Armor Alling the tires. As she was midway through her coat of Turtle Wax, she heard a vehicle coming up the drive. She adjusted her ballcap to see better.

The F-150 pulled up behind her and parked off to the side as to not block the drive. As Curt stepped out of the cab, Phoenix suddenly regretted her choice of wardrobe. It was a feeling of embarrassment she hadn't really experienced before, and she walked around to the other side of her car, keeping it between them.

"Afternoon, Phoenix!"

"Afternoon, Curt," she said, her smile a combination of shy and embarrassed.

"Washin' her up, huh? Looking good!" he said, inspecting her work. "What wax you using on her?"

"What? Oh, er, just some Turtle from a very old can I found in Liam's garage. Better than nothing, I figure, and I've been getting a fair amount of sap from pine needles."

"Yep. I'll bet. Not to mention the birds. Boy, they love my truck," he said, smiling back.

"Huh," she replied. Not a question, just a generic dumb response for which she chided herself. *Don't be so lame, Phoenix! Sheesh!*

The few seconds of awkward silence felt like a year before Curt said, "Liam home?"

"Yeah, uh, he's inside. I think he might be resting at the moment, though. He gets a little tired after he eats, it seems."

"Yeah, I've noticed that on occasion," he said, nodding, as he looked at his work boots.

"Yeah," she said, assessing her overdue pedicure. *Crikey.* "I, uh, could tell him you came by, maybe ask him to call you after he gets up?"

"Ah, no worries. Nothing urgent. I was just working on a neighbor's septic and thought I'd say hi."

"Cool," is the gem she came up with. *Shoot me now.*

"So…" he opened, manning up for his query. "I don't know if you have any plans for later, but, uh, would you be interested in joining me for dinner?" Again with the smile, which wasn't at all fair because he had those teeth.

Oh, my friggin' goodness! She tried not to let her ensuing panic show as she smiled back, completely off guard. "Wow…that's very nice of you to ask. You mean the three of us, right?"

"Well, actually, if it's just the same to you, and your grandfather, I was thinking of, uh, just you and me. Nothing fancy, and I don't mean it to sound forward or anything, but…I have a gift certificate I need to use, and I'd like to take you. If you're interested, of course." He smiled again, this time a little self-consciously, since he had hung himself out there.

A gift certificate. Actually, in some way, that qualifier seemed to have taken a little pressure from the offer, she thought.

She took the next three seconds to decide. What was she going to do otherwise, stay home and reorganize her five pairs of socks?

"Hey, why not? That'd be nice. Thank you for thinking of me," she said, her heart racing as she smiled through the blush. She was equal parts terrified and proud of herself for not immediately dropping the wax and running inside like a ninny. After all, he did have a gift certificate, and it wasn't like a real *date* or anything.

"Great!" he replied, his confidence restored somewhat. "How does…7:00 sound? I could pick you up."

"7:00, perfect. I'll feed Grandpa…Liam…dinner beforehand. 7:00!" she parroted herself. *Okay!*

"I'll see you then, Phoenix," he said over his shoulder as he returned to the truck.

"See you at 7:00!" she said, her face reddening like an Arizona sunset. She waved as he drove back out to the road. Phoenix had never, *ever* been asked out before, and she channeled her anxiety into the rubbing compound as she completed her car's makeover. A quick glance at her Timex told her she needed to get busy with a quick load of laundry, painting her toenails, and doing *something* with her hair.

While her dressy-casual blouse and best jeans were finishing up in the dryer, Phoenix applied a second coat of polish to her refreshed toes. They gleamed back with a shiny hue called Fluorescent Orange Crème, from Orly's "Melt Your Popsicle" line. It was the closest color match to her hair's highlights, which were absolutely popping now that she'd spent an hour with the curling iron.

Other than a subtle bit of eyeliner, and a translucent lip gloss, she wasn't guilty of wearing too much make-up. This was, after all, a gift certificate dinner.

"Thank you for the casserole, sweetheart!" Liam called from the kitchen.

"You're welcome, grandpa!" she called back from the bedroom's wicker chair. *Thank God for Tuna Helper.* "I'll be right there to take your plate."

"That would be fine, dear," he said, turning his attention back to the Arizona Diamondbacks game on the television. "Missing a good game, honey."

"I know…I'll catch the next one with you, how about that?" she said, joining him in the family room. As she began gathering his plate and utensils, the TV's volume ramped down to zero. When she looked up, she noticed Liam staring at her, slack-jawed, like he'd seen a ghost.

"What? What is it, Grandpa?"

He was slow to speak, as he'd never seen anything so beautiful, nor as close to his late daughter in appearance. "Phoenix," he said softly. "You look absolutely radiant!"

"Aww, c'mon," she said, not really believing it. "I'll bet you say that to all your long-lost granddaughters," she added with a little smile.

"No, I mean it. Absolutely the truth."

"Well, thank you, Grandpa. You're sweet. It's just a little dinner. Curt has a coupon that's going to expire, so we're going. Somewhere. Anyway, I'll be back in a little while. Don't feel you need to wait up, okay?" she said, giving him a peck on the cheek.

"Have a good time, honey. And a word to the wise: order the lobster!" he said with a laugh as she retreated to the kitchen and he restored the volume to the set. Randy Johnson fired another hundred-mile-an-hour fastball, striking out the side. "Ha! Grab some friggin' pine, dude!" he yelled out to the defeated batter.

Curt pulled up the drive at 7:00 sharp, popping a piece of Freshen Up chewing gum, and waiting for the little minty squirt to explode in his mouth before stepping out of the truck.

Phoenix stood in the hallway, next to the closed front door, taking a few slow, deep breaths. She might as well be stepping out onto the opera stage; she felt that nervous. She popped a peppermint Tic Tac and watched Curt's silhouette fill the door's glass panels as he stepped up onto the porch and rang the bell.

Ready...go. She closed her eyes for a moment, then sprung them wide as she swung the door open. "Hi, Curt," she said, smiling. "Right on time," she added with a nervous chuckle. She watched his expression turn from casual to what could only be construed as pleasant shock, as he looked back at this singularly beautiful creature. For a brief moment, he had to wonder if he'd pulled up at the wrong house, she was that stunning.

"Wow...uh, hello, Phoenix! Geez, you look...amazing," he confessed, suddenly feeling outgunned. He'd only spruced himself up to the extent of ironing a pleat in his Lands' End jeans, and putting on a fresh, long-sleeved, blue sun-washed shirt from the same catalog.

"You're sweet, thank you," she said, nailing him, without even knowing it, with her lip-gloss smile. The way she was standing there in the doorway, perfectly backlit by the hallway light, with her amazing head of hair cascading in a perfectly coiffed 'do that radiated a rainbow of red tones, like so many solar flares…he was completely transfixed. He looked nice too, she thought, and she tried not to notice the fact that he'd forgotten to zip his fly. "Well, I'm ready if you are."

"Uh, you bet!" he said, standing to the side as she made her way out and down to the car where he opened her door. "It's a little step up, there's a grab handle there," he said, pointing to it.

"Maybe a ladder, if you have one," she said, letting out a little laugh. "No, I'm fine," she added as she slid onto the upholstery and buckled herself. "Nice truck."

"Thanks, I like it," he said, entering on his side. "Three years from now, after my last payment, I'll like it even better," he confided, smiling at his ravishing guest. As the truck backed down the drive, Liam smiled as he watched this little scene play out from his unseen vantage point behind the door. He turned on the porch light for her and got back to his game.

They rode in silence for a couple of minutes before Curt pushed a CD into its slot. Phoenix hadn't anticipated the soft piano intro, especially coming from the music collection of Paul Bunyan. The piano then fused with a beautiful tenor voice, effortless in its range, and it was nothing short of warm velvet. The lyrics to "Silver Morning" began melting her to her seat.

"Very nice. Who is this?"

"Mm, Kenny Rankin. One of my favorites. You've never heard of him?"

"No, but he's on my radar now. Kinda surprised," she said, looking over at him with an approving smile.

Curt smiled back. "What do you mean?"

"I don't know. I guess I figured you for…I dunno…maybe more of a Molly Hatchet guy," she said, laughing nervously.

"Molly Hatchet?" he said, shaking his head, "Where'd that come from? Do I come across as somebody who's flirting with disaster?" he added, laughing now.

"I have no idea where that came from, and it was a silly generalization. Sorry… I guess I just didn't expect you to have such a…soft center," she replied, looking out the window for a moment before turning back. "It's nice. It's a good quality. Still waters run deep sometimes, right?"

"Hm, I've never been accused of being deep, but I appreciate your nod of approval," he said, turning down the music a little. "So, tell me, please. What kind of music do you like?"

"Me? Oh, man…."

"You're going to make me guess?"

"No, it's just…there's so much that I like! My tastes defy category. I listen to…gawd…everything from Abba to Zappa! Seriously, I kid you not. Just don't pop any rap into the player and we'll get along just fine."

"Same here. Especially the rap part," he offered. "And punk, death metal, not a fan. Still friends?"

"We're solid in our musical tastes," she said with a grin.

Before she knew it, they were entering territory that was at least somewhat familiar to her. They were back in Pacific Grove and pulling into a smallish parking lot outside a quaint looking place with a vibe of rustic elegance: Fandango!

"I hope you like this place. Truth be told, I've never been, but a client tipped me with a gift certificate, so here we are, we're living dangerously!" he said, climbing out of the truck. He came around to her side, and—other than when Pop Pop had done so—she was experiencing another in a series of firsts: having her door opened for her. *Chivalrous too!* He was scoring points left and right already. Curt offered his arm and Phoenix used it to brace herself as she made the big step down from the cab. It felt akin to Neil Armstrong taking his giant leap. "Whee!" she exclaimed as she stuck the landing.

As they approached the entrance, the red, lowercase font of the restaurant's logo greeted them, as did the window boxes exploding with fresh flowers. She liked it already, and this was going to be a far cry from the Olive Garden.

Formerly a residence, the restaurant's homey conversion was in keeping with a European flair, its small, inviting dining rooms welcoming them as special guests. They were warmly escorted to the table Curt had hoped to get, the highly coveted table for two at the far end, next to the exquisite stone fireplace. The fire was lit, literally and figuratively, as they took their seats.

"Will this work?" Curt asked, pushing in her seat for her.

"Oh, my goodness," Phoenix said, marveling at the ambiance. "I guess it'll have to do," she added with a chuckle. "Wow…."

The server introduced himself and asked for their drink orders. "Do you know what you'd like?" Curt asked his guest.

"To tell you the truth, I'm not a big drinker," she replied before turning to the server. "Do you have Sunny D?"

"Sunny D, I don't believe so, but I'll check with the bar," he said politely. "And for you, sir?"

"White wine for me, please, a house chardonnay, maybe? As long as it's not overly oaky."

"Absolutely, sir. May I recommend one from Santa Lucia Highlands in Monterey County that I think you may enjoy, a Hahn chardonnay. Not too heavy on the oak. I can bring you a taste, if you wish?"

"No, thank you. It sounds perfect. I'll go with your recommendation," he replied.

"Very well. I will check on the…*Sunny D* and be right back."

Once the server had left, Curt felt a need to explain. "Please don't get the wrong impression; I'm not a wine snob, believe me. I rarely even drink it and, if I do, I'm definitely an under-ten-bucks-a-bottle guy. It's just the last time I ordered a chardonnay, it was this intensely oaky, overly buttery monstrosity. I almost ended up dipping my crab legs in it, it was that much of a butter bomb. The stuff could've drowned last week's movie theater popcorn. Oy."

"Sounds delightful," Phoenix replied with a laugh, nearly choking on her water.

"Sorry, didn't mean to—"

She waved him off as she set down her glass. "So, if you don't mind my asking, other than your side jobs, what is it you do exactly?"

"Mm. Well, it's nothing glamorous. And it's not my chosen profession, but I recently took a gig with an outfit in Salinas," he said, pulling out a business card with his name and a company logo on it and handing it to her.

She studied the card, noting the company's diamond-shaped logo, with a capital letter "P" in the center of the diamond, all stamped in a yellow-gold ink. "Diamond P, huh?"

"Yep," he replied, pausing for a sip of water.

"And I see your last name's listed here as well: *Martinsen.* Curt Martinsen, yes?"

"The same," he confirmed. "I think it means, son of Martin, or something. I'm kind of a European mishmash of Dutch, North German, Danish, and Norwegian. Or so I've been told."

"Sounds very noble. Pleased to make your acquaintance, sir," she replied, duly impressed enough to wink at him.

"The pleasure's mine, m'lady," he countered.

"So, what kind of company is Diamond P? What do they do? What do you do?"

"Well, it started out as a manufacturer and installer of splashguards," he said, hoping she wouldn't plumb for more details. "But they're diversifying."

"Mm, splashguards. Like for cars, right?"

"Not exactly…more like, splashguards for urinals—urinal cakes, too—for men's public restrooms, y'know…."

This time, it was a full-on spit-take. "I'm sorry," she said, trying not to howl in such a nice place. "Did you say the company name was *Diamond Pee?*" she said, covering her mouth as she laughed. "Gotta give brownie points to the marketing department there," she managed, ramping it down to a hearty chuckle.

"Yeah, well, last month they moved me to, uh, collections. Less paperwork, but kinda crazy hours sometimes."

The beverages arrived and none too soon. The server poured a taster for Curt's approval.

"Perfect," he said, greenlighting the chardonnay. "Thank you."

"And, I'm sorry, but we don't seem to have any Sunny D tonight, ma'am. May I bring you something else? Perhaps a juice?"

"An orange juice would be just fine. Thank you," she said, smiling warmly.

"Very well. I'll give you both some time to look at the menus," he replied with a nod.

Phoenix let out a sigh of contentment as the server made his way back to the kitchen. "I think this may be the nicest place I've ever been," she confessed happily. "Some gift certificate!"

"I'd have to agree with you," he said, the flames from the fireplace casting them both in a warm glow. "Thanks for coming out to play tonight."

"The pleasure's mine," she said, flashing a grin before they picked up their menus.

It was a target-rich environment, this menu, and Phoenix found the goat cheese salad and pasta puttanesca to her liking. Curt indulged his inner carnivore with an appetizer of giant sea scallops, a spinach mimosa salad with chopped bacon and hard-boiled egg, and an entrée of couscous lamb shank.

"Thank you for not ordering the veal," she said to Curt. "As a vegetarian, I never judge anyone else's choices, but…veal…that's kind of where I draw the line."

"Totally understand that," he said, wiping his mouth. "I don't eat that other stuff either, that appetizer, gawd what's its name? Goose something or other."

"Foie Gras! Oh, my goodness. How anyone could order that on a good conscious is beyond me. You are a good human being, Curt," she said, putting her hand on his. It surprised her more than him, and she left it there for a moment longer before continuing with the last bites of her salad. "Do you like beets?"

"Love 'em," he said, "Best part of the salad bar, in my opinion!"

Phoenix looked him in the eye. "Oh, my goodness. You are like the only person, other than me, that's ever extolled the virtues of beets in a salad. Seriously. Most people complain, saying stuff like, *ewww... nasty...they taste like dirt.* Me? I friggin' love these. Want some?"

"No. I'm good. Thanks though," he said, popping the last bite of scallop in his mouth. "Oh, and you should eat those tomatoes. Good for your prostate, they say," he added, in all seriousness.

"Is that a fact?" she said, grinning, as she found the comment too cute to correct. They finished their salads in a comfortable silence, which became increasingly devoid of any awkwardness as time progressed. *So, this is what a perfect dinner date is supposed to be like.* They both thought it, they both felt it.

Their server poured a second glass of chardonnay and refilled her juice, which to Phoenix seemed to taste like from an especially fine crop. Maybe even from the Santa Lucia Highlands, she thought. Definitely fresh-squeezed, anyway.

"So, Liam tells me you're a dog person."

"Liam tells the truth there. Always had a soft spot for my furry companions. Since I was a kid, actually. I trust dogs more than most people, truth be told. Present company excluded, of course," she said with a friendly smile. "How about you? Are you a dog person? Any pets?"

"Me? No pets at the moment, unless you count my roomie," he said with a chuckle. "But I did have a dog, a terrier mix of some kind. Got away," he said with a trace of discernable sadness.

"Oh, no. What happened? The fence blow down or something?"

"No. Nothing like that. He split out the front door, all of a sudden like. Fast like a bunny. Next thing I knew, he was gone. Never found him."

"That is so sad. I'm sorry for your loss. You can never replace them, really."

"I know, but it's been a while now. I've been thinking about getting another dog, a rescue this time. I just don't want the same thing to happen again, you know?"

"Maybe you should rethink things a little."

"Oh?"

"Maybe get yourself a sloth!"

"A sloth?"

"Might solve the door-dash problem," she said, chuckling at her own suggestion.

"Yeah, well, I think I'll wait before I jump into anything…" Curt said, still wondering if she was serious or joking at his expense.

"You have any family in the area?" she ventured, changing the subject.

"No. Not nearby anyway. My dad, he lives in Castle Rock, Colorado. Tiny town, not too far from Colorado Springs. I was raised there, graduated high school. But that town didn't hold much for me. Other than their green chile, which is to die for. My mother left when I was pretty young, never knew her, really."

Phoenix nodded. She could relate to that part. "Any siblings?"

Curt shook his head. "Nope. Just me. I haven't seen my dad in a couple of years. We kind of had a bit of a falling out when I wanted to move to California."

"Mm…I'm sorry to hear that."

"Thanks. It's fine though. How about you? You said that you were getting reacquainted with your grandpa, Liam, right?"

"Long story, that. Not really re-acquainted, more like getting to know him—having never met him before—kind of acquainted, if you know what I mean. Funny, but we only really met a couple of days ago! Hard to believe," she said wistfully. Her whole life had changed so much, and in so many ways, these past days.

"Wow. Liam's great. He's had some issues, as you undoubtedly know by now, but he's got a heart of gold. I enjoy doing little projects for him, y'know. I don't even charge him half the time. I didn't know he had a granddaughter. Especially such a beautiful one," he said, chancing the compliment.

"You're sweet," she replied shyly.

"So, how about you? Any other family? Siblings?"

She tried to focus on swirling a bit of her pasta on her fork and failed miserably for the better part of a minute. She abandoned the mission and gently set down her fork. The dreaded question she'd never been asked, nor been tasked with answering. But it was a fair question, especially considering she had broached the subject first.

She looked Curt in the eyes. They were an azure blue. Kind eyes, non-judgmental eyes. And they felt...safe, even. She shook her head, then took a chance, hoping her response wouldn't be met with pity or, worse, disgust. She didn't want to ruin things.

"No, I can't say that I do, really. Well, other than Liam, of course. That's an entirely new connection I had no idea about until quite recently." She sighed, looking into the flames. To her surprise, she wasn't repulsed by them like she was accustomed to being.

"It's okay," Curt said, placing his hand on hers. It was warm, and so was the fireplace. She looked back at him; his features only expressed compassion and encouragement. "I didn't mean to put you on the spot, Phoenix."

"You didn't. You said nothing wrong. Please, it's okay," she said. "It's just—I've never had anybody ask me about my family, and here's the wack part: I've never really known about my family until, like, the last week. Liam wrote a letter.... Oh, I forgot to mention my awesome dad—well, adoptive dad, Pop Pop. That's what I call him anyway." She sighed loudly. "This is going to be confusing, but I'll try."

"Only if you want to," he said, pushing his plate off to the side and taking her hand in both of his.

"I'm—I'm flawed, Curt. I was adopted when I was about five, and Pop Pop and my adoptive mom—who left when I was young, not unlike yours—raised me. Up until recently, that was the long and short of it. Just me and Pop Pop, doing our little thing in the desert there. He has a car repair shop, and I help him out a few days a week," she said, pausing for a sip of water. "And that's all I knew. I had no siblings, and I didn't know anything about my birth mom. As far as a birth dad, no friggin' idea. Oh, and here's something interesting. My name was Phoebe up until last week!"

Curt didn't register surprise, nor anything to communicate he felt any less of her for what she was spilling. He gave her hand a squeeze. "That's…a lot," he said, nodding.

"You don't know the half of it yet. So there I am, living this happy-go-lucky lie for twenty years when, out of the blue, I get this letter from Liam. He says he has some information for me, and I'm like, hmm, okay…which prompts Pop Pop to do a little intel and, lo and behold, we find out that not only was I adopted—we knew that part already—but a new little tidbit of info nobody thought it important to pass along to me until now: I was…oh, gawd, I told myself I wasn't going to embarrass myself," she managed, before dabbing at her eyes. "It turns out…whew…"

"It's okay, Phoenix. Whatever it is, you can tell me, okay? But only if you want to."

She nodded as she wiped her eyes, surprised that, not only was all this coming to the surface, but she had, in this moment, decided it was safe to verbalize her deepest, darkest secret, and to a new acquaintance. "It turns out…whew…turns out—you ready for this? I survived an…I'm an abortion survivor. How do you like those apples?" She glanced over at the other tables, grateful that nobody seemed to have heard her.

Curt had to look off into the fire for several moments before he could attempt a response.

"I…I don't even know how to—I mean, I can't even imagine the pain you're experiencing with knowing this now, Phoenix," he said, his comforting voice registering slightly over a whisper. "Look, I didn't mean to upset you, and we can—"

"No, it's all right. You didn't upset me at all. And I know we only recently met, but we might as well lay it all out there now, right?"

His eyes were beautiful tranquil pools, offering her safe harbor from her inner storm, and assured her she could tell him anything, that there would be no judgment. He nodded for her to continue. She smiled weakly, then launched into it.

"Thank you. So, here's my unsavory story, the Cliff Notes version, warts and all: I survived an abortion attempt. I told you that. It was a successful abortion, don't get me wrong. I mean, there was another baby. A twin. A sister. She was aborted. And…they missed me. Completely…*surprise!* Can you believe it? I mean, how can a sonographer miss *that,* right? Details. Can you imagine my poor teenage mother? Holy cow. So, it turns out—and, again, I just found all this out—she tried to raise me in secret, because the father, I can't say "my father" because it was some strange, hostile sperm that was responsible, was an abusive guy. And she was scared to death of him, and what he would do to her, and to me, if he found out. So, she ran away from him, had me, and we were a reasonably happy family of two, at least I imagine we were, until—"

"Sorry to interrupt. Is everything to your liking?" the server asked.

"Oh, yes! Everything is perfect, thank you," Curt said, smiling up at him. "We're just a little full. Could you please box these plates for us?"

"Yes, sir. With pleasure." And he was on his way.

"So, you were saying...until—?" Curt said, refocusing his entire attention.

"Yes. Until...until he hunted her down. He found her, five years after he'd sent her off for the abortion—which he assumed was a done deal—and...and...the son of a bitch murdered my mother. Then he set her house on fire to cover it up."

"Oh, my God, Phoenix," he cried out softly, his own eyes welling up with tears. "I. Am. So. So. Sorry, sweetie," he said, and he came around to initiate a hug. Neither of them cared, at this point, what any other diners might be thinking. This was a moment that was unfolding between two people, two good people who were rapidly becoming very close friends, and nothing else mattered. Her shoulders shook as he held her, and he gave the top of her head a peck.

"I'll take care of the check," he whispered as he pulled the generous gift certificate, plus a hundred-dollar bill, from his wallet and left them on the table. "Let's get you home, okay?"

She nodded gratefully, and they navigated the dining room with their two containers of what would be tomorrow's dinner.

They drove in total silence for several minutes, taking a different route than how they'd come in. Phoenix eventually saw a sign indicating they were approaching the entrance to 17-Mile Drive.

"Would you mind?"

"I'm sorry?"

"Would it be okay if we take the long way back? That is, if you're not completely sick of me now. I'm not quite ready to get back yet," she confided.

"Absolutely," Curt replied. "I was kind of hoping we would. And, of course I'm not—nor could I ever be—sick of you," he added, placing his hand on hers once they'd made the first turn.

It had become a pitch-dark night, save the light from the full moon intermittently smiling through the trees. Curt knew this road like the back of his hand, having provided services to many of its residents. Still, it was slow going, and he relied on his high beams on occasion.

"I'm sorry for spoiling the evening," Phoenix said through a sigh. "Believe me, that was not the intention."

"Don't be silly. You didn't spoil anything. I appreciate your honesty, and I respect you even more for it."

"You mean it?" she asked, looking over at him.

"Scout's honor," he said, making a pledge gesture. "I hope you don't mind my saying so, Phoenix, but I think you're pretty amazing." The moon entered the cab momentarily, as if on cue, lighting up his very genuine smile. It offered all the confirmation she needed.

"You're sweet and, truth be told, I think you're kind of amazing as well, Curt," she said, completely gob-smacked at her newfound candor. She turned her head to the window, even though it was too dark to see much.

Curt smiled, refocusing his attention on the tricky roads. They continued in silence for a long while and as they reached the midpoint, Phoenix was able to get her bearings when the moon illuminated some familiar coastal landmarks, signaling their turn inland. A few minutes later, realizing they were getting close to Liam's driveway, he broke the silence.

"Okay, so now that we've determined we're both *amazing*, and we weren't in a screaming hurry to get back to Liam's, I have to ask you—as a friend now—where are we in this odyssey of yours? By that, I mean…are you making any headway in your pursuit of the truth about this person, the one who killed your mother? Is there a trail to follow? Do you have any idea if he's even still alive? Where he could be now?"

"Funny you should ask," she said, turning to him.

He couldn't chance taking his eye off the road, but he managed a glance at her. "Oh?"

"We just passed his place," she said, and her steely look told him she wasn't fooling.

They sat there, in Curt's truck, for close to an hour, their features barely illuminated from the pool of porch light Liam had left on for them.

"How sure are you?"

"I'm sure. Our intel is rock solid. In fact, I saw him drive in there the other day."

"Jeezus, Phoenix, this is…you have to be extremely careful with this guy. Based on what you've told me, he sounds extremely dangerous."

"I know. He is. Liam says we need to be smart and that we need to get a team. I'm not sure what he has in mind for that, but—"

"I'm in."

"What?"

"I'm in. I'm all in. I'm on your team," Curt said, looking at her with dead earnest.

"Oh, you don't want to get involved with—"

"Try and stop me. Not with what you've told me. Consider me on the team, and there's no way I'll be dissuaded."

Phoenix looked straight ahead, through the bug-laden windshield, over to the house.

"You don't have to do this, Curt. I don't want to put you in any jeopardy because of me," she said, turning to him. "I appreciate tonight, and for being so awesome, but—"

He cleared his throat, deliberately interrupting her. His look told her his mind wouldn't be changed.

"At least let me talk with Liam about it, okay?" she said, squeezing his hand.

"Fair enough."

"Gawd."

"Whatcha doin' tomorrow?" Curt asked, kissing her hand.

"Me? Hmm, oh, I don't know. Might just binge-watch a bunch of Primus music videos or something," she said, laughing at the sarcasm. "But seriously, no plans. Liam has the visiting nurse coming over in the morning, and I think they're supposed to be here for several hours. Why?"

"I think you ought to hang out with me at work tomorrow. I think you could use a little distraction," he said, handing her the card again.

She laughed at the suggestion. "You mean, like, hanging out in men's rooms? You're right; that would be a distraction!"

"Nah, not quite. C'mon. I can even get you paid for the day. What do you say? All you have to do is show up at the address on the card tomorrow morning. Dress code is casual. Very casual. But no flipflops. I'll take you to lunch too, after."

She looked at him, her brow scrunched as she bit her lip. The proposition sounded goofy on its face, yet the thought of making a little money didn't sound bad. Especially considering the tally she'd rung up on Pop Pop's credit card. "What will I be doing, exactly?"

"We'll go over it when you arrive. I'll be training another guy too. Piece o' cake…c'mon. Please?" he pleaded with his head cocked for effect. With those eyes, and his demeanor, she thought he looked like a huge puppy.

"You're serious."

"Very. 8:00. The address is on the card. It's in Salinas."

"*Silliness*," she corrected with a grin.

"*Silliness!*" he concurred. "Deal?"

"What the hey. Deal!" she blurted, and they sealed the deal with a fist bump.

Followed by a kiss.

It was unplanned. A completely innocent kiss and, devoid of any lasciviousness, it unfolded naturally and was deployed before either party could second guess anything. It started with the slightest contact, Curt's mouth brushing against her cheek, and Phoenix found herself a willing participant, turning to meet him, their lips drawn to each other's like magnets.

Phoenix's heart was racing and, after several moments, she

had to come up for air. She gently broke contact and pulled away slightly, just enough to be able to look in his eyes. In all of her years, she'd never even had so much as a practice run at this, and it was a heady, foreign experience. But a very nice one. Curt smiled at her and she reciprocated, like they were fourteen.

"I'm sorry…was…that all right?"

"Mm…no need to apologize. It was more than all right," she said, thankful that it was too dark out to see how much she was blushing. "I—I'd better get inside."

"Yes, probably a good idea," he said, kicking himself for how lame he sounded.

"Thank you for dinner, for…everything, really. I'm glad I came," she said, leaning in for the briefest peck of punctuation. "I'll see you tomorrow morning, okay?"

"Yes, please. 8:00. You still have the card, right?"

She held it up for him. "8:00," she confirmed as she opened her door, flooding the cabin with its cruel dome lighting. She grabbed her doggy bag dinner container from the floor. "Good night, Curt Martinsen," she said with an irrepressible smile.

"Good night, Phoenix," he said, returning one. He waited until she was safely inside, and the porch light extinguished, before he headed back down the drive.

Phoenix was thankful she'd had the foresight to cover Angus's cage, especially since it was in Liam's room, as she hadn't wanted to disturb him when she returned. She took the Prick out for a quick potty break, brushed her teeth and changed into jammies, at which point she looked in the mirror and smiled. She thought about the delicious experience she'd just had, proud to no longer be a member of the Virgin Lips club.

If this isn't a wish-list trip for the record books….

She set the alarm on the clock radio for 6:00 and was about to turn off the light when she noticed a lump on her bed. As she turned down the covers, she discovered something foreign on the adjacent pillow. Its very presence was mysterious, yet once she studied it, the auburn hair and striped pants made it immediately recognizable as the Mattel Honey Hill Bunch doll she'd been found with twenty years before. Liam had saved it all this time, for her! *Bless him!*

She switched off the light, hugging her bedmate closer. The hair still had that familiar smell, and channeling her inner five-year-old, she drifted off to sleep with a smile.

CHAPTER 22

NIGHTMARES OF A trailer park Christmas in flames hadn't helped her sleep one iota. *Mercy.* She didn't have time to make any coffee, so she'd have to grab some on the way.

She did her best not to disturb Liam's sleep as she got herself ready, hiking her hair into her trademark ponytail and affixing her ballcap. Curt had sounded adamant about not wearing flipflops, so she strapped on her walking shoes before taking the little guy out to piddle.

She placed the usual bowl of kibble for him in the kitchen and, for whatever reason, he wasn't having it. A couple of yips registered his displeasure.

"You want some cheese with that whine, mister? What's the matter? You love this chow," she said. He stared back at her, trying to exert his will on her. "In answer to frequently asked questions, no, I'm not giving you something else. Sheesh." After she'd put her foot down and left the kitchen, she watched from around the corner as he began eating.

She jotted a note for Liam, telling him of her plans and reminding him to please uncover the bird. She'd be home for dinner. She grabbed the Post-it note with Curt's number off the fridge, just in case.

She'd never been to a Starbucks before. She found the notion silly, as she'd often noted the lemmings sidling up to get their overpriced fixes. Sometimes several times a day. Not her. She was a drip coffee kind of girl, and she and Pop Pop never deviated from the home brew, which she found superior anyway.

But she didn't have the luxury of choice this morning, so she pulled off the freeway once she'd noticed the Starbucks signage. *Any port in the storm...oy.*

Once inside, she waited in line for several minutes before it was her turn at the counter. This gave her a few moments to peruse the vast menu of options, but none of it made much sense to her.

"What can I get for you?" the tattooed girl wonder asked, too disinterested to smile.

"Oh, um, let's see," Phoenix replied, looking at the menu board.

Tatt Girl rolled her eyes, which didn't go unnoticed. "Let me know when you're ready."

"Okay...how about a drip coffee, your Coffee of the Day, please," she said, opting for simplicity.

"What size?"

"A large coffee, please."

"Venti?"

"Excuse me?"

"Grande?" The barista seemed to be enjoying herself, and Phoenix wasn't in the mood.

"A *large* one. I don't know!" Phoenix said, a bit surprised at how annoyed she was becoming. "Whatever's your biggest, tallest, most grande vessel of coffee you guys offer, okay? Please, I don't have my Starbucks decoder ring on me! For Christ's sake!"

Another roll of the eyes, and a smug smile to a co-worker. "Room for cream?" she asked, grabbing the corresponding paper cup.

"Yes. Please," Phoenix said, sorry now that she'd come here against better judgment.

"She'll ring you up," the barista said with a trace of a smirk as she grabbed the Sharpie pen and clicked the corresponding boxcs. "Your name?"

Phoenix told her, and she scribbled on the cup.

How friggin' hard does it have to be? She forked over a fiver and glanced at her watch, and after several minutes she was handed her cuppa.

It wasn't until she gotten back on the freeway that she noticed the barista's annotation:

GINGER BITCH

Phoenix shook her head. *You want a ginger bitch? I'll* show *you a ginger bitch!*

Sadly, she didn't have time right now to turn around and throw it back in the chick's face, but she made a mental note of the location, and promised herself she'd make a return visit at some later date. With some Venti attitude.

It could be argued that she was developing a slightly heightened sense of right and wrong in recent days. Enough so that she was becoming aware of the fact, and if she were found on the Periodic Table, she might now be Promethium. Still, she tried her best to pick her battles. But there were times when they were picked for her. Like right now. She glanced at the rearview and couldn't help but notice the anomaly, and it couldn't be ignored.

Case in point, the self-important asshat that was weaving in and out of traffic, endangering all comers in the process, as he rapidly approached Phoenix's bumper in his late-nineties silver Mustang. He was pretty sure he was the shit, and he had to be doing spurts close to a hundred miles per hour. He decided he wanted to pass the Road Runner, even though there wasn't sufficient room for his vehicle in front of her.

He swung aggressively alongside, and his plans were now obvious as he swung left into Phoenix's lane, forcing her to do a hard braking maneuver as he forced his way into her lane. He'd cleared her by an inch, tops.

She laid into her horn, but its meager *Meep! Meep!* didn't sufficiently communicate her displeasure. "Oh, I don't *think* so, asshole!" she screamed, flipping him off with both hands, once she'd downshifted. "You don't *even* want to mess with the ginger bitch today!"

She might be a couple of minutes late for work, but this had to be done. As the idiot swung back into the other lane to weasel his way around the next car, Phoenix closed the gap, and once he saw he couldn't pass, he tried the same thing with Phoenix. She wasn't having it, and she was all but kissing the bumper of the minivan in front of her.

Phoenix looked over at the maniac next to her, surprised to find out it wasn't a *he*, but was instead a *she* driving like this. She was Latina, probably late twenties, and her music, if you could call it that, was up way too loud. The poor darling was stuck behind a series of transport trucks now and had nowhere to go. *Awwww.*

The Mustang made a series of jerking movements toward Phoenix's lane, despite the fact that there was absolutely no room for her. That didn't dissuade her, however, and Phoenix went out of her way—ten miles past her exit, in fact—maintaining her pole position, while assuring the chick was denied passage.

Eventually, the trucks exited, creating a window of opportunity, and the chick flipped Phoenix off, to which she only received a head shake and a smile in return. "Have a nice day, honey!" Phoenix yelled to her, laughing as she roared off. She was quaking with rage, but it had been entirely worth it. It was the principle of the thing.

It was 8:35 when she rolled into the parking lot below the tall, yellow/gold logo sign indicating she'd arrived at Diamond P. She hadn't had a sip of her coffee yet, so she brought it with her as she approached the open door to what looked like a warehouse garage.

There were several septic trucks parked in the space, and there were two guys seated in folding chairs facing Curt, who sneaked a glance at his watch. "Glad you could make it, Phoenix," he said. Thankfully he'd left any trace of sarcasm out of his voice because she didn't need anything else right now.

"Sorry I'm late. There was something that came up," she said, attempting a smile as she sat down in the other available chair.

"No problem," Curt said. "I was just explaining the different vehicles we have, their systems, and what capacities they have. I can fill you in on that later," he said. "Okay, guys, we need to head out, we've got a full day ahead."

The other two guys stood. The one nearest Phoenix was skinny, wearing a knit cap that covered his entire head and ears. He smiled at her, shyly. "Mornin'."

"Good morning," Phoenix said.

"Wingnut, you'll be riding in the other truck, with Bob. Phoenix, you'll ride with me, okay?" Curt said, checking his clipboard.

"Sure," she answered before turning to the thin man next to her. "Wingnut? Is that what they call you?"

He nodded, shrugging his shoulders.

"That's kind of—I don't know—do you mind me asking why they call you that?"

He pulled off his knit cap, liberating his enormous ears, which flopped into position as if spring-loaded. He smiled wider, and his goofy grin revealed two missing teeth. "I don't mind it. Curt's my roommate and he doesn't mean anything by it," he replied. "Real name's Jimmy. You can call me either one, makes no difference to me."

"Okay…Jimmy, nice to meet you. Have a good day out there."

"You do the same," he said over his shoulder as he walked over to his designated truck.

"Ready?" Curt said as he approached. "I see you've met Wingnut. Known him for a while. He's a good guy. Let's talk on the way," he said, leading them toward the larger of the two vehicles. It's enormous stainless-steel tank gleamed.

"Yep. Ready, for what, I have no idea, but, yeah. So, tell me: Wingnut? Really? I guess the names Dumbo and Dopey were already taken?" she said with a chuckle. An opportune chuckle at that, as she found herself smiling for the first time that morning. Just being around Curt seemed to improve her attitude, she found.

"Big step up," he said, as he opened her door. "Your chariot awaits!" he mused.

Phoenix grabbed a handle and swung her way into the seat. She placed her coffee in the cupholder and secured her belt. "Where to?"

Curt climbed in, secured himself, and adjusted the mirrors before starting the ignition. He glanced at his clipboard, then looked at her and smiled. "Do you like the circus?"

He hadn't been kidding.

It was a veritable big top, with three red and white striped tents occupying the fairgrounds. The crowds had gone the night before, ending a well-attended three-day run. Some sketchy looking carneys were dismantling some kiddie rides, while others were attending to the disassembly of the tents and rigging. The animal wagons had been dispatched to another location at the close of the show.

"Ha!" Phoenix blurted in disbelief as they pulled the truck around the back and alongside a long bank of port-a-potties. "Now I think I understand what you meant when you told me you were in *collections*. Tell me we're not involved with those," she said, pointing to the dozens of portable toilets.

"Aw, it's not as bad as you might think," he said, winking as he exited the cab and came around to her side. He swung the door open and offered his hand, which she took. It was a long step down for her. "Glad you wore some sensible shoes."

"Just following the boss's instructions," she said, chuckling as she reached back in for her coffee. He gently put his hand on her arm. "You might want to leave that in here for now."

She shrugged and closed the door behind her, praying she wouldn't be suffering the mother of all caffeine withdrawal headaches later.

"Here, you'll want to put these on," he said, handing her a pair of clear goggles. "And these should fit you." She put on the safety glasses and took the pair of well-used and very heavy rubber work gloves.

"Yee-haw," she said, grimacing. The doors to the units were still closed but her nostrils were already beginning to flare. "How much did you say I'd be getting paid today?"

"Not enough," he said with a laugh. "Follow me, I'll show you the rig." He walked around to the back of the truck and began extending a length of heavy-duty suction hose, attached to a long metal wand. He grabbed a bucket, threw in some chemicals, and carried it over to the closest unit, setting it off to the side. Phoenix was still standing at the truck, looking at the long line of blue boxes, fearing the worst.

"C'mon," he called over. "It's not that bad, once you've got a couple of 'em under your belt."

"If you say so," she replied through a cough. "Holy Hannah." She sighed as she stepped up to the door next to him.

"Gonna be a hot one." Curt wiped the sweat from his brow with his shirt sleeve. The day was shaping up to be rather muggy. Kinda felt like Hawaii, Phoenix imagined, but without all the totally awesome Hawaiian-y stuff that goes with it. "Ready?"

"Don't you tease me," she said, readying for the moment of truth, which came immediately once Curt grabbed the handle and swung the door wide.

"Jeezus!! Holy mother of—" she managed, her gag reflex working overtime as she tried not to toss her cookies. "Oh, my…gawd!

This…is…absolutely…horrible!!!" she cried, turning her head and gasping for fresh air and not really finding any.

Curt shook his head, trying not to laugh too hard. "Here, hold this," he said as he handed her the wand and walked back over to the truck. He flipped some levers and turned on a motor of some kind. The sound of industrial suction. He came back over to her and retrieved the wand, draping the suction hose across his shoulder and stepping inside. "C'mon, have a look."

Phoenix shook her head, wondering what she'd done to deserve this. "You're serious."

"Yeah, it's not a bad one. Have a look."

She reluctantly stepped forward, far enough to get her head and shoulders inside for a better view. Her worst fear was realized as she stared down into the hole—an absolute hellish abyss of body fluids and feces of various consistencies. There had to be several days' worth, and this was seriously uncool. She coughed loudly.

"Now, you want to stick the wand in like so," he said, demonstrating the proper technique before handing the wand to her. He maneuvered the suction hose so that it rested atop her right shoulder as she readied herself over the poop pit. "Flip that switch on the handle there," he said. "Stick in in there and move it around…stir it like coffee!" he said loudly over the whine of the suction machine.

"Jeezus…gawd," she whispered in protest as she moved the long wand about the waste chamber. The coiled, swollen pumping hose churned and twitched like an anaconda trying to digest its oversized meal, and she felt like she might become its next victim.

"You're doing great, Phoenix! Really, you've got a knack for this!" he said, laughing.

"Gee…thanks," she said through a grimace, trying to ignore the gloppy stuff she was sucking up. "Jeez, there's friggin' diapers and shit in here. I see a Kotex even!" she cried, not sure if she would be able to make it another minute before projectile vomiting into this stew. "Seriously, I'm pretty sure the clowns, the big cats…even the elephants took their dumps in here!"

"Here, let me spell you for a second. The hose gets clogged with those things sometimes. I'll take it," he said, relieving her of the snake as she stepped back out into the stifling heat. She hunched over, hoping to find a better pocket of fresh air between her knees. But it wasn't to be found.

"Found somebody's phone. Bet they were looking for that!" he called out to her with a laugh. He continued emptying the waste chamber for several minutes as he sung "Black Water" by the Doobies, while Phoenix tried to regain her faculties. Afterwards, Curt went about spraying down the seat, the floor, and the walls before adding chemicals to the pit.

Phoenix shuffled over to the truck and opened the door. She took off her gloves and reached for her coffee, but that had been ruined. Maybe forever.

"Okay. One down, nineteen to go," he said as he approached the truck. She wasn't smiling.

Curt finished stowing the hoses, then secured the bucket and attachments before joining Phoenix at the side of the truck, where they both washed their hands thoroughly. He set his clipboard on the dash as they climbed in and he started the ignition. "Good job today." His smile wasn't returned immediately, as she was too busy shooing away the millionth buzzing fly.

"What's with the friggin' flies!" she snipped, her annoyance at surface level.

"What about 'em? They're everywhere, not much we can do about 'em, right?"

"Well, I don't remember ever seeing anything close to this many in Arizona. Silliness is the new Amityville, I swear."

"Maybe so," he conceded. "Hey, I promised you lunch."

"Really? You could eat after *that*?!" she muttered in disbelief.

"Believe it or not, yeah. I've become pretty desensitized to this stuff. C'mon. At least join me for a cool beverage, okay? Escape the heat for a little bit?"

"Cool beverage sounds good," she said, pouring the contents of her Starbucks cup out the window as they pulled away. "That was the best second date ever," she said, rediscovering her sense of humor.

"Is that what it was?" he replied with a chuckle.

"Making memories!" she said, cocking her head back as she laughed hysterically. "Whew!"

"Yeah, well the day's still young. Besides, I owe you. I know a place, but first we've got to gas up the truck."

The filling station was a familiar one, as Diamond P had a company card with them, and they had long been their go-to place to refuel. As Curt pulled up to the commercial pumps, he noticed Wingnut's truck was parked on the side of the building with its small two-porta-potty trailer behind it.

Curt hopped out and began fueling up while Phoenix ran inside to use the restroom. She stood in line behind an older gentleman who had the same idea. He was well into his eighties and appeared to be in dire need and seemed to be more than a little confused as he shifted from one foot to the other during his inquiry, after which the attendant informed him that there were no indoor restrooms; he'd have to use the facilities located outside. Phoenix wasn't in any hurry, so she perused the snack aisle while he shuffled outside.

Several minutes later, Curt tapped the horn, signaling he'd finished fueling, and Phoenix decided she could wait, so she trotted out. She noticed Wingnut's crew had already left, and an older woman sitting in the passenger seat of a nearby Buick seemed a bit agitated.

They were ten minutes down the highway when they caught up to Wingnut's rig and they got into position alongside. Curt tapped the horn, and Phoenix gave a wave as they were adjacent to the trailer, at which time the porta potty door opened, and a very shocked senior citizen sat there with his pants around his knees.

"Oh, my goodness," Phoenix said, trying not to laugh. "That poor man!" she added, an involuntary chuckle escaping this time. Curt glanced at the rearview and saw an erratically driven Buick, with an old woman at the wheel, giving chase.

Curt grabbed his walkie and keyed the switch. "Wingnut. Curt."

Wingnut picked up his radio and keyed the switch to acknowledge. "Go for Wingnut."

"Dude, I need you to slow and pull off at the next exit. You have a stowaway."

They enjoyed a guilty laugh as they made their way along the treacherously curvy, two-laned rural bypass known as River Road. It was aptly named, since it mostly paralleled the rather serpentine Salinas River as it meandered through the rich farmlands there.

Phoenix was still amazed by the agricultural system of this fertile valley, and it seemed these land parcels produced everything from lettuce to strawberries with equal success. She stared out at the vast lettuce fields, which were in the process of being harvested.

Several open two-wheel trailers were parked along the edges of the fields. Each was laden with stacks of what Phoenix guessed to be fifty-plus lengths of long metal pipe.

"What's with all the metal pipes?"

"Above-ground irrigation. Sprinkler pipes—most likely three-inch pipes, twenty-foot long. They'll be moved into place, hooked together, then connected to their water source. Crops are thirsty!" he concluded with a chuckle.

"Ah…" she murmured in response. The pipe trailers reminded her of teeter totters because they were all tilted at forty-five-degree angles, either frontward or backward, and seemingly at random. There were also scores of laborers, all dressed in hoodies, doing backbreaking work, and this group seemed to be in a huge hurry to feed a very hungry machine.

"What's that gizmo?" she inquired.

"Oh, that? Lettuce harvester. Speeds up the process considerably," Curt replied, sneaking a look at the field. He had to keep his eyes on the road as there were very few guardrails here.

"Sure takes a lot of people," Phoenix added. "Why so many?"

"I'm no expert—and I can't look right now—but you'll probably see, like, maybe eight groups of three people working the machine."

"Yep, I see that."

"Harvesters cut the lettuce near the soil level with a long knife, trim the unwanted leaves off, then they toss it to the next guy who cuts the heads further before tossing it to the next guy who does the packaging. It only takes a few seconds for each head, and they can blow through a lettuce patch like crap through a goose. Always incredible to watch, and I've seen these guys a million times."

"They're so fast! Man, I have a new appreciation for what goes into the salad bar!"

"Yep, if people only knew," he affirmed.

Phoenix turned to Curt and smiled. "Thanks, Teach!"

"Don't mention it," he chuckled. "Almost there, by the way."

The Watering Hole, from the outside anyway, looked like an old saloon or a sketchy biker bar. The smattering of Harleys in the parking lot indicated it could be both. And it was.

Stepping inside was a bit like going back in time as the rustic, creaky swinging door gave way to eclectically decorated wood-paneled walls and the bar, which had to be a hundred years old if it was a day. The ceiling was littered with several dozen one-dollar bills, each with patrons' names scribbled on them and affixed with darts.

As they entered, they were both still having a guilty laugh at the old man's expense.

"That…that was the capper on the day!" Phoenix howled.

"That was a first, for sure," he said, joining in the laugh.

Curt pulled a single from his wallet and grabbed a Sharpie from the table by the entrance. After scribbling his name, he got a dart from the bartender, speared the bill, and tossed it upward, under-handed, joining its brethren on the overhead surface. "You want to do one?" he asked.

"Nah, I think I'm good," Phoenix replied. "I'm digging the vibe though. Now, if they have my Sunny D, you will have pretty much redeemed yourself," she said, punching his shoulder playfully.

"Fair enough," he answered, pulling out one of the two available barstools for her and taking the other. It appeared they were perhaps the only two non-biker types in this establishment.

Phoenix leaned over and softly sang, into Curt's ear, the title to the Steppenwolf song, "Born To Be Wild."

"Shhh," he whispered back, winking, as he turned to get the bartender's attention.

"Hey, what can I get ya?" the brawny, liberally tatted, spikey-haired barkeep asked him.

"Hi. Uh, a Sunny D—if you have it—and a Sierra Nevada, please."

"Sorry, no Sunny D today. Or any day, really. Not much call for that here. Have orange juice. Or apple, if that works."

"Orange would be fine, thanks," Phoenix interjected.

"You got it. Be right back," she said, disappearing into the reefer.

"So…" Curt began, picking up the small, laminated menu of available bar snacks, "sure you're not hungry?"

"Still good," Phoenix said, with a single nod for emphasis. "Get yourself something though. You worked up an appetite," she added with a giggle.

Curt shook his head in response as he scanned the short list. The barkeep set two napkins on the bar with their respective libations atop them. "What can I get ya?"

"Uh, how about the Buffalo wings and an order of onion rings, please."

"Perfect. Ma'am?"

Phoenix smiled and waved her off with a polite, nonverbal *No, thank you.*

"Okay, I'll get those goin' for you," she said, stepping behind a door to the kitchen.

Curt picked up his beer and brought it around to face Phoenix. She picked up her OJ and held it up in anticipation of his toast. "Thank you for today. I'm sorry it was kind of hinkey."

"Hinkey? I haven't heard that term in ages. Yep, I guess you could say today was kind of…hinkey!" she said, still laughing at the word choice.

"I just figured, after everything you shared with me last night, all that you've been through, you could probably use a little distraction today." He searched her face for a reaction. "Forgive me?"

"Consider me properly distracted and, yes, you are forgiven," she replied, a grin returning to her face.

"Whew!" he said, somewhat relieved. "Okay, then," he continued, gesturing with his glass. "Here's to good friends. To the survivors. To your team, of which I'm now a part, like it or not. To… finding answers. To…discovery, and new truths. And, to redemption. To you, m'lady. Cheers, Phoenix!"

She clinked his glass. "Thank you. I think that was the longest toast ever, by the way. Cheers, Curt, son of Martin!" They each took a thirst-quenching swig and set down their glasses.

"About last night…" Curt started to say.

"What about it? Are you having—?" Phoenix began, hoping he wasn't going to launch into how it'd all been a mistake. *Don't ruin it.*

"Let me finish, please… I was about to say that I really enjoyed our time together last night. All of it."

"I did too," she said, a small ripple of embarrassment trickling in as she thought about their kiss.

"And I feel really good about it. How it went, the whole evening." He paused to take a sip of his beer. "And, if you don't mind my saying so, I really enjoyed kissing you."

Phoenix locked into his eyes. He was speaking the truth, she could tell, and she'd be less than honest if she didn't concur with his assessment. "I had a really good time too, Curt. The whole night. And…especially the end. You were a true gentleman. Thank you," she said, smiling and surprising them both as she leaned over and planted another kiss on his lips. They held it for a second longer then smiled at each other. "I kinda like doing that," she confessed with a sheepish grin.

"I'm glad, 'cause so do I, truth be told."

"Cool. Now that we got that out of the way…" she said, feeling much relieved.

The bartender emerged from the kitchen carrying a plastic, wax paper-lined basket of greasy-yet-golden onion rings and another full of bright orange wings, with several celery sticks and a side of blue cheese dressing. "Here you go. Can I get you anything else?"

"No, we're good, thank you," Curt replied. He took inventory of the delights spread before him, and he was ravenous. As he slid the wings basket closer, an involuntary blast of saliva shot from his mouth, like a Rainbird, spritzing droplets across the bar's surface like it was a summer lawn. He prayed she hadn't just seen that. She had, but pretended not to.

"Bon appétit," she said with an impish grin.

"You don't mind?" he asked, turning to Phoenix.

"No, please. Dig in."

Having received the green light, Curt obliged, digging into the wings with reckless abandon, while Phoenix found secret amusement in the orange stains forming around his mouth. She enjoyed watching this gentle giant eat, and she snuck a couple of onion rings along the way.

As Curt was polishing off his last onion ring, a loud scream of agony came from a bearded and particularly burly-looking biker three seats down from them. He was holding his right shoulder with his left hand and staring down at the dart-speared dollar bill on the bar in front of him.

"Who the fuck's *CURT?!!*"

Phoenix's hand went to her mouth as she tried to suppress a giggle, while her date signaled for the check. "Wanna get out of here?" he asked, not needing an answer.

Back at the shop, Curt backed the truck up to the dump station at the rear of the lot.

"You may want to stay in here for this part. It's, uh, not pretty, and it'll take a little while. You okay?"

"Definitely think I'll take that advice, skipper, thanks. I'll be fine."

"Cool. Be back shortly," he said, stepping out of the cab and walking to the back of the rig, where he attached a ten-foot-long discharge hose to the six-inch valve and aligned it with the gaping target in the ground. The truck was also equipped with two thirty-foot hoses, but he sure didn't need those here. Satisfied with the trajectory, he opened the dump valve, and a roaring mudslide of upwards of fifteen-hundred gallons of circus poop began shooting out.

Phoenix's face scrunched up into a look of absolute horror as she listened to this tsunami, happy she'd been spared the visual this time.

Several minutes later, the discharge began slowing to a trickle of mud, signaling it had nearly finished purging its load of biowaste. Phoenix listened while she looked around the cab and all of its switches and knobs. She glanced over at the passenger side mirror and saw Curt removing the hose; then her gaze drifted to her own reflection briefly before shifting focus to the proximity warning etched in the bottom of the glass. She did a doubletake as, at first, it seemed to display:

OBJECTS IN MIRROR ARE MIGHTIER
THAN THEY APPEAR

And, just as quickly, it reverted to the standard warning. *Did that just happen?*

Curt opened the passenger door, helped her down, and tossed the clipboard on the dash. "That wasn't too bad. You should see this baby in action when we do the big jobs!" he said with a laugh.

"There are bigger jobs?"

"Oh, yeah. Once in a while we get the big ones. Actually, in a couple of days, we do the Salinas Rodeo. Three days, probably 40,000 people. I'll spare you the math word-problem, but it works out to be a lot of poop. We'll easily fill this 4,000-gallon tank, plus some."

"Good times!"

"Let's head inside and we'll get you paid," he said as he unlocked the steel door leading into the garage. The other crew's truck was already empty and parked inside, and they'd knocked off for the day. "Wait just a second, okay? Be right back," he said as he disappeared into the tiny, no-frills office.

Curt emerged with a company checkbook and began filling in

the date. "I'm sorry, Phoenix. I don't think you ever told me your last name. For the check."

"Oh. It's, uh, La Flamme. Two words: two ems and an e."

He looked at her, wondering if she was kidding, but she wasn't. "La Flamme. Phoenix La Flamme."

"I know. Wild, huh? Like I told you, I was known, until very recently, as Phoebe, and the adoptive last name didn't seem like such a tweaky anomaly, but there it is. Sounds kind of like a superhero, now that I hear you say it, though," she said, laughing.

"I like it," he said, his pen paused over the payee line. "So, for our purposes, should I make it out to Phoenix, or Phoebe LaFlamme?"

"Good catch! Make it out to Phoebe, please; I haven't had time to apply for the name change yet. Thanks."

"You got it," he said, tearing off the check and handing it to her.

She went almost slack-jawed when she looked at the amount. "Two hundred dollars? For that?" she said, not wanting her disbelief to be mistaken for being ungrateful. Two hundred bucks right now was huge.

"Call it stunt pay," he said with a chuckle. "Besides, you earned it. Hope it's okay."

She looked up from the check and smiled. "It's more than okay, it's perfect, and very timely! Thank you!"

"Okay, then. We've settled with the Accounts Payable department. If you ever feel like coming out with us again, I can probably bring you on. Just had a guy quit, so...."

"Really? Shocker!" she said.

"Yeah...like I said, we'll be pretty busy with the rodeo deal. Just let me know."

"I'll definitely let you know," she said, stuffing the check in her front pocket. "I appreciate it and, all things considered, I had fun today, working at Diamond Pee—and Poo."

"Ah, yes! DP&P! Perhaps I should have the business cards

changed," he said with a laugh. "And, gawd, I hope that poor guy at the bar's okay," Phoenix added, a guilty giggle escaping.

"Yeah. I'm sure he's fine. He looked pretty tough."

She glanced over at the shop's wall clock. "Oh, my goodness… I'd better get back and rustle up dinner for Grandpa Liam and assorted critters. Pretty sure we'll be splitting that leftover pasta puttanesca. Yum," she said, excited at the prospect.

"Sounds good. I'll be firing up my doggie bag stuff too. Definitely not splitting mine with Wingnut though," he said with a wink. "Can you find your way out of here okay?"

"Yeah, no problem. Think so, anyway."

"Okay, Phoenix La Flamme. Drive safe, and, uh…let me know if you and Liam come up with any ideas about…you know…any game plans. Secret team ops."

"I will, thanks."

Curt leaned in and this time gently cradled the side of her face with his enormous hand, which felt like a soft pillow, she thought. He bent down and kissed her, not once, but three times, pausing between each to look into her eyes before redeploying. Phoenix started to feel a bit light on her feet from this, and her head seemed to sink into his hand.

"Talk to you soon, okay?" Curt said, planting the fourth kiss on her forehead before disengaging.

Phoenix took a deep breath in through her nose and exhaled a sigh. She hoped she was okay to drive, because she felt almost drunk from all this. Not that she had anyone to compare against, but Curt was an excellent kisser.

"Sounds good, Curt Martinsen, son of Martin," she said, looking over her shoulder as she almost floated out through the shop door. "Talk to you later!"

CHAPTER 23

AN HOUR AND a half later, give or take, she pulled into her spot at Liam's, cut the ignition, and slumped back against the seat, trying to remember any cogent details from the drive back. She had nothing. She'd just experienced Day One of the rodeo's traffic, and she hoped not to get stuck in that mess again. At least it was still daylight. She was literally pooped, and Curt had dissolved whatever was left of her. With some effort, she shuffled into the house.

"Home, Grandpa!" she called out loudly before heading down the hall. "Gonna take a quick shower, then I'll make dinner!"

"Okay, sweetheart!" Liam acknowledged from the den office.

And with that, Phoenix rifled through the handful of clean options she could change into, momentarily considering burning the clothes she had on, but instead stuffed them in a large plastic bag to be attended to later. Right now, a long shower beckoned. She needed to wash away any trace evidence of the circus.

She emerged, some forty minutes later, squeaky clean, with her damp hair hiked in a ponytail, once again feeling like a member of the human race. Liam was in the family room, flipping channels, while she whipped together a couple of salads and heated up the leftover Fandango! goodness for them.

"A hundred channels and nothing's on. I swear I'm gonna cancel this cable," Liam groused from the other room.

"I know. Pretty soon they'll probably offer you a deal on an additional hundred channels, and there'll be twice as much of a wasteland. TV…I can't do it," she said, testing the pasta's warmth before serving.

"If it weren't for the ballgames…"

"Yeah, there's that," she said, carrying two plates of pasta, each accompanied by a thick slice of garlic bread and the side salads.

"Oh, look at this," Liam said, delighted by the beautiful food being set onto his TV tray.

"Just a little something I put together," she mused. "Leftovers from our dinner last night, actually. Should be pretty great. Dig in!" she said, pulling up her own tray.

"You were so quiet last night; I didn't even hear you come in," he said, twirling the pasta onto his fork in anticipation of that first bite. "Oh….my…sweet lord, this is lovely, dear!"

"Mm, I'm glad! Nice place in PG. Curt had a gift certificate, so it wasn't like a *date* date or anything. Nice time, though," she said, a tidal wave of saliva cuing up.

Other than the assortment of *oohs* and *ahhs*, the conversation lagged for several minutes while they happily enjoyed the meal. The two onion rings Phoenix had snuck earlier in the day hadn't really tided her over, so it was all she could do not to inhale this.

"I hope Angus didn't keep you awake last night," she managed with a mouthful.

"Angus? Nah, he was perfectly fine. Woke me up a couple of times, but it's a nice sound. Makes me miss my umbrella."

"I'll bet. After we're done here, I'll walk Gracie and Luke. Might bring the Prick too, but not sure yet. We'll see."

"That'd be fine, dear."

She was temporarily hypnotized as she watched the rapid-fire images whiz by on the muted TV. The blur of programming she saw Liam flipping through—most of it worse than what she'd seen at the circus earlier—served to remind her why she'd given up on "the boob tube" long ago.

"Nothing!"

"Yeah, well…" Another couple of minutes went by before she broached the subject. "So, Grandpa. Back to our conversation about what to do next."

"What's that?" He sounded distracted.

"You know. You said we need to play it smart. You said we need a team, remember?"

He flipped off the TV with both a one-figure gesture and the remote, then turned to her.

"I remember. A team, yes. Very important. Have you come up with any ideas?" he asked, his expression serious, focused.

"Well, yes, actually. I think I can say with confidence that our friend, Curt, wishes to be on the team."

"Curt," Liam said to himself, pondering the suggestion.

"Yes. In fact, he said—in no uncertain terms—that he wouldn't take 'no' for an answer."

Liam plucked a cherry tomato from his salad and popped it in his mouth, rolling it around with great ceremony before he responded. "He did, did he? Hm…that Curt, known him for a little while now. Good boy. I trust him. What do you think?"

"Absolutely. I mean, I've only recently met him, but I have no reservations with having him on the team. Not sure what you have in mind, exactly, but we need to put our heads together. He said he'll be busy with work coming up the next couple of days, but he's all in. He's solid."

"Next couple days, you say? Rodeo, I'll bet. Well, we may have to move up our timetable a little. Can't put my finger on it, but I'm getting the feeling the Pirate might be heading out of town again soon. He does that, and we don't want to let him slip through the cracks again."

"Indeed. So?"

"Doing anything tomorrow?"

"Tomorrow…other than an emergency load of laundry, I don't think so. Why?"

"I'll have a chat with Curt, see if we can get him over for a little powwow. Cool?"

"Cool, Grandpa." With that much settled, they finished their salads, and Phoenix cleared their plates as Liam restored the volume. Thank God there was a ballgame on.

Phoenix needed some fresh air. After the long day at DP&P, she owed her lungs an apology—plus the dogs were restless. She hadn't attempted walking the two shepherds and the Prick all together until now, so this would be a good trial run. Three leashes shouldn't be unmanageable, considering she'd had as many as seven pooches on a collective walk during her pet-sitting days.

It was a good excuse to clear her head a little too, as it was noisily buzzing—the kind that comes with a buttload of simultaneous life changes, individually and collectively brutal to process, and collectively—way beyond overwhelming. She'd been given the mother of all pop quizzes, for which there was no study guide.

"Hold still, Prick," she said as she clipped the leash to the metal ring of his tiny collar. "There you go. Okay, you two…Grace… good girl!" she said, praising the sweetest German shepherd she'd ever encountered. "And…your turn…sit, Luke! Sit! Luke!!" He was a great dog as well, though rough around the edges and still full of his puppy energy. She might as well have been tasked with nailing Jell-O to a tree during a monsoon. "Good boy!" she said, finally able to rein in the horses. And off they went.

At the end of the driveway, she directed the team to head right. The walking trails on this stretch weren't very wide, and the tourists tended to exceed the posted limits, so she did her best to keep Grace and Prick on relatively short leashes on her left, and Luke—who tended to be a puller—on a shorter leash at her right hip.

It was a pleasant time of day, just before dusk, and she was glad they'd been able to have an early meal, which allowed for a pre-dark walk. She couldn't blame the dogs too much for being squirrelly. They weren't accustomed to walking as a trio, and Luke seemed to stop every few feet to turn around and see if Prick was there. It was the herder in him. "Luke!" Phoenix called, giving his leash a firm yank. "Watch where you're going, mister! Sheesh!"

They were about a half mile into the hike when an opportune time presented itself for a potty break. A little clearing alongside a low, weathered fence line was chosen by Luke, having given it a thorough sniff test. He immediately arched his back and unleashed an impressive, steaming log cabin, which triggered Grace, and even Prick to join in. "Really? All of you?" Phoenix muttered as she tore a poop bag from the roll in her pocket. Getting this collective output into the bag was going to be iffy, but she managed to pick it all up. Securely closing the full bag would be another matter, however.

Phoenix carried it in her right hand, along with Luke's leash, as they returned to the roadside trail. Moments later, a red convertible Mustang came flying around the blind turn. Four teenagers, two couples, were whooping it up, probably celebrating their perfect day at Carmel Beach, but that didn't make it okay to be driving this road at twenty miles over the speed limit.

The curve wasn't negotiated particularly well, and it took a firm correction from the driver to avoid completely crossing over to the side where Phoenix and the dogs were. The car chirped to a stop several yards short of them. Gracie froze in her tracks while the Prick yipped bloody murder, and Luke jumped backward. "Slow down, asshole!!!" Phoenix yelled, negotiating three tight leashes and the terrified dogs attached to them.

"Ha!!" was the less-than-apologetic response from the driver, while the brunette girl in the back seat chimed in with, "Watch where you're walkin', loser!"

"Yeah, keep that little rat on the sidewalk!" her boyfriend added, not so cleverly.

The driver laughed and commenced a slow approach, the Mustang creeping toward the pack.

Phoenix's fury produced an instantaneous reaction before she could even think about it. In two quick movements, a split-second apart, she transferred Luke's leash into her left hand with the other two and, freeing up her right, hurled the weighty sack of droppings with a fierce delivery. Her catapult aim had been perfect, as the bag first made contact mid windshield, busting open the loose seal and delivering its contents across the glass, then cascading upwards over the lip of the open roof and into the faces of its occupants.

If only Abraham Zapruder could've been there to record the resplendent moment on his Bell & Howell eight-millimeter for later slow-motion analysis. Over some beers. It was that good.

The car lunged forward then jerked to the right and braked hard, noisily skidding to the side of the road before making just enough contact with a cypress to make explaining the dent in the hood to his parents something that would get him grounded for months. Add to that, the image of the four preppy teens trying to spit out small bits of gooey shrapnel. That was the extent of their injury: their pride and their tastebuds.

Phoenix, having assessed nobody was hurt, and that the car was probably still drivable, had already pulled herself and the troops to safer ground, a vantage point behind a line of trees, where she enjoyed a not-at-all-guilty, celebratory chuckle.

The driver, a bleach-blonde jock type, climbed out to inspect the damage and, despite his best efforts to maintain his alpha image, he was immediately reduced to tears. Phoenix didn't hear his exact words, as he was mumbling through sobs at this point, but she could ascertain that his parents were indeed going to kill him.

Shaking his head wildly, he got back in the car and backed away from the tree, pulling part of the fender away in the process. His girlfriend tried to comfort him, but to no avail. He waved her off and pulled away, wiping his tears and what was left of his self-esteem, and continued down the road with his cohorts, utterly defeated.

Phoenix waited a few minutes, then returned to the path with her pack. If only the girls' softball coach had been privy to her considerable pitching skills, she mused. A glance at her watch confirmed that they should be heading back before long. Just a little further, she decided, and then they'd turn around.

What happened next was weird, serendipitous, and something she hadn't prepared for. As she followed the path around the next turn, she found herself at the clearing she'd parked at earlier, just slightly cattycornered to the driveway leading to what her grandpa had called Pirate's Cove. She now knew why he called it that, of course, and she was a bit freaked out by the timing of the arrival of a certain black Corvette, which was slowing to a stop, just shy of the driveway's entrance.

Phoenix froze, and her heart started racing at the sight of him. The Prick, always a good judge of character, began growling quietly. Grace and Luke both tensed, sensing unknown threat.

She'd fully expected, and hoped, the roadster would make the immediate turn onto his property, but this time it wasn't the case. He was just sitting there, engine idling and, even though she couldn't see a face, she could feel the burn of his stare through the dark, tinted glass. He had seen her, she was certain, and she felt like her feet were cement blocks.

She couldn't stand here forever; she knew that much, so she pretended she hadn't noticed him, and slowly resumed walking in the same direction, the dogs on a tight leash. Keeping her eyes forward and on the path, she continued on a few yards and, as she was adjacent to the driveway, she heard the distinct sound of the Corvette's power window slowly going down. This got another growl from the Prick, and she immediately shushed him.

The voice froze her in her tracks.

"Lost?"

Even though a single word had been uttered, it was an utterly chilling sound, emanating from a decidedly evil source. The effect was instantaneous as an avalanche of ice shut down her nervous system, seemingly cooling her core to near zero, rendering her inert. It was unmistakable, and a sinister voice she'd heard once before as she'd witnessed the last breaths being squeezed from the throat of her dying mother all those years ago.

The moment felt like an hour, when in reality it had taken Phoenix several seconds to process a response. "Lost? Uh, no, no, thanks," she stammered. She turned her head ever so slightly toward the car, enough to get a peek at her adversary. He was wearing wraparound sunglasses, but his was the face from the photos and her indelible memories. He stared at her for several seconds.

"No? Hm, okay. Had to ask. I just, you just reminded me of somebody, that's all," he replied, with the slightest trace of what could be construed as a smile.

Phoenix silently chided herself for staring back longer than she should have. She half-smiled as she looked away. "Just walking the dogs. Nice day out. Got to get back…don't want my husband worrying," she said, truly pissed at herself for how lame that must have sounded, and utterly disgusted that she was having an exchange with this monster.

"Yes…I suppose so. Gets dark quickly this time of day," he hissed softly. "One can't be too careful out here, on this stretch of road…all alone," he added, punctuating what seemed like a veiled threat with a menacing smile from his lizard lips.

Phoenix's stomach began to quake. He seemed to savor the moment as he toggled a switch, and his face slowly disappeared behind a black curtain of glass as the 'Vette turned down the drive and vanished from view. Seconds later, the tsunami of acidic bile that had been building—and that, with concerted effort, she'd tried to calm—was given permission to crest, spilling out onto the roadside.

Phoenix had little to no memory of the journey back. She removed her walking shoes once she got to the front porch, as there were traces of vomit on them, and they'd need a cleaning.

After the dogs' water and food needs were met, she peeked into the family room where Liam was asleep in his recliner. She gently pried the remote from his hand and turned down the volume before disappearing down the hall.

She spent a longer than usual amount of time cleaning Angus's cage. There was little thought involved and, despite his best efforts to start a conversation, Angus's greetings were all but ignored. Her encounter on the road had left her in a deep mental fog, and she relied on muscle memory as she went about the tasks.

As she scrubbed the metal bars and replaced the newspaper liner, she paused to read the latest current events in the fresh, day-old *Carmel Pine Cone* that Liam had set aside for her. What got her attention was the front page story about a local teen whose body had been found, dumped near the polo field, near Stevenson Drive. Just a few miles from their location.

The photo of the young girl, only sixteen years of age, jarred Phoenix. She stopped breathing as she read the accompanying facts: an aspiring singer and daughter of a local police detective, her nude body had been discarded in a roadside ditch. Cause of death appeared to be strangulation. Aside from the ditch part, the parallels were too many, and she couldn't help but think about how her mother had been found.

Could it? Her thoughts went back to the encounter she'd had less than an hour before.

Oh, my God.

Unplanned tears found her cheeks, and her blood began a slow boil as she deliberately slid the tray back into the bottom of the cage, barely finding her breath as she covered it and whispered, "Goodnight, Angus."

It had taken some doing, but she managed to wake Liam, liberate him from his chair, and see him down the hall where she hugged him goodnight. He was tired, but not too much so to sense something was off.

"You okay, honey? Seem awfully quiet tonight."

"Mm, just...I'm just tired, Grandpa," she lied. His look told her he didn't seem to be buying it, but she nipped it in the bud for now. "Just need some sleep. See you in the morning, Grandpa. Love you."

"I love you too, kiddo," he replied, and as she started down the hall it prompted an afterthought: "Oh, and I got ahold of Curt." This stopped her in her tracks. "He's coming over tomorrow morning. Team meeting. 9:00. Hope you know how to make omelets."

CHAPTER 24

AFTER SEVERAL HOURS of flopping around like a rainbow trout on a riverbank, Phoenix gave up on the idea of getting any sleep. Her mind had been racing on a looped track, with pitstop thoughts of the young dead girl she'd read about, her facetime with the devil, and the anxieties that came with having no clue how to make an omelet.

It would be light soon, so she surrendered to the morning and set about scrubbing last night's dinner from her shoes. She'd planned on replacing her toothbrush anyway, so she made sure she had a freshy before soiling her old one. After several minutes, with a firm stroke and some mild soap, she managed to get the worst of it out.

She whispered to Prick that it was time for him to get up too, and he was not too pleased about it. Securing his leash, she liberated him from the warmth of his bed and took him outside, where the subtle, early hints of color promised to paint the sky in impressive fashion.

Returning inside, she began the mystical search for ingredients she could only imagine would occupy the folds of an omelet. She enjoyed eating them. In restaurants. But she'd never been tasked with replicating the construction of such a beast.

Pulling a fresh eighteen-pack of brown, cage-free eggs from the fridge, she began laying out the contenders: two avocados that, based on the squeeze test, needed to be used immediately; a smallish package of slightly beige, whole mushrooms; some fresh Cilantro; two large, ripe-enough Roma tomatoes; and an unopened bag of shredded pepperjack. That seemed like omelet material, right? Next order of business was locating a suitable pan, preferably a large, nonstick variety: *Check*. Spatula and rubber scraper: *Check*.

Rifling through the pantry, she found a small can of mild Ortega peppers and a bottle of mild green salsa that had expired a couple of months back. But it was unopened, and she made the executive decision to use it. *Why did he have to tell Curt I'm making friggin' omelets? Oy.*

Then the thought occurred to her that there should probably be something else on those plates, just in case the omelets completely blow. Thankfully, further search revealed some hash browns in the freezer and, while she was at it, she dug out a cast iron skillet that weighed as much as she did. A tube of biscuits with the little Poppin' Fresh dude on it. *Jam? Yep.*

A glance out the kitchen window treated her tired eyes and weary soul to a Technicolor kaleidoscope of purple, some vivid reds, and some intense yellows and oranges sneaking through them. *Thank you, God*, a reminder to be grateful in all things.

"Good morning, honey," the voice said, accompanied by the sound of a squeaky walker.

"'Morning, Grandpa. What are you doing up?" She glanced at the microwave clock. "It's a little after 6:00," she announced as she went about assembling a larger than usual pot of coffee.

"Tell that to Angus," he answered with a chuckle.

"Ooh, really? Sorry about that…I put him to bed early last night. Hope he wasn't too obnoxious."

"Nah…like I said, I miss my umbrella. Angus is good company and nothing like the howler monkey of a bird I used to have, believe me."

"Ah…," She yawned, her attention fixed on the scoops of Folgers. *Was that eleven or twelve?* She threw in a couple of extra scoops, just in case. "So, thanks for falsely advertising me as the Omelet Queen. Honestly, this will be a first, and I make no guarantees. Couldn't we have had our team meeting around bowls of cereal? I can cut up bananas with the best of 'em, you know."

"Looks like you've got some good ingredients, anyway," he replied, surveying the offerings atop the counter. "No onions, please. Gives me the runs something awful."

"No onions. Duly noted. And thanks so much for that special start to my day there, Grandpa," she said, shaking her head as she chuckled.

"Anything I can do?"

"Nah, coffee'll be up in a few minutes. Just put your feet up. I'll bring it in there to you."

"Can't argue with that arrangement. Thank you, dear," he said, shuffling into the next room.

Phoenix got out the carton of half & half and a sugar bowl. Today was going to call for extra additives, and she'd deliberately constructed a strong pot. She heard the TV's volume as it ratcheted up. Sounded like a local news channel.

"Oh, dear," Liam said.

"What's the matter, Grandpa?" she asked, peeking her head around the corner.

"Sixteen years old…" he said quietly, a world of dread just below the surface.

Phoenix came around next to his recliner and, standing there, felt the strength escape her legs as she turned her attention to the newscast. She plopped down onto the adjacent chair. There she was—the girl from the paper and now lining Angus's cage.

The blonde, and entirely too bubbly, news anchor went on to list the details Phoenix had already read about, and it became clear to her that her grandpa hadn't bothered to read yesterday's paper before volunteering its reuse.

"Such a shame," Liam said, barely above a whisper. "What kind of animal…?"

Phoenix listened as the reporter mentioned one last, new detail: the girl had last been seen at a karaoke restaurant down in the village, a couple of nights before she went missing.

"I think we know the answer to that one, Grandpa," Phoenix affirmed. "Oh, my gawd…."

Liam turned to look at his granddaughter. Somehow, he knew in his gut she had to be right.

"Do you think?" he wondered, but he knew the answer.

Phoenix stood, pacing in a circle as she addressed the jury. "The similarities…there are too many to ignore, grandpa! Think about it—this monster…he has a pattern! Young girl, an aspiring singer he can exploit…and then—" she paused, the prosecutor had a frog in her throat, "—and then…he strangles her. Just like…just like he did…to our Rose!" she said, resting her case.

Liam muted the TV as it switched to a story about JFK Jr.'s plane that was still missing off the coast of Martha's Vineyard. He shook his head slowly as the greatest pain he'd ever experienced in this life returned. The surface scab had been yanked off once again.

"Suppose you're right…."

"I've never felt so fucking right about something in my life, Grandpa. Excuse my French. But this has all the markings of the asshole you've been consumed with these past twenty years. And now, here I am, like you…all-consumed! I'm all in on this now, Grandpa—you know that—and I ran into that same sonofabitch yesterday, after dinner!"

Liam stared at her, slack-jawed, as he processed this last item.

"I know. More on that in a bit. Let me get your coffee."

He switched off the set, then finished his can of Tab before lighting up his first Kent of the day. That and a can of Slim Fast—the double chocolate one—was all the breakfast he needed.

They'd found the body quickly enough, not that he'd put much effort into concealing it. He'd been in a hurry, but they'd have nothing to connect him to it. As usual.

If there were a couple of things he really hated—and there were several—near the top of the list would be: being threatened and leaving loose ends. That little bitch had left him no choice, and she'd been easy enough to track down after she'd left that night. Sweet-talking her back into the car with an apology and fresh promises had been easy. After all, she was young, naïve, and desperate.

And he was a Pirate.

Occasionally, a rare nugget of self-awareness would present itself, and lately he'd found that coming off a fresh kill made him a little hungry for another. He might even have time for another quick conquest before he had to return to LA, as the new band he managed had just had their lead singer quit before they were to hit the road. He planned to teach that ungrateful little tart a lesson—and one she wouldn't survive—but that would have to wait. He had to find a replacement for her quick…or kiss the entire tour goodbye.

And that wasn't an option.

Phoenix had left Liam hanging with his coffee, and her newsflash, as she'd had to make herself presentable for their breakfast guest. Now, she had her game face on as she prepped her omelet ingredients and sequestered them into their respective bowls.

She had to guesstimate the number of eggs to use, factoring in three diners. Then she remembered to count Curt as two people, so she cracked open ten eggs. She was making it up as she went. Her thoughts momentarily returned to the news, her encounter with the evil one, and events of the past, as she channeled her fury into beating the eggs, whipping them with a fork into an almost liquid state of submission.

A knock on the door prompted her glance upward and, as she feared, it was 9:00 on the nose. She peeked in the oven to check the progress of the doughboy, wiped her hands, and went to answer the front door.

"Good morning," Curt said, his smile beaming as he handed her a white vase of fresh-cut flowers.

"Wow…good morning! Wow…these are beautiful! Thank you so much. Please, come in," she said, giving the giant a peck as he filled the doorway. *Another first: flowers!*

"He here?" Liam called from the family room.

"I am! Good morning, Liam," he acknowledged as he made his way to greet him. The men settled in as she brought them both fresh coffees.

"If you'll excuse me…" she said, "the cook called in sick today, so…." With a nervous smile she disappeared around the corner.

Phoenix's attention returned to the task at hand as she sprayed some nonstick schmutz into the largest of Liam's seemingly new and hopefully nonstick frying pans and turned on the gas burner to a medium-low setting. She spun on her heals at the sound of the oven timer and, with an economy of movement, slipped on the protective mitt, pulled out the tray of biscuits, and switched off the oven. They were probably one shade darker than optimal, but still edible. So what if "Poppin' Fresh" had a tan?

The ten eggs were dusted with some salt and pepper, and the mixture stirred, before being poured into the pan. It sure seemed like a lot of eggs, now that she saw them in their new habitat, and she hoped they'd reach their target consistency without being a slimy, undercooked mess.

Logic told her that the only way the entire egg population would get cooked was if they had equal opportunity to the heat source, so she threw up a Hail Mary and grabbed a rubber scraper from the utensil drawer. As the edges seemed to be cooking first, she teased them back with the scraper and tilted the pan to allow the more liquid-y parts to assume the position nearest the heat. As she went around the edges, she continued to push them back slightly and repeated the process for a couple of minutes until there was very little runny goo.

She lowered the heat, allowing the tiniest bit of blue flame, then added the various chopped veggies, careful to keep them toward the center of the pan so that she could, in a perfect world, fold the sides inward to approximate an omelet. Shredded cheese was last, then she grabbed two spatulas and went about tucking in the flaps. The cheese seemed to hold it together enough and after turning off the burner, it was the moment of truth. She slid a large platter into position and nudged the mass from the pan onto it. The thing was pretty massive, and she was pretty proud of the fact that it actually looked like something edible. A sprinkle of grated cheddar and a couple dollops of green salsa, and…*voila!* It went into the microwave for about twenty seconds to melt the cheese, and it was a thang.

"Breakfast is ready, boys!" she called as she carried the platter to the table, along with a pie server.

"Mm…we're coming!" Liam replied eagerly.

Once the taters and biscuits were staged, and everything was as ready as it would ever be, Phoenix wiped her hands on her apron and gave herself a pat on the back. She'd actually pulled this thing off, she thought, but knew the taste test still awaited.

"Grandpa, you're here," she said, pulling out his chair as he approached with the walker. "And, Curt, you're at the end here," she said, offering him a smile, which was both affectionate and from a sense of relief. Phoenix took the middle seat, between her men.

Food was passed around the table and, once they all began eating, there was very little uttered, other than the happy sounds associated with pleasure. Their "meeting" would be called to order afterward, and nobody would be taking minutes right now.

"Oh, my goodness. Phoenix. Seriously. Best omelet I've ever had," Curt said, wiping the salsa from the corner of his mouth. "I would *so* order this in a restaurant. Scout's honor."

"Got to agree, sweetheart! And *who* said they didn't know how to make an omelet?" Liam concurred with a laugh and wink to his granddaughter. "Brilliant."

Phoenix set down her fork and smiled at them both. She prayed she didn't have any cilantro stuck in her teeth. "Thank you, gentlemen. Truth be told, nobody's more surprised than me! I've never made anything like this before and, well…it *is* pretty brilliant, if I do say so myself!" she said, beaming. "Beginner's luck, right?" *Thank you, Lord!*

After they'd finished, Curt helped clear the table, and Phoenix set the dishes into the basin of soapy water to soak. Liam emerged from his office, his walker's basket laden with notepads, writing utensils, and his files. The meeting was about to start.

"Okay, first order of business," Liam said as they scooched in their chairs. "Curt. Thank you for coming, and thanks for offering your services as part of the team. Not sure what your role will be—or any of our roles will be—yet, but that's why we're here. To figure it out."

"Don't mention it, Liam. Really. There's no way I wasn't going to be involved, after what Phoenix told me."

"Yes, thank you, Curt," she said with a sigh, giving his hand a tiny squeeze. "You should know that, since we talked the other night about this, I had a…I ran into…you know who."

Curt's brow furrowed. "Okay, please explain."

"Late afternoon, yesterday. I was walking the dogs out on the road here, when outside of the creep's driveway, he pulled up and engaged me in conversation." She paused, shuddering at the thought. "I saw his face, and I heard his voice. I felt his…evil. I know it was a very long time ago, but it was definitely the man that I

243

saw—" her voice caught in her throat, and Curt squeezed her hand. She took a deep breath. "I am one hundred percent sure it was the man who killed my mother."

"Jeezus," Liam sighed. "You okay, sweetie? Need to take a break?"

"We just started, Grandpa. I'm fine. I just…it makes my skin crawl."

"And mine," Liam muttered as he opened up his thick case file. He turned to the clippings and police reports from the fire, then spun it around so Curt could better see it. He also spread out the photos he'd previously shown Phoenix. "This is our guy. This is my daughter's—and Phoenix's mother's—murderer. And there have been others, apparently."

"Not apparently…*definitely*," Phoenix corrected. "Turn on this morning's news, and you'll see what I'm talking about."

"I saw that! You think—?"

"I *know*," Phoenix blurted, cutting off Curt's query. "Don't have proof, yet, but it's definitely him. It clicks all the boxes."

"Wow," Curt whispered as he shuffled through the photos. "I think I've seen this guy, but never noticed the eye patch. Must've worn shades over it. I know his property. Did some work there about a year back. Guy looks like a friggin'—"

"Pirate?" Liam interrupted. "That's our nickname for this dip-shit. And, together, we need to find a way to take him down."

It took nearly forty-five minutes to bring him completely up to speed on the case, but when Curt had absorbed all the facts, and factored how it had brought such incalculable pain to these people whom he'd come to deeply care about, he closed the file and looked them both squarely in the eyes.

"Any thoughts?" Liam asked.

"Well…just thinking out loud here, but my initial thought would be for me to just drive right over there, introduce myself, and then break this one-eyed, wannabe pirate pissant into several pieces."

Curt noticed Phoenix's eyes get a little larger at hearing this. "But you tell me how you want to play this," he conceded.

"As lovely as that scenario sounds," she mused, "I think we need to take a different tack. Let's save your idea as our Plan B, but we need to be smart here. We need to exploit his vulnerabilities, if we can find them. We already know his penchant for young girls, and the ones he thinks he can exploit. And he seems to know where to find his current supply, right?"

"Yep," Liam agreed. "But where does that fit into...?"

"I was hoping you'd ask that," Phoenix offered. "There just might be a way to play him, to trip him up into incriminating himself somehow."

"And pray tell, how might we do that? My offer still stands to bust him up, by the way."

"Hear me out. I've given this a little thought here, though admittedly it's still a bit sketchy. Okay? So, where do we find a young girl to lure him?" she challenged, looking back and forth at them before raising her hand. "I volunteer!"

Their slack jaw reactions indicated they didn't much like the idea.

"There's no way my granddaughter is going to be used as bait," Liam exclaimed.

"I agree. You've been through enough, Phoenix, and this isn't somebody to mess with. I can't sign on to anything that could endanger you. Sorry."

"Well, thanks for thinking about it," she said, infusing her annoyance with sarcasm. "Look, I understand and appreciate your concern. And, believe me, I'm not interested in becoming another casualty here. But I think we just may have an opportunity—and maybe our last opportunity—to get him! There has to be a reasonably safe way to play this, and we need to put our heads together. *Please*...."

"Define reasonably safe. I don't know how that looks," Curt said, the concern evident on his face.

Liam squirmed in his chair, his fingers drumming the case file. He didn't like the risk, not at all. But he also knew their window of opportunity might be closing.

"What if..." he prefaced, looking at them both as he formulated his thoughts. "Suppose there was a way to set up a situation, like Phoenix is suggesting, but safely."

"You mean, like having police present, ready to jump in if everything goes south?" Curt interjected.

"No. Of course not. He'd smell cops a mile away. I'm talking about another safety mechanism. An electronic one."

"You mean, like a wire?" Phoenix probed.

"Something like that, yes. If there were a way to monitor what's going on—safely, of course—while maintaining stealth, we could possibly have a shot. And it might be the only way to get him to open up. Maybe even incriminate himself. There are ways to do it."

Curt turned to Phoenix. "So, you're thinking—you're both thinking, apparently—you want to set up a meeting with this guy. You wear a wire, or a recorder—whatever. And see if you can get him to spill the beans? Am I hearing this correctly?"

"I'd be willing to do that," Phoenix affirmed, displaying newfound resolve as she looked at Curt, then to Liam. "I want to do that."

"Listen to what you're saying, Phoenix. This could be very dangerous," Curt pleaded.

"If Liam, as a former detective, thinks it can be done—and yes, safely—I want to try it. Please..." she said, grabbing Curt's hand now, "Please support me in this... I've come too far just to see him get away again, and this isn't just about me. It's about my mother, and God knows how many others. I owe it to them to at least try," she begged. "I'll definitely need your help to get this guy, and this may be our only shot."

Curt bit his lip as he wrestled with the proposal. There was a lot on the line. He took a full minute before responding, yielding to the experienced party. "Liam?"

Phoenix walked Curt to the door. His eyes shifted around more than usual, and she could read the anxiety in his expression, even though he'd tried his best to hide it.

"Thanks for breakfast, Phoenix. It was pretty amazing," he said, adding a strained smile.

"You're welcome. Thanks for coming, Curt. Listen, I appreciate your concern, more than I can tell you, but please don't worry too much, okay? We'll try this…and be smart about it. It may or may not work, but we have to at least try. Maybe we'll get lucky, who knows." She stood on her tiptoes to kiss him on the lips, and he met her halfway.

"Yeah, let's hope. Okay, gotta go. Prunedale construction site needs our attention today. Things should quiet down slightly after the rodeo ends tomorrow night. Promise me you'll walk the dogs the other direction for now, okay? Promise?"

"Promise," she vowed, crossing her heart.

"Call you later, okay?" he said, kissing her hand as he stepped off the porch.

"'Kay," she affirmed. He gave the horn a tap of goodbye as he made his way down the driveway, and she reciprocated with a wave as he disappeared onto the main road. The corners of her smile caved a little, conceding to thoughts of unknown dangers. *What am I getting myself into?*

With the arrival of the visiting nurse, Phoenix elected to take the pooches on a shorter than usual walk, exiting left out of the driveway this time per her promise, before jumping in the car for an impromptu errand she felt compelled to do.

She'd spent nearly an hour online, searching for designs before printing up a copy of the one she liked best. The forty-minute drive into Seaside had given her ample to time to reconsider, but she was feeling committed as she pulled into the sketchy strip mall and entered the tattoo shop. *Am I nuts? (Don't answer that!)*

The resident artist was a very large man of Samoan descent. He had long, black hair and a thin, scraggly beard, but his pearly white teeth formed a smile the Cheshire Cat would've been envious of. "Ah, you must be the Phoenix, yes?"

"Yes, I am the Phoenix," she said, laughing at the title he'd given her. "Thank you for seeing me without an appointment."

"Ah, no problem. No problem.... You brought a picture, I see."

"Yes," she said, handing him the paper upon which was a black and white image, approximately three inches tall. She'd sifted through hundreds of pictures before landing on this one, which she found graceful, while exuding strength. And strength was what she needed right now.

"Ah, yes. The Phoenix wishes the Phoenix…very nice. I can do this, no problem," he said, his smile almost blinding her. He wore a tank top that provided easy viewing of his considerable body art, most of it tasteful.

"I was thinking, I don't know…maybe, like, around the size I printed there. And maybe right here," she said, pointing to the area below her left clavicle. "Would that look good?"

"I can put it anywhere, and I think it would look amazing there," he responded, again with the smile.

"Will…it…um…hurt much?" she asked, clenching her teeth in a grimace.

"Nah, it will be okay. You'll see. This will take maybe three hours, I think. Let's have a seat over here and get started, yes?"

He drew a privacy curtain around the workstation as she took a seat. "And, if you're okay, let's take off your shirt, please." She was thankful she'd remembered to wear a sports bra underneath. As nice as he probably was, she didn't want this guy to be the first to ever see her half-naked.

She hoped to save that experience for someone else someday.

The area was reddened, swollen, and tender, but Phoenix had no regrets. Quite the opposite, actually. She was now embellished, but it wasn't with some silly Disney character, nor an unsavory "tramp stamp" occupying her backside. She somehow felt emboldened, now that she was emblazoned with this symbol of who she had become, and this called for a re-cue of her namesake song by Mr. Fogelberg for the drive back.

There would be no cooking tonight, she decided, as she approached Carmel. Not after the clinic she'd put on that morning. She pulled into an unfamiliar pizza establishment and waited twenty minutes while they constructed her 50/50 pie, which gave her time to check in with Pop Pop.

As she waited for him to pick up, she prayed for some kind of sign, a next move, anything....

"Phoenix! There you are! You good, baby? Liam behaving himself?"

"Yes, I'm good," she replied, trying to deliver her smile across state lines. "We're getting along well, hashing some stuff out."

"Any movement...you know, new developments?" Pop Pop inquired.

"Um, not really," she lied, not wanting to concern him. "But I hope to have a good report for you soon. Lots of moving parts, you know?"

"I'll bet, honey...."

"What're you up to?" she asked, desperate to change the subject.

"Just grillin' some chicken pieces. Hey, before I forget: a package came for you today. Kinda heavy, marked *fragile*. I put it in the cottage for you."

Phoenix tried not to laugh, knowing it had to be the "three-piece set" she'd ordered for him. "Great, Pop Pop, thanks!"

"Any idea how long you'll be staying out there, honey? Just wondering, that's all. I know this is an important trip. Just miss you around here," he confessed.

"Not sure, Pop Pop. Hopefully not too much longer. I'll keep you posted though. Hope you're not missing me too much at the shop right now."

"We're getting by, but I have to watch the new kid kind of close. He almost forgot to put the lug nuts back on after doing a tire rotation on a Caddy yesterday. That would never happen with you around," he assured.

"Aww, well I hope to be back in the saddle soon, Pop Pop. I—"

The counter chime rang, and an especially cheery teenage surfer dude announced, "Phoenix, your order's up!"

"Hey, I've gotta go. My pizza's ready. Talk to you soon, okay? Love you!"

"Love you too, kiddo! Bye."

A pang of guilt hung over her as she pocketed her phone. Phoenix hated lying, even by omission, but even hinting at the latest developments would've seen Pop Pop on the next flight out, and he'd probably ground her for twenty years.

The pizza was smelling pretty righteous and as she set it on the passenger seat, she noticed a flyer taped to the box. That little karaoke/Italian restaurant venue in the village—and the Pirate's presumed local hunting grounds—was hosting an open mic/live band/local talent gig the following night. She reread the flyer three times, just to make sure she wasn't hallucinating from tattoo ink poisoning.

It was, indeed, going to be tomorrow.

Be careful what you ask for.

Thank you, Lord!!!

With their timetable having been moved up, and chosen for them, things were starting to get real. As Liam was no longer an active-duty detective—with *any* department—the tech resources at their disposal were seriously diminished.

While it would've been great to have Phoenix wear a real "wire," like in the movies, with an armed team monitoring the conversation from some clandestine laundry truck in the parking lot, their team would be having to resort to Plan C, which was decidedly old school. With Plan B being Curt's kind offer of opening up a can of whoop ass....

After Liam and Phoenix had polished off their last slices of pizza, she cleared plates while he navigated his squeaky-wheeled walker down the hall to his office. He returned several minutes later, carrying an old shoebox in one hand, which he set on the kitchen table.

"What's that, Grandpa?" she asked, wiping her hands on a dishtowel.

"C'mon over, I wanna show you something."

Phoenix pulled up her chair and watched with rapt curiosity as Liam liberated several vintage-looking gizmos from the box. He carefully laid out the items that looked like something she'd find at one of her estate sales.

"This might not be sexy, but it might be the only game in town."

"Is that, like, a...Walkman? I used to have one of those," she offered.

"Not quite. Different purpose. Different format. Different maker. *This* little beauty is an Olympus SD microcassette recorder, vintage 1977, and it's not for listening to music. I paid over two hundred bucks a piece for these back in the day, and there're two of 'em!" he mused.

"So, for lectures and stuff then?"

"Among other things, yes. I haven't tested 'em in about twenty years, but last time I used it, she worked like a charm." He held up a tiny TDK microcassette tape and handed it to her. "That little tape will record sixty minutes. Should be more than enough length for our purposes, and I've got a few extras here."

"What are those other things, Grandpa?" she asked, pointing to two metal, silver-toned, screw-on attachments.

"These? We won't be using these, but they're pretty nifty accessories. This one's an FM radio module, and the other's a voice actuator module. They each screw onto the bottom of the recorder, here, but we're going to have to go with the stripped-down version because the recorder's already a bit larger than is ideal. Especially since you'll have to stick in in your pocket. Here, hold it, and you'll see what I mean. Kind of a beast," he said, handing her the unit.

"Wow, solid! And…like you said, a beast!" she agreed, handing it back to him.

"I have some fresh batteries here, let's see if she still fires up," he said, wrestling with the battery compartment. "Say a little prayer, sweetie," he added, as he stabbed the play/record buttons.

"Please…."

"The wheels are turning, that much I can see. Here…say something; doesn't matter what. Regular voice, don't talk louder than would be normal."

"Okay…uh, testing…one, two…so, sir, how long have you been a pirate?" she said with a chuckle.

Liam hit the stop button, then rewound the tiny tape. "Moment of truth," he said as he hit play. The front-facing speaker crackled to life with a little distortion but surprising clarity:

"Okay…uh, testing…one, two…so, sir, how long have you been a pirate?" Her chuckle also came through clearly enough.

"Bingo," Liam declared. "We're in business. We'll put in another set of fresh batteries, just in case, and I'll give you a couple of extra tapes for backups. Thankfully we've got two of these, just in case. Regrettably, this rig comes with a couple of limitations though."

"Such as?"

"Such as, this won't transmit the conversation to anyone. It's simply a recorder. As a result, *we* can't monitor your conversation in real time, so it's very important that you're able to get something useable on tape."

"Gotcha. What's the other one?"

"If the environment has too much loud background noise, it makes it difficult to understand the voice. You'll need to select a time when, hopefully, there isn't a lot of extraneous clatter going on."

"Understood."

"So, that being said, I want you to take some time, right now, get very familiar with the buttons, switching out the tapes, and how to switch the record mode on and off by feel. *If* we get an opportunity to record this perp, you won't have the luxury of having the machine on the table in front of you. Got it?" He locked eyes with her, and his expression let her know he was deadly earnest.

"Got it, Grandpa."

"Good. Now what's for dessert?"

After their ice cream sandwiches, Liam assumed the position in his Lazy Boy and switched on the game. D-backs and Giants, with Randy on the mound.

Phoenix tried to find distraction in it, but lost interest after just half an inning. She gave Liam a peck goodnight and disappeared down the hall. Her mind was spinning with thoughts of vintage technology, pirate encounters, and deciding what she felt comfortable trying in front of a crowd.

She surveyed the redness surrounding her new ink and was careful not to agitate anything as she slipped into her jammies top. She was utterly exhausted, emotionally, and knew Curt had to be wiped out too, but she tried his phone one more time in hopes of reaching him before bed.

"Hey, Phoenix!" the voice said at the other end. "Sorry I missed your calls earlier. How are you?"

"Yay…glad you picked up. I'm mostly good, just tired. I can't even imagine what you must feel like. Rodeo's over, right?"

"Yep. Wingnut and I have been absolutely slammed. Just finished up here and driving out of the facility, with a very full truck. Had to use the big one!"

"Eww, I'll bet. Spare me the details, please," she teased.

"I will," he replied. "Hey…."

"Hey…."

"I've missed you," he said, his voice slightly above a whisper.

Wingnut's teasing voice could be heard in the background as he interrupted. "Ooh, I've missed you, my love!"

"Shut up, Wingnut, sheesh!" he blurted to his companion, then apologetically back to the phone, "Sorry about that. He's so mature."

Phoenix laughed at the exchange. *Boys....*

"Long day for everyone," she confessed. "So, a couple new developments, if you're not too tired to hear 'em."

"I'm wide awake and all ears," he replied.

"Hey! You makin' fun of my ears again?" Wingnut laughed. He'd long ago become immune to people's teasing.

"I'm sorry…again," Curt said, punching his companion in the shoulder as punctuation. "You were saying?"

Phoenix took the next twenty minutes explaining the details and the chain of events that had transpired since their last meeting. Curt held the Nokia tightly against his left ear, absorbing every detail as his own wheels turned. Wingnut was wise not to interrupt further, and only spoke when the call had finished.

"Everything okay?"

"Hmm? Oh, yeah," Curt answered, absently at first. A couple of miles of road went by before he turned to him. "Question…and you can totally say no."

"Shoot," his floppy-eared buddy replied.

"You up for a little adventure?"

Phoenix checked the batteries on the recorder for the third time, trying not to obsess about it.

"C'mon, Phoenix! Sheesh!" she snapped, her voice a loud whisper as she turned out the light on the nightstand. "Get some sleep, girl…."

Her thoughts went back to her too-brief, desert pitstop at the Mission San Xavier del Bac. It seemed like such a long while ago, but she knew she'd lost all sense of time since she'd embarked on this road trip odyssey of hers. She still felt bad that she'd rushed through her prayers that day, and felt compelled to revisit a psalm written around 1000 BC by King David. It was one of the few she still knew by heart, and it still seemed the most pertinent to her situation. She paused as she got to the fourth verse, repeating it over and over, until she fell asleep:

"Yea, though I walk through the valley of the shadow of death, I will fear no evil...."

PART SIX

MEEP!
MEEP!

CHAPTER 25

PHOENIX SLEPT LIKE the dead but woke early because Prick had to relieve his micro bladder. It was still dark out and she grimaced when she glanced at the clock's digital display.

"Really?" she said through a yawn. "It's 3:25, you little weasel. Okay...."

She stepped into her flipflops and wrapped herself in the tired terrycloth robe Liam had left in the closet for her. As the little guy did his business, Phoenix couldn't help but notice how incredibly bright the night/early morning sky was.

"Whoa," was all she could utter as her jaw hung slack. The pitch black was offset by seemingly billions of the brightest stars and constellations she'd ever seen. It was like she'd walked into a planetarium show, or stepped out into a spacewalk, and she had to stand there for a full ten minutes to take in the experience. A series of impatient yips brought her back to earth.

"Okay! Sheesh" she whispered, giving a tug on the leash.

After tucking him in again, she climbed back under the covers in hopes of resuming her slumber session, but after about fifteen minutes her eyes sprang open, and she realized it wasn't going to happen. Her stomach growled.

As quiet as a mouse on Christmas eve, Phoenix pulled a bowl from the cupboard and perused her grandpa's cereal collection. It was pretty impressive in its scope, as it offered nearly a dozen variations on bran, but no sugar bombs. Her early morning jones was hoping for some Lucky Charms, but she was denied. She settled on a box of Quaker product she'd never tried before and carried it to the table.

Yawning like a narcoleptic lion, Phoenix tried to shake her pre-caffeine cobwebs. Coffee would have to wait. As she sleepily poured milk onto her heaping bowl of Life, the irony didn't go unnoticed.

You trying to tell me something?

She knew it had to be that. As she started shoveling in her breakfast, she remembered a quote that had been attributed to Albert Einstein: *Coincidence is God's way of remaining anonymous.*

She was digging the cereal and was surprised when she poured herself a second bowl. *Guess that officially makes me pro-Life?* she mused, attributing her atypical giddiness to the early hour.

A mile down the road, it was also breakfast time at Pirate's Cove.

He stood in his black satin robe in the designer kitchen, feeling a bit lost and looking like a rookie as he fumbled with two of the six gas burners. He never used the thing, but he was out of his favorite microwave Jimmy Dean sausage sandwiches, so he'd have to—shudder—actually cook up his meal from scratch.

After mangling what was supposed to have been two fried eggs over easy, he began scrambling them while monitoring the second pan, which contained link sausages that were cooking at way too high a temperature. The pan spit out some volcanic sausage grease onto his exposed arm and he jumped back, pulling the egg pan with him, unable to prevent its noisy crash onto the tile at his feet.

"You bitch!!!!" he screamed out, perhaps to Jimmy Dean himself, as he turned off the burners and began cleaning up the floor. He was even more outraged because those had been his last two eggs, and he'd deliberately put off buying any more groceries until he came back from the road. *If* he even went on the road, now.

The sun wasn't up, and his day was already starting off to be a pisser. He lit up a Kent, plopped into his black leather dining chair, and washed down eight burnt sausage links with a room-temperature Tab.

A squeaky wheel alerted Phoenix to the fact that her grandpa was making his way down the hall. Somehow, she'd managed to get her best sleep right there at the kitchen table, and she was a bit disoriented when she realized it was light outside.

"Mornin', sweetheart," Liam said as his chariot's wheels hit the linoleum.

"Mornin', Grandpa," she answered through a passionate yawn. "Wow…what time is it?"

"Little after 8:00," he said, noticing the remnants of her breakfast on the table. "Guess I missed the party, eh?" he added with a chuckle.

"Hm? Oh, no…couldn't sleep. That is, until I fell asleep here at the table." She groaned, getting up to clear the evidence. "I'll start coffee. Can I make you some waffles? Scrambled eggs?"

"Yes, that would be great, please."

"Which…?"

"Both, since you mentioned 'em both. If that's okay," he replied, wheeling through to the family room where he sank into his lazy throne and flipped on the set.

"Sure. Of course, Grandpa…I'll bring it into you," she said, as she set about making an extra-large pot of java. She hit the brew button and watched the agonizingly slow trickles begin their journey into the pot. She momentarily wished she could just fill a syringe with the magical caffeinated nectar and jab it straight into her jugular. *No creamer necessary.*

"Rodeo's done," Liam called out from the other room, breaking her train of thought.

"Yeah, I know. Curt told me last night," she replied, loudly enough to be heard over the TV. The local newscaster's voice was blaring into the kitchen, and Phoenix wished her grandpa would entertain the idea of some good hearing aids. She heard the story topic change from the rodeo to the local dead girl, and carried the carton of eggs with her as she stepped into the family room to follow the story.

"Authorities still have no suspect in the case and continue to seek the public's help with any information that might lead to an arrest and conviction in her murder. The sheriff's hotline number is at the bottom of your screen, and a reward is—" Phoenix muted the TV.

"What are you doing?" Liam blurted. "I was listening—"

"I know. Sorry, I just can't hear any more right now. I'm freaked out enough already, just thinking about tonight," she confessed, handing him back the remote. "Gotta make waffles," she mumbled, retreating back to the kitchen.

Liam waited until he heard the telltale sounds of waffle batter being made before he unmuted the TV, which had now gone to commercial for a miracle vacuum cleaner attachment turned hair-cutting tool called the Flowbee.

"What the hell—?" he muttered to himself, as Phoenix appeared with a cup of coffee. She placed it on the ceramic coaster next to him.

"Want that for Christmas, Grandpa?" she asked, catching the sarcasm in her tone. It wasn't like her, and she hated sounding disrespectful. She made a note to attempt a nap later.

"Nah, I think I'm good," he replied, putting his fingers through his bedhead.

"Okay, then. Clear the decks; breakfast'll be up in five minutes," she said over her shoulder.

Phoenix was on her third cup of coffee as she watched her grandfather wipe up the last bit of his syrup with a perfectly constructed final bite of egg atop a tiny waffle raft. Mercifully, the TV was muted, and the silence was bliss. The caffeine was finally beginning to kick in, for which she was grateful, but that dashed any plans for an afternoon nap.

"I'll take that if you're done, Grandpa."

"Done, dear," he said, throwing back the last splash of his mango juice.

"Done done done?" she asked, seeking final-answer permission to grab his tray.

"Yes. Thank you, sweetheart."

"I'm going to clean things up and be back in a few, okay?"

"Sounds perfect. We can go over the plan again, fine-tune anything we need to," he said, reclining his chair.

"Okay," she agreed, disappearing into the kitchen. They'd gone over it pretty thoroughly already, she thought, but one more time couldn't hurt. He was right about there not being any room for error.

As she set his plate into the sink to soak off the Aunt Jemima sludge, she thought she heard a sound coming from the next room. She peeked through the doorway, and her suspicion was confirmed. Liam was snoring like a chainsaw.

With her grandpa crashed out, Phoenix decided to use the time constructively. She attended to both Angus's cage and his emotional needs, as she felt like she'd been ignoring him of late. After a twenty-minute *hello* fest, she took the three pooches for a short walk. She needed to budget time for laundry, plus she had to iron her one good blouse and her best jeans.

It was *showtime* tonight.

Curt and Wingnut had stopped by the shop on the way back from the rodeo, just long enough to put their radio on the charger and grab three fresh ones. It'd been after hours, and the rodeo gig was a done deal, so he was pretty sure nobody would miss them. Besides, the boss had given the crews a day off for their hard work.

Neither of them had gotten any sleep, as they'd had just enough time to stop by the apartment and take turns in the shower. Fresh clothes were their only luxury.

Wingnut, for a little guy, could eat like a horse—especially when someone else was paying for it. Curt ponied up for their chow at his roomie's establishment of choice: In-N-Out Burger. Curt went for the classic combo of a double cheeseburger, fries, and a chocolate shake, while Wingnut looked like he'd ordered his death row meal. Curt was pretty sure Wingnut had over-ordered, but was astonished as he watched his diminutive co-worker put it away.

As they sat in the F-150, Curt took his time, savoring every bite. It'd been a while, and it was a religious experience every time for him. "Dude, slow down a little. And don't get any in the truck, okay?"

"Mm, can't help it," dude answered, briefly coming up for air before chomping into his second double-double. He'd requested his burgers "animal style," which amounted to extra onions, extra spread, and probably extra heartburn. He shoveled a handful of fries into his mouth and attempted to talk over them, with mixed success. One of the fries escaped his grasp and fell out the truck window and onto the ground. He watched as a very well-fed sparrow snatched it immediately and hopped away with it. It was so fat it probably couldn't even achieve liftoff anymore.

"Man, if I came back as something else, y'know...in the next life, I mean, I think I'd be a sparrow," he said, pausing to actually chew his food.

"A sparrow," Curt said, shaking his head.

"Yeah… I mean, look at these little guys! It's French fry heaven, and an endless supply."

"Okay…all I can say is, be careful what you ask for, Wingnut," Curt replied, pausing to unclog his straw. Satisfied, he took a long pull on his milkshake.

"Yeah, I guess you're right," Wingnut said quietly, appreciative for the sage advice from his mentor. He consumed the remainder of his food in silence as he watched the birds and considered Curt's nugget of wisdom.

"You gonna want anything else?" Curt dared ask.

"Me? Nah, I'm good. Hey, thanks for treating."

"Least I could do, man. Hey, I appreciate your helping us out here. Not entirely sure how things will go, but we'll hope for the best. At least we have a plan, and we'll adjust if we have to."

"Ten four, skipper," Wingnut acknowledged, before noisily slurping the remnants of his shake, while Curt tossed their bags of trash into the receptacle. "What do we do now?"

"Now…now we wait."

He rewound the reel-to-reel tape again to the same spot he'd been rewinding it to for the past hour. It was just after the second guitar solo and the cue where the lead vocalist punched things up to the song's crescendo. It was a difficult vocal part, but she'd always been comfortable hitting the lofty high notes. She had a three-octave range, occupying that same rarified air as Heart's Ann Wilson in that regard and made it sound easy. It was anything but, however.

That's what was concerning the Pirate as he listened to it again. For about the fiftieth time. The musicians playing behind her were competent enough, sure, and they did have stage presence, but it was her voice that had launched Tramp Eez, and he was seething to think that she'd just walked away, especially when they were to head out on tour the following week.

Yes, he'd hunt her down. And, yes, he'd make her regret her decision. In fact, he'd make sure that tramp could never sing again—let alone breathe again—but that would have to wait.

He punched the remote button that tilted open the vent windows in his music room, then fired up a Kent. He took an extra-deep drag and watched the cigarette paper glow a bright orange, rapidly burning its way down the cancer stick. He exhaled his frustration, which rose in a billowy cloud toward the outside world, before slamming his fist down on the audio console.

"Bitch!!!"

It was useless, he determined, stabbing the stop button and killing the power to the board. He'd never be able to replace her. And if he did, it'd be all but impossible to get someone, with her range, who knew the songs well enough to jump in with both feet. And in a matter of days.

It was getting late in the afternoon, and he needed some air. And some food. The Italian joint in the village was having their Open Mic Night, but he held little hope for the level of talent that would be there. Still, you never knew. He made haste upstairs and grabbed his keys.

Curt had already dropped off Wingnut at his appointed post, having left him with one of the radios. He'd made sure to set the frequency on all the radios to the same, easy-to-remember channel and frequency of 12-25. Nobody forgets Christmas, he figured.

As he pulled into Liam's driveway, he saw that the Road Runner was still there. He had hoped it would be, as he wanted to see Phoenix again before the ball was set in motion.

As the F-150 came to a stop out front, Phoenix heard the car door slam, and she turned off the curling iron. She had done a pretty rockin' job on her hair, having spent over an hour on it, and with its multi-colored flaming curls, she'd be impossible to ignore. Her eye makeup was also dialed, as was her lip gloss. She ran to the front door as the bell rang and swung it open.

Curt's jaw fell to the ground. So did the radio, and he picked it up after catching his breath.

"Oh. My. Gawd…. I'm sorry, I think I must have the wrong house," he said, only half kidding. She looked every bit the rock star.

"Aren't you sweet!" She laughed, giving him a very appreciative kiss, followed by a peck on the cheek. "You might want to wipe that off," she said.

"Never!" he affirmed.

"Wanna come in? Grandpa Liam's almost ready. Just putting on his shoes, I think."

"Perfect. Yes, please," he said, stepping in next to her and turning to get another look. "How're you feeling? Are you up for—you know—tonight?"

"A nervous wreck, mostly, but ready as I'll ever be, I guess," she confessed as she shut the door behind them and led Curt to the family room. Liam was futzing with his laces and looked up to greet their guest.

"Hey, Curtis! And…wow!! Look at our girl!" he exclaimed as Phoenix sidled up next to him.

"Hi, Liam. Yeah, she looks amazing, doesn't she? And what's with *Curtis*? I haven't been called that since, like, the third grade," he added with a chuckle of embarrassment.

"Sorry, just came out that way. Forgive the ramblings of an old man," he replied, turning his attention to the ravishing Phoenix. "No second thoughts, lovey?" he asked as he cinched the final knot.

"Wouldn't do us much good now if I did, would it?" she replied, hoping her determination would supplant the underlying fear she still had.

"Guess you're right," Curt said. "Don't forget, we've got your back, and I think we've covered the bases."

Phoenix leaned over and gave him a long hug. "I know," she whispered in his ear. The long looks they gave each other once they broke the hug said more than words could have, each expressing their care for the other, and their mutual concerns.

"All right, good people," Liam said as he climbed out of his Venus fly trap of a recliner. "We can only postpone the inevitable so long, I suppose."

"Your grandpa and I will get a good parking place out front. And remember: if he tries anything, do not—under any circumstances—get into his car. Promise. We'll be there if you need us, or if anything goes south on us, okay?"

"Okay. Promise. I'm leaving in five minutes. Be right behind you," she said, looking them both in the eye as she patted the inside breast pocket of her denim jacket, which was occupied by the recording equipment. "Let's do this."

Five minutes into the drive, Curt's radio squawked to life. "Wingnut. That you?" he said, keying the button. A minute went by without a response. He hoped the range wasn't too great.

"Curt, this is Wingnut."

"Go ahead, buddy. What's up?"

"Yeah...uh, the Pirate's left the cove!"

"You're sure? You saw him leave?"

"That's affirmative. The package is in the open. Elvis has left the building. I saw him split a few minutes ago. Whacha want me to do?"

"Okay, well done. Um, listen, sit tight for another, say, twenty minutes. Make sure he didn't just step out for a quicky errand."

"So, wait twenty minutes? Then what?"

"Yes, don't do anything for twenty minutes, okay?" Curt hoped he didn't come across as condescending. It wasn't his intention. Wingnut was a reliable guy, as long as he was properly instructed, and he could trust him. "Then, I want you to go to the position we talked about, okay? Stay out of sight and let me know when you're there. If, for any reason, we lose contact on the radios, call me on my cell. Understood?"

"Your cell. Yep."

"Okay, buddy. Until you're better paid, thanks!"

"You're welcome," Wingnut responded. He appreciated being appreciated.

"Okay, Curt out."

A couple of minutes went by before Liam piped up: "Think he can handle it?"

Curt was on a straightaway piece of road, so he had the luxury of returning the look. "Yeah. I think so."

Phoenix strapped herself in for the drive, and for what she knew was to be a potentially dangerous encounter, the likes of which she could never have imagined.

She drove in silence for as long as she could, but her mind was racing in a thousand directions, none of them good. Her hands began to sweat against the wheel, and she couldn't bear it any longer. She nudged the cassette into the deck and turned up the volume in anticipation of whatever happened to serendipitously cue itself up.

As it turned out, the selection couldn't have matched her feelings any better.

The introductory acoustic guitar chords gave way to a much grungier sound as she immediately recognized the soulful song written by the Cranberries' Dolores O'Riordan. Phoenix knew the song had been written to describe the violence and suffering in the longstanding conflict between nationalists and unionists in Northern Ireland, and in memory of two young boys who'd been killed in an IRA bombing in England. Phoenix also remembered an interview where O'Riordan had described the song as "our cry against man's inhumanity to man, inhumanity to child."

For the purposes of Phoenix's inner struggle, and the pain she'd already endured at the hands of such an inhumane monster, she made the song her own and belted it out with reckless abandon, tapping into Dolores's signature keening and all of the requisite passion and horrible pain it was written to express. She indeed felt like she was in a "Zombie"-like state.

Another head hangs lowly
Child is slowly taken
And the violence, caused such silence
Who are we mistaken?

But you see, it's not me
It's not my family
In your head, in your head, they are fighting
With their tanks, and their bombs
And their bombs, and their guns
In your head, in your head they are crying

In your head, in your head
Zombie, zombie, zombie-ie-ie
What's in your head, in your head
Zombie, zombie, zombie-ie-ie, oh

Du, du, du, du
Du, du, du, du
Du, du, du, du
Du, du, du, du

Another mother's breaking
Heart is taking over
When the violence causes silence
We must be mistaken

It's the same old theme
Since nineteen-sixteen
In your head, in your head, they're still fighting
With their tanks, and their bombs
And their bombs, and their guns
In your head, in your head, they are dying

In your head, in your head
Zombie, zombie, zombie-ie-ie
What's in your head, in your head
Zombie, zombie, zombie-ie-ie
Oh oh oh oh oh oh oh, ay, oh, ya ya

Phoenix saw the parking lot on her left as the song wound down, its bass guitar, distorted guitar and percussion outro timing perfectly as she pulled up front and killed the engine.

She sat there with her head hung low and eyes closed for several minutes, processing everything. Thoughts went to her mother, to her sister, to a despicable evil who had robbed her of both.

And like a breaker had been flicked on, she raised her head, reopened her eyes, felt her breast pocket for the presence of her recording equipment, and stared at the game face looking back from the rearview.

It was showtime.

JAFE DANBURY

From their vantage point in Curt's truck, across the smallish parking lot out front, Curt and Liam had watched Phoenix pull up and seen her take pause as she psyched herself up to go inside the restaurant. The two men exchanged concerned looks, and Curt glanced at his watch but neither said a word. They just watched as the door closed behind her.

Even though Wingnut had reported the Pirate having left his home a half hour before, there had been no sign of him arriving at this location yet. The entire team understood that it was going to be a waiting game, with no guarantees that he'd even show up, but it was their best shot, and they'd have to exercise the same level of stealth—and patience—that a nature photographer would have in the wild.

A very polite young hostess with very teased hair and a painted-on black dress showed Phoenix to a small table with two chairs, about twenty feet from the corner makeshift stage where a local cover band was setting up their gear. She'd wanted to get there early enough to select her table, and her timing had been good as a few others were starting to dribble in.

She could spot the difference between the regular diner/spectators and those who were probably planning to partake in the open mic talent night. She wondered if she, too, stood out like a sore thumb in that regard, but she didn't care. She was singularly focused.

An exceedingly shy busboy poured some ice water into her glass, which she immediately consumed. Her mouth was feeling dry, and her pits were starting to perspire. She didn't really have the option to remove her denim jacket as it held her gear, so she prayed the air conditioning would kick in.

Scanning the room slowly and discreetly, she caught no sight of her adversary, but did get some lascivious stares from a couple of older men leering from their tables, both of whom got called out by their significant others' stink-eye reactions. It was still early, so she tried to distract herself by checking out the band.

It was a small corner that had been allotted them—only about eight feet deep by ten feet wide, she guesstimated. By the time the drums were set up, and a couple of amps, it left very little room for the three musicians. The drummer, a guitarist, and a bass player. *No keyboards. Bummer.* Her song choices would be limited. Moments later, another guy came in from the back door, however, carrying a medium-sized KORG keyboard. *Cool!* There was a retro-looking Shure microphone affixed to a stand out front. It was the "Elvis" mic they'd be using.

Another scan of the room and a refill of water. Her stomach started to growl, but the last thing she could think about was food right now. Probably because it felt like a million monarch butterflies were competing for space in her stomach.

She felt her breast pocket nervously, confirming the presence of her equipment. She reapplied her lip gloss, took a deep breath, and tried to calm her nerves. The place was starting to get busier now, and there was no turning back.

The guitarist was putting a stack of index cards and several pens on the tiny round table next to the stage. The sign taped to a wicker basket read:

PLEASE PLACE SONG
REQUESTS HERE.
3 REQUESTS MAX, PLEASE!

That seemed fair enough, she thought, and probably better than just having a clipboard where everyone could see what you were hoping to sing. Since nobody else had moved yet, she casually walked up to the table and grabbed a card and a pen. She smiled at each of the band guys, hoping they might consider at least one of her requests. They each tracked her back to her table, exchanging smiles.

As Phoenix began writing down some song options she prayed the band might know, a college-aged black girl with an impressive Diana Ross-esque perm approached, carrying a menu.

"Good evening," she said, smiling warmly. "My name's Diana, and I'll be your server this evening."

Phoenix almost choked on her water when she mentioned her name, because her 'fro was indeed *supreme.* "Thank you," she replied, returning the smile.

"Will there be anyone joining you for dinner…or will it just be you tonight?" she inquired, handing her the menu.

"Um, well, I'm kind of waiting for someone…not sure when they might show…or if, but if you could leave a second menu, that would be great. Thank you," she managed. Man, she hadn't planned for that question.

"Of course. Can I get you anything from the bar while you wait?"

"Um. Okay, this might be a weird request," she said, before lowering her voice to a whisper, "but do you have any Sunny D?"

"I'll have to check on that. Not a lot of requests, to be honest, but I'll be back in a moment. Excuse me." And she was off.

The tables were just about all taken now, and the modest dining room was feeling much more…intimate. For a small strip mall Italian place, this establishment had done their level best to create a cozy atmosphere with a few Italian-themed embellishments like plastic grape clusters, several of those empty straw-woven wrapped Chianti bottles, the requisite Leaning Tower of Pisa statuette, and a freestanding, painted menu board with a plump little Italian chef dude on it advertising the specials.

She finished scribbling her three songs on the card, for what it was worth, and dropped it in the basket on the way to the front entrance, where she peeked out the door and eventually made eye contact with Curt. She scrunched her shoulders and made one of those *Who knows?* gestures with her hands, before returning inside.

"I don't know," Curt said to Liam.

"Just give it a little more time," Liam said, as he craned his neck to scour the parking lot again. "If you had any idea how many hundreds of hours I've sat in cars doing stakeouts, you'd know what I'm talking about. That's where I got my hemorrhoids from, those stakeouts. We wait. We need to give it another hour, at least, before we think about pulling the plug on this."

"If you say so. I'll defer to your experience, sir."

"And enough with the *sir* crap. Okay. It's just Liam. We're just two people, here for the same reason...to protect the girl we love."

The girl we love.

This rendered Curt speechless, and he pretended not to hear that last part, but he couldn't help wondering if the feelings he was developing for Phoenix were that outwardly obvious. He pretended to futz with his walkie-talkie in an attempt to be convincing.

Multiple glasses of water were taking their toll on Phoenix, and she'd discovered her bladder's limitations. She had to pee. She gestured to Diana on the way to the restroom and let her know she'd be right back.

The women's room was empty, and she slipped into its single stall. There was barely enough room to turn around once you finished your business, and she took a moment to study the paper towel dispenser as she dried her hands. There was also an air hand dryer, but those blew.

As she exited the restroom, she could hear a microphone crackle to life and someone announcing the first "act" for the Open Mic Night. She hurried back to her table, just as Diana was setting down her glass of Sunny D. "Awesome. Thanks so much!"

"Let's give a warm welcome to—" the guitarist paused to look at the index card before continuing. "Please put your hands together for Ronnie!" he said, handing her the mic before assuming his position a scant two feet away.

Ronnie looked to be in her early forties, or maybe thirties but with high mileage, Phoenix thought. She was dressed in an ill-advised, mid-thigh spandex dress, that wasn't at all forgiving. Phoenix had to give her points for bravery, however, as the keyboard player began the opening chords to Streisand's "The Way We Were."

As the intro segued into the vocal, Ronnie began humming just a bit off tune, but not alarmingly so. The singing that followed, however, sounded like someone was torturing a cat. *Oh, my goodness!* The guitarist nodded his encouragement, hoping they'd all make it through the next four minutes without being pelted by dinner rolls, or tossed out into the parking lot.

Phoenix nursed her beverage and tried to offer up a smile when the singer made eye contact with her. She was suddenly feeling just a little less nervous about her own upcoming performance—that was, if it even happened. Still no sign of the creeper.

Several other acts of similar quality were to follow, with perhaps the highlight being a surprisingly good rendition of Metallica's "Enter Sandman" by a twenty-something local kid named Doug. The band trimmed the first minute of the intro before launching into the power chords and vocals. *No friggin' way!* Phoenix began playfully bobbing her head. *Music to choke on your pasta by.*

The band, especially the guitarist, seemed to enjoy this one in particular, as it was in their normal set list, and it gave them an opportunity to rock it. They ended up trimming another minute off the outro, making it a three-minute burner instead of a five-and-a-half-minute headbanger, much to the approval of several older diners. The crowd showed him some love as he returned to his seat.

"Please give it up for...Doug, everybody! Whoo-hoo!" the bass player announced, looking over to the guitarist who was in charge of picking the index cards. He handed him one.

Part of her was beginning to give up hope. She wasn't wearing a watch, but she guessed she'd probably been there for an hour and a half, with no sight of the Awful Man.

Maybe he didn't take the bait. Maybe he's already split town. Maybe our only shot is not happening. Her train of defeatist thought was interrupted by an announcement from the stage.

"Okay…seems we have time for one more performer before we take a short break, so next up is…Phoenix!"

"Oh, gawd…" she muttered to herself. "Really?"

"Where's Phoenix?" he said, scanning the room. When she stood, he added, "There she is! Come on up, Phoenix. Don't be shy!"

It wasn't shyness she was feeling, it was…disappointment. The whole reason she'd come here, and what the "team" had thought to be their best shot, was centered on the hope that a certain party might be in attendance. And it appeared he wouldn't be joining the gig. She almost waved off the invitation to sing, but figured she was already there, so what the hell.

The diners applauded as Phoenix approached the microphone. She turned to the band guys and they told her which of her three requested songs they'd be doing. The keyboard player, the newest addition to the band, had lobbied for it because he could nail the synth stuff. The rest of the guys were totally comfortable with it as well, as they'd already incorporated it into their set. *Bitchin'!*

She cleared her throat and the band launched right into the twenty-second synth/percussion intro immediately followed by the song's trademark power chords. *This is gonna be fun! Too bad the Awful Man isn't here to see it.*

Phoenix knew the song by heart, so she jumped in with both feet, taking the original John Schlitt vocal part to a new level, nudging it just a tad higher and with perfect pitch. It was an inspired song choice considering her vocal range, and the band guys all exchanged approving looks as she went for it. When they joined in with background vocals, the Head East experience was complete and utterly convincing.

After another synth break, as she was about to cruise into the second verse, she chanced a look out to her small audience. Their reaction indicated one hundred percent approval, with many smiles and bobbing heads. When two couples got up from their tables to dance, she knew she had them.

There was also a new patron, one she hadn't seen previously, standing by himself at the bar. He was wearing sunglasses and was dressed in all-black. He seemed to be studying her closely, though not expressing any emotion. She couldn't see an eyepatch, as he had on his wraparound shades, but his roughhewn face provided her all the confirmation she needed. That and the discernible pure evil vibe he radiated. *He must've come in the rear door! Shit!*

The blizzard of chill that came with seeing him momentarily threw her off her game, but she quickly recovered, kicking it up a notch as she channeled the lovechild of John Schlitt and Ann Wilson. The Pirate was here. And this was her only shot. She was going to take no prisoners.

> *Did you have any bad dreams? Did you break any glass?*
> *Would you be my companion? Is there even a chance?*
> *You've been talking in circles. Since I've been able to cry.*
> *There's never been any reason. For never telling me why, yeah, yeah.*
> *Save my life I'm goin' down for the last time...*

The effect was potent, and her delivery nothing short of incendiary. Phoenix more than delivered on the entire performance, and as she and the band hit the final crescendo five minutes later, it was the stuff of goosebumps.

Save my life, I'm goin' down—for—the—last—time....

It was a mic-drop moment, but it was the "Elvis" mic and too nice for that. An eruption of applause and whistles told her that it was the performance of the evening to beat. After an enthusiastic offer by the guitarist for her to join their band, for reals, she told them she'd think about it and thanked them all as she returned to her seat. She avoided any looks toward the bar area as she chugged a glass of water and buried her head in the menu.

"We're going to take a short break and will be back with more local open mic talent, so please stick around!" the guitarist announced. With that, the band left the stage area and gathered at the small bar.

The dining room got appreciably quieter, with most of the loudest sounds being those of low-level restaurant chatter and utensils shoveling pasta from plates. Phoenix was grateful for the break, as she needed to assess if the recording equipment would even have a chance to pick up speaking voices if given the chance. She was sure that it would, provided that the band wasn't performing during a hypothetical conversation.

Phoenix steeled herself for what might possibly become a literal *speak of the devil* moment.

The tables were indeed all occupied now, with the lone available seat being across from Phoenix at her small table. The devil whispered to a server and she nodded. He began his approach, like a rattler, sidewinding his way over to join her.

Even with her eyes fervently glued to her menu, Phoenix's peripheral vision couldn't ignore the pair of black cowboy boots as they came to a stop two feet away. She dug deep as she tried to ignore his presence, but the sound of his voice elicited a deep chill.

"Sorry to disturb you, but it seems like we've crossed paths once again," he said, his twisted smile trying to tamp down any sense of menace and replace it with that of a cool operator accustomed to getting what he wanted.

"I'm sorry?" Phoenix replied, looking up at him.

He studied her a moment longer, trying to decide if she was indeed the same girl who'd been walking her dogs outside his home. She'd worn a ballcap, but it was her, he was sure of it now. "Waiting for your husband, are you?" he said, noticing no ring on her finger.

"My husband? Mm, no…no. There is no husband," she replied, embarrassed to not have prepared for that either.

"Ah, then perhaps you're waiting for a friend then," he said. "I'm sorry to have bothered you, Miss…"

"Phoenix," she blurted out almost too quickly, not wanting him to walk away, even though her survival instinct wanted nothing more than to avoid any contact with the beast.

"It's no problem, actually. My friend…she didn't show up after all," she said, tapping into a shy smile. Mentioning a "she" friend hopefully indicated there was no significant other.

"Phoenix…" he repeated, absorbing the unusual name. "Phoenix. I like that," he said, trying on a bit of charm, like it was a new jacket. She saw straight through it. "So, Phoenix," he continued, looking around at the full dining room. "There's a very good turn-out tonight, and I arrived just a bit late…but…perhaps I arrived just in time. I was wondering if you might consider letting me join you at your table for a meal and maybe some conversation if you see fit. I'd be happy to pay for your meal if you'd show me this kindness."

A killer with manners!

She had to plant the hook now, or risk losing this prize fish. She pretended to scratch herself under her jacket, activating the recorder's buttons before she answered. "Hey, why not? Please." She gestured to the available chair.

"Very kind of you, thank you," he said as he took care not to drag the chair out too noisily. "Have you eaten here before, Phoenix?" he asked, settling in and motioning for the server's attention.

"No, actually. First timer. Here for the Open Mic thing," she confessed truthfully. "It's been…interesting, so far." She giggled for effect. She was secretly hoping not to lose bladder control with his arrival. As he'd entered from an unseen rear door—a contingency they hadn't planned for—she was reasonably sure her team hadn't become aware of his presence. *Shit.*

"I've been to a couple of these things and, to use your word, they are often *interesting* at best," he said, looking up as Diana arrived with a smile and a cocktail menu.

"Can I get you started with a drink, sir?"

"Yes, please. Um, I'd like one of your Tequila Mockingbirds, well shaken. What would the lady like?"

"Seriously, there's a drink called a tequila mockingbird?" she said with a chuckle. "Never heard of that one but I love the name. What's in it?"

"If you like watermelon, you'll love it. It's basically a spicy margarita, with watermelon and a little jalapeño for kick; we add a little white agave, some fresh lime juice, and some agave syrup, and… *voila!* Tequila mockingbird!" the server explained with the requisite enthusiasm to make the sale. It was a signature drink, and she got a small commission on every one of these sold here.

"Hey, sounds good. Just, uh, easy on the tequila on mine, please. Not much of a drinker," she confided. The Awful Man took note.

"You got it!" she said, scribbling on her small pad. "And have you had time to look at the menu?" she asked them both, but she directed her look to Phoenix.

"Oh, wow…what might you recommend for a vegetarian?"

"We have a nice pasta Alfredo, a Puttanesca spaghetti, and a Margherita pizza. All good choices."

"The pizza, please."

"Perfect," she said, scribbling again. "And you, sir?"

"I don't need to look at the menu. Bring me your veal, with a side of that pasta. Not the Alfredo, the other one. Thank you," he said thrusting the menu back at her more aggressively than intended.

"I'll get those started for you and be right back with your mockingbirds."

"Before we were interrupted, I meant to tell you how much I enjoyed your performance."

Phoenix took a small sip of her Sunny D and visualized the wheels turning the tiny microcassette buried in her breast pocket. It served to remind her that she'd need to initiate a line of questioning soon, before the music resumed.

"You're too kind. Thank you. It was…fun!"

"Have you ever considered doing this professionally?"

"What do you mean?" she replied.

"Professionally. I mean, beyond the cheesy strip mall Italian restaurant Open Mic night stuff. Like with a much bigger audience. Recording, touring even. Have you ever given it some thought?"

"Me?" she responded with a chuckle. "I…I don't know. I don't have any connections."

He wasn't going to let her off that easy, and he still had a big slot to fill. One that she might just be perfect for. "Maybe you do, and just don't know it yet," he said a bit cryptically.

"What do you mean? You know somebody in the biz?" she said, turning on the requisite naïveté.

"I don't just *know* somebody…I *am* somebody. I produce and manage some of the biggest names in music, Phoenix, and I have to say, you've got a great deal of talent. I think I could help you develop that. Get you out there." He'd dangled the carrot, and he'd circle back during the meal.

"Gosh…wow," she said, smiling back with the reaction she figured he'd want.

He was staring at her now, studying her face, the tiny cleft in her chin, the freckles, and mostly her fireball mane of hair. She suddenly felt like she was getting an x-ray by some creepy doctor. This threw her a bit, and she had to regroup. Thankfully, he opened things up.

"So, Phoenix… As I mentioned the other day, out on the road, you look…somehow…familiar to me. Are you sure we haven't met somewhere else?"

"Hm, I don't know. Have we? I think I would've remembered you."

"I get that a lot," he joked, then leaned in a little closer, his obscured eyes boring a hole in her. He was still seeking an answer to his puzzle. "I'm almost sure of it, but I can't exactly place it."

"I guess it depends."

"On?"

"Have you ever been to Arizona?" she probed. It seemed like an innocent enough question.

"Arizona!" he said, shaking his head. He seemed amused by her query. "Arizona… Oh, I've been to Arizona, all right. I'm from there originally but haven't been back there in a very long time."

"Really? Wow. How long ago did you leave there?" she asked, trying to chisel away delicately.

"If I had to guess, I'd say probably twenty-five years, give or take. Like I said, a long time ago."

"I see. Any family back there?"

"Not any longer," he said, looking away as he answered. Just as quickly, he returned his gaze to her. "No…nothing holding me back there," he added, his voice slightly trailing off.

"Well, that's where I'm from. But if you haven't been there in…what'd you say? Twenty-five years? That's how old I am, so we wouldn't have met, I'm afraid."

The drinks arrived, offering a brief distraction. "Cheers, Phoenix."

"Mm, Cheers—" She caught herself. She'd almost said his name, and he hadn't yet introduced himself.

"Forgive me. Name's Roger. Always hated the name, but there it is."

"Cheers, Roger," she offered, taking a sip of the watermelon concoction. "Oh. My. Goodness."

"Good, right?"

The Pirate didn't seem to think much about the timeline, and there had been no red flags hoisted yet, Phoenix thought. She couldn't let the topic end there just yet, so she forged ahead with some things she'd rehearsed earlier.

"Whereabouts did you live in Arizona?" she ventured. Maybe she could establish some locales and a timeline. Eliminate some alibis, even.

"Oh, here and there, really. Phoenix, Gilbert...let's see...Glendale, Peoria...bounced around a bit. You seem interested in the area, or are you just taking an interest in me?" he asked.

Ewwwwww...

"Yeah. Like I said, I'm from there. Just making conversation," she responded before blurting out the next part. "Ever been to Cave Creek?"

He half-smiled, and she wasn't sure if she'd hit a nerve or if he was just tiring of the questions. "Cave Creek? Huh...let me think. Yeah, I believe I've been to Cave Creek."

"Remember when?"

He shook his head before answering. "Aren't you just the inquisitive one," he said, playing along, but carefully. "Yeah, I do remember when. Just before I left for California. Christmas time, actually, so that'd make it probably 1978, maybe '79. Nine, I think," he declared, arriving at his choice.

"Nice." *Really, Phoenix? That's the best retort you've got? C'mon!*

"Yeah, *nice*," he said under his breath.

Their entrees arrived quicker than she'd imagined, and Diana went about placing their plates before them. "The Margherita pizza, and the veal, with a side of puttanesca."

"Thank you," Phoenix said.

Her tablemate studied his plate before signing off on it. "Okay. Yes, thank you," he said, dismissing her. He took a sip of his cocktail and realized he hadn't had a chance to use the facilities.

"I'll be right back, if you'll excuse me," he said, not waiting for an answer as he pushed in his chair and walked off.

Diana was back seconds later with a white bowl of grated cheese and a spoon. "Fresh Parmesan for you this evening?" she asked Phoenix.

"Yes, please!" she responded enthusiastically. She loved the stuff and had been hoping it would be offered. She watched as two generous spoonfuls of the fine powder settled onto her woodfired pizza. "Perfect."

"And the gentleman? Would he be taking any on his?"

"Um, no. I think not. Thank you."

"You're very welcome," Diana said, dashing off.

It so figures this asshole would order the veal. Just then she felt something she'd forgotten about in her side jacket pocket. Pulling it out, she discovered it was the baggy of foot shavings she'd collected, and meant to discard, back in Pacific Grove when she'd first arrived. *What better topping for this friggin'asshole's veal than a dash of ground calluses ala Phoenix?* She quickly opened the baggie's seal and sprinkled a generous snowy layer onto his meal, then stuffed the resealed bag where she'd found it. A wry smile formed on her face.

A moment later, he returned, surveying his dish. "What's with the damn cheese?"

"Oh, sorry," Phoenix replied. "I just assumed…blame it on me."

He furrowed his brow, processing his level of discontent, then looked up from his dish. "No problem," he said, letting go of his annoyance and offering his version of a smile again.

"Bon appétit!" she said, thankful that he hadn't jumped across the table and plunged a fork into her throat in a fit of rage. They ate quietly for several minutes, each taking delight in their food. Phoenix took added delight in watching every bite of dead epidermal dust the clueless psycho consumed. *Hope he gets a raging case of athlete's throat.* He was wolfing it down like he hadn't eaten in a week, and she still had more questions.

Her tequila mockingbird had plenty of tequila in it, she realized, even though she'd been gingerly sipping it. She wondered if the server had mistakenly ordered it as a double instead of light on the alcohol.

The band was finishing their beers at the bar and would soon be making their way back to their instruments. Phoenix knew it would soon be too loud to get any further recording done.

Roger set down his knife and fork as he savored the final piece of extremely tender veal. He barely even had to chew it, and Phoenix wondered why anybody had to order such a cruelly harvested foodstuff. *It goes against everything holy. But then, so does he.*

"You mind?" he said, pulling out his pack of Kents. "If so, I'll just duck outside."

She did mind, but she didn't tell him so. She needed him to relax and maybe open up.

"Me? No, no...not at all. Please," she said, setting down the remainder of her crust. On the repulsive scale, she found smokers to be just one notch above veal eaters, and she abhorred smoke.

He stuck the cigarette in his mouth, reaching into his pocket and pulled out his failing Bic lighter, striking it several times unsuccessfully. "Damn thing," he muttered.

"Here, allow me," she said, seizing on the opportunity. She reached into her left pocket and pulled out a very weathered and blackened Zippo, courtesy of Liam's evidence bag.

"Thank—" he managed, leaning in to oblige her offer, before getting a closer look at the lighter. It was charred, but the skull and crossbones embellishment remained recognizable. Phoenix picked up on his "tell" when his cigarette dipped slightly, involuntarily, as it dangled a little looser from his lips.

She turned the wheel with her thumb, producing a perfect flame on its first attempt. Liam had worked on rebuilding it, and she'd practiced with it until she was comfortable. The flame found the end of the cancer stick and she watched the tobacco begin to ignite, as its glow reflected in his sunglasses. His look went from the lighter to Phoenix's eyes as he leaned back and took a long drag.

"Interesting lighter you have there, Phoenix. Didn't figure you for a smoker. Not good for your health, you know. Saved the day there, didn't you?" he said, pulling off his sunglasses for the first time. There, in all its glory, was the patch he was famous for.

"Mm, not a smoker. Just something I found," she said coolly. She prayed that the recorder was getting every minute of this.

"I see," he said, evaluating the situation. Her earlier line of questioning was starting to call attention to itself. Phoenix observed him look around, as if checking to see if law enforcement were around.

She said nothing as she watched him, all leaned back in his chair, taking long drags on his grit, his wheels seemingly turning in a new direction now. The cat that ate the canary.

The Pirate held the smoke deep in his lungs as he regarded his tablemate. His opponent. His sparring partner. His...*set-up?* He exhaled a cloud in her direction, then leaned in closer. His breath smelled of veal, dead skin, and smoke. "What did you say your last name was, Phoenix?"

"I didn't. But, since you ask, it's—well, *was*—McGinn. Irish," she said almost defiantly as she flicked her red hair with her hand for emphasis. "Why do you ask? Sound familiar, maybe?"

He zeroed on the dimple in her chin again, only now remembering the last—and only—time he'd seen hair as flaming red as hers. He thought about the timeline she'd established, and the query about Cave Creek. He was staring at the face of a ghost. It was impossible....

She'd aborted it!

"I know what you're probably thinking," she dared. "How the hell? When you had her get an abortion. Am I close?" she added, thankful to be in a public place during this exchange. Otherwise, all bets were off.

Curiosity was killing this cat. He pulled out another cigarette and lit it with the glowing butt of his first. "Your mother."

"What about my mother?"

"I'm sure she had a name."

"You tell me. Maybe you two might've even known each other, back in Cave Creek, even. Small world 'n' all."

He verbalized his assessment of the situation. "Fucking impossible. Im-*possible.*"

"Oh? How's that? Care to expand on your Neanderthalic response there?" Her feisty side was coming out, and she had to remember she had a cobra by the tail. But she was in it to win it.

"Rose?"

"Rose," she parroted. "What about her?"

"She never had a child," he muttered, but resolutely.

"Never's a long time, you know. How would you know that––I'm sorry, what did you say her name was...*Rose?* How would you know that...Rose...never had a child? You said yourself you left Arizona some twenty-five years ago. Christmas, I think you said. So, what's to say that this person went childless for the rest of her days? Answer me that."

The bass player was starting to tune up and the drummer was taking his place on the throne. They'd be starting up in a couple of minutes, and then any hopes of continuing this conversation would be kaput.

"Because, if you have to know, Rose—that was indeed her name—aborted her child. Before she died."

"Oh, I'm sorry for your loss. I didn't know."

"Don't you be a smartass with me, Phoenix—if that's even your real name. How do I know your name's not...Ginger...or fucking Bambi? Regardless, you seem way too interested in my past, and in somebody you obviously didn't even know. You're just grasping at straws, and this was before your time, so let's leave it at that."

"You're right about one thing: I really don't know much about Rose, and I'll tell you why. Because—and you're right about *another* thing: she died. Rose, Rose McGinn to be exact was..." She paused for effect, or perhaps for an opportune drum roll from the band.

"Rose was my mother, you son of a bitch!" she exclaimed, but in a hushed tone reserved for him.

His mouth dropped at this truth nugget, but he didn't have a response on deck.

"And, believe it or not, you're right about a *third* thing. You ready? Yep, she did have an abortion! Wow, you got almost a perfect score on the exam, dickhead! Just one thing you probably weren't expecting to hear, but I'm gonna lay it on you anyway: *There were twins! Both girls. I...somehow...survived!!*" She had to laugh at the last part, not because it was funny, but because his expression was priceless.

"Who would believe you? You think you're so smart. Let me tell you a thing or two about being smart, Phoenix," he hissed, barely above a whisper. "You think I would've gotten this far if I wasn't smarter than my competition? Smarter, stronger than my adversaries? Huh? Do you?"

She shrugged.

"I thought not. Which brings me to my next question. If you think you're smarter than me—and believe me, you're not—what are you insinuating? What do you think you could prove? So, you found an old cigarette lighter. Big deal. It means nothing. Look at you. Bimbo redhead with a chip, but nothing to back up her absurd claims. You can't prove anything."

"Rose's last words. I heard them. While I watched you strangle her, in our kitchen, on Christmas Eve, and right before you set her, and our fucking house, on fire. I heard her. She screamed, '*Offermann!!*'—which, last time I checked, just happens to be *your* last name, you bastard."

This threw him. He flashed back to that memory, the vision of Rose cutting up some chicken when he'd slipped in the screen door. The Christmas tree, the music, the gifts. There had been someone else, and he'd been in too much of a hurry to check further.

"You..."

"Yeah…me. *Surprise!!!*"

She was definitely feeling an extra buzz kick in. Had he slipped something into her drink when she wasn't aware? All she knew was she had to pee.

"Hold that thought, 'kay. I've got to use the little girls' room. Be right back," she said, as she left him at the table, locking the restroom door behind her. Her knees almost gave way entirely. She pulled the recorder from her pocket and saw the wheels had indeed been turning all this time. She hit the stop button and ejected the tiny-but-mighty microcassette.

Phoenix was definitely starting to spin, and she was almost certain now that it wasn't just from the tequila mockingbird. He'd drugged her. *Shit!* She had to act fast, while she still had her faculties, and she pulled one of Liam's small evidence baggies from her pocket and stuffed the tape into it. She sealed it, then, per his instructions, jimmied the paper towel dispenser's lock with a nail file until it popped open.

She tried not to panic but her hands were shaking. She couldn't help feeling like Michael Corleone, desperately feeling for the pistol that was supposed to be taped behind the toilet in that restaurant scene from *The Godfather*.

She recovered enough to securely affix the envelope containing the tape to the inside of the dispenser door with two strips of duct tape he'd given her, then slammed it tight.

The evidence was there, and secure for now. Her vision was getting blurry, and even splashing cold water onto her face had no effect.

As Phoenix exited the restroom, the Pirate emerged from around the corner. He'd already settled the tab with a pile of twenties, and he surprised her when he grabbed her firmly by the elbow.

"How 'bout we go outside and get some air, shall we?" he ordered, not needing permission. Phoenix was beginning to feel more panicky and less in control by the second, and her voice was caught in her throat. She flashed back to the last thing Curt had emphatically made her promise, about getting into his car, but her senses and her muscles were betraying her, and she hated herself for it.

His car was precisely where the Pirate was leading her, and he'd parked behind a liquor store's Dumpster, about a hundred yards away from the rear door, so as not to be noticed. She was walking the friggin' plank now, and his grip had tightened on her arm. Bruises were the least of her worries, as she suddenly realized what the other young girl must've felt before she was murdered and cast aside, like so much rubbish on the side of the road. *Is this how it ends? After all this?*

She was powerless to affect the outcome now and she knew it. It was out of her hands. The Pirate opened the passenger door of the Corvette and stuffed Phoenix inside without a trace of resistance. He waited until after he'd climbed behind the wheel and, making sure they hadn't been noticed, backhanded her sharply across the mouth before exiting the alley.

Curt had reached his wit's end. He'd had enough of this stakeout, and he yanked on his door handle, stepping out of the truck. He shut the door and leaned in the open window, looking at Liam with resolve.

"Sorry, but this is bullshit. We've waited long enough, Liam. I'm going to check on her. Should've an hour ago. This was all for nothing."

Liam knew he was right, yet his professional training had dictated their need for patience and stealth. It was time to pull the plug at this point. "I know. Looks like he's a no-show. Okay. Go get her, and we'll all go back to my place and debrief."

"Be right back," he affirmed and marched across the parking lot. He disappeared inside. Liam rubbed his eyes. It'd been a long day, and it seemed that their hopes were now dashed. He didn't have anything cued up as a viable Plan B, and he let out a defeated sigh.

Seconds later, Curt flew out of the restaurant's door and sprinted back to the truck. His face was full of panic.

"What's wrong?!" Liam demanded.

"She's fucking gone! She's with him! He fucking took her—out a back door, off the alley!" he screamed. His eyes were wide with panic, fear, regret and anger as he paced outside the truck for a few seconds more.

"Good God, how could we have—?!" he managed, before Curt cut him off.

"Do me a favor, Liam. Wait here, okay?"

"What're you—"

"Here, take these," he said, tossing Liam the truck keys. Her car was faster. "Turn on the heat, lock the doors, I—I've—gotta go find her!!" he added, pulling out the spare Road Runner key Phoenix had given him. He grabbed his walkie off the seat and backed away from the truck and towards the orange Plymouth. "I'm gonna get her back, Liam! I'm gonna go get our girl!"

"I'm gonna call the—"

"No! No cops! Not yet!" Curt barked, clearly reading his mind. "You have my cell number if you hear anything, okay? You good?" He waited a split second for Liam's nod of affirmation before flashing a thumbs-up and sprinting for the car.

It cost Curt a few precious seconds to slide the seat back, about a foot, and do a quick tweak of the mirrors. He'd forgotten just how tiny she was. The Road Runner fired up with authority and, seconds later, screamed out of the lot, leaving a trail of burnt rubber in its path.

As the screech of the tires faded, Liam sent up a most earnest prayer.

"Dear Jesus, please bring back our precious girl."

Ten minutes went by without an update, an eternity to Liam. He'd also been sitting on his ass for hours and needed to pee like a racehorse, or risk soiling Curt's passenger seat. He locked the car and proceeded to the restaurant.

As he entered, Liam winced at the volume and had to yell his query about the restroom to the hostess over the loud "music." Some very slovenly guy was absolutely butchering "Miss You" by The Stones. As he made his way past the bar to the facilities, Liam noticed the sole empty table, where he assumed Phoenix had been seated. He cursed himself as he went down the short hall and knocked on the men's restroom door. Nobody answered and he went inside and locked the door.

After relieving himself, he washed his hands, dried himself with a couple of paper towels and stepped back out to the hall. Just then, a woman was exiting the ladies' room and Liam smiled as she stepped past him. No one else was around, so he stepped inside and flipped the lock.

He retrieved the short flathead screwdriver from his pocket, inserted the blade into the dispenser's cheap lock and began jimmying the door. "Please, God," he prayed, as the mechanism sprung open. He was astonished to see that Phoenix had remembered to—and had somehow found a moment to—tape the evidence to the inside of the door. Just like he'd told her.

"Good girl," he whispered, pocketing the baggie with the microcassette.

Curt was quickly assessing the considerable horsepower at his disposal and, with a few exceptions where pedestrians were present, ignored the posted limits altogether as he attempted to gain ground on his adversary. The Pirate had the benefit of a head start, but not by more than a few minutes according to the server he'd asked. Curt was hoping his guess was correct as to where they'd be going, and he was thankful for his familiarity with these roads. He stabbed the preset on his phone, and it picked up on the first ring.

"Anything at your end, Liam?" he pleaded.

"No sightings of them, if that's what you mean, but I checked out the restroom. Phoenix left us the cassette, like we hoped for. I've listened to a few minutes already, and our girl did a kickass job of interrogating the bastard!"

"Good," Curt acknowledged, slightly distracted as he downshifted to negotiate a sharp corner. "Okay, Liam, are you okay?"

"Yeah, I'm good. Where are you?"

"I'm thinking he might be headed for his place, and I hope to God I'm right. Listen, maybe you should go inside, grab something to eat, see if anyone else has anything to add. The truck'll be fine, just lock it up. I'll let you know more soon, 'kay? Gotta go!"

Liam heard a dial tone before he could give a response, but took no offense considering the pressure of the moment. He locked up the truck and took Curt's suggestion. The last thing on his mind was food, but his blood sugar was tanking, so he'd power down a plate of pasta if the kitchen was still open. And hopefully all that Godforsaken racket was over with.

The Pirate downshifted the Corvette as they approached Ocean Avenue and hung a left, taking them westbound onto the narrow surface streets toward Carmel Bay. There'd be no time to enjoy a beach view tonight, not that he ever did. He couldn't be bothered.

He had to get through the Carmel Gate in order to hit 17-Mile Drive. He hoped there'd been no alerts put out, but he had his new piece in the glovebox, and it was locked and loaded if he needed to persuade anyone. This Smith & Wesson SW99 Luger was a marked upgrade to his old .38 revolver and offered much more firepower with its 16+1 capacity.

He glanced over at Phoenix, or what was left of her. With the exception of some blood coming from her lip, she might as well have been a five-foot tall stuffed bear he'd won at the dime toss event.

"Not so cocky now are you, Phoenix?" he asked mockingly. "What's the matter? Cat got your tongue?"

She had no response. She looked straight ahead through glassy eyes, and her limbs seemed useless.

"You couldn't just play nice tonight, could you? You know... enjoy a nice meal, some pleasant conversation, maybe even take that untapped talent of yours and actually do something with it...." His voice trailed off as he regretted how the evening had ended, and without securing his singer. "You had to stick your nose where it doesn't belong, didn't you? Phoenix...."

They were approaching the gate and there weren't any signs of a police presence. Lucky for them. Luckier for the gate guard, because he wouldn't have hesitated to put a bullet between his eyes. He slowed as the guard waved.

"Good evening, Mr. Offermann."

"Good evening, Tommy."

"Heading home, are ya?"

Of course, I'm heading home, numb nuts! "Sure am."

"Okay then, have a good evening!"

"You do the same," he said as he entered and proceeded west toward Pebble Beach. He did a quick threat assessment as he checked his mirrors but saw nobody. He knew his little additive to Phoenix's cocktail would be wearing off soon, and he had a few more very important questions to ask before he killed her.

Curt slammed his fist against the steering wheel as the Road Runner found a congested patch of traffic. He wasn't too far from the Carmel Gate, but he was at the mercy of some stop-and-go, hoping it'd open up.

"C'mon!!" he screamed to no one in particular. He picked up his walkie from the seat and was curious if he was within range. Worth a try. He keyed the button.

"Wingnut, Curt. Do you read?"

While he waited for a response, he watched a foursome of idiot teens in front of him exiting their Datsun 510, each jumping out of their doors and attempting a "Chinese fire drill," where they all switch seats before the cars started moving again. "Really?! Not the time, morons!!" he screamed. Moments later some walkie static got his attention. He keyed the button. "Wingnut, Curt. Is that you? Over."

"Roger, Curt. Wingnut here. Man, where ya been? Bring any food with you? I'm—"

"Wingnut! Listen very carefully," Curt interrupted. "No time for food, man. Hey, I'm pretty sure the Pirate's heading your way. He's got Phoenix with him, and she's in danger! Acknowledge, buddy!"

Traffic eased up for about ten seconds before coming to a stop again. "Dammit!"

"Curt, Wingnut. Yeah, I copy that. What you want me to do? Should I call the—?"

"No man, no. No cops. We don't know how he'd react to that, and we can't risk it while he has Phoenix. Please copy!"

"Copy!"

"Okay, look… I'm in a little traffic right now, but I'm headed your way. I'm in Phoenix's car. Keep your radio on, but not too loud in case you see the Corvette drive up. Stay out of sight and wait for my call. Got it? Over."

"Roger that. Standing by, over."

"Wingnut, I owe you, man. Thanks for hanging in. Keep your eyes peeled, and if you see anything, lemme know, okay?"

"Will do. Out."

"Holy mother of God…." Curt sighed to himself. He bit his lip, wiped his sweaty hands on his jeans, and cursed the City of

Carmel for not creating enough room to pass these clowns. Not that it would do any good, but he laid into the horn. *MEEP! MEEP! Really??*

Wingnut patiently stood by, watching and listening from his hidden post on the back side of the property. It was exceedingly quiet, with not much company, save the chirping crickets and a hooting owl off in a tree somewhere. He was the point man now. He didn't want to miss anything, and he hoped Curt would soon make contact again.

A few minutes later, he thought he heard the sound of an engine off in the distance. He pulled off his knit cap and let his radar dish-like ears flop into position to get a better read. People could laugh all they wanted, but he could hear a mouse fart from across the room with those things. This wasn't a standard engine, but more akin to what he imagined a Corvette might sound like. He crept along the side of the house to get a better look at the driveway, silencing the crickets in the process.

The throaty drone was getting louder, and it sounded very close now. Hiding behind a dense shrub, Wingnut trained his binoculars on the entrance, racking the focus back and forth until it came sharply into view. Headlight beams swung across the road as the Corvette made the turn and came to a brief stop at the junction of the driveway. They were here.

He brought the walkie up to his lips and keyed the talk switch. "Curt, Wingnut."

The response was immediate, and he lowered the volume to a bare minimum. "Go for Curt. What's going on, Wingnut?" the voice crackled through the electronics.

"Yo. The Corvette is just pulling in from the road, over."

"You're sure it's them?"

"It's a black Corvette, yeah. Just a second…" he replied, picking up the binocs for another look. "I can see the eye-patch dude and…I can see Phoenix in the passenger seat. She looks pretty out of it."

"Wingnut. Listen, stay out of sight. Wait till they get out, see if Phoenix looks okay. When they go inside, get back to your first position and radio me. I'm slowly chugging my way there, not quite to the Carmel Gate yet. Keep me posted, buddy!"

"Roger that. Wingnut out."

The Corvette pulled up to the front of the house and the engine was killed. The headlights folded to their down position and the driver's door opened. Wingnut watched through the long lenses and could clearly see the Pirate as he came around to the passenger side. As he opened the door, he turned Phoenix's face toward him for a better look. Wingnut could see a trickle of blood visible near her lip, and her eyes appeared glassy.

"Shit...." he whispered to himself.

The Pirate undid her seatbelt and swung Phoenix' legs out through the open door. With a less than gentle touch, he helped her to her feet and propped her up before pushing the car door closed with his boot. They made the very slow walk to the front door and after keying in a code on the pad, proceeded inside.

Wingnut quickly and quietly made his way back to the rear of the house as instructed. He could see the kitchen's light flick on, but it was otherwise windowless back there, with the exception of the basement area's vent windows, which remained dark. He'd had time to do his site survey before sundown and, since they were propped open, had already taken a peek through those. There was some cool stuff in there.

He keyed his radio and whispered. "Curt, Wingnut."

"Go, Wingnut. What're you seeing? She okay?"

"They went inside, but Phoenix couldn't walk all on her own. Looks like a busted lip maybe too. Otherwise, yeah, but she might be drugged or something. What do ya want me to do now?"

"Hold tight, buddy. Watch and listen. I'm almost at the Carmel Gate. Should be there soon. Wait for my word, Wing. Copy?"

"Copy. Standing by. Hurry, man...."

The Pirate plopped Phoenix down on a kitchen chair, just long enough for him to retrieve a can of Tab from the fridge. He popped the top and took a long swig. *What a friggin' night.*

Phoenix watched him as he downed the rest of the can. She licked her lip and tasted blood. Her limbs were still feeling quite numb, but there was a little bit of sensation returning. She sure as hell wasn't going to let him know that. She stared straight ahead, wondering if anyone had noticed her missing yet. If not, she was likely going to end up as another victim quite soon.

"C'mon," he barked, setting down the can and approaching her chair. "Get up, I want to show you something." He draped her right arm over his shoulder and hoisted her to standing, then pushed an electronic switch that unlocked the door leading to the short staircase. She wondered if this was where he was planning to kill her.

Her feet barely moved at all as they descended the steps, and she did her best to provide as much dead weight as possible as he lifted her downstairs. Whatever he'd slipped into her drink had rendered her a zombie, but her faculties—especially her survival instincts—were slowly returning. *I've got to buy some time....*

The room was pitch dark as they reached the bottom, and he set her down on a soft barstool. She had no frame of reference until he flipped a bank of light switches, revealing a shrine of sorts. Her first instinct would've normally been to drop her jaw and exclaim something akin to, "Whoa!!" but she had to play it cool as she saw this resplendent toy shop of his. She recognized several of the iconic guitars, and it was all she could do to pantomime being catatonic as she took in the sight.

"Not a lot of people get to come down here, Phoenix," he said as he fired up a cigarette. The smoke went up toward the vented windows, which he'd forgotten to close when he'd left so hastily, and he made note of his security faux pas. No harm, no foul. "I guess you're just one of the lucky ones," he added with a chuckle Phoenix found disturbing.

"Lucky me," she mumbled, licking her lip.

He spun at the sound, not expecting to hear anything from her so soon. "Ah, good morning, Phoenix! Nice to have you with us!" he laughed. "Uh, sorry about the lip there, but you were getting a bit disrespectful toward the end of our wonderful meal, and I don't take kindly to that. I'm sure you can understand."

Wingnut had noticed the downstairs vent windows light up, signaling they'd entered his music room. He couldn't hear their conversation from where he was, but he did have a decent visual at least, thanks to the short length of sewer line camera he'd snaked through the vent before their arrival. It wasn't perfect, but it at least gave him a visual reference to their location, their activities, and Phoenix's well-being for now.

He stepped back several steps as to not be heard and keyed the walkie. "Curt, Wingnut."

"Talk to me, buddy."

"They're downstairs now, in that music room of his. Phoenix is sitting on a chair and he's hovering over her. I have eyes on them from the sewer cam. Where are you?"

"Getting closer, bud. I'm through the gate and still a few minutes out. Keep me posted if anything changes. And wait for me. Copy?"

"Copy," Wingnut acknowledged as he set down his walkie and crept closer to the small window.

The Pirate was pacing slowly now, and Phoenix felt like a doomed feeder mouse that had been dropped into a hungry snake's cage at mealtime. She stealthily glanced around to get her bearings, looking for a weapon or an opportunity—anything. She was becoming more lucid now and decided to engage in a little conversation to improve her chances, or at least buy a little time.

"Guess I'll pass on the tequila mockingbird next time," she muttered.

"Ah, glad you enjoyed it. Yes, they can be a little strong some-times," he quipped, stopping directly in front of her. He looked into her eyes, trying to assess her remaining level of impairment.

"Especially if somebody slips you a Mickey, I'll bet," she challenged.

"Moi? A Mickey? Now, why would I do that?" he jeered.

"Just figured it might be your M.O., and I'm basing that largely on personal experience," she said defiantly. "I'm also assuming that's what you did to that little sixteen-year-old last week as well. You know, the one you dumped along the roadside."

"Sometimes you're just a little too smart for your own good, Phoenix," he hissed, stepping in closer. "So, you enjoy playing detective, do you?" he snarled.

"Is that what you did to my mom too? To Rose? When you first met her, I mean. Because there's no possible way you could ever get laid otherwise," she scoffed. "Prove me wrong."

The Pirate slapped her hard across the face. It rang her bell, yet she stared back defiantly. "You think you know everything when, really, you don't know anything. You may have noticed that you're not in a position to be giving me any grief, and if you take one lesson to your grave—which will be very soon by the way—it should be to respect your elders."

This got a howl from Phoenix, and a punch to the stomach from her captor. "See what I mean? Respect. It's what I demand, it's what I deserve, and I'll accept nothing else from you, you petulant little brat."

As she caught her breath, Phoenix fired another shot across the bow. "Gee, I'm sorry. You're right. You deserve my *respect!*" she said, laughing at the absurdity of his declaration.

He grabbed her by her lapels and thrust her jacket open, expos-ing the recorder. His head tilted momentarily, like a dog's when it doesn't understand something. "Well, what do we have here, detective? Huh?" he said, pulling the device from her pocket. "If I didn't know better, I'd almost say you were trying to record me. Is that what this is, Phoenix?"

"Hey, it was Open Mic Night, what can I say?"

He inspected the machine more closely, popping open the microcassette tape door. "Oops! Looks like you forgot to put a tape in there," he derided. "Rookie mistake, Phoenix," he said with a laugh, as he set the machine down on the counter.

"Did I? Let me just tell you that I may be a rookie, but I'm not stupid enough not to have had a tape in there. Give me a little credit," she said, a little smirk forming.

Again, with the head tilt. It looked cute on a confused German shepherd, but not so much on an asshole. She continued, "Hm... I'll bet you're wondering...*where did she put that tape?* Am I right?"

"You're bluffing!" he barked, thrusting open her jacket. "How do I know you're not just pulling my chain? Or, perhaps, you're wearing a wire?! Is that it?" he snapped, roughly popping the buttons off her blouse as he yanked it open, exposing her bra, but not her tat.

"Like what you see there? What's the saying: *Incest is best?*" she retorted through clenched teeth.

He loosened his grip on her blouse, which fell further open upon release. "Glad you bring that subject up, because now that we're getting to know each other better, maybe we should decide what you're going to call me," he sneered, his eyes still on her chest. "How about *Dad...?*"

"Mm, that's rich. Let's see... No, I was thinking something more along the lines of... *murderous, a-hole, crater-faced, cyclops!*" she boomed, yanking off his eyepatch with one hand and thrusting the nailfile deep into his neck with the other.

The Pirate bellowed in pain as the blade sunk in behind his trachea, his eyes wide with surprise. Phoenix couldn't help but notice that his left eye—the one that'd been behind the patch— was *way* out of alignment and had long ago ceased looking for its true north. It seemed to be staring down at the floor. In that split second, she delivered a perfect kick to his testicles, which sent him to his knees, yowling in pain. "Hey, I'm up here!" she mocked.

Wingnut had seen enough, and he keyed the radio. "Curt, where the hell are you, man? We need to get her out of there now—before it's too late!" he panted.

"Right around the corner, Wing! Be there in two minutes!"

"It's GO-time, Curt! She's getting hurt, man!" he whispered urgently.

"Okay, on my mark…are you ready?" Curt shouted into the radio. He downshifted the Road Runner and made the final turn. The driveway was just ahead.

"Yeah, man. Say the word!" Wingnut shouted, awaiting the signal they'd agreed to earlier.

Curt came to a stop at the entrance to the driveway, dimming the lights and orienting the car as he made the turn. "Wingnut, GO!! I repeat…GO!!! *Release the crappin'!!!*" he commanded, tweaking a line Sir Laurence Olivier had all but phoned-in from one of his and Wingnut's favorite Ray Harryhausen movies, *Clash of the Titans*.

"Roger! *Release the crappin'!!!*" Wingnut confirmed, as he decisively thrust open the release valve from the truck. Instead of unleashing a mythical, scaly, four-armed colossal sea creature, like Zeus had, he'd summoned something much more fearsome. As the hose bucked in protest, over four thousand gallons of rodeo poop began roaring down the tube.

The Pirate slowly rose to the hunched-over position, still in acute pain as he held his crotch. More than a trickle of blood was escaping his neck as well. "You little bitch!" he wailed. A new sound captured the attention of both, and Phoenix thought she recognized it from her day at the circus.

"What the hell—?" he said, spinning around as the rumble got louder.

"Sorry, *Dad*. I've been *taking* shit my whole life, and…well…I think there comes a time when you just have to…*give a shit!*" And, as if on cue, several hundred gallons breached the space, pouring in through the dump hose that protruded through the window. The roar, and the instantaneous stench that came with it, had the desired effect of "shock and awe" as the muck shot across the walls, the floor, and found their targets: several prized, vintage, and irreplaceable guitars. It was a mudslide of biblical proportions, and the Pirate jumped to his feet as he witnessed the horror. "*NOOOOOOOOOOOO!!!!!!!!!!!!!*" he bellowed, rushing toward the carnage.

Wingnut had managed to pre-aim the hose and, factoring estimated pressure and trajectory, it was achieving maximum effect. The Pirate charged toward the sludge, his stomach heaving from the stench as he made his way to his "babies" like a protective mother in the wild. To his horror, the Rickenbacker, the Gretsches, and two Epiphone Casinos caught the brunt of the first wave, toppling them like so much driftwood and completely submerging them.

He grabbed for their necks but missed, losing his footing in the process, which resulted in the belly flop from Hell. His head rose from the muck and he saw his collection of Les Pauls and the heirloom Stratocasters take the plunge next. The first thousand gallons of sewage had hit their mark, and there were another three thousand rushing in right behind them.

Phoenix took in the malodorous mayhem from her as-yet untainted vantage point at the other end of the room. She listened to the muffling of her captor's screams, which were nearly being drowned out by the roar as well as by another sound, one very familiar to her: the Road Runner roaring toward the house! If there was any doubt, it was erased by the accompanying *MEEP!! MEEP!! MEEP!! MEEP!!*

The cavalry!!!

The moment had presented itself, and as much as it pained her to see these beautiful instruments suffer such a heinous fate, she felt absolutely no remorse for the flailing, screaming maniac caught in the riptide.

She pivoted toward the door and paused for a nanosecond as she saw a guitar case off to the side, all by itself, and adjacent to the exit. The nanosecond of decision passed, and she grabbed the heavy case's handle and turned toward the mayhem happening across the room.

"I'll just see myself out!" she yelled, and she bounded up the steps to the kitchen. She found the front door and hurriedly unlocked the myriad of deadbolts, flinging it open and sprinting toward the idling Road Runner, and to Curt who was outside the car.

Curt was running toward her as well and they collided in a messy embrace.

"Oh, my God…Oh, my God…Oh, my God…" was all she could say between kisses.

"You okay?!" Curt panted, searching her eyes, and closing up her jacket for her.

"I'm okay…I'm okay, yeah!" she managed, before adding, "I wasn't sure if you were going to get here in time!"

"C'mon, jump in! We gotta get out of here!!" he urged.

She flung open the passenger door, tossed the guitar case onto the backseat, and jumped in as the Road Runner screamed down the driveway like a bottle rocket.

Wingnut's radio squawked to life and he picked it up. "Wingnut, Curt! I've got Phoenix!! Do you read?!"

"Curt, Wingnut! Yeah!! Glad she's okay! Hey, the plan worked, but now that his toys are gone, it looks like he's heading out of the room!"

"Dammit!" Curt cursed. "Let me know if he jumps in his car, okay? And if he does, get the hell out of there after he leaves. Got it?!"

"Will do! Wait a second... Curt, he just went outside. He's climbing into the 'Vette, man! I think he's coming after you guys!"

"Okay, thanks for the heads-up! I'll watch my mirrors; you get yourself and the truck out of there as soon as he's gone, Wingnut! And hurry! Copy?"

"Copy! Be careful, man! Out."

The Corvette roared to life and barreled toward the road. The Pirate opened both windows, but it had the same effect as hanging up a cardboard pine air freshener outdoors at a dairy farm. He was coated, head to toe, and the car's until-then pristine interior was officially toast.

He'd always had a sensitive gag reflex, and he'd effectively dry-heaved his insides beyond dry. His nostrils flared as he took in the stench, which only served to further fuel his extreme rage. He was hellbent on catching them, and he would not be denied his vengeance. As he took a right turn onto the road, he grabbed his pistol from the glovebox.

Thankfully there weren't too many cars on this stretch of Stevenson Drive at the moment, and Curt shifted gears and stepped on the gas. He needed to put some distance between them and this dangerous psychopath. "Buckle up, Phoenix!" he advised. "We're not out of the woods yet."

As she clicked her seatbelt, she remembered what Pop Pop had said: "No coyote's gonna be able to catch you, sweetheart." She hoped to God he was right.

The Corvette gripped the road as it barreled along Stevenson. Its 354-horsepower, 5.7-liter V8 engine was made for this. As pissed as he was, he planned to relish the moment, and to make these executions as fun—and as painful—as possible.

Wingnut shut the dump valve and detached the hose. He hadn't emptied the tank completely, but it was mission accomplished just the same. There would be no time for cleanup. He went back to the window and retrieved the sewer camera and stowed the gear. He'd probably be fired from his job now, he figured, but, what the hell? In-N-Out was hiring.

The Road Runner had plenty of horsepower and ordinarily had no problem passing anything that crossed its path. The passing opportunities were few on this section of road, however, and Curt needed to make it past the Pacific Grove gate before he'd find more stretches of two-laned road. They needed to get to Highway 68. His eyes darted back and forth, from the road ahead to the rearview mirror, watching for any sign of a particular set of headlights.

"No sign of him yet, but we didn't get much of a head start," Curt advised.

"Here, try that switch. Under the dash there," she said, pointing to it. "Couldn't hurt."

Curt reached down and felt around for it. He activated the switch and was a bit amazed as the pop-up hood scoop deployed, seemingly from nowhere. Though he couldn't see it from there, and especially in the dark, the Air Grabber featured a shark graphic with *Air Grabber* spelled out in the mouth. It was a bad-ass option that not only looked cool, but also forced air directly into the engine via the scoop.

He wasn't sure if it was his imagination or not, but he liked to believe that the engine was delivering a little more oomph now.

"Bitchin'," he said.

"Yep. Bitchin'!" Phoenix agreed.

He glanced at the rearview again then looked at his damsel in distress. "What's in the case?"

"Not sure," she said with a shrug. "It was just standing there, saying 'Rescue me!' so I did. Figured he owed me that much. If we survive this thing, we can open it up together, later. Like a treasure hunt. Like Christmas, even."

"Yeah…" he said absently as another glance to the mirror revealed a new set of headlights, and they were matching their speed.

"We may have company. Hold on!" he said, stomping harder on the accelerator. The lights behind him stayed with them and seemed even to be closing.

"You think it's—?" Her question was interrupted by the sound of something hitting the rear of the car. Though neither of them had ever experienced this, they knew for certain that this was the sound of a bullet piercing the trunk.

"Holy—!" Phoenix managed, her head spinning around to look out the back window. "He's shooting at us!!"

Curt didn't have a verbal response to the obvious. He instead made a desperate maneuver, crossing over into the opposite lane for a moment in order to pass a pickup truck. It was something he would never consider doing under normal circumstances, but this situation was anything but normal. "He's keeping up with us, dammit!" he seethed. They weren't far from the gate now, and he just hoped he could keep out of range of another volley.

The Pirate had fired two shots, which was a bit difficult from the window, especially at these speeds. He'd recognized the distinctive slits of the Road Runner's taillights and had managed to get off a couple of rounds. He wasn't sure if he hit anything though, as they continued at a high speed. He needed to close the gap and put a round through the rear window. Maybe hit a tire. He knew they had to be heading for Highway 68, and he hoped to finish them before they reached it.

Curt's cell phone rang, and he answered without looking at the display.

"Yeah?" he said, sounding both distracted and out of breath.

It was Liam. "Everything okay? Where the hell are you?"

"Liam! Sorry I haven't called you—here, let me put Phoenix on!" he barked, handing her the phone.

"Wha—?"

"Grandpa!" she gushed, cutting him off. "Grandpa! I'm...okay! We're—just a sec," she said, turning to Curt. "Where are we?"

"Coming up on the junction of Highway 68!" he yelled, the stress clearly evident in his voice.

"Approaching Highway 68, Grandpa!" she advised, as a loud *plink* announced the arrival of another bullet to the trunk. "Shit!!"

"What's the matter, honey?"

"Nothing, Grandpa...hey, we'll call you in a few minutes, okay?!" She hung up before waiting for his response.

Curt saw the sign indicating *Highway 68/Salinas* and shot a glance to the mirror. The Corvette was closing on them. He down-shifted and took the exit at twice the posted speed and, coming out of the curve, hit the throttle hard.

Moments later, Curt saw the set of unwelcome headlights coming out of the curve and getting closer. Even though there was nearly thirty years' difference in age between the two vehicles, they were worthy opponents, and this was proving to be a life-or-death contest of horsepower, handling, and performance. And guts. Only one would emerge, of this Curt was sure, and there was zero room for error.

Both vehicles weaved around other cars as they played their deadly, high-speed game of cat and mouse past Toro Regional Park.

"We've got a decision coming up," he said, as they approached the exit sign that read *Reservation Rd./River Rd.*

"Okay...I'm gonna have to defer to you on that one."

The Road Runner came to a momentary stop at the t-inter-section. The two-way sign showed *Reservation Rd* with an arrow pointing left, and *River Rd* to the right. Same road, really, but a name change, and equally sporty s-curves—especially at night.

There was no time to deliberate further. Curt yanked the wheel to the left and they were on their way down Reservation.

Other than an occasional piece of ranch property and a few dilapidated old barn structures, there was precious little out here. The absence of any road lighting, or even any moonlight, as well as the absence of anything resembling proper guard railing, made this a potentially deadly stretch.

Add *being shot at* and all bets were off.

It was dark as hell, with no businesses to speak of but, being a continuation of the farmland they'd seen on River Road previously, Curt knew it to be vast fields of crops they were whizzing by. As they made haste around the curves, the Road Runner's headlights occasionally gave them momentary glimpses of pieces of broken wooden fence, acres of hooped white tents covering berry bushes, the occasional John Deere tractor, and trailers laden with piles of sprinkler pipe.

Plink!

"Shit! Keep your head down, Phoenix!"

"I think I'm gonna throw up!"

"Sorry...can't help it. I know the curves aren't helping, but his aim's getting better" he warned, casting a steely glare at the headlights creeping up on them. He had to use these curves to his advantage and get some distance before they ended up in Marina, and Highway 1.

The blast from a horn refocused his attention to an oncoming pickup in the opposite lane that didn't appreciate their encroachment and narrowly passed on their left, thanks to Curt's abrupt course correction.

"Still want me to keep my head down?!" Phoenix chimed defiantly, coming fully upright. As they came around the next turn, a beater Ford Falcon was chugging along in their lane, causing Curt to hit the brakes hard. If they stayed behind this guy, they were goners.

"Sorry! Hey, hold on, I've got to get around this guy!!" Curt warned, downshifting and giving the wheel a sharp left as he over-took the poor woman who'd probably just finished her brutal twelve-hour shift in the fields. A quick yank to the right put them in front now, having barely cleared her bumper. This got a weak honk, but it went unheard. Curt hit the gas as if their lives depended on it. And they did.

The Corvette came around the corner and skidded to an abrupt stop, nearly taking out the Falcon. The Pirate leaned on the horn, flashed his high beams repeatedly, and screamed out the window. "Move that piece of shit!!!"

The woman put her arm out the window and motioned for him to go around her, but he answered it with a nine millimeter round to her right taillight.

"¡Gringo loco!" she yelped, but she had nowhere to go; there was no shoulder. Another bright flash split the night and was accompanied by a loud report and a whooshing sound as his second bullet took out her left rear tire.

He didn't have time for this. He yanked the wheel hard and stepped hard on the throttle as he entered the single opposing lane. He couldn't see the Road Runner now, as he was entering a curve, but what he could see as he rounded the corner made his eye(s) go wide with panic:

An extremely rugged looking orange, diesel Ford water truck barreling right at him. *HONK!!*

The tenth of a second that he had to assess the danger told him that impact was imminent. His only choice was made involuntarily for him as he swerved back to the right and, having overcorrected, sent the Corvette airborne, flying off the raised dirt berm and into the dark unknown.

The sleek roadster briefly enjoyed some flight time, like a carrier-based F-14 launching with a failed engine, or that Thunderbird at the end of *Thelma & Louise*, its headlights offering nothing as they only seemed to scan the cloudy sky, with no frame of reference in the void. As the doomed vehicle's dreaded arc started its descent, the Pirate released his grip on the pistol and lifted his arm in a defensive move, across his forehead.

The wheels spun freely, uselessly, and for another couple of seconds, he drifted…seemingly in slow-motion, as something began to come into view ahead of him. In the briefest of moments, his mind seized on new visual information, and the last sound he uttered was a sick, high-pitched, girlish scream as the trailer load of sprinkler pipes violently invaded his windshield and turned his face and complete upper torso into an unrecognizable gooey mess. The front of the Corvette had simultaneously slid underneath the trailer, ripping the vehicle to shreds, like a beer can in a woodchipper.

Needless to say, the unenviable task of identifying the driver via dental records would likely involve flushing considerable flesh and bone from the dozens of three-inch irrigation pipes that now occupied what was left of the cabin.

As they approached Marina, and civilization, Curt dared another glance at the rearview. He slowed, just to make sure his eyes weren't playing tricks on him. He saw no lights. There was nothing back there. He pulled over to the shoulder.

"I think we might've lost him!" he crowed. He glanced over at Phoenix. who looked quite pale, but she mustered a weak smile at his news.

"Yeah? Ya think?" she begged, turning to look over her shoulder. There was only a smattering of light traffic, and it seemed to be obeying posted speeds. And nobody appeared to be brandishing firearms. She exhaled deeply and for what felt like the first time in an hour.

Phoenix unbuckled herself and leaned over to give her knight in shining armor a long, heartfelt hug. He reciprocated, neither of them saying anything. They locked in their embrace, just shaking with long-overdue release, and appreciation for their lives…for each other.

"Thank you, God," she whispered.

With that, and much to their surprise, the dashboard hula girl finally surrendered the last of her remaining suction and crashed noisily onto the console.

Whoa.

After their promised call back to Liam, who'd just polished off an enormous slab of lasagna, they gave lengthy statements at the police station, describing what had led up to the chase, and provided some help in identifying the shish kabobbed pirate they'd found in the field.

Curt felt enormous relief after his other call—to Wingnut. He'd gotten off the property immediately, as instructed, and had done the best he could at the self-service carwash, hosing off the truck and the gear. He'd meet them back at the restaurant, he said.

Curt and Phoenix drove in absolute silence for the long haul back to the restaurant to retrieve Liam, and Curt's F-150.

When they arrived, Curt instructed Phoenix to stay in the car and lock it while he went inside. A few moments went by before she saw the entry door swing open and her two men emerge. Liam was going as fast as his walker allowed, and Phoenix bolted from the car, rushing to meet this dear, dear man whom she didn't even know existed a couple of weeks before.

The two of them collided mid-parking lot, locking each other in a python-like embrace, their intense feelings deafeningly expressed, even though wordlessly. They both burst into tears, and that served as all the communication needed for the next several minutes.

As Curt was helping Liam back to his truck and stowing the walker, the now-gleaming septic truck pulled up alongside. Wingnut rolled down his window and greeted the group with his goofy grin.

"My main man!" Curt trumpeted at the sight of him. "Get

down here, Wing. Give me some sugar!" he added, spreading his arms wide in anticipation of their impending bro-hug. Wingnut obliged happily, and Phoenix joined in a group hug-a-thon.

As they came up for air, Phoenix planted a big kiss of thanks on Wingnut's cheek, sending him into a crimson flush. He'd never wash that cheek again; he was sure of it.

It was the goofiest of ragtag reunions, really, celebrating the most unbelievable string of events, and an improbable team victory none of them could have imagined, and would never ever forget.

The collective exhaustion they all felt was justified and individually acknowledged. It was agreed upon that they'd all regroup in the morning, at Liam's, for a post-game debrief.

Phoenix would be making omelets, Liam assured them.

CHAPTER 26

THE RESTAURANT WAS dark now and Curt and Phoenix were the last to leave the parking lot, as Wingnut had kindly volunteered to take Liam home before returning the rig to the yard. Having run on pure adrenaline all night—and now that the threat had been eliminated—they both realized they'd hit the wall. Near-death experiences had a funny way of doing that.

Phoenix unleashed a gaping yawn that would rival the MGM lion.

"Tired?" Curt teased. "I can't imagine why."

Her yawn continued for another couple of seconds before she could reply. "Ya think?

Her eyes were a bit bloodshot, and her lip was swollen. She knew she must look like she'd gone twelve rounds and lost. She looked down at her shoes, not wanting to be seen like this.

Curt's bearpaw-like hand slowly emerged from his pocket, his thumb caressing the dimple in her chin while he cupped her jaw in his palm. Bruises or not, he'd never seen anything so beautiful in his life. Phoenix closed her eyes, and he felt her head's weight settle into his hand, surrendering to the feeling of comfort and safety he provided. She almost appeared to be asleep, and there was only one way to make sure.

He leaned down closer, regarding the beauty he held there,

like he was inspecting a melon before purchase. Her eyes fluttered slightly behind their lids, perhaps replaying perilous scenes from their ordeal. He wanted to replace them with pleasant ones, and his lips tenderly settled on hers.

Her eyes remained closed, and he closed his now as they lost themselves in the moment, taking comfort in knowing they were now safe and that they truly cared for each other.

They held their embrace for several minutes before Phoenix slowly pulled her lips away and smiled. Her eyes opened as she looked at him. "I love you," she whispered.

Curt's eyes smiled back first, and the rest of his expression joined in. "I'm glad, because I love you too, Phoenix. More than I've ever loved anything in my whole life."

Phoenix felt like she'd been hit by a lightning bolt. The sensation was electrical, and her soul felt an intense energy the likes of which she'd never experienced. Like somebody had finally found her cord and plugged her in. *So, this is what love feels like!*

As they resumed their kiss, the sound of an approaching streetsweeper cleaning the parking lot provided them with the clue that they should probably be on their way.

"Wanna get outta here?" he asked.

"Yeah. Where to?"

"I know a place."

"Should I follow you or—?"

"Nah. You shouldn't be driving right now. We'll come back for your car," he replied with an irrepressible smile. He too had been zapped by said lightning bolt.

Wingnut had also kindly offered to spend the night at a buddy's apartment, as he'd recently acquired a new PlayStation. *Resident Evil 2* was on the menu, and it'd be an all-nighter, but he assured Curt he'd join up for omelets in the morning.

Curt's and Wingnut's apartment was a standard ground floor,

two-bedroom bachelor pad. Curt held the door for Phoenix as she stepped inside the dimly lit hovel, which was a testament to their apparent love of pizza and Snapple.

"Sorry, maid's day off," he chuckled.

"Yeah, well, good help's hard to find," she replied, wondering if she should put on protective gear.

Curt gave her the thirty-second tour, with the most important landmark being the location of the restroom, which she duly noted. Beyond that, down the extremely short hall, lay two doors. Curt opened Wingnut's door first, and a quick peek inside revealed several more beverage empties, an unmade single bed, and walls plastered with movie posters—all Ray Harryhausen flicks—including his beloved *Clash of the Titans* and several *Sinbad* movies. Curt flicked off the light and closed the door.

"And," he said, resting his hand on the other doorknob. "My humble abode. Forgive the mess," he added, swinging the door wide. He flipped the wall switch, which illuminated the lamp on the nightstand. His bed was a California king, which took up almost the entire space. At least he'd made his, she thought.

"Very nice. At least the housekeeper's visited your room." She smiled, noting the complete lack of foodstuffs and their packaging.

"Yeah, well, that's the nickel tour," he said, holding out his palm. "That'll be five cents, please."

"I'll have to owe you," she teased.

On the other nightstand, she noticed a small, framed color photo. She picked it up and smiled at the scene—from the early 'seventies, she guessed—of a very tall young couple and their maybe six-year-old son. Curt's smile hadn't changed over the years. The woman wasn't smiling, however.

"Your folks," she said, smiling as she looked at him.

"Yep…not long before Mom took off," he sighed. "I don't have many pictures of her."

Phoenix came over to him and cradled his face in her hands.

"I'm sorry, baby. If you'll excuse me, I need to use the little girl's room," she said, giving him a peck.

"You know where it is," he said, stepping out of her way as she passed.

"I hope I can find it," she chuckled. "Be right back."

Curt sat down on the edge of the bed. He grabbed the framed picture and placed it face-down, then allowed himself to lay back on the bed, just for a minute.

Phoenix surveyed her face in the mirror, which only confirmed what she'd feared. She dabbed a tissue in water and cleaned up her lip the best she could, then retrieved some Visine from her purse and squeezed a couple drops into each eye. It burned, but it was a good burn. A further search of her purse netted a piece of lifesaving Freshen-Up gum and her lip gloss, which she applied gingerly to the swollen side. Her shellacked hairdo had survived its epic car chase, and the overall effect was as good as one could expect.

She turned off the hall light and peeked into Curt's room. It sounded like dualling chainsaws on Lumberjacks' Day; his snoring was impressive. She stood there and regarded this gentle giant, this knight who'd slayed this damsel in distress's dragon, this beautiful sleeping man with whom she had now fallen in love.

She considered letting him sleep—God knew they both needed it—but, with their declarations tonight, she'd made up her mind. She'd brought her shiny new tattoo to Show & Tell night, and her audience of one was going to be the first to see it. And she might even check another box on her wish list tonight. She quietly closed the door behind her, dimmed the three-way light switch to its lowest setting, and removed her tattered blouse.

CHAPTER 27

LIAM SQUEAKED HIS way down the hall, pausing his walker at the open door to Phoenix's room. He'd left her in Curt's safekeeping when they parted ways the night before, and he didn't have a further worry. They were young, they'd been through a lot. They were allowed—it was 1999, for crying out loud.

As he went about making a jumbo pot of coffee, usually Phoenix's job, he heard a car approaching. Then another. He hit the brew button and peeked out the curtain. The Road Runner, plus the F-150.

He turned at the sound of a key rattling in the lock and, as the door swung open, he was overjoyed to see the two youngsters. Phoenix was dressed as she had been the night before, but she looked refreshed, somehow. The smile she beamed at him seemed of a higher wattage as well.

"Good morning, Grandpa!" she said with a gleam in her eye as she gave him a hug.

"Good morning, sweetheart!" Liam replied joyfully.

"'Mornin', Liam," Curt chimed in. "Sleep okay?"

"Like the dead, my friend. You?"

"Um…yeah, pretty much," he replied, with a secret wink to Phoenix. "Hey, we made a stop at McDonald's—hope you don't mind," he added, holding two large bags adorned with the yellow letter M.

"Yeah, Grandpa. Omelets? Really? We made an executive decision and picked up a ton of Egg McMuffins instead. Hash browns too," she said as Curt squeezed inside. "Just put 'em on the kitchen counter, honey. I'll distribute everything," she said to the big man.

Her term of endearment didn't go unnoticed by Liam and he gave her an approving wink. She winked back. "I'd better set the table. Wingnut should be here any minute too."

"Coffee's going. Hope I didn't mess it up," he joked.

It had shaped up to be a beautiful morning, and Phoenix decided to serve breakfast out on Liam's back patio. The metal table's tempered glass top was laden with paper plates, red Solo cups, two cartons of orange juice, coffee mugs, and some of Mickey D's finest breakfast offerings. Phoenix had no problem polishing off her two sans-meat sandwiches and a sleeve of breakfast potatoes.

Curt had called dibs on doing the dishes afterward, which would only involve putting mugs in the dishwasher.

The fragrant star jasmine was in bloom, as were several varieties of Liam's roses, and the coffee was...ahem...extra strong. The additional caffeine was appreciated by all and, with enough creamer, they went through a second pot.

"Release the crappin'!!" Wingnut howled at the memory.

"Dude...not while we're eating," Curt admonished.

Wingnut had politely removed his ever-present knit cap upon arriving and, as Liam sat across the table from him, he couldn't help but marvel at the lad's very prominent helical display.

Curt had finished his third sandwich and polished off an equal quantity of what he referred to as "Barbie potatoes." Wingnut had been good for four sandwiches but passed on the Barbies.

Liam ate his one-of-each slowly, quietly observing this fine group assembled before him. These young people had all joined an important cause, signed on for a dangerous mission, had risen to the occasion, seized the moment, vanquished a formidable enemy, and helped an old man solve a cold case that had nearly pickled him.

His thoughts went to Rose. He regretted that he hadn't been much of a father to her, but he was thankful that he'd at least found her justice.

With as little ceremony as possible, Liam wiped away a secret tear, and joined in the merriment.

PART SEVEN

BLOOM

CHAPTER 28

PHOENIX PULLED THE remaining cluster of colorful helium balloons from the trunk of the Road Runner, pausing to run her fingers over the long-restored panel of its trunk that had, years before, been bullet-ridden. You'd never know it now, as the body shop had done quality work.

She slammed the lid and tied the bunch to the fence railing. She stepped back and surveyed her work, satisfied that each of the three clusters she'd spread about the patio were equally festive with their bright primary colors.

Curt exited the kitchen, carrying a large casserole dish of baked beans with the aid of some oven mitts he'd found in the drawer. "Hot stuff. Where do these go, babe?"

"On the red trivet there," she replied, pointing to the spot on the table. "Next to the potato salad."

There were four places set at the picnic table. The tablecloth was one of those vinyl ones, adorned with a smattering of bright colored dots printed on it. It matched the balloons, which was important. The paper plates were heavy duty, with the three compartments, and the utensils plastic.

"Everything looks great, honey! Want me to go get the guest of honor?" Curt asked.

"Not just yet, a couple of minutes. I'm going to finish up the fruit salad. Keep the cake out of sight for now, okay?"

"It's already on top of the fridge, hidden behind a bag of chips."

"Perfect. Thanks, sweetheart," Phoenix said, dashing back inside. The screen door slammed loudly behind her. *Darn it…keep forgetting that!*

As she stood at the sink cutting up the strawberries, grapes, and remaining banana, Phoenix took pause. *If only Liam were here to see all this.*

It saddened her to think that, having finally brought his daughter's murderer to justice, Liam's heart had decided he'd served his purpose in this life. He'd died in his sleep, quite unexpectedly, during the night…on that very evening, after the team had enjoyed their celebratory McMuffins. Somehow, he'd apparently made his peace with everything and made his exit accordingly.

Phoenix missed her grandfather, and she wished he could've lived to meet the great granddaughter he'd never known about: Little Rose. It was her third birthday today, and, well…she wished there could be a fifth place setting.

As she stirred the heavy bowl of fruit with the salad tongs, she looked out the kitchen window and thought about all she was grateful for. She'd had three-plus years to process it all now, and she'd emerged from her California adventure with the realization that she had been truly blessed. In many ways.

Thanks to her grandpa, she'd had her whole world view opened up to her. It had all started with his letter. She was no longer just the bored, aimless, girl garage-monkey who lived for Saturday garage sales and little else. He'd given her the greatest of gifts!

Her quest for the truth, her longing for family, for connections, fulfilled. She now realized why she had been given the precious chance at life, something that had been denied her sister. She was *alive*, fully, and in every respect. Her prayers had been answered, every one of them, and it still gave her chills to think about her good fortune.

Not only had Liam left everything to Phoenix when he died, but he'd also created a separate savings account to fund her eventual wish-list dream vacation to Hawaii—something he felt strongly about. The hula girl on the dashboard had told him all he needed to know, and he made it so. Phoenix and Curt had been able to spend a weeklong honeymoon on Maui, and that amazing trip was the second-to-last box on her list to put a checkmark next to. It had exceeded expectations.

Liam's house—and California altogether, for that matter—held no attraction to Curt nor herself, and they decided to sit on the sales proceeds while they figured out their next move.

"I know a place," Phoenix had promised him. And, that place had lots of saguaros.

Little Rose had been conceived well before they'd gotten married, actually. It had been on that craziest of nights, after the car chase—at Curt's apartment. During Show & Tell. *Ahem.* Two months later, Phoenix had started feeling nauseous, which prompted her to take a home pregnancy test. That evening, after his grueling shift, Curt had almost blown it completely with his ill-advised response to her showing him the test result.

"Wow... So, what do you wanna do?" had been his initial, bordering-on-Neanderthalic response, which could have utterly doomed the relationship had she not given him another chance.

"I'm going to pretend you didn't just say that..." she'd fumed, storming out of his apartment.

The next evening, after much reflection, he'd used his *Get Out of Jail Free* card and got down on one knee as he pulled out a small velvety box containing a diamond engagement ring—the one he'd purchased on the way home. It had taken all of his savings, but his mulligan response, and the resultant excitement about their big news, had the desired effect. Their joy was mutual…and remained so.

As Phoenix stretched the plastic wrap across the bowl, she was greeted with a welcomed arm around her shoulder: Little Rose's grandpa, Pop Pop. He kissed the top of Phoenix's head.

"Great looking salad, kiddo. What do you want me to do?"

"You can grab your steamed veggies thing off the grill. We're all ready for the princess. I'm going to go get her now."

"Roger that," Pop Pop said, exiting to the patio. "C'mon, guys," he said to Gracie and Luke as they followed him outside. They loved to help with the barbeque. The Prick couldn't care less; he preferred to bask in the tiny sliver of sunshine that came in through the window.

Phoenix padded softly down the hall and slowly turned the doorknob to Pop Pop's music room/Princess's nap room. The carrot-topped toddler's eyes fluttered open and went wider at the sight of her mama. Phoenix stepped in and picked up her little bundle.

"How's my little ginger snap? Did you have a good nap, sweetie?" she cooed, holding her close and smothering her with kisses.

"Yes, Mommy! But the birdie kept talking to me, he wouldn't be quiet."

"Hello!!…Hello!!!" said Angus, as if to prove her point.

"Well, let's put on some shoes because it's time for your birthday party, special girl!"

"Yay!"

"Hello!!!!"

"Yes, I'll bring you a piece of apple, Angus."

As Phoenix helped slip on Rose's tiny shoes, she looked up at the wall and shook her head in disbelief. Her bass guitar was again displayed on its wall hanger. The only difference now was that it had a really bitchin' bullet hole in it, which would make for a great story at their next gig.

Additionally, she took pause at the sight of what hung next to it: a very shiny, all-aluminum, chrome plated Veleno guitar. It was "a gift from a friend," and Pop Pop's prize possession.

Well, that, and a certain blown glass three-piece set; a gift from Phoenix.

AUTHOR'S NOTE

FIRSTLY, I'D LIKE to thank you for taking a chance on my novel. I truly respect your time and appreciate your coming along for the ride! I'd also be remiss if I didn't give a huge shout out to my wonderful and very supportive wife, Martina. Danke, sweetheart! Lisl, at Great Land Services, you definitely made the work better! Additional thanks to Derek Holt and Tony Brinsley for your "sense of direction;" Jack Hudkins, for encouraging the project; and Sonja Riley, for your calligraphy skills. And Luke, our German shepherd… you've been awesome through all of this! There's extra duck jerky in your future, buddy!

If you enjoyed *Leaving Phoenix*, I hope you'll be so kind as to leave a review of it on Amazon. As you can imagine, your book reviews and referrals are as vital to an author's success as a good grade point average is to a student's. It only takes a moment, and your feedback not only helps the author, but it might also help another potential reader find the book as well. So, thank you in advance!

The writing process for *Leaving Phoenix* was an enjoyable one for me, even though it took me down some very dark paths. The characters were people I found interesting to explore, as were the locales in which the story unfolded. The magic of Arizona holds a very special place for me, as do the rich, fertile regions of Monterey County, California. Pacific Grove, Monterey, Carmel, Pebble Beach, the Salinas Valley…it's a beautiful area, resplendent with treasures, and it's truly a marvel.

Speaking of treasures, the mystical lemon-blueberry cheesecake I wrote of actually exists, though it hails from Hilltop Bakery, in

Prunedale, California; not Arizona. Forgive the dramatic license. It really is that special, and you can find them on Facebook! Tell them Jafe sent you.

Perhaps you've developed a new appreciation for commercial agriculture and, the next time you're at the salad bar, you can think about all of the efforts that go into bringing all of those wonderful fruits and veggies to your plate. It's an amazing process, and these workers are unsung heroes, really. And maybe you've benefited from my tutorials on crafting a mixed tape, or on omelet preparation… who knows? Ha!

In researching this story, I dug deep, considering it spans a twenty-five-year period, from the mid-1970s to the early 2000s. I wanted the topography to be accurate, so I procured vintage maps and road atlases of the regions, as I wanted them to be true to the time frames. The music references had to be accurate as well, and I took it to the next level by making sure the cassette playlists timed out properly. I know….

Current events of the periods were sprinkled into the mix for authenticity. Then, there were those cars. I've wanted that 1970 Road Runner since before I could drive! The most difficult part, certainly, was researching the very unsettling practice of saline abortions. It haunted my dreams.

I loved the period of which I wrote—especially the '70s—as I have a great deal of experience living it. It was a wonderful time to grow up; an era rich with culture, it had a very distinct personality, and…an innocence, even. I wouldn't trade it. In recent years, I've become much more thankful for everything, and where the path has led me, and…it's truly good to be *alive!*

MEEP! MEEP!

~ Jafe Danbury

maxell XL II

POSITION
IEC TYPE II • HIGH (CrO₂)

XL II

ⓉＡＣ ⇐ ＸＨ₵

maxell

Ⓐ DATE .
N R   YES ✗ NO

Ⓑ DATE .
N.R.   YES ✗ NO

A Side	B Side
HEAD EAST - There's Never Been Any Reason	AMBROSIA - Somewhere I've Never Travelled
.38 SPECIAL - Hold On Loosely	CLIMAX BLUES BAND - America / Sense of Direction
FLEETWOOD MAC - Miles Away	BLIND FAITH - Can't Find My Way Home
DAN FOGELBERG - Tullamore Dew / Phoenix	SAVOY BROWN - Tell Mama
COLLECTIVE SOUL - Precious Declaration	ERIC JOHNSON - Desert Rose
GRAND FUNK RAILROAD - Comfort Me	UNICORN - Keep On Going
STEVE MILLER BAND - Motherless Children	BAD CO. - Seagull
CHUCK MANGIONE - Land of Make Believe (LIVE)	LYNYRD SKYNYRD - Simple Man
	ROSSINGTON COLLINS BAND - Don't Misunderstand Me
	STING - If I Ever Lose My Faith In You

Ⓐ

Ⓑ

A DATE .   .   B DATE   .   .

  ⚡PHX⇐CA② maxell

A

ALICE COOPER-
Under My Wheels
TOM PETTY - Runnin'
Down A Dream
IAN MATTHEWS - Heatwave
TEARS FOR FEARS - Shout
SOUNDGARDEN-
Fell On Black Days
DURAN DURAN-
A View To A Kill
STABILIZERS-
One Simple Thing
LEE MICHAELS-
Stormy Monday (LIVE)
CRANBERRIES - Zombie
SLY & THE FAMILY STONE
- Dance To The Music
PRINCE - 1999

B

GLORIA GAYNOR-
J Will Survive
WHAM - Wake Me Up
Before You Go Go
CLIMAX BLUES BAND-
Mesopopmania (LIVE)
ELO - In The Hall of
the Mountain King
JACKSON BROWNE-
Somebody's Baby
PLAYER - Baby Come Back
FOUNDATIONS -
Baby, Now That I've
Found You
DURAN DURAN -
Come Undone
GUESS WHO - Undun
SEAL (w/Joni Mitchell) - If I Could

A   **B**

Photo by Debbie Sowle, taken at Downtown Book & Sound, Salinas, CA

ABOUT THE AUTHOR

Jafe Danbury hails from the trenches of the Hollywood production scene, where he spent decades as a camera operator, director of photography, and director. He has also worked as a teacher and is a decorated U.S. Navy veteran.

He continues his long reign as "King of the Mixed Tape."

He enjoys noodling on the guitar, long road trips, likes his bacon crispy, and loves a good dive bar—especially if it happens to have a twenty-two-foot shuffleboard table. He prefers a leisurely walk to running, unless being chased by a clown with a chainsaw.

Jafe and his lovely bride currently reside in central California and are fine-tuning their exit plan. Their children consist of several rescue dogs and a couple of cockatoos.

LEAVING PHOENIX is his second novel.

For more information, please visit his website: JafeDanbury.com

Also, follow the latest developments on his
JAFE DANBURY author page on Facebook!